Judgment Day

The qadi looked at me sternly. "It's much too late for denials," he said. His dark face didn't seem sturdy enough to support either his bulbous nose or the bushy growth attached to it. "I've already reached my verdict."

Papa began to look a trifle upset. "You've already made your decision, without letting us present our side of the story?"

The qadi slapped his handful of paper. "All the facts are here. What is your side of the story? That you deny committing this foul crime? Of course, that's what you'd have said to me. I didn't need to waste my time listening to it. I have all this!" Again he slapped the papers.

"Then you've reached a verdict," said Papa, "and you've found us guilty."

"Precisely," said the qadi. "Guilty as charged. Guilty in the eyes of Allah and your fellow man. However, the death penalty will be set aside because of an earnest petition from one of the city's most respected citizens."

"Shaykh Reda?" I said. My stomach was starting to bother me again.

"Yes," said the qadi. "Shaykh Reda appealed to me on your behalf. Out of respect for him, you will not be beheaded in the courtyard of the Shimaal Mosque as you deserve. Rather, you will be banished to the desert. . . ."

Books by George Alec Effinger

What Entropy Means to Me
Relatives
Mixed Feelings
Irrational Numbers
Those Gentle Voices
Felicia
Death in Florence
Dirty Tricks
Heroics
The Wolves of Memory
Idle Pleasures
The Nick of Time
The Bird of Time
Shadow Money
The Zork Chronicles

When Gravity Fails
A Fire in the Sun
The Exile Kiss

George Alec Effinger

The Exile Kiss

BANTAM BOOKS

NEW YORK · TORONTO · LONDON · SYDNEY · AUCKLAND

This edition contains the complete text of the original hardcover edition.
NOT ONE WORD HAS BEEN OMITTED.

THE EXILE KISS

A Bantam Spectra Book / published by arrangement with Doubleday

PRINTING HISTORY
Doubleday edition published May 1991
Bantam edition / March 1992

SPECTRA and the portrayal of a boxed "s" are trademarks of Bantam Books, a division of Bantam Doubleday Dell Publishing Group, Inc.

ISBN 0-553-29664-7

Published simultaneously in the United States and Canada

Bantam Books are published by Bantam Books, a division of Bantam Doubleday Dell Publishing Group, Inc. Its trademark, consisting of the words "Bantam Books" and the portrayal of a rooster, is Registered in U.S. Patent and Trademark Office and in other countries, Marca Registrada. Bantam Books, 666 Fifth Avenue, New York, New York 10103.

PRINTED IN THE UNITED STATES OF AMERICA
RAD   0 9 8 7 6 5 4 3 2 1

To the science fiction community of the South Central region, which has given me so much support and encouragement over the years. My thanks to ArmadilloCon in Austin, SwampCon in Baton Rouge, the New Orleans Science Fiction and Fantasy Festival, and CoastCon in Biloxi.

And special thanks to Fred Duarte and Karen Meschke for hospitality above and beyond the call of duty, while my car was in a near-fatal coma during the writing of this book.

Though it rain gold and silver in a foreign land and daggers and spears at home, yet it is better to be at home.

—Malay Proverb

O! a kiss
Long as my exile, sweet as my revenge!

—William Shakespeare
Coriolanus
Act 5, scene 3

The Exile Kiss

1

It never occurred to me that I might be kidnapped. There was no reason why it should. The day had certainly begun innocently enough. I'd snapped wide awake just before dawn, thanks to an experimental add-on I wear on my anterior brain implant. That plug is the one that gives me powers and abilities far beyond those of mortal men. As far as I know, I'm the only person around with two implants.

One of these special daddies blasts me into full consciousness at any hour I choose. I've learned to use it along with another daddy that supercharges my body to remove alcohol and drugs from my system at better than the normal rate. That way I don't wake up still drunk or damaged. Others have suffered in the past because of my hangovers, and I've sworn never to let that happen again.

I took a shower, trimmed my red beard, and dressed in an expensive, sand-colored *gallebeya*, with the white knit skullcap of my Algerian homeland on my head. I was hungry, and my slave, Kmuzu, normally prepared my meals, but I had a breakfast appointment with Friedlander Bey. That would be after the morning call to prayer, so I had about thirty minutes free. I crossed from the west wing of Friedlander Bey's great house to the east, and rapped on the door to my wife's apartment.

Indihar answered it wearing a white satin dressing gown I'd given her, her chestnut hair coiled tightly on the back of her head. Indihar's large, dark eyes narrowed. "I wish you good morning, husband," she said. She was not terrifically pleased to see me.

Indihar's youngest child, four-year-old Hâkim, clung to her and cried. I could hear Jirji and Zahra screaming at each other from another room. Senalda, the Valencian maid I'd hired, was nowhere in evidence. I'd accepted the responsibility of supporting the family because I felt partly to blame for the death of Indihar's husband. Papa —Friedlander Bey— had decided that in order to accomplish such a worthy goal without causing gossip, I also had to marry Indihar and formally adopt the three children. I couldn't remember another instance when Papa had cared at all about gossip.

Nevertheless, despite Indihar's outrage and my flat refusal, the two of us now found ourselves man and wife. Papa *always* got his way. Some time ago, Friedlander Bey had grabbed me by the scruff of the neck and shaken the dust off me and turned me from a small-time hustler into a heavy hitter in the city's underworld.

So Hâkim was now legally . . . my son, as queasy as that concept made me. I'd never been around kids before and I didn't know how to act with them. Believe me, they could tell. I hoisted the boy up and smiled in his jelly-smeared face. "Well, why are you crying, O Clever One?"

I said. Hâkim stopped just long enough to suck in a huge breath, then started wailing even louder.

Indihar gave an impatient grunt. "Please, husband," she said, "don't try being a big brother. Jirji is his big brother." She lifted Hâkim out of my arms and dropped him back to the floor.

"I'm not trying to be a big brother."

"Then don't try being a pal, either. He doesn't need a pal. He needs a father."

"Right," I said. "You just tell me what a father does, and I'll do it." I'd been trying my best for weeks, but Indihar had only given me a hard time. I was getting very tired of it.

She laughed humorlessly and shooed Hâkim toward the rear of the apartment. "Is there some actual point to this visit, husband?" she asked.

"Indihar, if you could just stop resenting me a little, maybe we could make the best of this situation. I mean, how awful could it be for you here?"

"Why don't you ask Kmuzu how *he* feels?" she said. She still hadn't invited me into the suite.

I'd had enough of standing in the hall, and I pushed by her into the parlor. I sat down on a couch. Indihar glared at me for a few seconds, then sighed and sat on a chair facing me. "I've explained it all before," I said. "Papa has been giving me things. Gifts I didn't want, like my implants and Chiriga's bar and Kmuzu."

"And me," she said.

"Yes, and you. He's trying to strip me of all my friends. He doesn't want me to keep any of my old attachments."

"You could simply refuse, husband. Did you ever think of that?"

How I wished it were that easy! "When I had my skull

amped," I said, "Friedlander Bey paid the doctors to wire the punishment center of my brain."

"The punishment center? Not the pleasure center?"

I grinned ruefully. "If he'd had the pleasure center wired, I'd probably already be dead. That's what happens to those wireheads. It wouldn't have taken me long, either."

Indihar frowned. "Well, then, I don't understand. Why the punishment center? Why would you want—"

I raised a hand and cut her off. "Hey, *I* didn't want it! Papa had it done without my knowledge. He's got lots of little electronic gimmicks that can remotely stimulate my pain centers. That's how he keeps me in line." Learning recently that he was truly my mother's grandfather had not disposed me more favorably toward him. Not as long as he refused to discuss the matter of my liberty.

I saw her shudder. "I didn't know that, husband."

"I haven't told many people about it. But Papa's always there looking over my shoulder, ready to jam his thumb on the agony button if I do something he doesn't like."

"So you're a prisoner, too," said Indihar. "You're his slave, as much as the rest of us."

I didn't see any need to reply. The situation was a trifle different in my case, because I shared Friedlander Bey's blood, and I felt obliged to try to love him. I hadn't actually succeeded in that yet. I had a difficult time dealing with that emotion in the first place, and Papa wasn't making it easy for me.

Indihar reached out her hand to me, and I took it. It was the first time since we'd been married that she'd relented any at all. I saw that her palm and fingers were still stained a faint yellow-orange, from the henna her friends had applied the morning of our wedding. It had been a very unusual ceremony, because Papa had declared that it wouldn't be appropriate for me to marry anyone but a maiden. Indihar was, of course, a widow with three children, so he had her declared an honorary virgin. Nobody laughed.

The wedding itself was a mixture of customs observed in the city as well as those from Indihar's native Egyptian village. It pretended to be the joining of a young virgin and a Maghrebi youth of promising fortune. Friedlander Bey announced that it wasn't necessary to fetch Indihar's family to the celebration, that her friends from the Budayeen could stand in for them.

"We'll pass over the ritual certification, of course," Indihar had said.

"What's that?" I asked. I was afraid that at the last minute, I was going to be required to take some kind of written test that I should've been studying for ever since puberty.

"In some backward Muslim lands," explained Friedlander Bey, "on the wedding night, the bride is taken into a bedroom, away from all the other guests. The women of both families hold her down on the bed. The husband wraps a white cloth around his forefinger, and inserts it to prove the girl's virginity. If the cloth comes out stained with blood, the husband passes it out to the bride's father, who then marches around waving it on a stick for all to see."

"But this is the seventeenth century of the Hegira!" I said, astonished.

Indihar shrugged. "It's a moment of great pride for the bride's parents. It proves they've raised a chaste and worthy daughter. When I was first married, I wept at the indignity until I heard the cheers and joy of the guests. Then I knew that my marriage had been blessed, and that I'd become a woman in the eyes of the village."

"As you say, my daughter," said Friedlander Bey, "in

this instance such a certification will not be required."
Papa could be reasonable if he didn't stand to lose anything by it.

I'd bought Indihar a fine gold wedding band, as well as the traditional second piece of jewelry. Chiri, my not-so-silent partner, helped me select the gift in one of the expensive boutiques east of the Boulevard il-Jameel, where the Europeans shopped. It was a brooch, an emerald-encrusted lizard made of gold, with two rubies for eyes. It had cost me twelve thousand kiam, and it was the most expensive single item I'd ever purchased. I gave it to Indihar the morning of the wedding. She opened the satin-lined box, looked at the emerald lizard for a few seconds, and then said, "Thank you, Maríd." She never mentioned it again, and I never saw her wear it.

Indihar had not been well-off, even before her husband was killed. She brought to our marriage only a modest assortment of household furnishings and her meager personal belongings. Her contribution wasn't materially important, because I'd become wealthy through my association with Papa. In fact, the amount specified as her bride-price in our marriage contract was more than Indihar had ever seen in her lifetime. I gave two thirds of it to her in cash. The final third would go to her in the event of our divorce.

I merely dressed in my best white *gallebeya* and robe, but Indihar had to endure much more. Chiri, her best friend, helped her prepare for the ceremony. Early in the day, they removed the hair from Indihar's arms and legs by covering her skin with a mixture of sugar and lemon juice. When the paste hardened, Chiri peeled it off. I'll never forget how wonderfully fresh and sweet-smelling Indihar was that evening. Sometimes I still find myself getting aroused by the fragrance of lemons.

When Indihar finished dressing and applying a modest

amount of makeup, she and I sat for our official wedding holos. Neither of us looked especially happy. We both knew that it was a marriage in name only, and would last only as long as Friedlander Bey lived. The holographer kept making lewd jokes about wedding nights and honeymoons, but Indihar and I just watched the clock, counting the hours until this entire ordeal would be finished.

The ceremony itself took place in Papa's grand hall. There were hundreds of guests; some were friends of ours, and some were sinister, silent men who stood watchfully at the edges of the crowd. My best man was Saied the Half-Hajj, who in honor of the occasion was wearing no moddy at all, something remarkable in its own right. Most of the other club owners in the Budayeen were there, as well as the girls, sexchanges, and debs we knew, and such Budayeen characters as Laila, Fuad, and Bill the cab driver. It could have been a truly joyous occasion, if Indihar and I had loved each other and wanted to get married in the first place.

We sat face to face before a blue-turbaned shaykh who performed the Muslim marriage ceremony. Indihar was lovely in a beautiful white satin dress and white veil, with a bouquet of fragrant blossoms. First the shaykh invoked the blessings of Allah, and read from the first sûrah of the noble Qur'ân. Then he asked Indihar if she consented to the marriage. There was a brief pause, when I thought I saw her eyes fill with regret. "Yes," she said in a quiet voice.

We joined our right hands, and the shaykh covered them with a white handkerchief. Indihar repeated the words of the shaykh, stating that she married me of her own free will, for a bride-price of seventy-five thousand kiam.

"Repeat after me, Marîd Audran," said the shaykh. "I accept from thee your betrothal to myself, and take thee under my care, and bind myself to afford thēe my protection. Ye who are present bear witness of this." I had to say it three times to make it work.

The shaykh finished it off by reading some more from the holy Qur'ân. He blessed us and our marriage. There was an instant of peace in the hall, and then from the throats of all the women came the shrill, trilling sound of the *zagareet*.

There was a party afterward, of course, and I drank and pretended to be happy. There was plenty to eat, and the guests gave us gifts and money. Indihar left early with the excuse that she had to put her children to bed, although Senalda was there to do just that. I left the celebration not long afterward. I went back to my apartment, swallowed seven or eight tabs of Sonneine, and lay on my bed with my eyes closed.

I was married. I was a husband. As the opiates began to take effect, I thought about how beautiful Indihar had looked. I wished that I had at least kissed her.

Those were my memories of our wedding. Now, as I sat in her parlor, I wondered what my real responsibilities were. "You've treated me and my children well," Indihar said. "You've been very generous, and I should be grateful. Forgive me for my behavior, husband."

"You have nothing to be sorry for, Indihar," I said. I stood up. The mention of the children reminded me that they could run squawking and drooling into the parlor at any moment. I wanted to get out of there while I still could. "If there's anything you need, just ask Kmuzu or Tariq."

"We're well provided for." She looked up into my eyes, then turned away. I couldn't tell what she was feeling.

I began to feel awkward myself. "Then I'll leave you. I wish you a good morning."

"May your day be pleasant, husband."

I went to the door and turned to look at her again before I left. She seemed so sad and alone. "Allah bring you peace," I murmured. Then I closed the door behind me.

I had enough time to get back to the smaller dining room near Friedlander Bey's office, where we had breakfast whenever he wanted to discuss business matters with me. He was already seated in his place when I arrived. The two taciturn giants, Habib and Labib, stood behind him, one on either side. They still eyed me suspiciously, as if even after all this time, I might still draw a naked blade and leap for Papa's throat.

"Good morning, my nephew," said Friedlander Bey solemnly. "How is your health?"

"I thank God every hour," I replied. I seated myself across the table from him and began helping myself from the breakfast platters.

Papa was wearing a pale blue long-sleeved shirt and brown woolen trousers, with a red felt *tarboosh* on his head. He hadn't shaved in two or three days, and his face was covered with gray stubble. He'd been hospitalized recently, and he'd lost a lot of weight. His cheeks were sunken and his hands trembled. Still, the sharpness of his mind hadn't been affected.

"Do you have someone in mind to help you with our datalink project, my darling?" he asked me, cutting short the pleasantries and getting right to business.

"I believe so, O Shaykh. My friend, Jacques Dévaux."

"The Moroccan boy? The Christian?"

"Yes," I said, "although I'm not sure that I completely trust him."

Papa nodded. "It's good that you think so. It's not wise to trust any man until he's been tested. We will talk about this more after I hear the estimates from the datalink companies."

"Yes, O Shaykh."

I watched him carefully pare an apple with a silver knife. "You were told of the gathering this evening, my nephew?" he said.

We'd been invited to a reception at the palace of Shaykh Mahali, the amir of the city. "I'm startled to learn that I've come to the prince's attention," I said.

Papa gave me a brief smile. "There is more to it than joy over your recent marriage. The amir has said that he cannot permit a feud to exist between myself and Shaykh Reda Abu Adil."

"Ah, I see. And tonight's celebration will be the amir's attempt to reconcile you?"

"His *futile* attempt to reconcile us." Friedlander Bey frowned at the apple, then stabbed it fiercely with the knife and put it aside. "There will be no peace between Shaykh Reda and myself. That is quite simply impossible. But I can see that the amir is in a difficult position: when kings do battle, it is the peasants who die."

I smiled. "Are you saying that you and Shaykh Reda are the kings in this case, and the prince of the city is the peasant?"

"He certainly cannot match our power, can he? His influence extends over the city, while we control entire nations."

I sat back in my chair and gazed at him. "Do you expect another attack tonight, my grandfather?"

Friedlander Bey rubbed his upper lip thoughtfully. "No," he said slowly, "not tonight, while we're under the protection of the prince. Shaykh Reda is certainly not that foolish. But soon, my nephew. Very soon."

"I'll be on my guard," I said, standing and taking my leave of the old man. The last thing in the world I wanted to hear was that we were being drawn into another intrigue.

During the afternoon I received a delegation from Cappadocia, which wanted Friedlander Bey's help in declaring independence from Anatolia and setting up a people's republic. Most people thought that Papa and Abu Adil made their fortunes by peddling vice, but that was not entirely true. It was a fact that they were responsible for almost all the illicit activities in the city, but that existed primarily as employment for their countless relatives, friends, and associates.

The true source of Papa's wealth was in keeping track of the ever-shifting national lineup in our part of the world. In a time when the average lifespan of a new country was shorter than a single generation of its citizens, someone had to preserve order amid the political chaos. That was the expensive service that Friedlander Bey and Shaykh Reda provided. From one regime to the next, they remembered where the boundaries were, who the taxpayers were, and where the bodies were buried, literally and figuratively. Whenever one government gave way to its successor, Papa or Shaykh Reda stepped in to smooth the transition—and to cut themselves a larger chunk of the action with each change.

I found all of this fascinating, and I was glad that Papa had put me to work in this area, rather than overseeing the lucrative but basically boring criminal enterprises. My great-grandfather tutored me with endless patience, and he'd directed Tariq and Youssef to give me whatever help I needed. When I'd first come to Friedlander Bey's house, I'd thought they were only Papa's valet and butler; but now I realized they knew more about the high-level goings-on throughout the Islamic world than anyone else, except Friedlander Bey himself.

When at last the Cappadocians excused themselves, I

saw that I had little more than an hour before Papa and I were expected at the amir's palace. Kmuzu helped me select an appropriate outfit. It had been some time since I'd last put on my old jeans and boots and work shirt, and I was getting used to wearing a more traditional Arab costume. Some of the men in the city still wore Euram-style business suits, but I'd never felt comfortable in one. I'd taken to wearing the *gallebeya* around Papa's house, because I knew he preferred it. Besides, it was easier to hide my static pistol under a loose robe, and a *keffiya,* the Arab headdress, hid my implants, which offended some conservative Muslims.

So when I'd finished dressing, I was wearing a spotless white *gallebeya* suitable for a bridegroom, beneath a royal blue robe trimmed in gold. I had comfortable sandals on my feet, a ceremonial dagger belted around my waist, and a plain white *keffiya* held by a black rope *akal.*

"You look very handsome, *yaa Sidi,*" said Kmuzu.

"I hope so," I said. "I've never gone to meet a prince before."

"You've proven your worth, and your reputation must already be known to the amir. You have no reason to be intimidated by him."

That was easy for Kmuzu to say. I took a final glance at my reflection and wasn't particularly impressed by what I saw. "Marîd Audran, Defender of the Downtrodden," I said dubiously. "Yeah, you right." Then we went downstairs to meet Friedlander Bey.

Tariq drove Papa's limousine, and we arrived at the amir's palace on time. We were shown into the ballroom, and I was invited to recline on some cushions at the place of honor, at Shaykh Mahali's right hand. Friedlander Bey and the other guests made themselves comfortable, and I was introduced to many of the city's wealthy and influential men.

"Please, refresh yourself," said the amir. A servant offered a tray laden with small cups of thick coffee spiced with cardamom and cinnamon, and tall glasses of chilled fruit juices. There were no alcoholic beverages because Shaykh Mahali was a deeply religious man.

"May your table last forever," I said. "Your hospitality is famous in the city, O Shaykh."

"Rejoicings and celebrations!" he replied, pleased by my flattery. We conversed for about half an hour before the servants began bringing in platters of vegetables and roasted meats. The amir had ordered enough food to stuff a company five times our size. He used an elegant, jeweled knife to offer me the choicest morsels. I've had a lifelong distrust of the rich and powerful, but despite that, I rather liked the prince.

He poured a cup of coffee for himself and offered me another. "We live in a mongrel city," he told me, "and there are so many factions and parties that my judgment is always being tested. I study the methods of the great Muslim rulers of the past. Just today I read a wonderful story about Ibn Saud, who governed a united Arabia that for a time bore his family's name. He, too, had to devise swift and clever solutions to difficult problems.

"One day when Ibn Saud was visiting the camp of a tribe of nomads, a shrieking woman ran to him and clasped his feet. She demanded that the murderer of her husband be put to death.

" 'How was your husband killed?' asked the king.

"The woman said, 'The murderer climbed high up on a date palm to pick the fruit. My husband was minding his own business, sitting beneath the tree in the shade. The murderer lost his grip in the tree and fell on him, breaking my husband's neck. Now he is dead and I am a poor widow with no way to support my orphaned children!'

"Ibn Saud rubbed his chin thoughtfully. 'Do you think the man fell on your husband intentionally?' he asked.

" 'What difference does it make? My husband is dead all the same!'

" 'Well, will you take an honest compensation, or do you truly demand the death of this man?'

" 'According to the Straight Path, the murderer's life belongs to me.'

"Ibn Saud shrugged. There was very little he could do with such an obstinate woman, but he said this to her: 'Then he will die, and the manner of his death must be the same as the way he took your husband's life. I command that this man be tied firmly to the trunk of the date palm. You must climb forty feet to the top of the tree, and from there you shall fall down upon the neck of the man and kill him.' The king paused to look at the woman's family and neighbors gathered around. 'Or will you accept the honest compensation, after all?'

"The woman hesitated a moment, accepted the money, and went away."

I laughed out loud, and the other guests applauded Shaykh Mahali's anecdote. In a short time I'd completely forgotten that he was the amir of the city and I was, well, only who I am.

The pleasant edge was taken off the evening by the grand entrance of Reda Abu Adil. He came in noisily, and he greeted the other guests as if he and not the amir were the host of the party. He was dressed very much as I was, including a *keffiya*, which I knew was hiding his own corymbic implant. Behind Abu Adil trailed a young man, probably his new administrative assistant and lover. The young man had short blond hair, wire-rimmed spectacles, and thin, bloodless lips. He was wearing an ankle-length white cotton shift with an expensively tailored silk sport coat over it, and blue felt slippers on his feet. He glanced around the room and turned a look of distaste on everyone in turn.

Abu Adil's expression turned to joy when he saw Friedlander Bey and me. "My old friends!" he cried, crossing the ballroom and pulling Papa to his feet. They embraced, although Papa said nothing at all. Then Shaykh Reda turned to me. "And here is the lucky bridegroom!"

I didn't stand up, which was a blatant insult, but Abu Adil pretended not to notice. "I've brought you a fine gift!" he said, looking around to be certain that everyone was paying attention. "Kenneth, give the young man his gift."

The blond kid stared at me for a brief moment, sizing me up. Then he reached into his jacket's inner pocket and took out an envelope. He held it out toward me between two fingers, but he wasn't going to come close enough for me to take it. Apparently he thought this was some kind of contest.

Personally, I didn't give a damn. I went to him and grabbed the envelope. He gave me a little quirk of the lips and raised his eyebrows, as if to say "We'll sort out where we stand later." I wanted to throw the envelope in the fool's face.

I remembered where I was and who was watching, so I tore open the envelope and took out a folded sheet of paper. I read Abu Adil's gift, but I couldn't make any sense of it. I read it again, and it wasn't any clearer the second time. "I don't know what to say," I said.

Shaykh Reda laughed. "I knew you'd be pleased!" Then he turned slowly, so that his words would be heard easily by the others. "I have used my influence with the *Jaish* to obtain a commission for Marîd Audran. He's now an officer in the Citizen's Army!"

The *Jaish* was this unofficial right-wing outfit that I'd run into before. They liked to dress up in gray uniforms and parade through the streets. Originally their mission was to rid the city of foreigners. As time passed, and as more of the paramilitary group's funding came from people such as Reda Abu Adil—who himself had come to the city at a young age—the aim of the *Jaish* changed. Now it seemed that its mission was to harass Abu Adil's enemies, foreigner and native alike.

"I don't know what to say," I said again. It was a pretty bizarre thing for Shaykh Reda to have done, and for the life of me, I couldn't figure what his motive had been. Knowing him, however, it would all become painfully clear soon enough.

"All our past disagreements have been settled," said Abu Adil cheerfully. "We'll be friends and allies from now on. We must work together to better the lives of the poor *fellahîn* who depend on us."

The assembled guests liked that sentiment and applauded. I glanced at Friedlander Bey, who only gave me a slight shrug. It was obvious to us both that Abu Adil had some new scheme unfolding before our eyes.

"Then I toast the bridegroom," said Shaykh Mahali, rising. "And I toast the ending of conflict between Friedlander Bey and Reda Abu Adil. I am known among my people as an honest man, and I have tried to rule this city with wisdom and justice. This peace between your houses will make my own task simpler." He lifted his cup of coffee, and everyone else stood and followed suit. To all but Papa and me, it must have seemed a hopeful time of reconciliation. I felt nothing but a growing knot of dread deep in my belly.

The remainder of the evening was pleasant enough, I guess. After a while I was quite full of food and coffee, and I'd had enough conversation with wealthy strangers to last me many days. Abu Adil did not go out of his way to cross our paths again that night, but I couldn't help noticing that his blond pal, Kenneth, kept glancing at me and shaking his head.

I suffered through the party for a little while longer, but then I was driven outside by boredom. I enjoyed Shaykh Mahali's elaborate gardens, taking deep breaths of the flower-scented air and sipping an iced glass of Sharâb. The party was still going strong inside the amir's official residence, but I'd had enough of the other guests, who came in two varieties: men I'd never met before and with whom I had little in common, and men I did know and whom I just wanted to avoid.

There were no female guests at this affair, so even though it was nominally a celebration of my marriage, my wife Indihar was not present. I'd come with Kmuzu, Friedlander Bey, his driver, Tariq, and his two giant body-guards, Habib and Labib. Tariq, Kmuzu, and the Stones That Speak were enjoying their refreshments with the other servants in a separate building that also served as the amir's garage and stables.

"If you wish to return home, my nephew," said Fried-lander Bey, "we may take leave of our host." Papa had always called me "nephew," although he must have known of our true relationship since before our first meeting.

"I've had my fill of this amusement, O Shaykh," I said. Actually, for the last quarter hour I'd been watching a meteor shower in the cloudless sky.

"It is just as well. I've grown very tired. Here, let me lean on your arm."

"Certainly, O Shaykh." He'd always been a bull of a man, but he was old, nearing his two-hundredth birthday. And not many months before, someone had tried to mur-der him, and he'd required a lot of sophisticated neuro-surgery to repair the damage. He'd not yet completely recovered from that experience, and he was still weak and rather unsteady.

Together we made our way up from the beautiful formal gardens and back along the cloistered walk to the softly lighted ballroom. When he saw us approaching, the amir rose and came forward, extending his arms to embrace Friedlander Bey. "You have done my house great honor, O Excellent One!" he said.

I stood aside and let Papa take care of the formalities. I had the sense that the reception had been some kind of meeting between those two powerful men, that the celebration of my marriage had been entirely irrelevant to whatever subtle discussions they had conducted. "May your table last forever, O Prince!" said Papa.

"I thank you, O Wise One," said Shaykh Mahali. "Are you leaving us now?"

"It is after midnight, and I'm an old man. After I depart, you young men may get on with the serious revelry."

The amir laughed. "You take our love with you, O Shaykh." He leaned forward and kissed Friedlander Bey on both cheeks. "Go in safety."

"May Allah lengthen your life," said Papa.

Shaykh Mahali turned to me. *"Kif oo basat!"* he said. That means "Good spirits and cheer!" and it kind of sums up the city's attitude toward life.

"We thank you for your hospitality," I said, "and for the honor you've done us."

The amir seemed pleased with me. "May the blessings of Allah be on you, young man," he said.

"Peace be with you, O Prince." And we backed away a few steps, then turned and walked out into the night.

I had been given a veritable hillock of gifts by the amir and by many of the other guests. These were still on display in the ballroom, and would be gathered up and delivered to Friedlander Bey's house the next day. As Papa and I emerged into the warm night air, I felt well fed and content. We passed through the gardens again, and I admired the carefully tended flowering trees and their shimmering images in the reflecting pool. Faintly over the water came the sound of laughter, and I heard the liquid trickle of fountains, but otherwise the night was still.

Papa's limousine was sheltered in Shaykh Mahali's garage. We'd begun to cross the grassy courtyard toward it, when its headlights flashed on. The ancient car—one of the few internal combustion vehicles still operating in the city—rolled slowly toward us. The driver's window slid silently down, and I was surprised to see not Tariq but Hajjar, the crooked police lieutenant who supervised the affairs of the Budayeen.

"Get in the car," he said. "Both of you."

I looked at Friedlander Bey, who only shrugged. We got in the car. Hajjar probably thought he was in control, but Papa didn't seem the least bit worried, even though there was a big guy with a needle gun in his hand facing us on the jump seat.

"The hell's this all about, Hajjar?" I said.

"I'm placing both of you under arrest," said the cop. He pressed a control, and the glass panel slid up between him and the passenger compartment. Papa and I were alone with Hajjar's goon, and the goon didn't seem interested in making conversation.

"Just stay calm," said Papa.

"This is Abu Adil's doing, isn't it?" I said.

"Possibly." He shrugged. "It will all be made clear according to the will of Allah."

I couldn't help fretting. I hate being helpless. I watched Friedlander Bey, a prisoner in his own limousine, in the hands of a cop who'd taken the pay of both Papa and his chief rival, Reda Abu Adil. For a few minutes, my stomach churned and I rehearsed several clever

and heroic things I'd do when Hajjar let us out of the car
again. Then, as we drove through the twisting, narrow
back streets of the city, my mind began searching for
some clue as to what was happening to us now.

Soon the pain in my belly really began to gripe me,
and I wished I'd brought my pillcase with me. Papa had
warned me that it would be a serious breach of etiquette
to carry my cache of pharmaceuticals into the amir's
house. This was what I got for turning into such a respect-
ful guy. I got kidnapped, and I had to suffer through every
little physical discomfort that came my way.

I had a small selection of daddies on a rack in the
pocket of my *gallebeya*. One of them did a great job of
blocking pain, but I didn't want to find out what the goon
would do if I tried to reach inside my robe. It wouldn't
have cheered me up to hear that things would soon get a
lot worse before they got better.

After what seemed like an hour of driving, the limousine came to a stop. I didn't know where we were. I
looked at Hajjar's goon and said, "What's going on?"

"Shut up," the goon informed me.

Hajjar got out of the car and held the door open for
Papa. I climbed out after him. We were standing beside
some buildings made of corrugated metal, looking at a
private suborbital shuttle across a broad concrete apron,
its running lights flashing but its three giant thrusters cool
and quiet. If this was the main airfield, then we were
about thirty miles north of the city. I'd never been there
before.

I was getting worried, but Papa still had a calm look
on his face. Hajjar pulled me aside. "Got your phone on
you, Audran?" he said quietly.

"Yeah," I said. I always wear it on my belt.

"Let me use it a minute, okay?"

I unclipped my phone and handed it to Hajjar. He

grinned at me, dropped the phone to the pavement, and stomped it into tiny broken pieces. "Thanks," he said.

"The fuck is going on?" I shouted, grabbing him by the arm.

Hajjar just looked at me, amused. Then his goon grabbed me and pinned both of my arms behind my back. "We're going to get on that shuttle," he said. "There's a qadi who has something to tell the both of you."

We were taken aboard the suborbital and made to take seats in an otherwise empty front cabin. Hajjar sat beside me, and his goon sat beside Friedlander Bey. "We have a right to know where you're taking us," I said.

Hajjar examined his fingernails, pretending indifference. "Tell you the truth," he said, gazing out the window, "I don't actually know where you're going. The qadi may tell you that when he reads you the verdict."

"Verdict?" I cried. "What verdict?"

"Oh," said Hajjar with an evil grin, "haven't you figured it out? You and Papa are on trial. The qadi will decide you're guilty while you're being deported. Doing it this way saves the legal system a lot of time and money. I should've let you kiss the ground good-bye, Audran, because you're never going to see the city again!"

2

Honey Pílar is the most desirable woman in the world. Ask anybody. Ask the ancient, wrinkled imam of the Shimaal Mosque, and he'll tell you "Honey Pílar, no question about it." She has long, pale hair, liquid green eyes, and the most awe-inspiring body known to anthropological science. Fortunately, she's attainable. What she does for a living is record personality modules of herself during sex play. There are Brigitte Stahlhelm and other stars in the sex-moddy industry, but none of them come close to delivering the super-light-speed eroticism of Honey Pílar.

A few times, just for variety, I told Yasmin that I wanted to wear one of Honey's moddies. Yasmin would grin and take over the active role, and I'd lie back and experience what it felt like to be a hungry, furiously responsive woman. If nothing else, the moddy trade has helped a lot of people get some insight into what makes the eight opposite sexes tick.

After we'd finished jamming, I'd keep Honey's moddy chipped in for a while. Honey's afterglow was just as phenomenal as her orgasms. Without the moddy, I might have rolled over and drifted off to sleep. With it, I curled up close to Yasmin, closed my eyes, and just bathed in physical and emotional well-being. The only other thing I can compare it to is a nice shot of morphine. The way the morphine makes you feel after you're done throwing up, I mean.

That's just how I felt when I opened my eyes. I didn't have any memory of supersonic sex, so I assumed that somewhere along the line I'd run into a friendly pharmaceutical or two. My eyelids seemed stuck together, and when I tried to rub the gunk out of them, my arm wouldn't work. It felt like a phony arm made out of Styrofoam or something, and it didn't want to do anything but flop around on the sand next to me.

Okay, I thought, I'm going to have to sort all this out in a minute or two. I forgot about my eyes and sunk back into delicious lethargy. Someday I wanted to meet the guy who invented lethargy, because I now believed he hadn't gotten enough credit from the world at large. This was exactly how I wanted to spend the rest of my life, and until somebody came up with a reason why I couldn't, I was just going to lie there in the dark and play with my floppy arm.

I was lying with my back on the earth, and my mind was floating in Heaven somewhere, and the dividing line seemed to run right through my body. Right through the part that hurt so much. I could feel the ragged pain thrumming down there, beneath the opiate haze. As soon as I realized what kind of agony I'd feel when the drug wore off, I began to get very afraid. Fortunately, I couldn't keep my mind on it for more than a few seconds, and then I was grinning and murmuring to myself again.

I suppose I fell asleep, although in that state it was very hard to tell the difference between consciousness and dreams. I remember trying again to open my eyes, and this time I could move my hand to my chin and kind of walk the fingers across my lips and nose to my eyelids. I wiped my eyes clean, but I was so tired from that exertion that I couldn't move my hand back down. I had to rest for a minute or so with my fingers blocking my vision. Finally I tried to focus on my surroundings.

I couldn't see much. It was still too much trouble to raise my head, so all I could make out was what was directly in front of me. There was a bright triangle with a narrow base on the ground, rising up to a sharp point a few feet high. All the rest was blackness. I asked myself if I'd ever been put in mortal danger by a bright triangle. The answer was slow in coming: no. Good, I thought, then I can forget about it. I went back to sleep.

The next time I woke up, things were different. Not pleasantly different. I had a tremendous, throbbing misery in my head, and my throat felt as if a tiny little man in goggles had crawled down there and sandblasted it. My chest ached as if I'd inhaled a couple of pounds of mud and then had to cough it all up again. Every joint in my body shrieked with soreness whenever I made the slightest movement. My arms and legs were in particular agony, so I decided never to move them again.

Cataloguing all the discomfort occupied me for a few minutes, but when I got to the end of the list—when I realized that most of my skin surface was sizzling with pain, proof that I'd been flayed alive by some madman before he got around to cracking my bones—there were only a few choices: I could lie there and appreciate the totality of my suffering, I could try cataloguing again to see if I'd missed anything, or I could attempt to make myself feel better.

I opted for number three. I decided to get out my pillcase, even though that act would probably cost me a lot in terms of further distress. I remembered what my doctors told me in times like this: "Now," they always said, "this might sting a little." Uh huh.

I gently moved my right hand down across my belly, until it was resting flat beside me. Then I sort of worm-walked my fingers down my *gallebeya* toward the pocket where I kept my drugs. I made three rapid observations. The first was that I wasn't wearing my *gallebeya*. The second was that I was wearing a long, filthy shirt with no pockets. The third was that there was no pillcase.

I've been confronted by maniacs whose immediate concern was ending my life on the spot. Even in those most desperate hours, I never experienced the sheer, cold emptiness I felt now. I wonder what it says about me, that I'd prefer to risk death than endure pain. I suppose, deep down, I'm not a brave man. I'm probably motivated by a fear that other people might learn the truth about me.

I almost began to weep when I couldn't find my pill-case. I'd counted on it being there, and on the tabs of Sonneine inside to take away all this horrible pain, at least for a while. I tried to call out. My lips were as crusted over as my eyelids had been. It took a little effort even to open my mouth, and then my throat was too hoarse and dry for me to speak. At last, after much effort, I managed to croak "Help." Uttering the single syllable made the back of my throat feel as if someone had hacked my neck open with a dull knife. I doubted that anyone could have heard me.

I don't know how much time passed. I grew aware that in addition to my other discomforts, I was also suffering from great hunger and thirst. The longer I lay there, the more I began to worry that I'd finally gotten myself into trouble I wouldn't survive. I hadn't yet begun to speculate on where I was or how I'd got there.

I noticed after a while that the bright triangle was getting dimmer. Sometimes I thought the triangle seemed obscured, as if someone or something was passing in front of it. At last, the triangle almost completely disappeared. I realized that I missed it very much. It had been the only actual thing in my world besides myself, even though I didn't really know what it was.

A spot of yellow light appeared in the gloom where the bright triangle had been. I blinked my eyes hard a few times, trying to make them focus more clearly. I saw that the yellow light was coming from a small oil lamp, in the hand of a small person swathed almost completely in black. The black-clothed person came toward me through the triangle, which I now guessed must be the opening of a tent. A truly evil-smelling tent, I realized.

My visitor held the lamp up to let the light fall upon my face. *"Yaa Allah!"* she murmured when she saw that I was conscious. Her other hand quickly grasped the edge of her head cloth and pulled it across her face. I had seen her only briefly, but I knew that she was a solemn, pretty, but very dirty girl, probably in her late teens.

I took as deep a breath as I could with the pain in my chest and lungs, and I croaked out another "Help." She stood there, blinking down at me for a few moments. Then she knelt, placed the lamp on the level sand beyond my reach, stood up again, and ran from the tent. I have that effect on women sometimes.

Now I began to worry. Where exactly was I, and how did I get here? Was I in the hands of friends or enemies? I knew I must be among desert nomads, but which desert? There are quite a number of sand seas throughout the geographic expanse of the Islamic world. I could be anywhere from the western edge of the Sahara in Morocco to the fringes of the Gobi in Mongolia. I might have been only a few miles south of the city, for that matter.

While I was turning these thoughts over in my troubled mind, the dark-shrouded girl returned. She stood beside me and asked me questions. I could tell they were questions by the inflections. The trouble was that I could make out only about one word in ten. She was speaking some rough dialect of Arabic, but she might as well have been jabbering in Japanese for all I could tell.

I shook my head, once slightly to the left, once to the right. "I hurt," I said in my dead voice.

She just stared at me. It didn't seem that she'd understood me. She was still holding her head cloth modestly across her face, just below her nose, but I thought her expression—that part of it that was visible—was very kind and concerned. At least, I chose to believe that for the moment.

She tried speaking to me again, but I still couldn't understand what she was saying. I managed to get out "Who are you?" and she nodded and said "Noora." In Arabic, that means "light," but I guessed it was also her name. From the moment she'd come into the tent with her lamp, she'd been the only light in my darkness.

The front flap was thrown roughly aside and someone else entered, carrying a leather bag and another lamp. This was not a large tent, maybe twelve feet in diameter and six feet high, so it was getting kind of crowded. Noora moved back against the black wall, and the man squatted beside me and studied me for a moment. He had a stern, lean face dominated by a huge hooked nose. His skin was lined and weathered, and it was difficult for me to guess his age. He wore a long shirt and he had a *keffiya* on his head, but it wasn't bound with a black rope *akal*, merely twisted around with its ends stuffed in somehow. In the dancing shadows he looked like a murderous savage.

Matters weren't made any better when he asked me a few questions in the same dialect Noora had used. I think one of them had to do with where I'd come from. All I could do was tell him about the city. He may have then asked me where the city was, but I couldn't be sure that's what he said.

"I hurt," I croaked.

He nodded and opened his leather bag. I was surprised when he pulled out an old-fashioned disposable syringe and a vial of some fluid. He loaded the needle and jammed it into my hip. I gasped in pain, and he patted my wrist. He clucked something, and even ignorant of his dialect I could tell it was "There, there."

He stood up and regarded me thoughtfully for a while longer. Then he signaled to Noora and they left me alone. In a few minutes, the injection had taken effect. My expertise in these matters told me that I'd been given a healthy dose of Sonneine; the injectable variety was much more effective than the tabs I bought in the Budayeen. I was tearfully grateful. If that rough-skinned man had come back into the tent just then, I would have given him anything he asked.

I surrendered myself to the powerful drug and floated, knowing all the while that the relief from pain would soon end. In the illusory moments of well-being, I tried to do some serious thinking. I knew that something was terribly wrong, and that as soon as I was better I'd need to set things right again. The Sonneine let me believe that nothing was beyond my power.

My drug-deluded mind told me that I was in a state of grace. Everything was fine. I'd achieved a separate peace with the world and with every individual in it. I felt as if I had immense stores of physical and intellectual energy to draw upon. There were problems, yes, but they were eminently solvable. The future looked like one golden vista of victory after another: Heaven on Earth.

It was while I was congratulating myself on my good fortune that the hawk-faced man returned, this time without Noora. I was sort of sad about that. Anyway, the man squatted down beside me, resting his haunches on his heels. I could never get the hang of sitting like that for very long; I've always been a city boy.

This time when he spoke to me, I could understand him perfectly. "Who are you, O Shaykh?" he asked.

"Ma—" I began. My throat tightened up. I pointed to my lips. The man understood me and passed me a goatskin bag filled with brackish water. The bag stunk and the water was the most foul-tasting I'd ever encountered. *"Bismillah,"* I murmured: in the name of God. Then I drank that horrible water greedily until he put a hand on my arm and stopped me.

"Marîd," I said, answering his question.

He took back the water bag. "I am Hassanein. Your beard is red. I've never seen a red beard before."

"Common," I said, able to speak a little better now that I'd had some water. "In Mauretania."

"Mauretania?" He shook his head.

"Used to be Algeria. In the Maghreb." Again he shook his head. I wondered how far I'd wandered, that I'd met an Arab who had never heard of the Maghreb, the name given to the western Muslim lands of North Africa.

"What race are you?" Hassanein asked.

I looked at him in surprise. "An Arab," I said.

"No," he said, *"I* am an Arab. You are something else." He was firm in his statement, although I could tell that it was made without malice. He was truly curious about me.

Calling myself an Arab was inaccurate, because I am

half Berber, half French, or so my mother always told me. In my adopted city, anyone born in the Muslim world and who spoke the Arabic language was an Arab. Here in Hassanein's tent that relaxed definition would not do. "I am Berber," I told him.

"I do not know Berbers. We are Bani Salim."

"Badawi?" I asked.

"Bedu," he corrected me. It turned out that the word I'd always used for the Arabian nomads, Badawi or Bedouin, was an inelegant plural of a plural. The nomads themselves preferred Bedu, which derives from the word for desert.

"You treated me?" I said.

Hassanein nodded. He reached out his hand. In the flickering lamplight, I could see the dusting of sand on the hairs of his arm, like sugar on a lemon cake. He lightly touched my corymbic implants. "You are cursed," he said.

I didn't reply. Apparently he was a strict Muslim who felt that I was going to hell because I'd had my brain wired.

"You are doubly cursed," he said. Even here, my second implant was a topic of conversation. I wondered where my rack of moddies and daddies was.

"Hungry," I said.

He nodded. "Tomorrow, you may eat, *inshallah*." If God wills. It was hard for me to imagine that Allah had brought me through whatever trials I'd endured, just to keep me from having breakfast in the morning.

He picked up the lamp and held it close to my face. With a grimy thumb he pulled down my eyelid and examined my eye. He had me open my mouth, and he looked at my tongue and the back of my throat. He bent forward and put his ear on my chest, then had me cough. He poked and prodded me expertly. "School," I said, pointing at him. "University."

He laughed and shook his head. He slowly bent my legs up and then tickled the soles of my feet. He pressed on my fingernails and watched to see how long it took for the color to return.

"Doctor?" I asked.

He shook his head again. Then he looked at me and came to some decision. He grabbed his *keffiya* and pulled it loose. I was astonished to see that he had his own moddy plug on the crown of his skull. Then he carefully wrapped the *keffiya* around his head again.

I looked at him questioningly. "Cursed," I said.

"Yes," he said. He wore a stoic expression. "I am the shaykh of the Bani Salim. It is my responsibility. I must wear the mark of the *shaitan*."

"How many moddies?" I asked.

He didn't understand the word "moddies." I rephrased the question, and found out that he'd had his skull amped so that he could use just two modules: the doctor moddy, and one that made him the equivalent of a learned religious leader. Those were all he owned. In the arid wilderness that was home to the Bani Salim, Hassanein was the wise elder who had, in his own eyes, damned his soul for the sake of his tribe.

I realized that we were understanding each other thanks to grammar and vocabulary built into the doctor moddy. When he took it out, we'd have as much trouble communicating as we'd had before. I was getting too weary to keep up this conversation any further, though. Any more would have to wait until tomorrow.

He gave me a capsule to help me sleep through the night. I swallowed it with more of the water from the goatskin. "May you arise in the morning in well-being, O Shaykh," he said.

"God bless you, O Wise One," I murmured. He left the lamp burning on the sand floor beside me, and stood up. He went out into the darkness, and I heard him drop the tent flap behind him. I still didn't know where I was, and I didn't know a damn thing about the Bani Salim, but for some reason I felt perfectly safe. I fell asleep quickly and woke up only once during the night, to see Noora sitting crosslegged against the black wall of the tent, asleep.

When I woke again in the morning, I could see more clearly. I raised my head a little and stared out through the bright triangle. Now I could see a landscape of golden sand and, not far away, two hobbled camels. In the tent, Noora still watched over me. She had awakened before me, and when she saw me move my head, she came closer. She still self-consciously drew the edge of her head scarf across her face, which was a shame because she was very pretty.

"Thought we were friends," I said. I didn't have so much trouble talking this morning.

Her brows drew together and she shook her head. I wasn't having trouble talking, but I was still having trouble being understood. I tried again, speaking more slowly and using both hands to amplify my words.

"We . . . are . . . friends," she said. Each word was strangely accented, but I could decipher the dialect if she gave me a little time. "You . . . guest . . . of . . . Bani Salim."

Ah, the legendary hospitality of the Bedu! "Hassanein is your father?" I asked. She shook her head; I didn't know if she was denying the relationship or if she just hadn't understood my question. I repeated it more slowly.

"Shaykh . . . Hassanein . . . father's . . . brother," she said.

After that, we both got used to speaking simply and putting space between our words. It wasn't long before we weren't having any trouble following each other, even at normal conversational speed.

"Where are we?" I asked. I had to find where I was in relation to the city, and how far from the nearest outpost of civilization.

Noora's brow wrinkled again as she considered her geography. She poked a forefinger into the sand in front of her. "Here is Bir Balagh. The Bani Salim have camped here two weeks." She poked another hole in the sand, about three inches from the first. "Here is Khaba well, three days south." She reached across the much greater distance between us and made another hole with her finger. "Here is Mughshin. Mughshin is *hauta.*"

"What's *hauta?*" I asked.

"A holy place, Shaykh Marîd. The Bani Salim will meet other tribes there, and sell their camel herd."

Fine, I thought, we were all headed for Mughshin. I'd never heard of Mughshin, and I imagined it was probably just a little patch of palm trees and a well, stuck in the middle of the awful desert. It most likely didn't have a suborbital shuttle field nearby. I knew I was lost somewhere in the kingdoms and unmarked tribal turfs of Arabia. "How far from Riyadh?" I asked.

"I don't know Riyadh," said Noora. Riyadh was the former capital of her country, when it had been united under the House of Saud. It was still a great city.

"Mecca?"

"Makkah," she corrected me. She thought for a few seconds, then pointed confidently across my body.

"That way," I said. "Good. How far?" Noora only shrugged. I hadn't learned very much.

"I'm sorry," she said. "The old shaykh asked the same questions. Maybe Uncle Hassanein knows more."

The old shaykh! I'd been so wrapped up in my own

misery that I'd forgotten about Papa. "The old shaykh is alive?"

"Yes, thanks to you, and thanks to the wisdom of Uncle Hassanein. When Hilal and bin Turki found the two of you on the dunes, they thought you were both dead. They came back to our camp, and if they hadn't told Uncle Hassanein about you later that evening, you surely *would* be dead."

I stared at her for a moment. "Hilal and bin Turki just left us out there?"

She shrugged. "They thought you were dead."

I shivered. "Glad it crossed their minds to mention us while they were sitting comfortably around the communal fire."

Noora didn't catch my bitterness. "Uncle Hassanein brought you back to camp. This is his tent. The old shaykh is in the tent of bin Musaid." Her eyes lowered when she mentioned his name.

"Then where are your uncle and bin Musaid sleeping?" I asked.

"They sleep with the others who have no tents. On the sand by the fire."

That naturally made me feel a little guilty, because I knew the desert got very cold at night. "How is the old shaykh?" I asked.

"He is getting stronger every day. He suffered greatly from exposure and thirst, but not as greatly as you. It was your sacrifice that kept him alive, Shaykh Marîd."

I didn't remember any sacrifice. I didn't remember anything about what we'd been through. Noora must have seen my confusion, because she reached out and almost touched my implants. "These," she said. "You abused them and now you suffer, but it saved the life of the old shaykh. He wants very much to speak with you. Uncle Hassanein told him that tomorrow you may have visitors."

I was relieved to hear that Friedlander Bey was in better shape than I was. I hoped that he might be able to fill in some of the gaps in my recollection. "How long have I been here?"

She did some mental figuring, then replied, "Twelve days. The Bani Salim planned to remain in Bir Balagh only three days, but Uncle Hassanein decided to stay until you and the old shaykh were fit to travel. Some of the tribe are angry about that, especially bin Musaid."

"You mentioned him before. Who is this bin Musaid?"

Noora lowered her eyes and spoke in a low voice. "He desires to marry me," she said.

"Uh huh. And how do you feel about him?"

She looked into my face. I could see anger in her eyes, although I couldn't tell if it was directed at me or her suitor. She stood up and walked out of the tent without saying another word.

I wished she hadn't done that. I'd meant to ask her for something to eat, and to pass the word to her uncle that I'd like another jolt of Sonneine. Instead, I just tried to find a comfortable position to lie in, and I thought about what Noora had told me.

Papa and I had almost died in this wilderness, but I didn't yet know whom to blame that on. I wouldn't be surprised if it was all connected to Lieutenant Hajjar, and through him to Reda Abu Adil. The last thing I remembered was sitting on that suborbital shuttle, waiting for it to take off. Everything that came after—the flight itself, the arrival at the destination, and whatever events had led me into the middle of the desert—was still missing from my memory. I hoped it would all come back as I got stronger, or that Papa had a clearer idea of what had happened.

I decided to focus my rage on Abu Adil. I knew that although I felt peaceful enough now, I was still in deadly peril. For one thing, even if the Bani Salim permitted us to accompany them to Mughshin—wherever the hell *that* was—it would be very difficult to arrange our travel back to the city. We couldn't just show up again without risking arrest. We'd have to avoid Papa's mansion, and it would be very dangerous for me to set foot in the Budayeen.

All that was in the future, however. We had more immediate things to worry about. I had no real assurance that the Bani Salim would remain friendly. I guessed that Bedu hospitality required them to nurse Papa and me back to health. After that, all bets were off. When we were able to fend for ourselves again, the tribe might even capture us and turn us over to our enemies. There might be reward money in it for them. It would be a mistake to let our guard down too far.

I knew one thing for certain: if Hajjar and Abu Adil were responsible for what happened to us after we left the shuttle, they would pay dearly for it. I would swear an oath to that effect.

My grim thoughts were interrupted by Hassanein, who gave me a cheerful greeting. "Here, O Shaykh," he said, "you may eat." He gave me a round, flat piece of unleavened bread and a bowl of some ghastly white fluid. I looked up at him. "Camel's milk," he said. I'd been afraid he was going to say that.

"Bismillah," I murmured. I broke a piece of bread and ate it, then sipped from the bowl. The camel's milk wasn't bad, actually. It was certainly much easier to get down than the water in the goatskin bag.

Shaykh Hassanein squatted on his heels beside me. "Some of the Bani Salim are restless," he said, "and they say that if we wait here too long, we won't get as much money for our camels in Mughshin. Also, we must find somewhere else to graze the animals. You must be ready to travel in two days."

"Sure, be ready when you are." Ha ha, I thought. I was just putting up a noble front.

He nodded. "Eat some more bread. Later, Noora will bring you some dates and tea. Tonight, if you wish, you may have a little roasted goat."

I was so hungry that I'd have gnawed an uncooked carcass. There was sand in the bread and grit in the milk, but I didn't care.

"Have you used this time to ponder the meaning of what has happened to you?" asked Hassanein.

"Yes, indeed, O Wise One," I said. "My mind is empty of the details, but I've thought long and hard about why I came so near to death. I've looked ahead, too. There will come a harvesting."

The leader of the Bani Salim nodded. I wondered if he knew what I was thinking. I wondered if he would recognize the name of Reda Abu Adil. "That is well," he said in a carefully neutral voice. He stood up to leave.

"O Wise One," I said, "will you give me something for the pain?"

His eyes narrowed as he looked down at me. "Are you truly still in such pain?"

"Yes. I'm stronger now, all praise be to Allah, but my body still suffers from the abuse."

He muttered something under his breath, but he opened his leather bag and prepared another injection. "This will be the last," he told me. Then he jabbed me in the hip.

It occurred to me that he probably didn't have a vast store of medical supplies. Hassanein had to tend to all the accidents and illnesses that struck the Bani Salim, and I had probably already consumed much of his pain-relieving medication. I wished I hadn't selfishly taken this last shot. I sighed as I waited for the Sonneine to take effect.

Hassanein left the tent, and Noora entered again.

"Anyone ever told you you're very beautiful, my sister?" I said. I wouldn't have been so bold if the opiate hadn't chosen that instant to bloom in my brain.

I could see that I'd made Noora very uncomfortable. She covered her face with her head scarf and took her position against the wall of the tent. She did not speak to me.

"Forgive me, Noora," I said, my words slurring together.

She looked away from me, and I cursed my stupidity. Then, just before I drifted off into warm, wonderful sleep, she whispered, "Am I truly so beautiful?" I grinned at her crookedly, and then my mind spun away out of this world.

3

When my memory began to come back, I recalled that I'd been sitting next to Hajjar on the suborbital ship, and facing us had been Friedlander Bey and Hajjar's goon. The crooked cop had derived a lot of enjoyment from looking at me, shaking his head, and making little snotty chuckling noises. I found myself wondering how hard I'd have to twist his scrawny neck before his head would pop off.

Papa had maintained his air of calm. He simply wasn't going to give Hajjar the satisfaction of troubling him. After a while, I just tried to pretend that Hajjar and the goon didn't exist. I passed the time imagining them suffering all sorts of tragic accidents.

About forty minutes into the flight, when the shuttle had boosted to the top of its parabola and was coasting down toward its destination, a tall man with a thin face and a huge black mustache jerked aside the curtains to the rear cabin. This was the qadi, I imagined, the civil judge who had reached a decision in whatever case Papa and I were involved in. It did my mood no good to see that the qadi was dressed in the gray uniform and leather boots of an officer in Reda Abu Adil's *Jaish*.

He glanced down at a sheaf of papers in his hand. "Friedlander Bey?" he asked. "Marîd Audran?"

"Him and him," said Lieutenant Hajjar, jerking his thumb at us in turn.

The qadi nodded. He was still standing beside us in the aisle. "This is a most serious charge," he said. "It would have gone better for you if you'd pleaded guilty and begged for mercy."

"Listen, pal," I said, "I haven't even heard the charge yet! I don't even know what we're supposed to have done! How could we have pleaded guilty? We weren't given a chance to enter a plea at all!"

"Say, your honor?" said Hajjar. "I took the liberty of entering their pleas for them. In the interest of saving the city time and money."

"Most irregular," muttered the qadi, shuffling through his papers. "But as you entered both pleas of innocent, I see no further problem."

I slammed my fist on my seat's armrest. "But you just said it would have gone better for us if—"

"Peace, my nephew," said Papa in his imperturbable voice. He turned to the qadi. "Please, your honor, what *is* the charge against us?"

"Oh, murder," said the distracted judge. "Murder in the first degree. Now, as I have all the—"

"Murder!" I cried. I heard Hajjar laugh, and I turned and gave him a deadly look. He raised his hands to protect himself. The goon reached across and slapped my face, hard. I turned toward him, raging, but he just waved the barrel of his needle gun under my nose. I subsided a little.

"Whom were we supposed to have killed?" asked Papa.

"Just a moment, I have it here somewhere," said the qadi. "Yes, a police officer named Khalid Maxwell. The crime was discovered by an associate of Shaykh Reda Abu Adil."

"I knew Abu Adil's name would come into this," I growled.

"Khalid Maxwell," said Papa. "I've never had any contact at all with anyone by that name."

"I haven't either," I said. "I've never even heard of the guy."

"One of my most trusted subordinates," said Hajjar. "The city and the force have suffered a great loss."

"We didn't do it, Hajjar!" I shouted. "And you know it!"

The qadi looked at me sternly. "It's much too late for denials," he said. His dark face didn't seem sturdy enough to support either his bulbous nose or the bushy growth attached to it. "I've already reached my verdict."

Papa began to look a trifle upset. "You've already made your decision, without letting us present our side of the story?"

The qadi slapped his handful of paper. "All the facts are here. There are eyewitness accounts and reports from Lieutenant Hajjar's investigation. There's too much documented evidence to allow for even the slightest doubt. What is your side of the story? That you deny committing this foul crime? Of course, that's what you'd have said to me. I didn't need to waste my time listening to it. I have all this!" Again he slapped the papers.

"Then you've reached a verdict," said Papa, "and you've found us guilty."

"Precisely," said the qadi. "Guilty as charged. Guilty in the eyes of Allah and your fellow man. However, the

death penalty will be set aside because of an earnest petition from one of the city's most respected citizens."

"Shaykh Reda?" I said. My stomach was starting to
bother me again.

"Yes," said the qadi. "Shaykh Reda appealed to me on
your behalf. Out of respect for him, you will not be beheaded in the courtyard of the Shimaal Mosque as you
deserve. Rather, your sentence is banishment. You're for-
bidden ever to return to the city, under pain of arrest and
summary execution."

"Well," I said sourly, "that's a relief. Where are you
taking us?"

"This shuttle's destination is the kingdom of Asir,"
said the qadi.

I looked across at Friedlander Bey. He was doing his
serene old wise man routine again. I felt a little better,
too. I didn't know anything about Asir other than it bordered the Red Sea south of Mecca. Asir was better than
some places they could have shipped us, and from there
we could begin drawing on our resources to prepare our
return to the city. It would take time and a lot of money
passed under a lot of tables, but we'd come home eventually. I was already looking forward to my reunion with
Hajjar.

The qadi glanced from me to Papa, then nodded and
retired again to the rear cabin. Hajjar waited for him to
leave, then let loose a loud guffaw. "Hey!" he cried.
"What you think of that?"

I grabbed his throat before he could duck out of the
way. The goon rose out of his seat and threatened me
with the needle gun. "Don't shoot!" I said with feigned
terror, all the while squeezing Hajjar's larynx tighter.
"Please, don't shoot me!"

Hajjar tried to say something, but I had his windpipe

shut off. His face was turning the color of the wine of Paradise.

"Release him, my nephew," said Friedlander Bey after a moment.

"Now, O Shaykh?" I asked. I still hadn't let go.

"Now."

I flung Hajjar away from me, and the back of his head bounced off the bulkhead behind him. He gasped and choked as he tried to force air into his lungs. The goon lowered his needle gun and sat down again. I got the impression that he was no longer personally concerned with how Hajjar was feeling. I took that to mean that he didn't have a much higher opinion of the lieutenant than I did, and as long as I didn't kill Hajjar outright, I could pretty much do whatever I wanted to him without the goon interfering.

Hajjar glared at me hatefully. "You're gonna be sorry you did that," he said in a hoarse voice.

"I don't think so, Hajjar," I said. "I think the memory of your red, pop-eyed face will sustain me through all the difficulties to come."

"Sit in your seat and shut up, Audran," Hajjar uttered through clenched teeth. "Make a move or a sound, and I'll have your friend over there break your face."

I was getting bored, anyway. I put my head back and closed my eyes, thinking that when we arrived in Asir, I might need my strength. I could feel the maneuvering engines roar to life, and the pilot began turning the giant shuttlecraft in a long, slow arc toward the west. We descended rapidly, spiraling down through the night sky.

The shuttle began to tremble, and there was a long booming noise and a high-pitched wail. Hajjar's goon looked frightened. "Landing gear locking into place," I said. He gave me a brief nod.

And then the shuttle was down and screaming across a

concrete field. There were no lights outside that I could see, but I was sure we must have been surrounded by a great airfield. After a while, when the pilot had braked the shuttle to what seemed like a crawl, I could see the outlines of hangars, sheds, and other buildings. Then the shuttle came to a complete stop, although we hadn't arrived at a terminal building.

"Stay in your seats," said Hajjar.

We sat there, listening to the air-conditioning whining above our heads. Finally, the qadi reappeared from the rear cabin. He still clutched his sheaf of papers. He held up one page and read from it:

" 'Witness, that regarding the acts of members of the community, which acts are certain crimes and affronts to Allah and all brothers in Islam, those in custody identified as Friedlander Bey and Marîd Audran are herein found guilty, and their punishment shall be exile from the community which they so grievously offended. This is a mercy shown unto them, and they should count the remainder of their days a blessing, and spend them in seeking the nearness of God and the forgiveness of men.' "

Then the qadi leaned against the bulkhead and put his signature to the paper, and signed a duplicate copy so that Papa could have one and I could have the other. "Now, let's go," he said.

"Come on, Audran," said Hajjar. I got up and moved into the aisle behind the qadi. The goon followed me with Papa behind him. Hajjar brought up the rear. I turned to look back at him, and his expression was oddly mournful. He must have thought that soon we'd be out of his hands, and so his fun was almost over.

We climbed down the gangway to the concrete apron. Papa and I stretched and yawned. I was very tired and getting hungry again, despite all the food I'd eaten at the amir's celebration. I looked around the airfield, trying to learn something of value. I saw a big hand-painted sign that said *Najran* on one of the low, dark buildings.

"Najran mean anything to you, O Shaykh?" I asked Friedlander Bey.

"Shut up, Audran," said Hajjar. He turned to his goon. "Make sure they don't talk or do anything funny. I'm holding you responsible." The goon nodded. Hajjar and the qadi went off together toward the building.

"Najran is the capital city of Asir," said Papa. He completely ignored the goon's presence. For his part, the goon no longer showed much interest in what we did, as long as we didn't try streaking across the landing field toward freedom.

"We have friends here?" I asked.

Papa nodded. "We have friends almost everywhere, my nephew. The problem is getting in touch with them."

I didn't understand what he meant. "Well, Hajjar and the qadi will be getting back aboard the shuttle in a little while, right? After that, I guess we're on our own. Then we can contact these friends and get some nice, soft beds to spend the rest of the night in."

Papa gave me a sad smile. "Do you truly think our troubles end here?"

My confidence faltered. "Uh, they don't?" I said.

As if to justify Papa's concern, Hajjar and the qadi came out of the building, accompanied now by a burly guy in a cop-like uniform, carrying a rifle slung under his arm. He didn't look like a particularly intelligent cop or a well-disciplined cop, but with his rifle he was probably more than Papa and I could handle.

"We must speak soon of revenge," Papa whispered to me before Hajjar reached us.

"Against Shaykh Reda," I replied.

"No. Against whoever signed our deportation order. The amir or the imam of the Shimaal Mosque."

That gave me something else to think about. I'd never learned why Friedlander Bey so scrupulously avoided harming Reda Abu Adil, whatever the provocation. And I wondered how I'd respond if Papa ordered me to kill Shaykh Mahali, the amir. Surely the prince couldn't have received us so hospitably tonight, knowing that when we left his reception we'd be kidnapped and driven into exile. I preferred to believe that Shaykh Mahali knew nothing of what was happening to us now.

"Here are your prisoners, Sergeant," Hajjar said to the fat-assed local cop.

The sergeant nodded. He looked us over and frowned. He wore a nameplate that told me his name was al-Bishah. He had a gigantic belly that was pushing its way to freedom from between the buttons of his sweat-stained shirt. There were four or five days of black stubble on his face, and his teeth were broken and stained dark brown. His eyelids drooped, and at first I thought it was because he'd been awakened in the middle of the night; but his clothes smelled strongly of hashish, and I knew that this cop passed the lonely nights on duty with his *narjîlah*.

"Lemme guess," said the sergeant. "The young guy pulled the trigger, and this raggedy-looking old fool in the red *tarboosh* is the brains of the operation." He threw his head back and roared with laughter. It must have been the hashish, because not even Hajjar cracked a smile.

"Pretty much," said the lieutenant. "They're all yours now." Hajjar turned to me. "One last thing before we say good-bye forever, Audran. Know what the first thing is I'm gonna do tomorrow?"

His grin was about the most vicious and ugly one I'd ever seen. "No, what?" I said.

"I'm gonna close down that club of yours. And you know what's the second thing?" He waited, but I refused to play along. "Okay, I'll tell you. I'm gonna bust your

Yasmin for prostitution, and when I got her in my special, deep-down hole, I'm gonna see what she's got that you like so much."

I was very proud of myself. A year or two ago, I'd have smashed his teeth in, goon or no goon. I was more mature now, so I just stood there, looking impassively into his wild eyes. I repeated this to myself: the next time you see this man, you will kill him. The next time you see this man, you will kill him. That kept me from doing anything stupid while I had two weapons trained on me.

"Dream about it, Audran!" Hajjar shouted, as he and the qadi climbed back up the gangway. I didn't even turn to watch him.

"You were wise, my nephew," said Friedlander Bey. I looked at him, and I could tell from his expression that he had been favorably impressed by my behavior.

"I've learned much from you, my grandfather," I said. That seemed to please him, too.

"Aw right," said the local sergeant, "come on. Don't wanna be out here when they get that sucker movin'." He jerked the barrel of his rifle in the direction of the dark building, and Papa and I preceded him across the runway.

It was pitch black inside, but Sergeant al-Bishah didn't turn on any lights. "Just follow the wall," he said. I felt my way along a narrow corridor until it turned a corner. There was a small office there with a battered desk, a phone, a mechanical fan, and a small, beat-up holo system. There was a chair behind the desk, and the sergeant dropped heavily into it. There was another chair in a corner, and I let Papa have it. I stood leaning against a filthy plasterboard wall.

"Now," said the cop, "we come to the matter of what I do with you. You're in Najran now, not some flea-bitten village where you got influence. You're nobody in Najran, but I'm somebody. We gonna see what you can do for me, and if you can't do nothin', you gonna go to jail."

"How much money do you have, my nephew?" Papa asked me.

"Not much." I hadn't brought a great deal with me, because I didn't think I'd need it at the amir's house. I usually carried my money divided between the pockets in my *gallebeya*, just for situations like this. I counted what I had in the left pocket; it came to a little over a hundred and eighty kiam. I wasn't about to let the dog of a sergeant know I had more in the other pocket.

"Ain't even real money, is it?" complained al-Bishah. He shoved it all into his desk drawer anyway. "What about the old guy?"

"I have no money at all," said Papa.

"Now, that's too bad." The sergeant used a lighter to fire up the hashish in his *narjîlah*. He leaned over and took the mouthpiece between his teeth. I could hear the burbling of the water pipe and smell the tang of the black hashish. He exhaled the smoke and smiled. "You can pick your cells, I got two. Or you got somethin' else I might want?"

I thought of my ceremonial dagger. "How about this?" I said, laying it in front of him on the desk.

He shook his head. "Cash," he said, shoving the dagger back toward me. I thought he'd made a bad mistake, because the dagger had a lot of gold and jewels stuck on it. Maybe he didn't have anywhere to fence an item like that. "Or credit," he added. "Got a bank you can call?"

"Yes," said Friedlander Bey. "It will be an expensive call, but you can have my bank's computer transfer funds to your account."

Al-Bishah let the mouthpiece fall from his lips. He sat up very straight. "Now, that's what I like to hear! Only, *you* pay for the call. Charge it to your home, right?"

The fat cop handed him the desk phone, and Papa spoke a long series of numbers into it. "Now," said Papa to the sergeant, "how much do you want?"

"A good, stiff bribe," he said. "Enough so I *feel* bribed. Not enough, you go to the cell. You could stay there forever. Who's gonna know you're here? Who's gonna pay for your freedom? Now's your best chance, my brother."

Friedlander Bey regarded the man with unconcealed disgust. "Five thousand kiam," he said.

"Lemme think, what's that in real money?" A few seconds passed in silence. "No, better make it ten thousand." I'm sure Papa would have paid a hundred thousand, but the cop didn't have the imagination to ask for it.

Papa waited a moment, then nodded. "Yes, ten thousand." He spoke into the phone again, then handed it to the sergeant.

"What?" asked al-Bishah.

"Tell the computer your account number," said Papa.

"Oh. Right." When the transaction was completed, the fat fool made another call. I couldn't hear what it was all about, but when he hung up, he said, "Fixed up some transportation for you. I don't want you here, don't want you in Najran. Can't let you go back where you come from, either, not from this shuttle field."

"All right," I said. "Where we going, then?"

Al-Bishah gave me a clear view of his stumpy, rotted teeth. "Let it be a surprise."

We had no choice. We waited in his reeking office until a call came that our transportation had arrived. The sergeant stood up from behind his desk, grabbed his rifle and slung it under his arm, and signaled us that we were to lead the way back out to the airfield. I was just glad to get out of that narrow room with him.

Outside under the clear, moonless night sky, I saw

that Hajjar's suborbital shuttle had taken off. In its place was a small supersonic chopper with military markings. The air was filled with the shriek of its jet engines, and a strong breeze brought me the acrid fumes of fuel spilled on the concrete apron. I glanced at Papa, who gave me only the slightest shrug. There was nothing we could do but go where the man with the rifle wanted us to go.

We had to cross about thirty yards of empty airfield to the chopper, and we weren't making any kind of resistance. Still, al-Bishah came up behind me and clubbed me in the back of the head with the butt of his rifle. I fell to my knees, and bright points of color swam before my eyes. My head throbbed with pain. I felt for a moment as if I were about to vomit.

I heard a drawn-out groan nearby, and when I turned my head I saw that Friedlander Bey sprawled helplessly on the ground beside me. That the fat cop had beaten Papa angered me more than that he'd slugged me. I got unsteadily to my feet and helped Papa up. His face had gone gray, and his eyes weren't focused. I hoped he hadn't suffered a concussion. Slowly I led the old man to the open hatch of the chopper.

Al-Bishah watched us climb into the transport. I didn't turn around and look at him, but over the roar of the aircraft's motors I heard him call to us. "Ever come to Najran again, you're dead."

I pointed down at him. "Enjoy it while it lasts, motherfucker," I shouted, "because it won't last long." He just grinned up at me. Then the chopper's co-pilot slammed the hatch, and I tried to make myself comfortable beside Friedlander Bey on the hard plastic bench.

I put my hand under the *keffiya* and gingerly touched the back of my head. My fingers came away bloody. I turned to Papa and was glad to see that the color had come back into his face. "Are you all right, O Shaykh?" I asked.

"I thank Allah," he said, wincing a little. We couldn't say anything more because our words were drowned out as the chopper prepared for takeoff. I sat back and waited for whatever would happen next. I entertained myself by entering Sergeant al-Bishah on my list, right after Lieutenant Hajjar.

The chopper circled around the airfield and then shot off toward its mysterious destination. We flew for a long time without changing course in the slightest. I sat with my head in my hands, keeping time by the excruciating, rhythmic stabs in the back of my skull. Then I remembered that I had my rack of neural software. I joyfully pulled it out, removed my *keffiya*, and chipped in the daddy that blocked pain. Instantly, I felt a hundred percent better, and without the adverse effects of chemical painkillers. I couldn't leave it in for very long, though. If I did, sooner or later there'd be a heavy debt to repay to my central nervous system.

There was nothing I could do to make Papa feel better. I could only let him suffer in silence, while I pressed my face to the plastic port in the hatch. For a long time I hadn't seen any lights down there, not a city, not a village, not even a single lonely house stuck far away from civilization. I assumed we were flying over water.

I found out how wrong I was when the sun began to come up, ahead of us and a little to starboard. We'd been flying northeast the entire time. According to my inaccurate mental map, that meant that we'd been heading out over the heart of Arabia. I hadn't realized how unpopulated that part of the world was.

I decided to remove the pain daddy about half an hour after I chipped it in. I popped it, expecting to feel a wave of renewed agony wash over me, but I was pleasantly surprised. The throbbing had settled down to a normal, manageable headache. I replaced my *keffiya*. Then I got up from the plastic bench and made my way forward to the cockpit.

"Morning," I said to the pilot and co-pilot.

The co-pilot turned around and looked at me. He took a long look at my princely outfit, but he stifled his curiosity. "You got to go back and sit down," he said. "Can't be bothering us while we're trying to fly this thing."

I shrugged. "Seems like we could've been on autopilot the whole way. How much actual flying are you guys doing?"

The co-pilot didn't like that. "Go back and sit down," he said, "or I'll take you back and cuff you to the bench."

"I don't mean any trouble," I said. "Nobody's told us a thing. Don't we have a right to know where we're going?"

The co-pilot turned his back on me. "Look," he said, "you and the old guy murdered some poor son of a bitch. You ain't got any rights anymore."

"Terrific," I muttered. I went back to the bench. Papa looked at me, and I just shook my head. He was disheveled and streaked with grime, and he'd lost his *tarboosh* when al-Bishah bashed him in the back of the head. He'd regained a lot of his composure during the flight, however, and he seemed to be pretty much his old self again. I had the feeling that soon we'd both need all our wits about us.

Fifteen minutes later, I felt the chopper slowing down. I looked out through the port and saw that we'd stopped moving forward, hovering now over reddish-brown sand dunes that stretched to the horizon in all directions. There was a long buzzing note, and then a green light went on over the hatch. Papa touched my arm and I turned to him, but I couldn't tell him what was going on.

The co-pilot unbuckled himself and eased out of his

seat in the cockpit. He stepped carefully through the cargo area to our bench. "We're here," he said.

"What do you mean, 'we're here'? Nothing down there but sand. Not so much as a tree or a bush."

The co-pilot wasn't concerned. "Look, all I know is we're supposed to turn you over to the Bayt Tabiti here."

"What's the Bayt Tabiti?"

The co-pilot gave me a sly grin. "Tribe of Badawi," he said. "The other tribes call 'em the leopards of the desert."

Yeah, you right, I thought. "What are these Bayt Tabiti going to do with us?"

"Well, don't expect 'em to greet you like long-lost brothers. My advice is, try to get on their good side real fast."

I didn't like any of this, but what could I do about it? "So you're just going to set this chopper down and kick us out into the desert?"

The co-pilot shook his head. "Naw," he said, "we ain't gonna set it down. Chopper ain't got desert sand filters." He pulled up on a release lever and slid the hatch aside.

I looked down at the ground. "We're twenty feet in the air!" I cried.

"Not for long," said the co-pilot. He raised his foot and shoved me out. I fell to the warm sand, trying to roll as I hit. I was fortunate that I didn't break my legs. The chopper was kicking up a heavy wind, which blew the stinging sand into my face. I could barely breathe. I thought about using my *keffiya* the way it was meant to be used, to protect my nose and mouth from the artificial sandstorm. Before I could adjust it, I saw the co-pilot push Friedlander Bey from the hatch opening. I did my best to break Papa's fall, and he wasn't too badly hurt, either.

"This is murder!" I shouted up at the chopper. "We can't survive out here!"

The co-pilot spread his hands. "The Bayt Tabiti are coming. Here, this'll last you till they get here." He tossed out a pair of large canteens. Then, his duty to us at an end, he slammed the hatch shut. A moment later, the jet chopper swung up and around and headed back the way it had come.

Papa and I were alone and lost in the middle of the Arabian Desert. I picked up both canteens and shook them. They gurgled reassuringly. I wondered how many days of life they held. Then I went to Friedlander Bey. He sat in the hot morning sunlight and rubbed his shoulder. "I can walk, my nephew," he said, anticipating my concern.

"Guess we'll have to, O Shaykh," I said. I didn't have the faintest idea what to do next. I didn't know where we were or in which direction to start traveling.

"Let us first pray to Allah for guidance," he said. I didn't see any reason not to. Papa decided that this was definitely an emergency, so we didn't have to use our precious water to cleanse ourselves before worship. In such a situation, it's permissible to use clean sand. We had plenty of that. He removed his shoes and I took off my sandals, and we prepared ourselves for seeking the nearness of God as prescribed by the noble Qur'ân.

He took his direction from the rising sun and turned to face Mecca. I stood beside him, and we repeated the familiar poetry of prayer. When we finished, Papa recited an additional portion of the Qur'ân, a verse from the second sûrah that includes the line "And one who attacketh you, attack him in like manner as he attacked you."

"Praise be to Allah, Lord of the Worlds," I murmured.

"God is Most Great," said Papa.

And then it was time to see if we could save our lives. "I suppose we should reason this out," I said.

"Reason does not apply in the wilderness," said Papa. "We cannot reason ourselves food or water or protection."

"We have water," I said. I handed him one of the canteens.

He opened it and swallowed a mouthful, then closed the canteen and slung it across his shoulder. "We have *some* water. It remains to be seen if we have *enough* water."

"I've heard there's water underground in even the driest deserts." I think I was just talking to keep his spirits up —or my own.

Papa laughed. "You remember your mother's fairy tales about the brave prince lost among the dunes, and the spring of sweet water that gushed forth from the base of the mountain of sand. It doesn't happen that way in life, my darling, and your innocent faith will not lead us from this place."

I knew he was right. I wondered if he'd had any experience in desert survival as a younger man. There were entire decades of his early life that he never discussed. I decided it would be best to defer to his wisdom, in any case. I figured that if I shut up for a while, I might not die. I also might learn something. That was okay, too.

"What must we do, then, O Shaykh?" I asked.

He wiped the sweat from his forehead with his sleeve and looked around himself. "We're lost in the very southeastern portion of the Arabian Desert," he said. "The Rub al-Khali."

The Empty Quarter. That didn't sound promising at all.

"What is the nearest town?" I asked.

Papa gave me a brief smile. "There are no towns in the Rub al-Khali, not in a quarter million square miles of

sand and waste. There are certainly small groups of nomads crossing the dunes, but they travel only from well to
well, searching for grazing for their camels and goats. If
we hope to find a well, our luck must lead us to one of
these Bedu clans."

"And if we don't?"

Papa sloshed his canteen. "There's a gallon of water
for each of us. If we do no walking at all in the daylight
hours, manage our drinking carefully, and cover the greatest possible distance in the cool of the night, we may live
four days."

That was worse than even my most pessimistic esti-
mate. I sat down heavily on the sand. I'd read about this
place years ago, when I was a boy in Algiers. I thought the
description must have been pure exaggeration. For one
thing, it made the Rub al-Khali sound harsher than the
Sahara, which was our local desert, and I couldn't believe
that anyplace on Earth could be more desolate than the
Sahara. Apparently, I was wrong. I also remembered what
a Western traveler had once called the Rub al-Khali in his
memoirs:

The Great Wrong Place.

4

According to some geographers, the Arabian Desert is an extension of the Sahara. Most of the Arabian peninsula is uninhabited waste, with the populated areas situated near the Mediterranean, Red, and Arabian seas, beside the Arabian Gulf—which is our name for what others call the Persian Gulf—and in the fertile crescent of old Mesopotamia.

The Sahara is greater in area, but there is more sand in the Arabian Desert. As a boy, I carried in my mind the image of the Sahara as a burning, endless, empty sandscape; but that is not very accurate. Most of the Sahara is made up of rocky plateaus, dry gravel plains, and ranges of windswept mountains. Expanses of sand account for only 10 percent of the desert's area. The portion of the Arabian Desert called the Rub al-Khali tops that with 30 percent. It might as well have been nothing but sand from one end to the other, as far as I was concerned.

What the hell difference did it make?

I squinted my eyes nearly shut and looked up into the painfully bright sky. One of the minor advantages of being stranded in such a deadly place was that it was too deadly even for vultures. I was spared the unnerving sight of carrion birds circling patiently, waiting for me to have the courtesy to die.

I was pretty determined *not* to die. I hadn't talked it over with Friedlander Bey, but I was confident he felt the same way. We were sitting on the leeward side of a high, wind-shaped dune. I guessed that the temperature was already a hundred degrees Fahrenheit or more. The sun had climbed up the sky, but it was not yet noon—the day would get even hotter.

"Drink your water when you're thirsty, my nephew," Papa told me. "I've seen men dehydrate and die because they were too stingy with their canteens. Not drinking enough water is like spilling it on the ground. You need about a gallon a day in this heat. Two or three quarts won't keep you alive."

"We only have one gallon each, O Shaykh," I said.

"When it's gone, we'll have to find more. We may stumble across a trail, *inshallah*. There are trails even in the heart of the Rub al-Khali, and they lead from water hole to water hole. If not, we must pray that rain has fallen here not long ago. Sometimes there is damp sand in the hollow beneath the steep side of a dune."

I was in no hurry to try out my Desert Scout skills. All the talk of water had made me thirstier, so I unscrewed the cap of my canteen. "In the name of Allah, the Compassionate, the Merciful," I said, and drank a generous quantity. I'd seen holograms of Arab nomads sitting on the sand, using sticks to make tents of their *keffiyas* for shade. There weren't even sticks in this landscape, however.

The wind changed direction, blowing a fine curtain of grit into our faces. I followed Friedlander Bey's example and rested on my side, with my back to the wind. After a few minutes, I sat up and took off my *keffiya* and gave it to him. He accepted it wordlessly, but I saw gratitude in his red-rimmed eyes. He put on the head cloth, covered his face, and lay back to wait out the sandstorm.

I'd never felt so exposed to the elements before in my life. I kept telling myself, "Maybe it's all a dream." Maybe I'd wake up in my own bed, and my slave, Kmuzu, would be there with a nice mug of hot chocolate. But the broiling sun on my head felt too authentic, and the sand that worked its way into my ears and eyes, into my nostrils, and between my lips didn't feel at all dreamlike.

I was distracted from these annoyances by the blood-curdling cries of a small band of men coming over the shoulder of the dune. They dismounted from their camels and ran down on us, waving their rifles and knives. They were the scruffiest, most villainous-looking louts I'd ever seen. They made the worst scum of the Budayeen look like scholars and gentlemen by comparison.

These, I assumed, were the Bayt Tabiti. The leopards of the desert. Their leader was a tall, scrawny man with long stringy hair. He brandished his rifle and screamed at us, and I could see that he had two snaggled teeth on the right side of his upper jaw, and two broken teeth on the left side of his lower jaw. He probably hadn't celebrated occlusion in years. He hadn't taken a bath in that long, either.

He was also the one we were supposed to trust with our lives. I glanced at Friedlander Bey and shook my head slightly. Just in case the Bayt Tabiti felt like murdering us where we sat instead of leading us to water, I got to my feet and drew my ceremonial dagger. I didn't really think that weapon was of much value against the Bedu's rifles, but it was all I had.

The leader came toward me, reached out, and fingered my expensive robe. He turned back to his companions and said something, and all six of them broke up with laughter. I just waited.

The leader looked into my face and frowned. He slapped his chest. "Muhammad Musallim bin Ali bin as-Sultan," he announced. As if I was supposed to recognize his name.

I pretended to be impressed. I slapped my own chest. "Marîd al-Amîn," I said, using the epithet I'd been given by the poor *fellahîn* of the city. It meant "the Trustworthy."

Muhammad's eyes grew wide. He turned to his buddies again. "Al-Amîn," he said in a reverent tone. Then he doubled over with laughter again.

A second Bayt Tabiti went over to Friedlander Bey and stood looking down at the old man. *"Ash-shaykh,"* I said, letting the stinking nomads know that Papa was a man of importance. Muhammad flicked his eyes from me to Papa, then back again. He spoke some rapid words in their puzzling dialect, and the second man left Papa alone and went back to his camel.

Muhammad and I spent some time trying to get answers to our questions, but their rough Arabic slowed down our communication. After a while, though, we could understand each other well enough. It turned out that the Bayt Tabiti had received orders from their tribal shaykh to come find us. Muhammad didn't know how his shaykh knew about us in the first place, but we were where they expected us to be, and they'd seen and heard the military chopper from a long way off.

I watched as two of the filthy rogues pulled Friedlander Bey roughly to his feet and led him to one of the camels. The camel's owner prodded the knees of the beast's forelegs with a stick, and made a sound like "khirr, khirr!" The camel roared its displeasure and didn't seem willing to kneel down. Papa said something to the Bayt Tabiti, who grabbed the animal's head rope and pulled it down. Papa placed a foot on the camel's neck, and it lifted him up where he could scramble into the saddle.

It was obvious that he'd done this before. I, on the other hand, had never ridden a camel in my life, and I didn't feel the need to start now. "I'll walk," I said.

"Please, young shaykh," said Muhammad, grinning through his sparse dentition, "Allah will think we are being inhospitable."

I didn't think Allah had any misconceptions at all about the Bayt Tabiti. "I'll walk," I said again.

Muhammad shrugged and mounted his own camel. Everyone started off around the dune, with me and the Bedu who'd given his camel to Papa walking alongside.

"Come with us!" cried the leader of the party. "We have food, we have water! We take you to our camp!"

I had no doubt that they were heading back to their camp, but I had serious misgivings that Papa and I would arrive there alive.

The man walking beside me must have sensed my thoughts, because he turned to me and winked slowly. "Trust us," he said with a cunning expression. "You are safe now."

You bet, I thought. There was nothing to do but go along with them. What would happen to us after we arrived at the main camp of the Bayt Tabiti was in the hands of God.

We traveled in a southerly direction for several hours. Finally, as I was reaching exhaustion—and about the time my canteen ran out of water—Muhammad called a halt.

"We sleep here tonight," he said, indicating a narrow gap between two linked chains of sand dunes.

I was glad that the day's exertions were over; but as I sat beside Papa and watched the Bedu tend to their animals, it occurred to me that it was strange they didn't push on to rejoin the rest of their tribe before dark. Their shaykh had sent them out to find us, and they arrived only a few hours after we'd been dumped out of the chopper. Surely, the main camp of the Bayt Tabiti couldn't have been far away.

They went about their chores, whispering to each other and pointing at us when they thought we weren't watching. I started toward them, offering to help unload their camels. "No, no," said Muhammad, blocking me off from the animals, "please, just rest! We can see to the packs ourselves." Something was wrong here. And Friedlander Bey sensed it, too.

"I do not like these men," he said to me in a low voice. We were watching one of the Bedu put handfuls of dates in wooden bowls. Another man was boiling water for coffee. Muhammad and the rest were hobbling the camels.

"They haven't shown any outward signs of hostility," I said. "At least, not since they first ran down on us, yelling and screaming and waving their weapons."

Papa gave a humorless laugh. "Don't be fooled into thinking that we've won their grudging admiration. Look at that man dividing the dates. You know the packs on the camels are loaded with far better food than that. These Bayt Tabiti are too greedy to share it with us. They will pretend they have nothing better to eat than old, stone-hard dates. Later, after we're gone, they'll prepare themselves a better meal."

"After we're gone?" I said.

"I don't believe there is a larger camp within a day's

journey from here. And I don't believe the Bayt Tabiti are willing to offer us their hospitality much longer."

I shivered, even though the sun had not yet set, and the heat of the day had not yet dissipated. "Are you afraid, O Shaykh?"

He pursed his lips and shook his head. "I'm not afraid of these creatures, my nephew. I'm wary—I think it would be wise to know what they're up to at every moment. These are not clever men, but their advantages are that they are more than we, and that they know this terrain."

Further discussion was interrupted when the Bedu we'd been watching came to us and offered us each a bowl of rancid-smelling dates and a dirty china cup filled with weak coffee. "These poor provisions are all we have," said the man in a flat voice, "but we'd be honored if you'd share them with us."

"Your generosity is a blessing from Allah," said Friedlander Bey. He took a bowl of dates and a cup of coffee.

"I am quite unable to express my thanks," I said, taking my own supper.

The Bedu grinned, and I saw that his teeth were just as bad as Muhammad's. "No thanks are needed, O Shaykh," he replied. "Hospitality is a duty. You must travel with us and learn our ways. As the proverb says, 'Who lives with a tribe forty days becomes one of them.'"

That was a nightmarish thought, traveling with the Bayt Tabiti and becoming one of them!

"*Salaam alaykum,*" said Papa.

"*Alaykum as-salaam,*" the man responded. Then he carried bowls of dates to his fellows.

"In the name of Allah, the Compassionate, the Merciful," I murmured. Then I put one of the dates in my mouth. It didn't stay there long. First, it was completely coated with sand. Second, it was almost hard enough to crack my teeth; I wondered if these dates had been the downfall of the Bayt Tabiti's dental work. Third, the piece of fruit smelled as if it had been left to decay under a dead camel for a few weeks. I gagged as I spat it out, and I had to wash away the taste with the gritty coffee.

Friedlander Bey put one of the dates in his mouth, and I watched him struggle to maintain a straight face as he chewed it. "Food is food, my nephew," he said. "In the Empty Quarter, you can't afford to be fastidious."

I knew he was right. I rubbed as much sand as I could from another date, and then I ate it. After a few of them, I got used to how rotten they tasted. I thought only about keeping my strength up.

When the sun slipped behind the ridge of a western dune, Friedlander Bey removed his shoes and got slowly to his feet. He used my *keffiya* to sweep the sand in front of him. I realized he was preparing to pray. Papa opened his canteen and moistened his hands. Because I didn't have any more water in my own canteen, I stood beside him and extended my hands, palms up.

"Allah yisallimak, my nephew," said Papa. God bless you.

As I executed the ablutions, I repeated the ritual formula: "I perform the Washing in order to cleanse myself from impurity and to make myself eligible for seeking the nearness to Allah."

Once again, Papa led me in prayer. When we finished, the sun had completely disappeared and the sudden night of the desert had fallen. I imagined that I could already feel the heat leaching out of the sand. It would be a cold night, and we had no blankets.

I decided to see how far I could push the false hospitality of the Bayt Tabiti. I went over to their small fire of dried camel dung, where the six bandits were sitting and talking. "You pray to Allah," said Muhammad with a sarcastic grin. "You're good men. We mean to pray, but sometimes we forget." His tribesmen cackled at his wit.

I didn't pay any attention to that. "We'll need water for tomorrow's journey, O Shaykh," I said. I suppose I could've phrased that more politely.

Muhammad thought about it for a moment. He couldn't very well refuse, but he wasn't happy about parting with any of his own supply. He leaned over and muttered something to one of the others. The second Bedu got up and fetched a goatskin bag of water and brought it to me. "Here, my brother," he said with a blank expression. "May it be pleasant to you."

"We're obliged," I said. "We'll just fill our canteens, and return the rest of the water to you."

The man nodded, then reached out and touched one of my corymbic implants. "My cousin wants to know what these are," he said.

I shrugged. "Tell your cousin that I like to listen to music on the radio."

"Ah," said the Bayt Tabiti. I don't know if he believed me. He came with me while I filled my canteen and Papa's. Then the Bedu took the goatskin bag and returned to his friends.

"The sons of bitches didn't invite us to join them by the fire," I said, sitting down on the sand beside Papa.

He only turned one hand over. "It means nothing, my nephew," he said. "Now, I must sleep. It would be well if you remained awake and watchful."

"Of course, O Shaykh." Papa made himself as comfortable as he could on the hard-packed sand of the desert floor. I sat for a little while longer, lost in thought. I remembered what Papa had said about revenge, and from the pocket of my *gallebeya* I took the paper the qadi had given me. It was a copy of the charges against Friedlander Bey and me, the verdict, and the order for our deportation. It was signed by Dr. Sadiq Abd ar-Razzaq, imam of the Shimaal Mosque and adviser to the amir on the interpretation of *shari'a,* or religious law. I was happy to see that Shaykh Mahali had apparently played no part in our kidnapping.

Finally, I decided to lie down and pretend to be asleep, because I realized that the Bayt Tabiti were watching me, and that they wouldn't retire for the night until I did. I stretched out not far from Friedlander Bey, but I didn't close my eyes. I was sleepy, but I didn't dare drift off. If I did, I might never awaken again.

I could see the top of a gracefully curved dune about a hundred yards away. This particular sand hill must have been two hundred feet high, and the wind had blown it into a delicate, sinuous fold. I thought I could see a stately cedar tree growing from the very crest of the dune. I knew the mirage was a product of my fatigue, or perhaps I was already dreaming.

I wondered how the cedar tree could live in this waterless place, and I told myself that the only answer was that someone must be cultivating it. Someone had planned for that cedar to be there, and had worked very hard to make it grow.

I opened my eyes and realized that there was no cedar tree on that dune. Maybe it had been a vision from Allah. Maybe God was telling me that I had to make plans, and work very hard and persevere. There was no time now for rest.

I lifted my head a little, and saw that the Bayt Tabiti had thrown themselves on the ground near their fire, which had died down to pale, weakly glowing embers. One of the Bedu had been ordered to keep watch, but he sat against a wall of sand with his head thrown back and his mouth open. His rifle lay discarded beside him on the ground.

I believed all six of them were sound asleep, but I did not stir. I did nothing for another hour but stare at the seconds as they flicked by in the window of my watch. When I was certain that all the Bayt Tabiti were in deep slumber, I sat up quietly and touched Friedlander Bey on the shoulder. He came awake quickly. Neither of us said a word. We picked up our canteens and rose as silently as we could. I agonized for a few moments about trying to steal food and rifles, but at last I knew it would be suicidal to approach the camels or the sleeping Bedu. Instead, Papa and I just slipped away into the night.

We marched westward for a long time before either of us spoke. "Will they follow us when they find we're missing?" I asked.

Papa frowned. "I can't say, my nephew. Perhaps they'll just let us go. They're sure we'll die in the desert anyway."

There wasn't much I could say to that. From then on, we just concentrated on putting as much distance between us and them as we could, heading off at a right angle to the direction we'd traveled with them during the day. I prayed that if we crossed a desert track in the night we'd see it. It was our only hope of finding a well.

We had the stars as guides, and we trudged westward for two hours, until Papa announced that he had to stop and rest. We'd been traveling against the dunes, which ran from west to east, due to the prevailing winds. The westward slope of each dune was smooth and gradual, but the east side, which we'd have to climb, was usually high and steep. Consequently, we were making long detours as we tried to cross each hill at one of its low shoulders. It was slow, tiring, zigzag progress, and we couldn't have covered more than a mile or two as the sand grouse flies.

We sat panting beside each other at the base of yet another monstrous cliff of sand. I opened my canteen and gulped down a mouthful before I realized how brackish and alkaline it was. "Praise Allah," I groaned, "we'll be lucky if this water doesn't kill us before the sun does."

Papa had drunk his fill, too. "It is not sweet water, my nephew," he said, "but there is very little sweet water in the desert. This is the water the Bedu drink almost every day of their lives."

I'd known that the nomads lived harsh, desperate lives, but I was beginning to learn that I'd undervalued their skill at forcing a living from this most inclement environment. "Why don't they just go somewhere else?" I asked, capping my canteen again.

Papa smiled. "They are proud people. They get satisfaction in their ability to exist here, in a place that means death for any outsider. They scorn the softness and luxury of villages and towns."

"Yeah, you right. Luxuries like fresh water and actual food."

We stood up and started walking again. It was now about midnight. The path across the dunes didn't get any easier, and in a little while I could hear Papa's heavy breathing. I worried about the old man's condition. My own body was beginning to protest this unaccustomed exercise.

The stars turned slowly overhead, and when I looked at my watch again, it was half past one. Maybe we'd come another mile.

Papa estimated that the Rub al-Khali was about seven hundred and fifty miles west to east, and three hundred miles north to south. I figured it was likely that the military chopper had dropped us smack in the middle, so figuring a generous mile per hour, walking eight hours a night, we could get out of the Empty Quarter in, oh, just under forty-seven days. If we could also have a gigantic caravan of support equipment and supplies trailing along behind us.

We rested again, drank some more of the bitter water, and headed off on the last leg of the night's journey. We were both too tired to talk. I lowered my head against the wind, which was constantly flinging sand into our faces. I just kept putting one foot in front of the other. I told myself that if Friedlander Bey had the resolve to keep moving, so did I.

We reached our limit about four o'clock, and collapsed in utter exhaustion. The sun wouldn't rise for another hour or so, but the idea of going any farther that night was out of the question. We stopped beneath the vertical face of a gigantic dune, which would give us some protection from the wind. There we drank as much water as we could hold, and then prepared to sleep. I removed my beautiful royal blue robe and covered Papa with it. Then I huddled in a fetal position within my *gallebeya* and fell into cold, restless sleep.

I kept waking and falling back to sleep, and I was troubled by confused, anxious dreams. I was aware after a while that the sun had risen, and I knew the best thing would be to stay asleep as long as possible during the hot day. I pulled the *gallebeya* up over my head, to protect my face and scalp from burning. Then I pretended that everything was just fine, and closed my eyes.

It was about ten o'clock when I realized that I wasn't going to be able to sleep any later. The sun was beating down on me, and I could feel the exposed areas of skin burning. Friedlander Bey woke up then, too, and he didn't look as if he'd rested any better than I had.

"Now we must pray," he said. His voice sounded peculiar and hoarse. He struck the sand in front of him with his palms, and rubbed the sand on his face and hands. I did the same. Together we prayed, thanking Allah for giving us His protection, and asking that if it was His will, we might survive this ordeal.

Each time I joined in worship with Papa, I was filled with peace and hope. Somehow, being lost in this wilderness had made the meaning of our religion clear to me. I wish it hadn't taken such a drastic demonstration to make me understand my relationship to Allah.

When we'd finished, we drank as much water as we could hold. There wasn't much left in our canteens, but we didn't see any reason to discuss that fact. "My nephew," the old man said, "I think it would be wise to bury ourselves in the sand until evening."

That sounded crazy to me. "Why?" I asked. "Won't we bake ourselves like a lamb pie?"

"The deeper sand will be cooler than the surface," he said. "It will keep our skin from burning any further, and it will help reduce our loss of water through perspiration."

Once again, I shut up and learned something. We dug shallow pits and covered ourselves over with the sand. At one point, I noted to myself how very like graves they were. I was surprised to find that my body seemed to enjoy the experience. The warm sand soothed my aching muscles, and I was able to relax for the first time since we'd been snatched at the amir's celebration. In fact, after a while, listening to the murmurous buzzing of insects, I dozed off into a light sleep.

The day passed slowly. I had my *gallebeya* pulled up over my head again, so I couldn't see anything. There was nothing to do but lie there in the sand and think and plan and indulge in fantasies.

After a few hours, I was startled to hear a low vibrating hum. I couldn't imagine what it could be, and at first I thought it was only a ringing noise in my ears. It didn't go away, however, and if anything it got louder. "Do you hear that, O Shaykh?" I called.

"Yes, my nephew. It is nothing."

By now I was convinced that it was the warning whine of an approaching aircraft. I didn't know if that was good news or bad. The sound grew louder, until it was almost a shriek. I couldn't stand not being able to see, so I pushed my hands up out of the sand and pulled down the neck of my *gallebeya*.

There was nothing there. The buzzing had increased in volume until the aircraft should have been visible above our heads, but the sky was empty and blue. Then suddenly, as the wind shifted direction, everything fell silent again. The loud noise did not fade away but disappeared abruptly. "What was that?" I asked, bewildered.

"That, O Clever One, was the famous 'singing sands.' It is a very rare privilege to hear it."

"The sand made that sound? It was like the roaring of an engine!"

"They say it is made by one layer of sand slipping over another, nothing more."

Now I felt dumb for getting so upset over a little humming noise created by a sand dune. Papa, however, was not one to laugh or mock me, and I was grateful for that. I covered myself in the sand again and told myself not to be such a fool.

About five o'clock, we emerged from our sandy beds and prepared for the night's exertions. We prayed and drank the brackish water, and then headed off toward the west again. After we'd walked for half an hour, I had a brilliant idea. I took out my rack of neuralware and chipped in the special daddy that blocked thirst. Immediately, I felt refreshed. This was a dangerous illusion, because although I didn't feel thirsty—and wouldn't again, as long as I had that daddy chipped in—my body was still dehydrating at the same rate. Still, I felt that I could go on without water longer now, and so I gave my canteen to Papa.

"I can't take this from you, my nephew," he said.

"Sure you can, O Shaykh," I said. "This add-on will keep me from suffering for as long as our canteens do the same for you. Look, if we don't find more water soon, we'll both die anyway."

"That's true, my darling, but—"

"Let's walk, my grandfather," I said.

The sun began to set and the air began to get cooler. We took a rest stop some time later, and we prayed. Papa finished all the water in one of the canteens. Then we pushed on.

I was beginning to feel very hungry, and I realized that except for the crummy dates of the Bayt Tabiti, the last meal I'd eaten had been almost forty-eight hours ago, at the amir's palace. I was lucky, because I had a daddy that blocked hunger, too. I chipped it in, and the hollow pangs in my belly disappeared. I knew that Papa must be ravenous, but there was nothing I could do about that. I put everything out of my mind except making tracks across the remainder of the Empty Quarter.

Once, when we'd topped the crest of a high dune, I turned to look back. I saw what I thought was a smudge of dust rising in the pale moonlight from behind a distant dune. I prayed to Allah that it wasn't the Bayt Tabiti coming after us. When I tried to point it out to Friedlander Bey, I couldn't find the dust cloud again. Maybe I'd imagined it. The vast desert was good for that kind of hallucination.

After the second hour, we had to rest. Papa's face was drawn and haggard. He opened his other canteen and drained it dry. All our water was now gone. We looked at each other wordlessly for a moment. "I testify that there is no god but God," said Papa in a quiet voice.

"I testify that Muhammad is the Prophet of God," I added. We got up and continued our march.

After a while, Papa fell to his knees and began retching. He had nothing in his belly to vomit, but his spasms were long and violent. I hoped he wasn't losing much water. I knew that nausea was one of the first signs of severe dehydration. After a few minutes, he waved a hand weakly to let me know he wanted to keep going. From then on, I was more frightened than ever. I had no more illusions that we'd be able to save ourselves without a miracle.

I began to experience severe muscle cramps, and for the third time I turned to my moddy rack. I chipped in the pain-blocking daddy, knowing that I was going to be in pretty terrible shape if I ever lived to pop it out again. As my friend Chiriga likes to say, "Paybacks are a bitch."

About midnight, after another rest period, I noticed that Papa had begun to stagger. I went up to him and touched his shoulder. He faced me, but his eyes seemed unfocused. "What is it, my son?" he said. His voice was thick and his words indistinct.

"How are you feeling, O Shaykh?"

"I feel . . . strange. I'm not hungry anymore, which is a blessing, but I have a terrible headache. There are many little bright spots in front of my eyes; I can barely see in front of me. And there is the most annoying tingling in my arms and legs. Unfortunate symptoms."

"Yes, O Shaykh."

He looked up at me. For the first time in all the time I'd known him, he had genuine sadness in his eyes. "I do not wish to walk anymore."

"Yes, O Shaykh," I said. "Then I will carry you."

He protested, but he didn't do a very good job of it. I begged his forgiveness, then picked him up and slung him over my shoulder. I wouldn't have been able to haul him fifty yards without the daddies, which were damping out every last unpleasant signal my body was sending to my brain. I went on with a blithe, completely false sense of well-being. I wasn't hungry, I wasn't thirsty, I wasn't tired, and I didn't even ache. I even had another daddy I could use if I started to feel afraid.

In a little while, I realized that Papa was muttering deliriously. It was up to me to get us both out of this mess. I just gritted my teeth and went on. My amped brain was ridiculously confident that I'd emerge victorious against the most murderous desert in the world.

The night passed. I plodded my way through the swirling sand like a robot. All the while, my body was suffering the same debilitating effects of dehydration that had struck down Papa, and fatigue poisons were building up in my muscles.

The sun came up behind me, and I felt the heat grow on the back of my head and neck. I trudged on through the morning. Papa was no longer making any sounds at all. Once, about 8 A.M., my arms and legs just gave out. I dropped Papa heavily to the ground and fell down beside him. I let myself rest there for a little while. I knew I'd been abusing my body. I thought perhaps lying there motionless for a few minutes would be helpful.

I suppose I was unconscious, because the next time I checked my watch, two hours had passed. I got to my feet and picked up Papa and put him across my other shoulder. Then I walked some more.

I kept going until I collapsed again. This became a pattern, and soon I lost all track of time. The sun rose in the sky, the sun went away. The sun rose, the sun went away. I have no idea how far I managed to get. I have a vague memory of sitting on the side of a large dune, patting Friedlander Bey's hand and weeping. I sat there for a long time, and then I thought I heard a voice calling my name. I picked up Papa and stumbled on, in the direction of the voice.

This time, I didn't get far. I crossed two, maybe three great dunes, and then my muscles quit on me again. I could only lie on the ground, my face half-pressed into the hot, red sand. I could see Papa's leg from the corner of my eye. I was pretty sure that I was never going to get up again. "I take refuge . . ." I murmured. I didn't have enough saliva to finish. "I take refuge with the Lord of the Worlds," I said in my mind.

I passed out again. The next thing I knew, it was night. I was probably still alive. A man with a stern, lean face dominated by a huge hooked nose was bending over me. I didn't know who he was, or even if he was really there. He said something to me, but I couldn't understand his words. He wet my lips with water, and I tried to grab the goatskin bag out of his hands, but I couldn't seem to work my arms. He said something more to me. Then he reached forward and touched my implants.

With horror, I realized what he was trying to do. "No!" I cried in my cracked voice. "Please, for the love of Allah, no!"

He pulled his hand back and studied me for another few seconds. Then he opened a leather bag, removed an old-fashioned disposable syringe and a vial of some fluid, and gave me an injection.

What I really wanted was about a quart of clean, fresh water. But the shot of Sonneine was okay, too.

5

I was now clear on the events between the kidnapping and our rescue by the Bani Salim. The days after that, however, were probably lost forever in a fog of delirium. Shaykh Hassanein had sedated me, and then pulled free the daddies. My mind and body had immediately been overwhelmed by a ravaging flood of agony. I was grateful to Hassanein for keeping me knocked out with Sonneine until I'd begun to recover.

Noora was awake and watchful when I sat up and stretched in the morning. It took me a few seconds to recall where I was. The front and back flaps of the goat-hair tent had been thrown open, and a fresh, warm breeze passed through. I bowed my head and prayed, "Oh, that this day may be fortunate; give Thou that we see not the evil!"

"Blessings of Allah be on you, O Shaykh," said Noora. She came nearer, carrying a bowl of camel's milk and a plate of bread and *hummus,* a paste made of chick-peas and olive oil.

"*Bismillah,*" I murmured, tearing off a piece of bread. "May your day be pleasant, Noora." I began wolfing down the breakfast.

"It's good to see that your appetite is back. Would you like some more?"

My mouth was crammed full, so I just nodded. Noora went out of the tent to fetch a second helping. I took a few deep breaths and experimented with moving my limbs. There was still a deep soreness in my muscles, but I felt that I could get up soon. I remembered what Hassanein had told me, that the Bani Salim would need to find new grazing for their animals very soon. I wasn't thrilled by the prospect of walking a couple of hundred miles with them, so it was probably time that I learned how to ride a camel.

Noora returned with another plate of bread and *hummus,* and I attacked it hungrily. "The old shaykh will visit you when you're finished eating," she said.

I was glad to hear that. I wanted to see how well Friedlander Bey had survived our ordeal. It wasn't over by any means, though. We still had a long distance to travel, and the conditions would be just as harsh. The lifesaving difference was that we'd be traveling with the Bani Salim, and they knew where all the wells were. "Papa and I have much to talk over," I said.

"You must plan your vengeance."

"What do you know of that?" I asked.

She smiled. I realized that she was no longer holding her head scarf over her face. "You've told me many times about the amir and the qadi and the imam and Shaykh Reda. Most of the time, you just babbled; but I understood enough of what you were saying, and the old shaykh told me much the same story."

I raised my eyebrows and mopped up the last dollop of *hummus* with a chunk of bread. "What do you think we should do?"

Her expression turned solemn. "The Bedu insist on revenge. We practically make it a necessary part of our religion. If you didn't return to your city and slay those who plotted against you, the Bani Salim wouldn't be your friends when you returned to us."

I almost laughed when I heard her speak of my returning to the Rub al-Khali. "Even though the man responsible is a revered imam? Even though he's beloved by the *fellahîn* of the city? Even though he's known for his goodness and generosity?"

"Then he is an imam of two faces," said Noora. "To some, he may be wise in the worship of Allah, and kind to his brothers in Islam. Yet he did this evil to you, so his true nature is corrupt. He takes the coins of your enemy, and unjustly sentences innocent men to an exile that is almost surely death. The second face renders the first false, and is an abomination in the eyes of God. It's your duty to repay his treachery with the penalty accorded by tradition."

I was startled by her vehemence. I wondered why this matter between Papa and me, on the one side, and Dr. Abd ar-Razzaq, on the other, disturbed her so much. She saw me studying her, and she blushed and covered her face with her head cloth.

"The tradition of the Bedu may not be legal in the city," I said.

Her eyes flashed. "What is 'legal'? There's only right and wrong. There's a story the Bedu women tell their children, about the evil imam in the well."

"Noora, if it had been an accountant who'd done us harm, this story would be about the evil accountant in the well, right?"

"I don't even know what an accountant is," she said. "Listen, then. Maybe there was, and maybe there wasn't an evil imam of Ash-Shâm, which you call Damascus, when Ash-Shâm was the only city in the world. The Bedu have no need of imams, because every member of the tribe prays to God as an equal and defers to no other. The weak city folk needed an imam to help them, because they'd forgotten what it was to find their own water and make their own food, and they'd come to depend on other people to supply these things. So, too, had they come to depend on an imam to lead the way to Allah.

"Now, many of the people of Ash-Shâm still thought the evil imam was wise and good, because he made sure everyone who heard him preach gave money to their needy brothers. The imam himself never gave any of his own money, because he'd grown very fond of it. He loved gold so much that he sold his influence to one of Ash-Shâm's most corrupt and ambitious citizens.

"When Allah realized that the imam's heart had turned black, He sent one of His angels down to earth. The angel's instructions were to take the imam away into the desert, and imprison him so that he might never lead any of the people of Ash-Shâm astray. The angel found the imam in his secret treasury, stacking up his piles of gold and silver coins, and cast a spell over the imam that made him fall into a deep sleep.

"The angel picked up the evil imam and carried him in the palm of his hand, and brought him to the very heart of the Rub al-Khali. The imam knew nothing of this, because he was still fast asleep. The angel built a deep, deep well, and put the imam down at the very bottom, where there was only the most bitter and foul water. Then the angel caused the imam to awaken.

" 'Yaa Allah!' cried the evil imam. 'Where am I, and how did I come to this place?'

" 'It is too late to call on God, O Son of Adam,' said the angel. His stern voice cracked like thunder in the air, and the walls of the well shook around the imam.

" 'Let me out,' said the imam fearfully, 'and I promise to change my ways! Have mercy on me!'

"The angel shook his head, and his eyes loosed terrible flashes of lightning. 'It is for me neither to judge nor to have mercy. The One Judge has already condemned you to this place. Think on your deeds and repair your soul, for you have still to meet your God on the Last Day.' Then the angel departed, and left the evil imam all alone.

"A day came when the evil imam's successor, whose name was Salim and who was the founder of our tribe, came upon the well in his travels. Salim had never known the evil imam, and he was as different from him as the sun and the moon. This young man was truly kind and generous, and well beloved of all the people of Ash-Shâm, who had appointed him to be their imam in recognition of his virtues.

"As Salim bent forward to peer into the well, he was startled to see that a number of creatures had fallen into it and were trapped with the evil imam. The animals begged him to release them from the deep well. Salim felt so sorry for the animals that he unwound his *keffiya* and lowered it into the dark hole.

"The first animal to climb up the cloth ladder to freedom was a lizard, the one the Bedu call 'Abu Qurush,' or Father of Coins, because the end of this lizard's tail is flat and round. Abu Qurush was so grateful to be rescued that he shed a piece of his skin and gave it to Salim, saying, 'If ever you need help in a desperate situation, burn this piece of skin and I will come to you.' He began to run away across the hot sands, but he called back to Salim, 'Beware the Son of Adam who is in the well! He is an evil man, and you should leave him down there!'

"The next creature Salim pulled out was a she-wolf. The wolf was just as overjoyed as the lizard had been. She pulled out two of her whiskers and gave them to Salim, saying, 'If you should be in such a difficult place as that from which you rescued me, burn these and I will come to you.' She bounded away, but she too called back to him, 'Know, O Man, that the Son of Adam in the well is most evil.'

"Salim finished pulling out all the rest of the animals, and he listened to their warnings. Then he began to wrap his *keffiya* around his head once more. His countryman, the evil imam, shouted up to him in a heartbreaking voice. 'How can you save all those creatures, yet leave me to face my death in this pit of darkness? Are we not brothers according to the holy words of the Prophet, may the blessings of Allah be on him and peace?'

"Salim was torn between the warnings of the animals and his own good nature. He decided that he shared a bond of humanity with the unseen prisoner, and he once again lowered his *keffiya* down into the well. When he'd freed the evil imam, he took up his journey again, and many weeks later returned to Ash-Shâm."

"This is a great story, Noora," I said, yawning, "but it sounds like it's going to go on forever, and I remember your uncle telling me that the Bani Salim needed to move on to the next well soon. Surely, you don't want your camels and goats to die of starvation while you spin out this wonderful Bedu folklore for me."

Noora sighed. "I will finish it quickly," she said. I could see that she really loved telling stories. Maybe it was unkind of me to cut her off, but I had the feeling she was trying to make some special point. If she had some wisdom to impart, she could do it just as well in fifty words as five thousand.

I knew, of course, that in the story Salim represented

me, and the evil imam must be Dr. Abd ar-Razzaq. I thought I could guess what was going to happen. "So Salim gets in some kind of trouble, and it's the evil imam's fault, and he calls the lizard and the wolf."

"Actually," she said, trying to stay ahead of me, "Salim didn't get into trouble at first. He burned the lizard's skin, and Abu Qurush appeared before him before the last lick of gray smoke faded in the air. 'What do you wish?' asked the lizard.

" 'I'd like to be as rich as a king,' said Salim.

" 'The solution to that is simple. You must do as I tell you. Take the basket your servant uses to fetch bread, and leave it outside the city gates tonight. Then you must get up before the sun and bring it home again.' Salim did just as he was instructed, and he left the empty basket against the walls of the king's palace, and when he went to get it in the morning, it was filled with gold."

"Is that how Salim gets in trouble?" I asked.

Noora patted the air impatiently. "Wait, wait. So for a few days, Salim lived well. He ate the best food in the city, he bought himself a new wardrobe, he enjoyed all the pleasures of Ash-Shâm that Allah did not forbid. After a time, however, the king noticed that a part of his treasury was missing. He was outraged and furious, and he put out a decree: 'Whoever finds the robber of the king's gold shall have the king's beautiful daughter in marriage, and half the kingdom besides!'

"With that reward being offered, many wise and clever men came to examine the king's vaults. All were bewildered, and without exception they told the king that no man could have entered the treasury and stolen the gold. Finally, the cleverest of all asked that many arm-loads of dry palm fronds be put in the treasury. The king asked no questions, but did as the clever man said. Then the clever man set fire to the palm fronds and led the king and his courtiers outside the building. In a few minutes, all could see a black ribbon of smoke rising from a slender breach in the foundation of the palace wall. The clever man stepped closer and examined the ground itself, where he saw tiny footprints in the dust. 'Behold, your majesty!' he said. 'The thief was no man, but a lizard!'

"The king, who had little patience with clever men, thought this one was trying to make a fool of him, and so he ordered the clever man to be taken away and beheaded. And that was the end of the clever man."

"Is there supposed to be a moral in that for me?" I asked.

Noora smiled. "No, the story isn't even finished. The clever man wasn't important at all. I didn't even give him a name. Anyway, word of all this ran through the city of Ash-Shâm, until it reached the ears of the evil imam. The evil imam realized that the hand of the king's daughter and half the kingdom could be his, because he'd heard the words of Abu Qurush at the well. He ran to the king's audience chamber and cried, 'Your thief is your own imam, Salim!'

"Well, the king doubted this was true, but he sent his soldiers to Salim's house, where they found the rest of the gold. They arrested Salim and brought him in chains to the king's deepest, foulest dungeon. Salim knew who'd betrayed him, and he cursed his foolishness in ignoring the warnings of the animals and setting the evil imam free.

"Salim languished in his gloomy cell for a day and a night, and a day and a night, and then he remembered the words of the she-wolf. He took out the wolf's whiskers and burned them. In the blink of an eye, the she-wolf stood before him. 'What do you want of me?' she asked.

" 'Only for you to get me out of this dreadful prison, just as I released you from the well,' said Salim.

" 'Tonight you will be free,' said the wolf, and she squeezed beneath the door of his cell and was gone.

"Many hours passed, until it was the darkest watch of the night. Suddenly, there came screams of terror from the bedchamber of the king's young son and heir. The king ran into the room and saw the wolf with the boy's head gripped between her long, sharp teeth. Whenever the king or one of his soldiers or advisers tried to approach, the wolf let loose a loud, fierce growl. No one could do anything to save the young prince.

"Eventually, the news spread throughout the palace. The dungeon guards discussed it loudly, and Salim overheard them. 'Take me to the king,' he called, 'and I will save the life of the prince.'

"The guards laughed at him, saying the bravest of their number could do nothing, so what could this mere preacher hope to accomplish? At last, Salim persuaded the guards to bring him before the king. They hurried up to the prince's chamber. As soon as Salim entered, the wolf began wagging her tail and making sounds like a dog pleased to see its master. 'The she-wolf will depart without harming the boy,' said Salim, 'but only if you offer it the heart of the former imam of Ash-Shâm.'

"The king commanded his soldiers to hurry, and they ran out into the city and found the evil imam. They arrested him and dragged him back to the palace and cut off his head. Then they hacked open his chest, cut out his heart, and put it in a golden bowl. Salim placed the golden bowl before the she-wolf. The animal licked his hand, took the heart of the evil imam in her mouth, and ran from the palace to freedom.

"The king was so pleased that he pardoned Salim, and then gave him his daughter's hand in marriage!"

I waited a moment to be sure the story was finally

over. "I'm supposed to cut Dr. Sadiq Abd ar-Razzaq's heart out?" I said.

"Yes, and feed it to a dog," said Noora fiercely.

"Even though we don't do that kind of thing in the city anymore? I mean, we're talking about a theologian here. Not Hitler or Xarghis Khan."

Noora looked at me blankly. "Who are they?" she asked.

I smiled at her. "Never mind."

She took the empty plate and bowl from me and went out of the tent. Friedlander Bey entered almost immediately. He sat down beside me on the sand and clasped my hand. "How are you feeling, my darling?" he asked.

I was glad to see him. "It is as Allah pleases, O Shaykh," I said.

He nodded. "But look, your face is badly burned by the sun and the wind. And your hands and arms, from carrying me!" He shook his head. "I came to see you every day, even when you were unconscious. I saw the pain you suffered."

I let out a deep breath. "It was necessary, my grandfather."

Again he nodded. "I suppose I'm trying to express my gratitude. It's always—"

I raised my free hand. "Please, O Shaykh, don't make us both uncomfortable. Don't thank me. I did what I could to save our lives. Anyone would have done the same."

"Yet you pushed yourself beyond endurance, and you damaged your body and mind for my sake. I gave you those cursed implants, and I made you my weapon. Now you've repaid me with boundless courage. I feel shame."

I closed my eyes for a few seconds. If this went on much longer, it would be as unendurable as the walk in the desert had been. "I don't wish to talk about that anymore," I said. "We don't have time to indulge our emotions. The only hope we have of living through this trouble and returning to the city, and then restoring ourselves to our proper place, is to keep our minds focused clearly on a plan of action."

Papa rubbed his cheek, where his gray stubble was turning into a patchy beard. I watched him chew his lip as he thought. Evidently, he arrived at a decision, because from then on he was the old Friedlander Bey we all knew and feared back in the Budayeen. "We are in no danger from the Bani Salim," he said.

"Good," I said, "I didn't know where they stood."

"They've accepted responsibility for our well-being until we get to Mughshin. We'll be treated as honored guests and receive every courtesy. We must be careful not to abuse their hospitality, because they'll give us their food even if it means they themselves must go hungry. I don't want that to happen."

"Neither do I, O Shaykh."

"Now, I've never heard of Mughshin before, and I suppose it's just a community of huts and tents around a large well, somewhere to the south. We were wrong in thinking the sergeant in Najran arranged to have us dropped in the center of the Empty Quarter. The chopper traveled much farther than we thought, and we were thrown out in the northeastern part of the Sands." I frowned. "That's what the Bedu call this huge desert," Papa explained, "simply the Sands. They've never heard of the Rub al-Khali."

"Where we were didn't make any difference to us," I said. "If the Bani Salim hadn't found us, we'd have died long ago."

"We should have walked in the opposite direction, to the east. We're closer to Oman than we are to the western edge."

"We couldn't have made it to Oman, either. But we're still going to travel south with the Bani Salim?"

"Yes, my nephew. We can trust them. That counts for more in our situation than time or distance."

I drew up my knees experimentally, just to see if they still worked. They did, and I was happy about it, although they felt very weak after two weeks of enforced rest. "Have you planned our future after we reach Mughshin?"

He looked up, over my head, as if gazing into the distance toward the Budayeen and our enemies. "I do not know where Mughshin is, and even the shaykh, Hassanein, cannot show me. There are no maps or books among the Bani Salim. Several of the Bedu have assured me that beyond Mughshin, it is not a difficult journey across the mountains to a coastal town called Salala." Papa smiled briefly. "They speak of Salala as if it were the most wonderful place on earth, with every kind of luxury and pleasure."

"Mountains," I said unhappily.

"Yes, but not great mountains. Also, Hassanein promised to find us trustworthy guides in Mughshin to take us onward."

"And then?"

Papa shrugged. "Once we reach the coast, then we travel by ship to a city with a suborbital shuttle field. We must be extremely careful when we return home, because there will be spies—"

Noora returned, this time carrying some folded garments. "These are for you, Shaykh Marîd," she said. "Would you like to put on clean clothes, and take a walk with me?"

I wasn't in a hurry to put my aching muscles to work, but I couldn't refuse. Papa stood up and went outside the tent. Noora followed him and dropped the flaps in the front and the back, so I could dress in privacy.

I stood up slowly, ready to quit for the day in case I experienced any severe stabs of pain. I shook out the clean garments. First, there was a threadbare loincloth that I wrapped around myself. I wasn't exactly sure how the Bani Salim men wore them, and I wasn't about to find out. Over that I pulled a long, white smock, which the Bedu called a *thobe*. The poor men of the city wore something very similar, and I knew that Friedlander Bey often dressed in one, betraying his origins. On top of the *thobe* I wore a long, white shirt that was open all the way down the front, with wide, long sleeves. For my head there was a clean cotton *keffiya*, but my *akal* had been lost somewhere; I wound the head cloth around and tucked it in as these southern Bedu wore it. Then I drew on my now-tattered and travel-stained blue robe, which the Bayt Tabiti had so admired. There were no sandals with the rest of the clothes; I figured I could go barefoot.

It felt good again to be up and dressed and ready for action. When I stepped outside the tent, I was a little self-conscious because my outfit made me look like a wealthy shaykh from the decadent, feeble world beyond the Rub al-Khali. I was aware that the eyes of everyone in the camp were on me.

Waiting for me were Friedlander Bey, Noora, and her uncle Hassanein. The shaykh of the Bani Salim greeted me with a broad smile. "Here," he said, "I have your belongings. I took these for safekeeping. I feared that a few of our younger men might have been tempted to borrow them." He handed me my sandals, my ceremonial dagger, and my rack of moddies and daddies. I was extremely glad to get all these things back.

"Please, O Shaykh," I said to Hassanein, "I would be most honored if you would accept this gift. It can only begin to repay the great debt we owe." I presented him with the gorgeous jeweled dagger.

He took it in his hands and stared at it. He did not speak for a few moments. "By the life of my eyes," he said at last, "this is not for me! This is for some noble prince, or a king."

"My friend," said Papa, "you are as noble as any prince in the land. Accept it. This dagger has a long history, and it will do you honor."

Hassanein did not stammer out effusive thanks. He just nodded to me and tied the woven belt around his waist. In the Bedu manner, he wore the dagger directly in front, over his stomach. He said nothing more about it, but I could see that the gift had greatly pleased him.

We walked slowly among the black goat-hair tents. I could see the faces of the men turn to follow us. Even the women peeked at us as we passed, while they tended to the day's work. Not far away, the young boys herded the camels and goats toward the low, scrubby salt-bushes. This wasn't the best food for the animals, but in this desolate place it would have to do. I understood immediately what Hassanein had meant about moving on. There was little sustenance here for the animals.

The camp consisted of a dozen tents. The terrain around Bir Balagh was the same as that Papa and I had traveled through. There were no shade trees here, no date palms, no real oasis at all. All that recommended this low, flat stretch in a hollow between two chains of dunes was a single wide hole in the ground—the well. Whenever a traveler came upon one of these wells, he sometimes had to spend hours digging it out, because it didn't take the shifting sands long to fill it in.

I realized how helpless Papa and I would've been, even if we'd stumbled across such a muddy hole. The water was often ten feet or more below the surface, and there were no buckets or ropes. Each wandering Bedu band carried its own rope for the purpose of drawing out the life-giving water. Even if Allah had granted us the good fortune to find one of these brackish trickles, we might easily have died of thirst only ten vertical feet from the water.

That thought made me shudder, and I murmured a prayer of thanks. Then the four of us continued our walk. In one of the nearby tents, a few men were relaxing and drinking coffee from small cups little bigger than thimbles. This was the normal occupation of Bedu males in the camp. One of the men saw me and said something, throwing his coffee cup to the ground. A commotion arose among his friends, and he leaped to his feet and rushed toward me, yelling and gesturing madly.

"What is this?" I asked Hassanein.

The shaykh moved to intercept the angry young man. "These are our guests," said Hassanein. "Be silent, or you will dishonor us all."

"There's the one who brings dishonor!" cried the furious Bedu. He pointed one long, bony finger at me. "He's doing it right beneath your nose! He's trying to spoil her! He's seducing her with his unholy city ways! He's no true Muslim, may his father's infidel religion be cursed! He cares nothing for her, and he'll ruin her and leave her to go back to his *hareem* of unclean women!"

Hassanein was having no success restraining the young man, who kept shouting and waving his fist at me. I tried to ignore him, but soon the entire tribe had gathered around us. The whole thing was rapidly getting out of hand.

Noora's face grew pale. I caught her eye, and she looked away. I was afraid she would break out into tears. "Don't tell me," I said to her, "that's bin Musaid, your secret admirer, right?"

She looked into my face helplessly. "Yes," she said softly. "And now he's decided to kill you."

I thought how much better things would've been if I'd declined Shaykh Mahali's invitation, and just gone out and gotten drunk instead.

6

I watched the Bani Salim pack up their camp. It didn't take them long. Each person in the tribe had his particular task, and he went about it quickly and efficiently. Even the sullen Ibrahim bin Musaid, who'd been restrained and persuaded not to murder me where I stood, was busy rounding up the pack camels.

He was a dark, brooding young man about twenty years old, with a long, narrow face. Like some of the younger Bani Salim, he didn't wear a *keffiya,* and his head was framed by his wild, stringy hair. His upper jaw thrust forward, giving him an unfortunate foolish expression, but his black eyes glared at the world beneath knotted brows.

The situation between him and Noora was more complicated than I'd thought. It wasn't just a matter of unrequited love, which in the closed community of a Bedu tribe would be bad enough. Hassanein told me that bin Musaid was the son of one of the shaykh's two brothers, and Noora was the daughter of the other. Among the Bani Salim, a girl is betrothed at birth to her first cousin, and cannot marry anyone else unless he releases her. Bin Musaid had no intention of doing that, even though Noora had made it clear that she wanted to marry another young man named Suleiman bin Sharif.

I'd made everything worse, because bin Musaid had focused all his jealousy on me. I guess I was an easier target than bin Sharif, because I was an outsider and a civilized weakling. Bin Musaid made it abundantly clear that he resented the hours Noora had spent with me, particularly those long nights while I was recuperating. It didn't make any difference to him that I'd been unconscious most of that time. He still hinted at all kinds of unseemly behavior.

This morning, though, there wasn't time for more accusations. The camels lay couched on the ground, while the men of the Bani Salim stacked the folded tents and packs of belongings and supplies nearby. The air was filled with the loud grunting and roaring of the camels, who were aware of what was going on and were unanimous in their displeasure. Some turned their heads and snapped at their owners, who were trying to adjust the loads, and the Bedu had to be quick to dance out of the way.

When everything was divided and properly stowed, we were ready to travel. Bin Sharif, Noora's boyfriend, brought a small female camel named Fatma to me. The tribe had a few dozen camels in its herd, but only two or three were bulls. Bin Sharif explained to me that they sold or ate the rest of the bulls, because they didn't believe in giving food and water to an animal that wouldn't return milk.

I saw one of the men mounting a camel that was already on the move. He did this by climbing up one of the animal's forelegs, gripping it above the knee with his toes, and then pulling himself up over the camel's neck and into the saddle. I wasn't ready to display that kind of nonchalance, and I waited until bin Sharif couched Fatma by tapping behind her front knees with a stick, and making the same "khirr, khirr!" noise I'd heard the Bayt Tabiti use. Then I dragged myself awkwardly into the sheepskincovered wooden saddle. Bin Sharif got the animal to her feet and handed me the head rope and a riding stick. I saw that Friedlander Bey had been helped onto another small camel.

"In the name of Allah, the Compassionate, the Merciful!" cried Shaykh Hassanein, leading the Bani Salim south from Bir Balagh.

"*Allahu akbar!* God is Most Great!" shouted his tribesmen. And then we were off on the three-day journey to Khaba, the next well.

Papa maneuvered his camel alongside me on the left, and Hilal, one of the two Bani Salim who'd found us in the desert, rode on my right. I was not enjoying the experience, and I couldn't imagine staying in that saddle for the three days to Khaba, let alone the two weeks it would take to reach Mughshin.

"How do you feel, my nephew?" asked Papa.

I groaned. "I hate this," I said.

"These saddles aren't as comfortable as those of the northern Bedu. Our muscles will hurt tonight."

"Look," said Hilal, "we don't sit in our saddles like city people. We kneel." He was, in fact, kneeling on the back of the camel. I was having enough trouble maintaining my balance, wedged into the wooden saddle and hanging on for dear life. If I'd tried to kneel like Hilal, I would've rolled off and fallen the ten feet to the ground with the camel's next lurching step. Then I would've had a broken neck to go along with my aching back.

"Maybe I'll just get off and walk," I said.

Hilal grinned and showed me his strong white teeth. "Be cheerful, my brother!" he said. "You're alive, and you're with friends!"

Actually, I've never been among such horribly cheerful people as the Bedu. They chanted and sang the whole way from Bir Balagh to Khaba. I suppose there was little else to pass the time. Now and then, one of the young men would ride up to one of his cousins; they'd have a wrestling match atop their camels, each trying to topple the other to the ground. The possibility of broken bones didn't seem to daunt them.

After about an hour and a half, my back, neck, and legs began to complain. I couldn't stretch adequately, and I realized it was only going to get worse. Then I remembered my daddies. At first, I hesitated to chip in the pain blocker again, but my argument was that it was only the abuse of drugs and daddies that was dangerous. I took out the daddy and chipped it in, promising myself that I wasn't going to leave it in any longer than necessary. From then on, the camel ride was less of a strain on my cramped muscles. It never got any less boring, though.

For the remainder of the day, I felt pretty good. As a matter of fact, I felt almost invincible. We'd survived being abandoned in the Rub al-Khali—with the help of the Bani Salim, of course—and we were on our way back to punish Reda Abu Adil and his tame imam. Once more, I'd shown Friedlander Bey that I was a man of honor and courage; I doubted that he'd ever again resort to blasting my brain's punishment center to get my cooperation. Even if at the moment all wasn't right with the world, I was confident that it soon would be.

I felt as if a strong current of dynamic force was flowing into me from some mystic source. As I sat uneasily astride Fatma, I imagined Allah inspiring our allies and creating confusion for our foes. Our goals were honest and praiseworthy, and I assumed God was on our side. Even before the abduction, I'd become more serious about my religious obligations. Now when the Bani Salim paused for prayer at each of the five prescribed times, I joined in with sincere devotion.

When we came into a valley between two parallel ridges of sand, Hassanein called a halt for the evening. The men couched the camels and unloaded them. Then the boys herded the beasts toward some low, dead-looking shrubs. "Do you see the *haram,* the salt-bush?" said Suleiman bin Sharif. He and Ibrahim bin Musaid had unloaded Fatma and Papa's camel.

"Yes," I said. The *haram* had dead-looking reddish-green leaves, and was as unhappy as any plant I'd ever seen.

"It's not dead, although it looks like dry sticks poking up out of the sand. No water has fallen in almost two years in this part of the Sands, but if it rained tomorrow, the *haram* would flower in a week, and then it could stay alive another two years."

"The Bani Salim are like the *haram,*" said bin Musaid, looking at me with a contemptuous expression. "We aren't like the weak city-dwellers, who can't live without their Christian ornaments." "Christian" seemed to be the worst insult he could think of.

I had a response to that, something to the effect that bin Musaid did indeed remind me of the *haram,* but I couldn't imagine him all covered with flowers because he'd need to bathe first. I decided not to say it aloud, because I could just picture the headlines: BUDAYEEN CLUB OWNER DIES IN SALT-BUSH MASSACRE.

The women put up the goat-hair tents for the night, and Hassanein generously offered to let Papa and me use his. "Thank you, O Shaykh," I said, "but I'm well enough now to sleep by the fire."

"Are you sure?" asked Hassanein. "It reflects badly on my hospitality for you to sleep under God's sky tonight. I'd truly be honored—"

"I accept your most kind invitation, Shaykh Hassanein," said Friedlander Bey. "My grandson wants to experience the life of the Bedu. He still entertains romantic notions of the nomadic existence, no doubt put in his mind by Omar Khayyám. A night by the fire will be good for him."

Hassanein laughed, and went to tell his wife to make room in their tent for Papa. As for me, I hoped it wouldn't get too cold that night. At least I'd have my robe to help keep me warm.

We shared a simple supper of dried goat meat, rice porridge, bread, coffee, and dates. I'd gotten plenty hungry during the day, and this food was as satisfying as any meal I could remember. Some of the enjoyment came from the company. The Bani Salim had unanimously welcomed Papa and me, and it was as if we'd been born among them.

Well, the acceptance was *almost* unanimous. The lone dissenter, of course, was Ibrahim bin Musaid. Noora's cousin didn't have any problem with Friedlander Bey, but he still gave me the fishy eye and muttered under his breath whenever he caught me looking at him. I was under the protection of Shaykh Hassanein, however, and therefore completely safe from his nephew. And bin Musaid was bright enough to realize that if he just waited long enough, I'd go away again.

After I finished eating, I popped out the pain daddy. Except for some soreness in my neck and back, I felt pretty good. I watched some of the men get up to make sure the boys had hobbled the camels properly for the

night. There were still five or six of us at the fire, and a
good-humored story-telling session began, concerning the
men who had wives to prepare their meals and tents to
sleep in. One man told some gossip about bin Shahira
who, like many of the Bani Salim, had been named after
his mother rather than his father. "Bearing his mother's
name has made him crazy all his life," said the narrator.
"All the years we were boys together, he complained
about what a strict tyrant his mother was. So who does he
marry? Old Wadood Ali's daughter. Badia the Boss we
used to call her. Now he's the most henpecked man who
ever rode a camel. Tonight at prayers, I think I heard him
ask Allah to let the Bayt Tabiti raid us and carry her off.
Just her and nothing else!"

"Min ghayr sharr," said one of the other men, who
wasn't amused. That was a superstitious formula to avoid
the evil bin Shahira had wished for.

No one was safe from the loose tongues of the Bani
Salim, except of course the other men who sat by the
campfire. Even Shaykh Hassanein came in for some sarcastic comments about how he was handling his hot-
headed nephew, bin Musaid, and his beautiful niece,
Noora. It was clear that bin Musaid and bin Sharif weren't
the only men of the tribe who had their eyes on Noora,
but because bin Musaid was her first cousin, he had an
unshakable claim on her.

The talk drifted in one direction and then another.
One of the older men began a recitation of some long-ago
battle in which he'd distinguished himself. The younger
men complained that they'd heard the story a hundred
times before, but that didn't dismay the speaker. Hilal and
bin Turki got up from their places and came to sit beside
me.

"Do you remember us, O Shaykh?" asked Hilal, who'd
ridden beside me most of the day.

"Yes, of course," I said. "You're the clever young men who found us in the desert."

Hilal and bin Turki grinned at each other. "My cousin would like to ask you a question," said Hilal.

"Sure," I said.

Bin Turki was a handsome, shy youth. Even by the firelight I could see that he was blushing furiously. "O Shaykh," he said, "when you return to your city, will you be far from China?"

I wondered what he meant. "Very far, bin Turki," I said. "Why?"

"Ten days' march?" he asked. "Twenty?"

I stopped to do some quick calculation. The camels made a steady three miles an hour, and the Bani Salim put in about twelve hours of travel per day. Call it thirty-six miles, then. Now, the distance from the city to China . . . "Hundreds of days, O my friend, across deserts and seas and great mountains."

Bin Turki just blinked at me a few times. "O Shaykh," he said in a quavering voice, "even Allah's world is not so big."

He thought I was lying to him, but he couldn't bring himself to accuse a guest of his tribe. "Indeed it is so big. The Sands are only a portion of Arabia, and all of Arabia is to the world as . . . as one she-camel to the entire herd."

"*Wallâhi!*" murmured Hilal, which means "By Almighty God," and is one of the Bani Salim's strongest oaths. I rarely heard them resort to obscenity.

"What is your curiosity about China, bin Turki?" I asked. These were people who had never heard of England, Nuevo Tejas, or even the western lands of the Muslim world.

"Does not the Prophet—may the blessings of Allah be on him and peace—say, 'Seek knowledge even unto

China'? I thought maybe I could return with you to your city, and then go from there to China."

Hilal laughed. "Bin Turki's hungry for knowledge," he said in a teasing voice. "He's already eaten all the knowledge there is to be had in the Sands."

"You don't have to go to China," I said. "If you're serious about learning, maybe you could travel with us after we reach Mughshin. Would you like that?"

I could see that bin Turki was trembling. "Yes, O Shaykh," he said softly.

"Is there any reason why you couldn't come with us? Do the Bani Salim need you? Might Shaykh Hassanein forbid you to go away for a few months?"

"I haven't yet discussed this with the shaykh," said bin Turki.

"The Bani Salim won't need you," said Hilal. "You never do anything useful anyway. It will be one less belly to fill with water from the wells of the Sands. Seriously, my brother, Shaykh Hassanein will let you go with his blessing."

There were a few moments of quiet while bin Turki thought over the consequences of what he wanted to do. We listened to dead limbs of the mimosa-like *ghaf* trees spit and crackle in the fire. Then the young man worked up his courage. "If Shaykh Hassanein gives his permission," he asked, "would I be welcome to join you?"

I smiled at the young man. "Do you know the way across the mountains from Mughshin to that coastal town?"

"To Salala?" said bin Turki. "Yes, I've been there many times. Two or three times, anyway."

"Well, then, we'd be glad of your company. Talk it over with Shaykh Hassanein and see what he has to say. It's a big, strange world out there, and you may wish you never left the Bani Salim."

"If that happens, I will come back to the Sands, *in-shallah*."

Hilal looked from bin Turki to me, realizing that his friend might soon be leaving their community for the unimaginable life beyond the desert. *"La illah ill'Allah,"* he said in astonishment. "There is no god but God."

Bin Musaid came to the fire and stared down at me for a few seconds. "You don't have to sleep here on the sand tonight," he said. "You're welcome to share my tent."

His sour expression belied the generosity of his offer. I wondered why he was making this overture. Maybe Hassanein had had a little talk with him. "May Allah reward you, bin Musaid," I said, "but tonight I wish to sleep under the stars."

"Good," he said. He wasn't going to try to talk me out of it. One of the others passed him a goatskin of camel's milk, and he squatted down to drink. It's considered shameful for a Bedu to drink standing up. Don't ask me why.

Noora joined us, but she didn't even glance at bin Musaid. "My uncle wishes to know if there's anything you need," she said.

There was a time not long ago when I would have weakened and asked the shaykh for some medication. "Tell Hassanein that I feel very well," I said.

"Noora," said Hilal, "tell us about the time Abu Zayd was rescued by the Bayt Tabiti!"

"There *is* no story about Abu Zayd and the Bayt Tabiti," said one of the other men.

"Give Noora a minute or two and there will be," said bin Turki.

Bin Musaid grunted in disgust, got up, and stalked away into the deepening darkness.

"He better be hung like a bull camel," said Hilal, "because his wife won't get any happiness from him any other way." There was an uncomfortable silence, while we all tried hard not to look at Noora.

"Well, does anybody want to hear about Abu Zayd?" she said at last.

"Yes!" came several voices. Abu Zayd is a popular hero of Arabian folklore. His mythical tribe is responsible for everything from the Roman ruins in North Africa to the mysterious petroglyphs in the Rub al-Khali.

"All you who love the Prophet," Noora began, "say, 'May Allah be pleased with him and grant him salvation.' Now, one day Abu Zayd found himself lost in a part of the Sands he had never traveled before. There were no familiar landmarks, and he did not know that he was on the edge of the terrible gypsum flat called Abu Khawf, or Father of Fear. He led his faithful camel, Wafaa, down onto the flat, which stretched ahead of him for eight days' journey. After three days, Abu Zayd had drunk all of his water. By the end of the next day, when he'd reached the very middle of Abu Khawf, he was suffering from thirst, and even Wafaa, his camel, was beginning to stumble.

"Another day passed, and Abu Zayd was afraid for his life. He prayed to God, saying that if it was the will of Allah, he'd much prefer getting out of Abu Khawf alive. Just then, he heard a loud voice. Coming toward him, leading two camels loaded with bulging goatskin bags, was a man of the Bayt Tabiti. '*Salaam alaykum,* my brother!' cried the stranger. 'I am Abduh bin Abduh, and I will give you water!'

" '*Alaykum as-salaam,*' said Abu Zayd, overcome with relief. He watched as the Bayt Tabiti took several bags of water and slung them on Wafaa. Then Abduh bin Abduh gave him a bag of camel's milk, from which Abu Zayd drank greedily. 'You've done me a great service,' he said. 'You've kept me from dying in this miserable gypsum flat.

No man has ever shown me greater hospitality and generosity. I insist that you turn your camels around and return with me to the nearest oasis. There I will give you a suitable reward.'

" 'Of course,' said Abduh bin Abduh, 'I had no thought at all of reward. Still, if you insist.' And he did turn his camels around, and together the two men made their away across the remainder of Abu Khawf, the Father of Fear. Two days later, they arrived at Bir Shaghir, a settlement around a well of the sweetest water in all the Sands. Abu Zayd made good on his promise, buying a huge load of flour, butter, dates, coffee, rice, and dried meat, and giving it all to Abduh bin Abduh. Afterward, the two men expressed gratitude and good wishes to each other, and then they parted, going their separate ways.

"A year later to the very day, Abu Zayd again found himself lost in the Sands, and this time he stumbled into Abu Khawf from a different direction. After three days passed, he realized that fate had led him into the very same situation he'd endured the year before. He prayed for God, saying, '*Yaa Allah*, how like a woven web of spider silk is Your will. All glory be to God!'

"And on the fifth day, when Abu Zayd and his camel, Wafaa, were growing weak without water, who should come toward them across the gypsum flat but the very same Bayt Tabiti! 'God bless you!' cried Abduh bin Abduh. 'All year, I've told my friends of your generosity. I hoped we'd meet again, so you could know that your name is legendary for gratitude among my people.'

"Abu Zayd was amazed, but once again he persuaded Abduh bin Abduh to turn his camels and go back with him to Bir Shaghir. This time he bought the Bayt Tabiti so much flour, butter, dates, coffee, rice, and dried meat that he also needed to buy the man a third camel to help carry it all. Then they swore undying friendship to each other and went off in opposite directions.

"Before Abduh bin Abduh disappeared from view, however, Abu Zayd turned and shouted after him. 'Go with safety, my brother,' he called, 'and enjoy my gifts to you, because for a second time you saved my life. I will never forget what you've done, and as long as my sons and my sons' sons draw breath, they will sing your praises. But listen, O fortunate one: I am not a rich man. If you come upon me next year in Abu Khawf, pass me by and let me die of thirst! I can't afford to thank you one more time!' "

All the men at the campfire laughed loudly, and Noora stood up, smiling and looking pleased. "Good night, my brothers," she said. "May you arise in the morning in health."

"And you are the daughter of well-being," said bin Sharif. That's a Bedu idiom, possibly even an exclusively Bani Salim idiom. Noora raised a hand, and then crossed the open area of the camp to her father's tent.

Morning would come early, and the unmarried men soon settled in for the night. I wrapped myself in my cloak and tried to relax, knowing that there would be another long day of travel tomorrow. Before I fell asleep, I entertained myself with stories of what would happen when I got back to the city. I imagined that Indihar and Chiri and Yasmin ran to me, tears of joy streaming down their faces, praising Allah that I was alive and well. Imagined that Reda Abu Adil sat in his lonely palace, gnashing his teeth in fear of the retribution that would soon come. I imagined that Friedlander Bey rewarded me with tons of money, and told me that he was hiring an outside contractor to deal with Dr. Sadiq Abd ar-Razzaq, and that I needn't concern myself with him.

Breakfast in the morning was rice porridge, dates, and coffee. It wasn't very appetizing, and there wasn't enough of it. There was still plenty of water from Bir Balagh; but it had started out brackish, and after a day in the goatskin bags, it had begun to taste like, well, goatskin. I was already looking forward to getting to Khaba well, which the Bani Salim all talked about as the last sweet well before the long haul to Mughshin.

Friedlander Bey rode beside me again on the second day. "I've been thinking of the future, my nephew," he said, yawning. I'm sure it had been years since he'd had to sleep on the ground and share such meager rations, yet I hadn't heard him complain.

"The future," I said. "Imam ar-Razzaq first, and then Abu Adil? Or maybe the other way around?"

Papa didn't say anything for a little while. "Haven't I made it clear that you are not to harm Shaykh Reda under any circumstances?" he said. "Neither him nor his sons, if he has sons."

I nodded. "Yes, I know all that. How do you mean 'harm'? Do you mean physically? Then we won't raise a hand against him. Surely you won't mind if we destroy his business and influence in the city. He deserves that much at least."

"He deserves that much, Allah knows it. We can't destroy his influence. We don't have the means."

I laughed without humor. "Do I have your permission to try?"

Papa waved a hand, dismissing the entire subject. "When I spoke of the future, I meant our pilgrimage."

This wasn't the first time he'd brought up the trip to Mecca. I pretended I didn't know what he was talking about. "Pilgrimage, O Shaykh?" I said.

"You're a young man, and you have decades yet to fulfill that duty. I do not. The Apostle of God, may the blessings of Allah be on him and peace, laid upon us all the obligation to travel to Mecca at least once during our lifetime. I've put off that holy journey year after year, until now I'm afraid that I have very few years left. I'd planned to go this year, but when the month of the pilgrimage came, I was too ill. I strongly desire that we make definite plans to do it next year."

"Yes, O Shaykh, of course." My immediate concern was returning to the city and reestablishing ourselves; Friedlander Bey had thought past all that, and was already making plans for when life got back to normal. That was an outlook I wished I could learn from him.

The second day's march was much like the first. We pressed on over the high dune walls, stopping only to pray at the required times. The Bani Salim took no lunch breaks. The rocking gait of Fatma, my camel, had a lulling effect, and sometimes I dozed off into uneasy sleep. Every now and then, out of the blue, one of the men would shout "There is no god but God!" Others would join in, and then they'd all fall silent again, absorbed in their own thoughts.

When the tribe stopped for the second evening, the valley between the dunes looked identical to our camp of the previous night. I wondered how these people actually found their way from place to place in this huge desert. I felt a quick thrill of fear: what if they really couldn't? What if they only *pretended* they knew where they were going? What would happen when the water in the goat-skins gave out?

I forgot my foolishness as I waited for Suleiman bin Sharif to couch Fatma. I slipped down her bulging side and stretched my aching muscles. I'd ridden the whole day without the aid of my daddy, and I was proud of myself. I went to Papa and helped him off his mount. Then the two of us pitched in to help the Bani Salim set up the camp.

It was another peaceful, lovely night in the desert. The

first disturbing moment came when Ibrahim bin Musaid came up to me and put his nose about an inch from mine. "I watch you, city man!" he shouted. "I see you looking at Noora. I see her looking shamelessly at you. I swear by the life of my honor and by Almighty God that I'll kill her, rather than let you mock the Bani Salim!"

I'd had just about all I could take from bin Musaid. What I really wanted to do was knock the son of a bitch down, but I'd learned that the Bedu take physical violence very seriously. A crummy punch in the nose would be enough of a provocation for bin Musaid to kill me, and he'd have the sympathy of all the other Bani Salim. I grabbed my beard, which is how the Bedu swear their oaths, and said, "I haven't dishonored Noora, and I haven't dishonored the Bani Salim. I doubt anyone could dishonor you, because you have no honor to speak of."

There was a loud murmur on all sides, and I wondered if I'd gone a little too far. I have a tendency to do that sometimes. Anyway, bin Musaid's face darkened, but he said nothing more. As he stormed away, I knew I had a lifelong enemy in him. He paused and turned to face me again, raising his thin arm and pointing a finger at me, shaking in rage. "I'll kill her!" he cried.

I turned to Hilal and bin Turki, but they just shrugged. Bin Musaid was my problem, not theirs.

It wasn't long before another loud altercation broke out. I looked across the fire to the far side of the camp. There were five people involved in a shouting match that was getting louder and more violent by the moment. I saw bin Musaid and Noora waving their arms wildly at each other. Then bin Sharif, the young man Noora wished to marry, came to her defense, and I thought the two young men would begin strangling each other right there. An older woman joined them, and she began firing accusations at Noora, too.

"That's Umm Rashid," said Hilal. "She has a temper like a fennec fox."

"I can't make out what she's saying," I said.

Bin Turki laughed. "She's accusing Noora of sleeping with her husband. Her husband is too old to sleep with anybody, and all the Bani Salim know it, but Umm Rashid is blaming her husband's inattention on Noora."

"I don't understand. Noora is a good, sweet child. She's done nothing to deserve all this."

"Being good and sweet in this life is enough to attract evil," said Hilal, frowning. "I seek refuge with the Lord of the Worlds."

Umm Rashid screeched at Noora and flapped her arms like a crazed chicken. Bin Musaid joined in, practically accusing Noora of seducing the old woman's husband. Bin Sharif tried to defend her, but he could barely get a word in edgewise.

Then Noora's father, Nasheeb, was finally stirred to action. He came out of his tent, yawning and scratching his belly. "What's this all about?" he said.

That got Umm Rashid yelling in one of his ears, and bin Musaid in the other. Noora's father smiled lazily and waved his hands back and forth. "No, no," he said, "it can't be. My Noora is a good girl."

"Your Noora is a slut and a whore!" cried Umm Rashid. That's when Noora felt she'd had enough. She ran —not into her father's tent, but into her uncle Hassanein's.

"I won't let you call her that," said bin Sharif angrily.

"Ah, and here's her pimp!" said the old woman, putting her hands on her hips and cocking her head sideways. "I warn you, if you don't keep that bitch away from my husband, you'll wish you had. The Qur'ân allows me that. The Straight Path permits me to kill her if she threatens to break up my household."

"It does not," said bin Sharif. "It doesn't say that anywhere."

Umm Rashid paid him no attention. "If you know what's good for her," she said, turning back to Nasheeb, "you'll keep her away from my husband."

Noora's father just smiled. "She's a good girl," he said. "She's pure, a virgin."

"I hold you responsible, my uncle," said bin Musaid. "I'd rather see her dead than spoiled by the likes of that infidel from the city."

"*What* infidel from the city?" asked Nasheeb in confusion.

"You know," said Hilal thoughtfully, "for someone as good and kind as Noora, there sure are an awful lot of people ready to hurt her."

I nodded. The next morning, I remembered what he said when I discovered Noora's lifeless body.

7

The Bani Salim were standing crowded together in the hollow of a horseshoe-shaped dune near their camp, grouped in a semicircle around Noora's corpse. She lay on her back with her right arm up on the hill of sand as if reaching toward Heaven. Her eyes were wide open, staring up at the cloudless sky. The girl's throat had been slashed from ear to ear, and the golden sand was darkly stained with her blood. "Like an animal," murmured bin Turki. "She's been butchered like a goat or a camel."

The Bedu had gathered into several groups of people. Friedlander Bey and I stood with Hilal and bin Turki. On one side were Nasheeb and his wife, who were on their knees and shrieking their grief. Nasheeb looked dazed and kept repeating "There is no god but God. There is no god but God." Not far from them stood Ibrahim bin Musaid and Suleiman bin Sharif, who were engaged in a fierce argument. I saw bin Sharif point sharply toward Noora's body, and bin Musaid raised both his hands as if to ward off a blow. Shaykh Hassanein stood aside with a grim expression, nodding as his brother, Abu Ibrahim, spoke to him. Everyone else contributed to the noise and confusion, all loudly speculating, debating, and praying.

There was a lot of scriptural citation going on, too. " 'He who is wrongfully slain,' " quoted Hilal, " 'We have given license to his heir, but let him not revenge himself in too great a measure. Behold! he will be helped.' "

"All praise be to Allah," said bin Turki, "but what heir did Noora have to settle this blood-debt?"

Hilal shook his head. "Only Nasheeb, her father, but I don't think he'll do very much. He doesn't have the temperament for vengeance."

"Perhaps her uncles," I said.

"If not them, then *we* will take up this matter," said Friedlander Bey. "This is a needless tragedy. I liked the young woman a great deal. She was very kind to me while I recovered."

I nodded. I felt the flame of rage burning in me, the same hot, frightening feeling I've gotten whenever I've witnessed the scene of a murder. Those other times, however, were back home. In the Budayeen, crime and violent death are daily occurrences; they barely raise an eyebrow among my hardened friends.

This was different. This was a killing among close-knit people, a tribe that depended on each member for the continued well-being of all. I knew that the justice of the desert people was more sure and swift than the justice of the city, and I was glad. Vengeance would not bring Noora back, but it helped a little to know that her murderer's hours were numbered.

It wasn't immediately clear who her killer was, however. The two likely candidates, based on their loudly publicized threats the previous evening, were bin Musaid and Umm Rashid.

Shaykh Hassanein raised his arms and called for attention. "This girl must be buried by sundown," he said. "And her murderer must be identified and punished."

"And the blood-price paid!" cried the grief-stricken Nasheeb.

"All will be done in accordance with the Book," Hassanein assured him. "Abu Ibrahim, help me carry our niece back to the camp. Hilal, you and bin Turki must begin digging a grave."

"May God have mercy on her!" someone said, as Hassanein and his brother wrapped Noora in a cloak and lifted her up. We made a slow procession from the horseshoe dune through a narrow gully to the campsite. The shaykh chose a spot for Noora's final resting place, and Hilal and bin Turki fetched two folding shovels and began digging down through the hard belly of the desert.

Meanwhile, Hassanein disappeared into his tent for a few minutes. When he returned, his *keffiya* was arranged more carefully on his head. I guessed that he'd also chipped in one of his two moddies, probably the one that loaned him the wisdom of a Sunni Muslim religious leader.

The Bani Salim were still upset and angry, and there were many loud discussions going on, trying to make sense of the killing. The only one who wasn't involved was bin Musaid. He seemed to be holding himself apart. I looked at him, and he stared back at me across the open space. Finally he turned his back on me, slowly and insultingly.

"Shaykh Marîd," said Hassanein, "I'd like to speak with you."

"Hm? Sure, of course." He led me into his shady tent. He invited me to sit down, and I did.

"Please forgive me," he said, "but I must ask you some questions. If you don't mind, we'll do without the preliminary coffee and conversation. Right now, I'm only interested in learning how Noora died. Tell me all about how you found her this morning."

I felt a lot of anxiety, although Hassanein probably didn't consider me a prime suspect. I was one of those kids who, when the teacher came in and asked who'd written the dirty word on the blackboard, even though I hadn't done it, I'd blush and look guilty. All I had to do now, I told myself, was take a deep breath and tell the shaykh just what had happened.

I took the deep breath. "I must've gotten up a little before dawn," I said. "I had to relieve myself, and I remember wondering how long it would be before old Hamad bin Mubarak woke us with his Call to Prayer. The moon was low on the horizon, but the sky was so bright I didn't have any trouble following the little alleys among the dunes east of camp. When I finished, I stumbled back toward the fire. I must've taken a different path, because I hadn't seen Noora before. She was stretched out in front of me, just as you saw her. The pale moonlight made her drained face look ghastly. I knew immediately that she was dead. That's when I decided to come straight to your tent. I didn't want to disturb the others until I told you."

Hassanein just regarded me for a few seconds. With the imam moddy in, his behavior and speech were more deliberate. "Did you see signs of anyone else? Were there footprints? The weapon, perhaps?"

"Yes," I said, "there was footprints. I can't read footprints in sand as well as footprints in mud, O Shaykh. I imagine they were Noora's footprints and her killer's."

"Did you see long tracks, as if she'd been dragged to the place?"

I thought back to that moonlit scene. "No," I said, "I

definitely didn't see tracks. She must've walked there and met the other person. Or maybe she was carried. She was alive when she got there, because there was no trail of blood leading back to camp."

"After you told me about Noora," he said, "did you tell anyone else?"

"Forgive me, O Shaykh, but when I got back to the fire, bin Turki was awake and asked me if I was all right. I told him about Noora. He was very upset, and our talking roused Hilal, and then in a little while everyone had heard the news."

"All is as Allah wills," said Hassanein, holding up his hands with his palms out. "Thank you for your truthfulness. Would you do me the honor of helping me question some of the others?"

"I'll do whatever I can," I said. I was surprised that he asked for my help. Maybe he thought city Arabs were more accustomed to this sort of thing. Well, at least in my case he was right.

"Then fetch in my brother, Nasheeb."

I went back outside. Hilal and bin Turki were still digging the grave, but were making slow progress. I went to Nasheeb and his wife, who were kneeling on the ground beside the cloak-wrapped body of their daughter. I bent down and touched the old man on his shoulder. He looked up at me with a vacant expression. I was afraid he was in shock. "Come," I said, "the shaykh wishes to speak to you."

Noora's father nodded and got slowly to his feet. He helped his wife get up, too. She was shrieking and beating her chest with her fist. I couldn't even understand what she was crying. I led them into Hassanein's tent.

"The peace of Allah be upon you," said the shaykh. "Nasheeb, my brother, I'm with you in your grief."

"There is no god but God," muttered Nasheeb.

"Who did this?" his wife shouted. "Who took my baby from me?"

I felt like an intruder witnessing their anguish, and it made me uncomfortable that there wasn't anything I could do to help them. I just sat quietly for about ten minutes, while Hassanein murmured soothing things and tried to get the couple into a frame of mind to answer some questions.

"There will come a Day of Resurrection," said Hassanein, "and on that day Noora's face will be bright, looking on her Lord. And the face of her murderer will be full of fear."

"Praise be to Allah, the Lord of the Worlds," prayed Umm Noora. "The Compassionate, the Merciful. Owner of the Day of Judgment."

"Nasheeb—" said Hassanein.

"There is no god but God," said the shaykh's brother, hardly aware of where he was.

"Nasheeb, who do you think killed your daughter?"

Nasheeb blinked once, twice, and then sat up straight. He ran his long fingers through his gray beard. "My daughter?" he whispered. "It was Umm Rashid. That crazy woman said she'd kill her, and now she has. And you must make her pay." He looked straight into his brother's eyes. "You must make her pay, Hassanein, swear it on the grave of our father!"

"No!" cried his wife. "It wasn't her! It was bin Musaid, that jealous, evil-minded murderer! It was him!"

Hassanein shot me a pain-filled glance. I didn't envy him his responsibility. He spent another few minutes calming Noora's parents, and then I led them out of the tent again.

Hassanein next wanted to speak to Suleiman bin Sharif. The young man entered the shaykh's tent and sat down on the sandy floor. I could tell that he was barely keeping himself under control. His eyes darted from one side to the other, and his fists clenched and unclenched in his lap.

"*Salaam alaykum,* O good one," said Hassanein. His eyes narrowed, and I saw that he was observing bin Sharif carefully.

"*Alaykum as-salaam,* O Shaykh," said the boy.

Hassanein paused for a long moment before he said anything more. "What do you know of this?" he asked at last.

Bin Sharif sat up straight, as if he'd been pricked. "What do *I* know of it?" he cried. "How should I come to know anything of this terrible thing?"

"That is what I must find out. How did you feel toward Noora bint Nasheeb?"

Bin Sharif looked from Hassanein to me and back again. "I loved her," he said flatly. "I suppose all the Bani Salim knew that."

"Yes, it was common knowledge. And do you think she returned your affection?"

He didn't hesitate. "Yes," he said. "I know it."

"But your marriage was impossible. Ibrahim bin Musaid would never allow it."

"God blacken the dog's face!" shouted bin Sharif. "God destroy his house!"

Hassanein held up a hand and waited until the young man calmed down again. "Did you kill her? Did you murder Noora bint Nasheeb, rather than see her belong to bin Musaid?"

Bin Sharif tried to answer, but no sound emerged. He took a breath and tried again. "No, O Shaykh, I did not kill her. I swear this upon the life of the Prophet, may the blessings of Allah be on him and peace."

Hassanein stood up and put a hand on bin Sharif's

shoulder. "I believe you," he said. "I wish I could do something to lessen your grief."

Bin Sharif looked up at him with tormented eyes. "When you discover the murderer," he said in a low voice, "you must let me be the instrument of his destruction."

"I'm sorry, my son. That hard duty must be mine alone." It didn't look like Hassanein was looking forward to that responsibility, either.

Bin Sharif and I went back outside. Now it was Umm Rashid's turn. I went to her, but as I approached, she cowered away from me. "Peace be with you, O lady," I said. "The shaykh wishes to speak with you."

She stared at me in horror, as if I were an *afrit*. She backed away across the open ground. "Don't come near me!" she shrieked. "Don't talk to me! You're not of the Bani Salim, and you're nothing to me!"

"Please, O lady. Shaykh Hassanein wishes—"

She fell her to her knees and began praying. "O my Lord! My trials and tribulations are great, and my sorrows and sufferings are deep, and my good deeds are few, and my faults lie heavily upon me. Therefore, my Lord, I implore Thee in the name of Thy greatness—"

I tried to raise her up, but she began screaming at me again and pummeling me with her fists. I turned helplessly to Hassanein, who saw my difficulty and came out of his tent. I stepped back, and Umm Rashid fell to her knees again.

The shaykh stooped and murmured to her. I could see her shake her head vigorously. He spoke to her again, gesturing with one hand. His expression was mild and his voice was pitched too low for me to hear his words. Again the woman shook her head. At last, Hassanein put his hand beneath her elbow and helped her to her feet. She began to weep, and he escorted her to her husband's tent.

He returned to his own tent and began gathering his coffee-brewing equipment. "Whom do you wish to speak to next?" I asked.

"Sit down, Shaykh Marîd," he said. "I'll make coffee."

"The only other real suspect is Ibrahim bin Musaid."

Hassanein acted as if he hadn't heard me. He poured a large handful of coffee beans into a small iron pan with a long handle. This he set on the glowing coals of the cooking fire his wife had built that morning. "If we get a good start in the morning," he said, "we should reach Khaba well by evening prayers tomorrow, *inshallah.*"

I looked out at the camp, but I didn't see Friedlander Bey. The two young men were still digging the dead girl's grave. Some of the Bani Salim were standing nearby, arguing every aspect of the situation, but the rest had already returned to their tents or were seeing to the animals. Bin Musaid stood all by himself to one side, with his back still turned toward us, as if none of this affected him at all.

When the coffee beans had been roasted to Hassanein's satisfaction, he let them cool. He stood up and got a small goatskin bag and brought it back to the cook fire. "Here," he said, "my wife makes fresh *laban* for me every morning, no matter what happens." This was curdled camel's milk, sort of like yogurt.

I took the goatskin bag and murmured *"Bismillah."* Then I drank some, thinking how odd it was that everyone from my mother to Shaykh Hassanein tried to push curdled camel's milk on me. I really didn't like it very much, but I pretended to enjoy it out of respect for his hospitality.

I gave him back the bag, and he swallowed a little *laban.* By then, the coffee beans had cooled, and he put them in a brass mortar and crushed them with a stone pestle. He had two coffeepots; one was bright brass, shiny and polished, and the other was black with soot. He opened the sooty pot, which contained the leftovers of the morning's coffee, and dumped in the freshly ground beans. He added some water from another goatskin bag, and a pinch of powdered cardamom. Then he put the blackened pot in the fire, and carefully stirred the coffee until it boiled.

"Let us give thanks to Allah for coffee!" said Hassanein. He poured it from the black pot into the shiny pot, back into the black pot, and then into the shiny pot again. This let most of the coffee grounds settle and stay behind. Finally, he jammed a piece of hemp into the spout of the bright coffeepot to act as a filter.

"Il hamdu lillah!" he said. Praise be to God. He set out three small coffee cups.

I took one of the cups. "May your table last forever, O Shaykh," I said.

He filled my cup, then looked up. "Ibrahim bin Musaid," he called. "Come! There is coffee!"

Bin Musaid turned and regarded us. His expression said that he didn't understand what the shaykh was doing. He walked slowly toward us. "O Shaykh," he said suspiciously, "don't you have more important duties?"

Hassanein shrugged. "There is time for everything. The Bani Salim have plenty of time. Now is the time for coffee. Be refreshed!" He gave one of the cups to the young man.

We drank a cup of coffee, and then another. Hassanein chatted idly about his favorite camel, whose feet had grown tender and probably wouldn't be able to carry him across the gravel plains to the south.

It's customary to drink three small cups of coffee, and then signal by waggling the empty cup that you've had enough. After the third cup, Hassanein sat back and looked at bin Musaid. The silence became thick and threatening. Finally, bin Musaid laughed out loud. "This is some trick, O Shaykh. You hope to shame me with your coffee and your hospitality. You think I'll clasp your knees and beg forgiveness of Allah. You think I murdered Noora."

He got to his feet and angrily threw the china coffee cup to the ground, where it shattered into scattered fragments. I saw Hassanein wince. "I've mentioned nothing to you about that," he said.

"Look elsewhere for your murderer, O Shaykh," said bin Musaid fiercely. "Look to your guest here, the infidel from the city. Maybe only he and Allah know the truth." He turned and strode off across the camp, disappearing into his own black tent.

I waited for Hassanein to speak. Several minutes passed, and he just sat outside his tent with a sour expression, as if he'd just tasted something rotten. Then, when my patience was about ended, he let out his breath in a heavy sigh. "We've learned nothing," he said sadly. "Nothing at all. We must begin again."

He got slowly to his feet, and I joined him. We crossed to where Hilal and bin Turki were digging in the ground. "A little deeper yet, O excellent ones," said Hassanein. "But when you've dug the grave, don't lay the poor girl in it."

"We should bury her soon," said bin Turki, looking up and shading his eyes with his hand. "The noble Qur'ân—"

Hassanein nodded. "She'll be laid to rest before sunset, as the Wise Mention of God prescribes. But do not lower her into the ground until I tell you."

"Yes, O Shaykh," said Hilal. He glanced at bin Turki, who just shrugged. None of us had any idea what Hassanein had in mind.

"In the Hadhramaut, which is the shaykhdom in the heel of the boot of Arabia," said Hassanein, "a murderer is sometimes made to undergo a trial by fire. Of course, that's all superstition, and the value of such an ordeal is only as great as the belief in its power."

I saw that he was leading me out of the camp, toward the herd of camels. Young boys had scrambled up into the *ghaf* trees that grew in the narrow valleys between the dunes. They'd cut loose the tops of the trees, and the camels were grazing contentedly on the vegetation.

Hassanein continued with his story of justice in the Hadhramaut. "The ceremony always takes place in the morning, after the dawn prayers. The master of ordeals assembles the accused killer, the witnesses, the victim's family, and anyone else who has an interest in the matter. The master uses a knife blade which has been heated in a fire. When he decides that the knife is sufficiently hot, he makes the accused man open his mouth and stick out his tongue. The master wraps his own hand in his *keffiya,* and grasps the accused man's tongue. With his other hand, he takes hold of the fiery knife and strikes the man's tongue, first with one flat side and then the other."

"What's the point of that?" I asked.

Hassanein went to his favorite camel and patted her neck. "If the man is innocent, he'll be able to spit right then and there. The master usually gives him a couple of hours' grace, though. Then the accused man's tongue is examined. If it looks badly burned, then he's judged guilty. He'll be executed immediately, unless the victim's family accepts a reasonable blood-price. If there's no sign of burns, or only minor discoloration, the man is declared innocent and given his freedom."

I wondered what the shaykh was up to. He'd couched the camel and had begun saddling her. "And that's not the custom among the Bani Salim?"

Hassanein laughed. "We're not superstitious like the wild men of the Hadhramaut."

I thought the Bani Salim were plenty superstitious, but I didn't think it was wise to say anything. "Are you going on a journey?" I asked.

"No," said Hassanein. He threw two palm-fiber pads on the camel's back behind the hump, and then laid the wooden frame of his saddle over them. He tied the frame securely in place over the beast's withers, in front of the hump. Next he put a thick palm-fiber pad over the wooden frame, fitting it behind the hump and tying it with a string. This pad rose up high in the rear, and made a kind of uncomfortable backrest. Next, Hassanein draped a blanket over the pad, and then a heavy sheepskin over the blanket. He used stout woolen cords to hold everything firmly in place.

"Good," he said, stepping back and examining his handiwork. He grasped the camel's head rope, got her to stand up, and led her back into the middle of the camp.

"Do you know who the murderer is?" I asked.

"Not yet, but soon," he said. "I once listened to a man in Salala talk about how criminals are caught and punished in other countries." He shook his head ruefully. "I didn't think I'd ever need to try one of those methods."

"You're going to use this camel?"

He nodded. "You know, the Arabs aren't the only shrewd and clever people in the world. Sometimes I think our pride gets in the way of adopting ideas that might truly help us."

He brought the camel right up to the edge of the grave, where Hilal and bin Turki were scrambling up out of the hole. "I need the help of all three of you," said the shaykh, couching the camel again. He indicated the cloak-covered body of Noora.

"You want to put her in the saddle?" asked Hilal.

"Yes," said Hassanein. The three of us looked at each other, and then at the shaykh, but we bent and helped him lift the dead girl into place. He used some more cords to tie her securely, so that she wouldn't fall to the ground when the camel stood up. I didn't know what he was up to, but I thought it was pretty bizarre.

"Get up, Ata Allah," Hassanein murmured. His camel's name was "God's Gift." He gave her a little more urging and she complained, but slowly she rocked to her feet. The shaykh pulled on her head rope and began leading her around the broad circumference of the camp, beyond all the tents.

Hilal, bin Turki, and I watched in astonishment as Hassanein led the camel away. "Is this some custom of the Bani Salim?" I asked. "Like a moving wake, where the relatives stay in one place and the corpse does the traveling?"

"No," said bin Turki, frowning, "I've never seen the shaykh behave like this. Maybe he's been driven mad by the murder of his niece."

"Are there a lot of murders among the Bedu?" I asked.

The two young men looked at each other and shrugged. "As common as anywhere else, I guess," said bin Turki. "One tribe raids another, and men die. Blood must be avenged, and feuds begin. Sometimes the feuds last for years, decades, even generations."

"But there's rarely murder within a tribe, like this," said Hilal. "This is unnatural."

Hassanein called back over his shoulder. "Come, Shaykh Marîd, walk with me!"

"I don't understand what he's doing," said Hilal.

"I think he expects to figure out who the murderer is this way," I said. "I can't imagine how." I hurried after Ata Allah and her macabre burden.

By now, many of the Bani Salim were standing outside their tents, pointing at Hassanein and the camel. "My baby! My child!" shrieked Noora's mother. The woman flung herself away from her husband's grasp and ran stumbling in the path of the camel. She shouted prayers and accusations until she collapsed in tears to the ground. Nasheeb went to her and tried to help her to her feet, but she would not be comforted. Noora's father stared down dumbly at his wife, then up at the bundled figure of his daughter. He didn't seem to know exactly what was going on.

Suleiman bin Sharif cut across the camp and intercepted us. "What are you doing? This is disgraceful!" he said.

"Please, O excellent one," said Hassanein, "you must trust me."

"Tell me what you're doing," bin Sharif demanded.

"I'm making sure everyone knows what happened to Noora, the light of our days."

"But there isn't anyone in the tribe who hasn't heard the news," said bin Sharif.

"Hearing the news is one thing. Seeing the truth is another."

Bin Sharif threw his hands up in disgust, and let the shaykh lead the camel on around the circle.

We came abreast of Umm Rashid's tent, and the old woman just shook her head. Her husband, who was indeed far too old to be dallying with any woman, poked his head out of the tent and whined to be fed. Umm Rashid mouthed a prayer in Noora's direction, then went inside.

When we'd gotten three-quarters of the way around, I saw that Ibrahim bin Musaid was watching us with an expression of absolute hatred. He stood like a statue carved from sandstone, turning only his head a little as we drew nearer. He said nothing as we passed him and came again to the grave Hilal and bin Turki had carved into the desert floor.

"Is it time to bury her now, O Shaykh?" I asked.

"Watch and learn," said Hassanein.

Instead of stopping, he led Ata Allah past the grave and started a second perambulation of the camp. A loud sigh went up from the Bani Salim who were watching us, who were just as bewildered as I was.

Noora's mother stood beside our path and shouted curses at us. "Son of a dog!" she cried, hurling handfuls of sand at Hassanein. "May your house be destroyed! Why won't you let my daughter have peace?"

I felt sorry for her, but Hassanein just went on, his face empty of expression. I didn't know what his reasoning was, but it seemed to me that he was being unnecessarily cruel. Nasheeb still stood silently beside his wife. He seemed to be more aware now of what was happening around him.

Bin Sharif had had a while to think about what Hassanein was doing. He'd lost some of the edge of his anger. "You're a wise man, O Shaykh," he said. "You've proved that over the years, leading the Bani Salim with a sure and equitable hand. I defer to your knowledge and experience, but I still think what you are doing is an affront to the dead."

Hassanein stopped and went to bin Sharif. He put a hand on the young man's shoulder. "Perhaps someday you'll be shaykh of this tribe," he said. "Then you'll understand the agony of leadership. You're right, though. What I'm doing is an unkindness to my sweet niece, but it must be done. *Ham kitab.*" That meant "It is written." It didn't really explain anything, but it cut off bin Sharif's argument.

Bin Sharif looked into the shaykh's eyes, and finally his gaze turned down to the ground. As we took up our progress again, I saw that the young man had begun walking back to his tent with a thoughtful expression on his face. I hadn't had much opportunity to talk with him, but I'd gotten the impression that he was an intelligent, serious young man. If Hassanein were correct and bin Sharif would someday succeed him, I guessed that the Bani Salim would remain in very capable hands.

I just stared ahead, a little unhappy about being part of this strange procession. It was another typical day in the Empty Quarter, and the hot wind blew sand into my face until I was grumbling under my breath. I'd had just about enough of all this; and despite what Friedlander Bey thought, I didn't find the Bedu way of life romantic in the least. It was hard and dirty and entirely without pleasure, as far as I was concerned, and they were welcome to it. I prayed that Allah would let me get back to the city soon, because it had become very obvious to me that I would never make a very good nomad.

Along the last part of the loop, bin Musaid was still watching us with hooded eyes. He stood in the same place as before, his arms folded across his chest. He hadn't said a word and he hadn't moved an inch. I could almost see him trembling with the effort to keep himself under control. He looked as if he were ready to explode. I didn't want to be near him when he did.

"Enough, O Shaykh?" said bin Turki as we drew abreast of the grave. Already it was beginning to fill in with fine sand blown across the desert floor.

Hassanein shook his head. "Another circle," he said. My heart sank.

"Will you explain what you're doing, O Shaykh?" I said.

Hassanein looked toward me, but his gaze was over my head, into the distance. "There were people on the back of the world," he said in a tired voice. "People as poor as we, who also led lives of wandering and hardship. When one of their tribe was killed, the elders carried the corpse around their camp five or six times. The first time, everyone in the tribe stopped whatever they were doing to watch, and they joined together in mourning the unfortunate victim. The second time, half the tribe watched. The third time, only a few people were still interested. By the fifth or sixth time, there was only one person who was still paying close attention to the progress of the body, and that was the killer himself."

I looked around the camp area, and I saw that almost everyone had gone back to his chores. Even though a popular young woman had died that morning, there was still hard work that had to be done, or there would be no food or water for the Bani Salim or for their animals.

We led Ata Allah slowly around the circle, with only bin Musaid and a few others observing our progress. Noora's father looked around for his wife, but she'd gone into their tent much earlier. Nasheeb leaned against a taut rope and stared at us with vacant eyes.

As we drew near bin Musaid, he blocked our way. "May Allah blight your lives for this," he growled, his face dark with fury. Then he went to his tent.

When we came up to the two young men this time, Hassanein gave them instructions. "You must look for the murder weapon," he told them. "A knife. Hilal, you look for it where Shaykh Marîd discovered Noora's body. Bin Turki, you must search around the tent of her parents." We went by the grave and started our final circuit. As Hassanein had predicted, there was only one person watching us now: Nasheeb, his brother, Noora's father.

Before we reached him, Hilal ran up to us. "I found it!" he cried. "I found the knife!"

Hassanein took it and examined it briefly. He showed it to me. "See?" he said. "This is Nasheeb's mark."

"Her own father?" I was surprised. I would've bet that the killer was bin Musaid.

Hassanein nodded. "I suspect he'd begun to worry that the loose talk and gossip might have some basis in truth. If Noora had been ruined, he'd never get her bride-price. He probably killed her, thinking that someone else would be blamed—my nephew Ibrahim, or old Umm Rashid—and at least he'd collect the blood money."

I looked at Nasheeb, who was still standing blank-faced beside his tent. I was horrified that the man could kill his own daughter for such a foolish reason.

The Bedu system of justice is simple and direct. Shaykh Hassanein had all he needed to be convinced of the murderer's identity, yet he gave Nasheeb a chance to deny the evidence. When we stopped beside him, the rest of the Bani Salim realized that we'd found the killer, and they came out of their tents and stood nearby, to witness what would happen next.

"Nasheeb, my father's son," said Hassanein, "you've murdered your own daughter, the flesh of your blood and the spirit of your spirit. 'Slay not your children, fearing a fall into poverty,' it says in the noble Qur'ân, 'we shall provide for them and for you. Lo! the slaying of them is great sin.'"

Nasheeb listened to him with his head bowed. He seemed to be only vaguely aware of what was happening. His wife had collapsed on the ground, weeping and calling on Allah, and some of the other women in the tribe were tending to her. Bin Musaid had turned away, and his shoulders shook. Bin Sharif just stared at Nasheeb in bewilderment.

"Do you deny this accusation?" asked Hassanein. "If you wish, you may swear your innocence on the great shrine of Shaykh Ismail bin Nasr. Remember that it was only a year and a year ago that Ali bin Sahib swore falsely on that holy shrine, and within a week he was dead of a snakebite." This was the same Shaykh Hassanein who'd assured me earlier that the Bani Salim weren't superstitious. I wondered how much he believed in the swearing-on-shrines stuff, and how much was purely for Nasheeb's benefit.

The murderer, Noora's own father, spoke in a voice so low that only Hassanein and I could hear. "I will swear no oath," he said. That was his admission of guilt.

Hassanein nodded. "Then let us prepare Noora for her rest unto the Day of Judgment," he said. "Tomorrow at sunrise, Nasheeb, you'll be allowed to pray for your soul. And then I will do what I must do, *inshallah.*"

Nasheeb only closed his eyes. I've never seen such pitiful anguish on a man's face before. I thought he might faint on the spot.

We brought Noora back to the grave site. Two of the women fetched a white sheet to use as a shroud, and they wrapped the girl in it and wept and prayed over her. Hassanein and Abu Ibrahim, Noora's uncles, lowered her into the grave, and the shaykh prayed for her. Then there was nothing to do but cover her over and mark the place with a few stones.

Hassanein and I watched Hilal and bin Turki finish that work, and neither of us spoke. I don't know what the shaykh was thinking, but I was asking myself why it is that so many people seem to think that murder can be a solution to their problems. In the crowded city or here in the empty desert, can life really become so unbearable that someone else's death will make it better? Or is it that deep down inside, we never truly believe that anyone else's life is worth quite as much as our own?

As the two young men completed their sad task, Friedlander Bey joined us. "May the blessings of Allah be on her and peace," he said. "Shaykh Hassanein, your brother has fled."

Hassanein shrugged, as if he knew it would happen. "He seeks his own death in the desert, rather than from my sword." He stretched and sighed. "Yet we must track him and fetch him back, if God wills. This tragedy is not yet over."

8

Well, as much as I hated the idea, my time among the Bani Salim had changed my life. I was almost sure of it. As I drowsed aboard Fatma, I daydreamed about what things might be like when I got back to the city. I especially liked the fantasy of bursting in on Reda Abu Adil and giving him the big kiss, the one that Sicilian crime lords knew as the mark of death. Then I reminded myself that Abu Adil was off-limits, and I turned my attention elsewhere.

Whose neck would I most like to wring? Hajjar's? That went without saying, but dusting Hajjar wouldn't give me the true satisfaction I was looking for. I'm sure Friedlander Bey would expect me to aim higher.

A fly landed on my face, and I gave it an annoyed swipe. I opened my eyes to see if anything had changed, but it hadn't. We were still slowly rocking and rolling across the sand mountains called the Uruq ash-Shaiba.

These were indeed mountains, not just hills. I'd had no idea that dunes could rise so high. The sand peaks of the Uruq ash-Shaiba towered six hundred feet, and they stretched on and on toward the eastern horizon like waves of frozen sunlight.

It was sometimes very difficult for us to get the camels up the backs of those dunes. We often had to dismount and lead the animals by their head ropes. The camels complained constantly, and sometimes we even had to lighten their loads and carry the stuff ourselves. The sand on the slopes was soft, compared with the firm, packed sand on the desert floor, and even the surefooted camels had trouble struggling up to the crest of the high dunes. Then, on the leeward side, which of course was much steeper, the beasts were in danger of tumbling and seriously injuring themselves. If that happened, it might cost us our lives.

There were six of us in the chase party. I rode beside Hassanein, who was our unspoken leader. His brother, Abu Ibrahim, rode with bin Musaid, and Suleiman bin Sharif rode with Hilal. When we stopped next to rest, the shaykh squatted and drew a rough map in the sand.

"Here is the track from Bir Balagh to Khaba well to Mughshin," he said, drawing a crooked line from north to south. He drew another line parallel to it, about a foot to the right. "Here is Oman. Perhaps Nasheeb thinks he can beg the safety of the king there, but if so, he's badly mistaken. The king of Oman is weak, under the thumb of the amir of Muscat, who is a fierce defender of Islamic justice. Nasheeb would live no longer there than if he returned to the Bani Salim."

I indicated the space between the desert track and the Omani border. "What is this?" I asked.

"We've just entered this area," said Hassanein. He patted the honey-colored sand. "This is the Uruq ash-

Shaiba, these high dune peaks. Beyond it, though, is something worse." Now he ran his thumbnail in the sand along the border with Oman. "The Umm as-Samim."

That meant "Mother of poison." "What kind of a place is it?" I asked.

Hassanein looked up at me and blinked. "Umm as-Samim," he said, as if just repeating the name explained everything. "Nasheeb is my brother, and I think I know his plans. I believe he's heading there, because he'd rather choose his own way to die."

I nodded. "So you're not really anxious to catch up to him?"

"If he intends to die in the wilderness, I'll allow it. But just the same, we should be prepared to head him off if he tries to escape, instead." He turned to his brother. "Musaid, take your son and ride to the northern limits of the Umm as-Samim. Bin Sharif, you and Hilal ride to the south. This noble city man and I will follow Nasheeb to the edge of the quicksands."

So we split up, making plans to meet again with the rest of the Bani Salim at Mughshin. We didn't have a lot of extra time, because there were no wells in the Uruq ash-Shaiba. We had only the water in our goatskin bags to last us until we caught up with Nasheeb.

As the day wore on, I was left alone again with my thoughts. Hassanein was not a talkative man, and there was very little that needed discussion. I'd learned quite a lot from him. It seemed to me that in the city, I sometimes paralyzed myself, worrying over right and wrong and all the gray shades in-between. That was a kind of weakness.

Here in the Sands, decisions were clearer. It could be fatal to delay too long, debating all the sides of a course of action. I promised myself that when I got back to the city, I'd try to maintain the Bedu way of thinking. I'd reward good and punish evil. Life was too short for extenuating circumstances.

Just then, Fatma stumbled and recovered her footing. The interruption in the rhythmically swaying ride jolted me from my introspection and reminded me that I had more immediate matters to think about. Still, I couldn't help feeling that it was the will of Allah that I should have this lesson. It was as if Noora's murder had been arranged to teach me something important.

Why Noora had to die for it, I couldn't begin to understand. If I'd asked the deeply religious Friedlander Bey about it, he'd only have shrugged and said, "It's what pleases God." That was an unsatisfactory answer, but it was the only one I'd get from anyone. The discussion of such matters always devolved into late-adolescent speculation about why Allah permitted evil in the world.

Praise Allah the Unknowable!

We rode until sundown, then Shaykh Hassanein and I stopped and made camp in a small flat area between two immense dunes. I'd always heard it was wiser to travel by night and sleep during the hot afternoon, but the Bani Salim felt it was safer to reverse the conventional wisdom. After all, Fatma had enough trouble with her balance in the daytime, where she could see where she was going. In the dark, we'd be courting disaster.

I unloaded Fatma and staked her down with a long chain that let her find her own spare dinner. We needed to travel light, so our own meal wasn't much better. We each chewed two or three strips of dried goat meat while Hassanein prepared hot mint tea over a small fire.

"How much further?" I asked, staring into the flickering fire.

He shook his head. "That's hard to say, without knowing Nasheeb's plans. If, indeed, he's attempting a crossing of the Umm as-Samim, then our task will be completed by noon tomorrow. If he tries to elude us—which he cannot do, since his life depends on finding water soon—we'll have to close in on him from three sides, and there may be a violent confrontation. I trust that my brother will do the honorable thing, after all."

There was something I didn't understand. "O Shaykh," I said, "you called the Umm as-Samim 'quicksands.' I thought they existed only in holoshows, and then usually along some unlikely jungle trail."

Hassanein gave one short, barking laugh. "I've never seen a holoshow," he said.

"Well, the quicksand usually looks like thick mud. Seems to me that if you can tread water, you ought to be able to stay above the surface in an even denser medium. You aren't sucked down immediately."

"Sucked down?" asked the shaykh. He frowned. "Many men have died in the Umm as-Samim, but none of them were sucked down. 'Fall through' is a better choice of words. The quicksands consist of a swampy lake of undrinkable water, over which is a crust of alkaline crystals washed by streams from the hills along the Omani border. In some places, the crust can bear the weight of a man. The crust is hidden from observation, however, by the desert sands that have drifted over it. From a distance, the Umm as-Samim looks like a quiet, safe floor at the edge of the desert."

"But if Nasheeb tries to travel across it—"

Hassanein shook his head. "May Allah have mercy on his soul," he said.

That reminded us that we'd delayed our sunset prayers, although only for a few minutes. We each cleared a small area of desert bottom, and performed the ritual ablutions with clean sand. We prayed, and I added a prayer asking for a blessing on Noora's soul, and guidance for all the rest of us. Then it was time to sleep. I was exhausted.

I had strange dreams all through the restless night. I can still recall one—something to do with a strong father figure giving me stern lectures about going to the mosque on Friday. In fact, the father figure wouldn't permit me to choose any old mosque; it had to be the one he attended, and he wouldn't tell me which one that was. It wasn't until I awoke that I realized he wasn't even my father, he was Jirji Shaknahyi, who had been my partner during the brief time I worked for the city's police department.

I was deeply troubled by that dream for two reasons: now and then, I still blamed myself for Shaknahyi's death, and I wondered how he came to represent strict and harsh behavior in my dreams. He hadn't been like that at all. Why was he troubling my rest now, instead of, say, a dream Friedlander Bey?

We had another meal of dried goat meat and tea before we loaded the camels and went off in pursuit of Nasheeb. Normally, breakfast was only rice porridge and dates. "Eat what you will," said Hassanein. "This will be a day filled with happenings that will not be pleasant. Eat and drink your fill, because we will not stop again until my brother is dead."

Yipe, I thought. How can he speak so calmly about such a thing? I'd thought that *I* was hard, yet this desert chieftain was showing me what real strength and toughness were.

I threw the elaborate saddle over Fatma's back, and she made her obligatory, halfhearted objections. I hung half of our supplies from the saddle, and then I got the camel to her feet. This was no simple task, believe me. More than once I'd wished that the Bani Salim had turned out to be one of those desert clans who speed across the landscape on beautiful horses. Instead, I got this balky, foul-smelling beast instead. Oh well, it was as Allah pleased.

We urged our camels on toward the east, toward the Umm as-Samim. Hassanein was right: this was going to be an unpleasant day. Yet at the end of it, there'd be a resolution that would prove cathartic for the shaykh, *inshallah*.

Neither of us spoke. We were each wrapped in dark thoughts as we sat on our camels, rocking slowly toward our appointment with Nasheeb. A few hours passed this way, until I heard an exclamation from the shaykh. *"Allahu Akbar!"* he said fiercely. "There he is!"

I looked up at once. I guess I'd been dozing, because I hadn't before noticed the broad, sparkling plain ahead of us. Standing at the western edge was a man, unloading his camel as if he planned to camp there.

"Well," I said, "at least he isn't going to take the poor animal with him."

Hassanein turned to glare at me. All his usual good humor had been burned away. His expression was hard and perhaps a little vindictive.

We urged our camels to their highest speed, and rode down out of the high dunes like a Bedu raiding party. When we were only fifty yards from Nasheeb, he turned to look at us. His face held no fear or anger, but only a kind of immense sadness. He raised an arm and gestured toward us. I didn't know what it meant. Then he turned and ran toward the bright crust of Umm as-Samim.

"Nasheeb!" cried Hassanein in despair. "Wait! Return with us to the Bani Salim, where at least you may be forgiven before I must execute you! Isn't it better to die in the bosom of your tribe, than out here in this desolate place, all alone?"

Nasheeb didn't acknowledge his brother's words.

We'd almost caught up with him as he took his first hesitant step onto the sand-covered crust.

"Nasheeb!" shouted Hassanein. This time the murderer did turn around. He touched his chest above the heartbeat, brought his fingers to his lips and kissed them, then touched his forehead.

Finally, after what seemed like the longest moment in the history of the world, he turned again and took a few more steps across the crusted alkaline surface.

"Maybe he'll—" My words were silenced by Nasheeb's cry of utter hopelessness, as his next step broke through the crust, and he fell helplessly into the marshy lake below. His head reappeared briefly, but he was thrashing about helplessly. Knowing how to swim is not high in the list of the Bani Salim's necessary survival skills.

"In the name of Allah, the Beneficent, the Merciful," wailed Hassanein. "May the blessings of Allah be on him and peace."

"I testify that there is no god but God," I said, almost as shaken as my companion. I closed my eyes, even though there was nothing to see now but the small hole Nasheeb had broken in the salt crust. There was never any other sign of him. He'd died very quickly.

There was nothing else to do here, and the harshness of the environment dictated that we had to find the rest of the tribe at Mughshin as quickly as possible. Hassanein understood that truth better than I did, and so without speaking another word he dismounted and took the head rope of Nasheeb's camel, leading it across the whistling sand to his own mount. If there was grieving to be done, the shaykh would do it quietly, as we lurched our way to the southwest.

I don't recall sharing a single word with Hassanein during the remainder of that day. He pushed our little party to the utmost, and we rode for an hour or two after night fell, stopping only to pray at sunset. The shaykh explained the situation tersely. "The southern part of the Sands is hungry now," he said. "There is little water and little grazing for the camels. This part of the desert is going through a drought."

Well, hell, I was about to ask him how a place as dry as the Empty Quarter could have a drought. I mean, how could you tell? You could probably hold the entire annual rainfall for the region in a ten-ounce tumbler. I could see that Hassanein was not yet in a mood for talking, so I kept my peace.

About two hours after we'd made camp, eaten our meager dinner, and spread our blankets near the fire, we were joined by Hilal and bin Sharif. I was cheered to see them, although the recent events hung over this small reunion like the fear of God.

The two newcomers prepared their places near the fire. "We could see you and Nasheeb from a long way," said Hilal. "As soon as we saw you leave the edge of Umm as-Samim, we realized that Nasheeb must have killed himself. Then we angled across the Sands to intercept you. We would've met you sooner, but you must have kept up an exhausting pace."

"I don't wish to spend any more time here than necessary," said Hassanein in a grim voice. "Our food and water—"

"Is sufficient, I think," said bin Sharif. "You just want to leave what happened behind."

The shaykh stared at him for a long moment. "Are you judging me, Suleiman bin Sharif?" he asked in the fiercest of voices.

"*Yaa salaam*, I wouldn't dare," said the young man.

"Then spread your blanket and get some sleep. We have a long way to travel in the morning."

"As you say, O Shaykh," said Hilal. In a few minutes,

we were all dreaming beneath the cold, black sky of the Rub al-Khali.

The next morning, we broke camp and started off across the desert, with no track to guide us but Hassanein's memory. We traveled for days like that, no one but Hassanein speaking, and he wouldn't utter a word unless it was necessary: "Time to pray!" or "Stop here!" or "Enough for today!" Otherwise, I had plenty of time for introspection, and believe me, I used it all. I'd come to the conclusion that not only had my time among the Bani Salim changed me, but when I got back—not *if* I got back —to the city, some drastic changes in my behavior were in order. I'd always been fiercely independent, yet somehow I'd come to desire the approval of this rough clan and its taciturn leader.

Finally, we'd traveled so far, over so many days, that thoughts of the city faded from my mind. I thought only of getting safely to another town, another Bedu village on the southern edge of the Sands. And therefore I was immensely happy when Hassanein stopped us and pointed to the horizon, slightly south of southwest. "The mountains," he announced.

I looked. I didn't see any mountains.

"These are the last miles of the Sands. We are in Ghanim now."

Sure, O Shaykh, if you think so. Nothing looked any different at all to me. But we turned a little to the south, and soon we found the centuries-old path worn from Khaba well to Mughshin on the far side of the Qarra Mountains. Mughshin was our goal, where we'd meet the rest of the tribe. The Bani Salim talked about Mughshin as if it were a treasure house of wonders, as if it were Singapore or Edo or New York. I'd already told myself that I'd withhold judgment until I had a chance to wander its alleys myself.

In another two or three days' travel the terrain began to rise, and I no longer doubted that the shaykh knew where he was going. At the base of the mountains that separated us from the seacoast was Mughshin. I'd imagined the place completely, from the stories of my companions, so I wasn't prepared for the shock of the truth. Mughshin consisted of fifty or sixty tents—commercial, European-made tents—strewn across a broad plain so that each occupant had sufficient privacy. A strong, gritty wind blew across the village, and no one was in sight.

Bin Sharif and Hilal were overjoyed to see the village come into view, and they stood on the backs of their camels, waved their rifles, and shouted the conventional pious phrases. "Go," said Hassanein, "and see if our tribe is there. Our usual camping ground looks empty."

"We may well have beaten them here," said bin Sharif. "We can travel faster than the slow procession of the Bani Salim."

The shaykh nodded. "And then we'll abide here until they arrive."

Hilal knelt in his saddle and shouted something I didn't understand. Then he prodded his camel into high gear, followed closely by bin Sharif.

Hassanein pointed toward the village. "Is your city greater than even this?" he asked.

That startled me. I stared at the handful of green and gray tents. "In some ways, yes," I said. "In some ways, definitely no."

The shaykh grunted. The time for talking had ended. He kicked up his camel, and I followed at a moderate pace. I began to feel a great sense of victory, in that I'd survived in this extremely low-tech environment. My skull-amping had been of very little use since my rescue by the Bani Salim; I'd even tried to stop using the pain, hunger, and thirst blockers, because I wanted to prove to myself that I could bear everything that the unmodified Bedu could.

Of course, I wasn't nearly as disciplined as they were. Whenever the pain, hunger, or thirst grew too great, I retreated thankfully behind the numb shield of my intracranial software. There was no point in overdoing anything, especially if only pride was at stake. Pride seemed too expensive in the Sands.

It was true that the Bani Salim had not yet arrived. Shaykh Hassanein led us to the tribe's usual stopping place, and we pitched a temporary, shelterless camp. How I stared longingly at the permanent tents! I'd have given a lot of money to rent one for myself, because the wind was chill and it carried a full weight of sand in its teeth. An earlier version of Marîd Audran would've said, "To hell with this!" and gone to rest within one of the tents. Now it was only my pride, my expensive pride, that kept me from abandoning Hassanein and the two young men. I was more concerned with what they'd think of me than with my own comfort. That was something new.

The next day I was very bored. We had nothing to do until the Bani Salim caught up with us. I explored the village, an accomplishment that took little time. I did discover a small *souk* where the more ambitious of the Mughshin merchants had spread blankets on the ground covered with various items. There was fresh meat and semifresh meat, vegetables, dates and other fruits, and the staples of the Bedu diet: rice and coffee and dried meat and cabbage, carrots, and other vegetables.

I was rather surprised to see one old man who had just seven little squares of plastic on his blanket: daddies brought across the mountains from Salala, imported from who-knows-where. I examined them with great curiosity, wondering what subjects this canny old fellow thought might sell to the few blazebrains who wandered the Rub al-Khali.

There were two Holy Imam daddies, probably the same as that owned by Hassanein; two medical daddies; a daddy programmed with various Arabic dialects spoken in the southern part of Arabia; an outlaw sex manual; and a compendium of *shari'a*, or religious law. I thought the latter might make a good gift for the shaykh. I asked the old man how much it cost.

"Two hundred fifty riyals," he said, his voice faint and quavery.

"I have no riyals," I admitted, "only kiam." I had almost four hundred kiam that I'd kept hidden from Sergeant al-Bishah in Najran.

The old man gave me a long, shrewd look. "Kiam, eh? All right, one hundred kiam."

It was my turn to stare. "That's ten times what it's worth!" I said.

He just shrugged. "Someday, someone will think it's worth a hundred, and I'll sell it for a hundred. No, no. Because you're a guest in our village, I'll give it to you for ninety."

"I'll give you fifteen for it," I said.

"Go then, see to your companions. I don't need your money. The Almighty Lord will provide for me in my state of want, *inshallah*. Eighty kiam."

I spread my hands. "I cannot afford such a steep price. I'll give you twenty-five, but that's as high as I can go. Just because I'm a stranger, that doesn't mean I'm rich, you know."

"Seventy-five," he said, without blinking an eye. His bargaining routine was more of a social custom than a true attempt to extort money from me.

This went on for a few more minutes, until I finally bought the legal-advice daddy for forty kiam. The old man bowed to me as if I were some grand shaykh. Of course, from his point of view, I was.

I took the daddy and headed back toward our campsite. Before I'd walked twenty yards, one of the other villagers intercepted me. "*Salaam,*" he said.

"*Alaykum as-salaam,*" I replied.

"Would you be interested, O Excellent One, in trying out some particularly fine and rare personality modules?"

"Well," I said, curious, "maybe."

"We've got some so . . . unusual that you won't find their like anywhere, not in Najran or across the mountains in Salala."

I gave him a patient smile. I didn't come from some near-barbarous town like Najran or Salala. I thought I'd tested out some of the strangest and most perverted moddies in the world. Still, I was interested in seeing what this tall, thin camel jockey had by way of merchandise. "Yes," I said, "show them to me."

The man was very nervous, as if he were afraid someone might overhear us. "I could have my hand cut off for showing you the kind of moddies we sell. However, if you go in without any money, it will protect us both."

I didn't quite understand. "What do I do with my money?"

"The merchant who sold you the daddy has some metal cash boxes, O Shaykh. Give him your money, and he'll put it away safely, give you a receipt, and a key to the cash box. Then you go inside my tent, experiment with our moddies as long as you like. When you've decided to buy or not to buy, we come back and get your money. This way, if someone in authority interrupts the demonstration, we can prove you had no intention of buying, and I had no intention of selling, because you won't have any money on your exalted person."

"How often are your 'demonstrations' interrupted?" I asked.

The Bedu hustler looked at me and blinked a couple of times. "Now and then," he said, "now and then, O Shaykh. It's a hazard of this industry."

"Yes, I know. I know very well."

"Then, O Excellent One, come with me and deliver your money to Ali Muhammad, the old merchant."

I was a little suspicious of the younger man, but the old merchant had struck me as honest in an old-fashioned way.

We walked to his blanket. The younger man said, "Ali Muhammad, this lord desired to inspect our stock of number-one moddies. He's prepared to deposit his money with you."

Ali Muhammad squinted at me. "He's not the police or some other kind of troublemaker?"

"Just in speaking to this noble shaykh," the nervous man said, "I've come to trust him completely. I promise you on the shrines of all the imams that he will make no trouble."

"Eh, well, we'll see," said Ali Muhammad grumpily. "How much cash does he have."

"I know not, O Wise One," said my new friend.

I hesitated a moment, then brought out most of my roll. I didn't want to give him all of it, but both men seemed to know I'd do that.

"You must keep none in your pocket," said Ali Muhammad. "Ten riyals would be enough to earn severe chastisement for all three of us."

I nodded. "Here, then," I said, giving him the remainder of the money. In for a penny, in for a pound, I told myself. Except I was in for a few hundred kiam.

The old merchant disappeared inside a nearby tent.

He was gone only two or three minutes. When he returned, he handed me a key and a written receipt. We thanked each other in the conventional manner, and then my fidgety guide led me toward another tent.

Before we'd covered half the distance, he said, "Oh, did you pay the five-kiam deposit on the key, O Shaykh?"

"I don't know," I said. "What deposit? You didn't mention the deposit before."

"I'm truly sorry, my lord, but we can't let you see the moddies unless you've paid the deposit. Just five kiam."

A warning chill settled into my belly. I let the skinny weasel read my receipt. "Here," I said.

"There's nothing about the deposit here, O Shaykh," he said. "But it's just five kiam more, and then you can play all day with the moddies of your choice."

I'd been too easily seduced by the idea of X-classification moddies. "Right," I said angrily, "you witnessed me giving every damn kiam I had to your old man. I don't have another five kiam."

"Well, that worries me, O Wise One. I can't show you the moddies without the deposit."

I knew right then I'd been had, that there probably were no moddies. "Right," I said fiercely. "Let's go back and get my money."

"Yes, O Shaykh, if that's what you wish."

I turned and headed back to Ali Muhammad's blanket. He was gone. There was no sign of him. Guarding the entrance to the tent that housed the cash boxes was a gigantic man with a dark, glowering face. I went to him and showed my receipt, and asked to be let in to retrieve my money.

"I cannot let you in unless you pay the five-kiam deposit," he said. He growled more than a human being should, I thought.

I tried threatening, pleading, and promises of a large stipend when Friedlander Bey arrived with the rest of the Bani Salim. Nothing worked. Finally, acknowledging that I'd been out-scammed, I turned to my nervous guide. He was gone, too.

So I was left holding a worthless receipt, a key—which probably holds the world record for Most Expensive Worthless Key—and the knowledge that I'd just been given a lesson in pride. It was a very costly lesson, but a lesson nonetheless. I knew that Ali Muhammad and his young confederate were probably halfway across the Qarra Mountains already, and as soon as I turned my back on Mr. Bedu Muscles, he'd vanish, too. I began to laugh. This was an anecdote I'd never tell Friedlander Bey. I could claim that someone robbed me one night while I slept. It was virtually the truth.

I just walked away, mocking myself and my lost superiority. Dr. Sadiq Abd ar-Razzaq, who'd condemned us to this horrible place, had actually done me a favor. More than one, as I was stripped of many illusions about myself. I'd come out of the desert a vastly different man from the one I was when I dropped in.

In four or five days the Bani Salim arrived, and there were many loud celebrations and reunions. I confirmed that Friedlander Bey was none the worse for the trek, and he seemed happier and healthier than ever. At one of the celebrations, Shaykh Hassanein embraced me as he would a family member, and formally adopted Friedlander Bey and myself into his clan. We were now full-fledged Bani Salim. I wondered if that would ever come in handy. I gave Hassanein the *shari'a* daddy, and he was greatly pleased.

The next day, we prepared for our departure. Bin Turki was coming with us, and would guide us across the mountains to the coastal town of Salala. From there we'd book passage aboard the first ship bound for Qishn, about two hundred miles to the west, the nearest city with a suborbital-class airfield.

We were going home.

9

Aboard the suborbital craft *Imam Muhammad al-Baqir*, the amenities were hardly superior to those on the ship that had flown us to Najran, into exile. We weren't prisoners now, but our fare didn't include a meal or even free drinks. "That's what we get for being stranded at the ends of the Earth," I said. "Next time, we should work to be stranded in a more comfortable place."

Friedlander Bey only nodded; he saw no joke in my statement, as if he foresaw many such kidnappings and strandings to come. His lack of humor was something of a trademark with him. It had raised him from a penniless immigrant to one of the two most influential men in the city. It had also left him with an exaggerated sense of caution. He trusted no one, even after testing people again and again over a period of years. I still wasn't entirely sure that he trusted me.

Bin Turki said hardly a word. He sat with his face pressed against the port, occasionally making excited comments or stifled exclamations. It was good to have him with us, because he reminded me of what it was like before I'd become so jaded with modern life. All of this was new to bin Turki, who'd stuck out like a hayseed hick in the poor crossroads town of Salala. I shuddered to think what might happen to him when he got home. I didn't know whether to corrupt him as quickly as possible—so he'd have defenses against the wolves of the Budayeen—or protect his lovely innocence.

"Flight time from Qishn to Damascus will be forty minutes," the captain of the suborbital announced. "Everyone on board should make his connections with plenty of time to spare."

That was good news. Although we wouldn't have the leisure time to explore a bit of Damascus, the world's oldest continually inhabited city, I was glad that travel time back to our city would be at a minimum. We'd have a layover in Damascus of about thirty-five minutes. Then we'd catch another suborbital direct to the city. We'd be home. We'd be powerless to move around in complete freedom, but at least it would be home.

Friedlander Bey stared out of his port for a long while after takeoff, thinking about matters I could only guess at. Finally, he said, "We must decide where we're going when the ship from Damascus to the city touches down."

"Why don't we just go to the house?" I asked.

He regarded me with a blank expression for a few seconds. "Because we're still criminals in the eyes of the law. We're fugitives from what passes for 'justice' there."

I'd forgotten all about that. "They don't know the meaning of the word."

Papa waved impatiently. "In the city, as soon as we

showed our faces, your Lieutenant Hajjar would arrest us and put us on trial for that unexplained murder."

"Does everyone in the city speak that mutilated Arabic gibberish?" asked bin Turki. "I can't even make out what you're saying!"

"I'm afraid so," I told him. "But you'll get the hang of the local dialect quickly." I turned back to Papa. His sobering insight had made me realize that our troubles were far from over. "What do you suggest, O my uncle?" I asked.

"We must think of someone trustworthy, who'd be willing to house us for a week or so."

I couldn't follow his idea. "A week? What will happen in a week?"

Friedlander Bey turned the full power of his terrifying cold smile on me. "By then," he said, "we'll have arranged for an interview with Shaykh Mahali. We'll make him see that we've been cheated of our final legal recourse, that we're entitled to an appeal, and that we strongly urge the amir to protect our rights because in doing so he'll uncover official corruption under his very nose."

I shuddered, and then I thanked Allah that I wasn't going to be the target of the investigation—at least, not long enough to get nervous about. I wondered how well Lieutenant Hajjar slept, and Dr. Abd ar-Razzaq. I wondered if they foresaw events closing in on them. I got a delicious thrill while I imagined their imminent doom.

I must've drifted off to sleep because I was awakened some time later by one of the ship's stewards, who wanted bin Turki and me to make sure that our seat belts were securely fastened prior to landing. Bin Turki studied his and figured out how to work the catch. I cooperated because it seemed to please the steward so much. Now he wouldn't have to worry about my various separated limbs flying toward the cockpit, in case the pilot planted the aircraft up to its shoulders in the sand dunes beyond the city's gates.

"I think it's an excellent opportunity, O Shaykh," I said.

"What do you mean?" said Papa.

"We're supposed to be dead already," I explained. "We've got an advantage then. It might be some time before Hajjar, Shaykh Reda, and Dr. Abd ar-Razzaq realize that their two abandoned corpses are poking around in matters they don't want brought to light. Maybe we should proceed slowly, to delay our eventual discovery as long as possible. If we go charging into the city with banners and bugles, all our sources will dry up immediately."

"Yes, very good, my nephew," said Friedlander Bey. "You are learning the wisdom of reason. Combat rarely ever succeeds without logic to guide the attack."

"Still, I also learned from the Bani Salim the dangers of hesitancy."

"The Bani Salim would not sit in the dark and hatch plans," said bin Turki. "The Bani Salim would ride down upon their enemies and let their rifles speak. Then they'd let their camels trample the bodies in the dust."

"Well," I said, "we don't have any camels to trample with. Still, I like the Bani Salim's approach to the problem."

"You have indeed been changed by our experiences in the desert," said Papa. "Yet we won't be hesitating. We'll go forward slowly but firmly, and if it becomes necessary to dispatch one of the key players, we must be ready to commit that deed without regret."

"Unless, of course, the player is Shaykh Reda Abu Adil," I said.

"Yes, of course."

"I wish I knew the whole story. Why is Shaykh Reda

spared when better men—I'm thinking of his pet imam—may be sacrificed to our honor?"

A long sigh came from Papa. "There was a woman," he said, turning his head and gazing out the port again.

"Say no more," I said. "I don't need to hear the details. A woman, well, that alone explains so much."

"A woman and an oath. It appears that Shaykh Reda has forgotten the oath we took, but I have not. After I am dead, you will be released from that oath, but not before."

I let my breath out heavily. "Must've been *some* woman," I said. This was the most he'd ever discussed the mysterious ground rules of his lifelong conflict with his rival, Abu Adil.

Friedlander Bey did not deign to respond to that. He just stared out at the blackness of the sky and the darkness of the planet we were hurrying to meet.

An announcement came over the PA system instructing us to remain seated until the suborbital came to a complete stop and then underwent the quarter-hour cooling-down procedure. It was frustrating in a way, because I'd always wanted to visit Damascus, and we'd be there but I wouldn't get a chance to see anything but the terminal building.

The *Imam Muhammad al-Baqir* slipped into its landing configuration, and in a few more minutes we'd be on the ground. I shuddered a little in relief. I always do. It's not that I'm afraid of being shot into the sky in a rocket; it's just that when I'm aboard, suddenly I lose all my faith in modern physics and suborbital-craft design. I always fall back on a frightened child's thought, that they'll never be able to get so many tons of steel into the air, and even if they do, they'll never be able to keep it there. Actually, the time I'm most worried is during takeoff. If the ship doesn't explode in glittering smithereens, I figure we've got it licked and I relax. But for a few minutes, I keep waiting to hear the pilot say something like "Ground Control has decided to abort this flight once we're far enough downrange. It's been a real pleas—"

We came to a nice, smooth landing in Damascus, and then stared out the ports for fifteen minutes while the suborbital shrunk back to its IAA-approved tolerances. Papa and I had only three small bags between us, and we carried them across the tarmac to the terminal. It didn't take us long to figure out where we had to go to catch the suborbital that would take us home.

I went to the small souvenir shop, thinking to buy something for myself and maybe something for Indihar and something for Chiri. I was disappointed to discover that nearly all the souvenirs had "Made in the Western Reserve" or "Made in Occupied Panama" stickers on them. I contented myself with a few holocards.

I began writing one out to Indihar, but I stopped. No doubt the phones in Papa's palace were now tapped, and the mail was probably scrutinized by unfriendly eyes as well. I could blow our cover by sending a holocard announcing our triumphant return.

No doubt weeks ago Indihar and all my friends had reconciled themselves to my tragic demise. What would we find when we got back to the city? I guessed I'd learn a lot about how people felt toward me. Youssef and Tariq were probably maintaining Friedlander Bey's estate, but Kmuzu must have seen his liberation in my death, and would be long gone.

I felt a thrill as I climbed aboard the second suborbital. Knowing that the *Nasrullah* would ferry us back to the city made me tingle with anticipation. In under an hour, we'd be back. The uneasy alliances and conspiracies that had tried to kill us would be shaken, perhaps shaken to death, as soon as we got down to work. I looked forward eagerly to our vengeance. The Bani Salim had taught me that.

It turned out to be the shortest long flight I'd ever taken. My nose was pressed right up against the port, as if by concentrating with all my might, I could help steer the *Nasrullah* and give it a little extra acceleration. It seemed that we'd just passed through Max Q when the steward came by to tell us to buckle up for landing. I wondered if, say, we should plummet back to Earth and plow a crater a hundred feet deep, would the seat belt provide enough protection so that we could walk away unharmed, through the fireball?

The three of us didn't spend much time in the terminal, because Friedlander Bey was too well known to go long without being recognized, and then the word would get back to Abu Adil, and then . . . Sand Dune City again. Or maybe one shot through four cerebral lobes.

"What now, O Shaykh?" I asked Papa.

"Let us walk a bit," he said. I followed him out of the terminal, to a cab stand. Bin Turki, anxious to make himself useful, carried the bags.

Papa was about to get into the first cab in line, but I stopped him. "These drivers have pretty good memories," I said. "And they're probably bribable. There's a driver I use who's perfectly suited to our needs."

"Ah," said the old man, "You have something on him? Something that he doesn't want to come to light?"

"Better than that, O Shaykh. He is physically unable to remember anything from one hour to the next."

"I don't understand. Does he suffer from some sort of brain injury?"

"You could say that, my uncle." Then I told him all about Bill, the crazy American. Bill had come to the city long before I did. He had no use for cosmetic bodmods—appearances meant nothing to Bill. Or for skull-wiring, either. Instead, he'd done a truly insane thing: he'd paid one of the medical hustlers on the Street to remove one of Bill's lungs and replace it with a sac that dripped a constant, measured dose of lightspeed RPM into his bloodstream.

RPM is to any other hallucinogen as a spoonful of crushed saccharin is to a single granule of sugar. I deeply regret the few times I ever tried it. Its technical name is *l*-ribopropylmethionine, but nowadays I hear people on the street calling it "hell." The first time I took it, my reaction was so fiercely horrible that I had to take it again because I couldn't believe anything could be *that* bad. It was an insult to my self-image as the Conqueror of All Substances.

There isn't enough money in the world to get me to try it again.

And this was the stuff Bill had dripping into his arteries day and night, day and night. Needless to say, Bill's completely and permanently fried. He doesn't look so much like a cab driver as he does a possessed astrologer who'll probably seduce the entire royal family and end up being assassinated in an icy river at midnight.

Riding with Bill was a lunatic's job, too, because he was always swerving to avoid things in the road only he could see. And he was positive that demons—the *afrit*—sat beside him in the front, distracting him and tempting him and being just enough of a nuisance that it took all his concentration to keep from dying in a fiery crash on the highway. I always found Bill and his muttered commentaries fascinating. He was an anti–role model for me. I told myself, "You could end up like him if you don't stop swallowing pills all the time."

"And yet you recommend this driver?" said Friedlander Bey dubiously.

"Yes," I said, "because Bill's total concentration could

pass through the eye of a needle and leave enough room for a five-tier flea pyramid to slide by above. He has no mind. He won't remember us the next day. He may not even remember us as soon as we get out of the cab. Sometimes he zooms off before you can even pay him."

Papa stroked his white beard, which was desperately in need of trimming. "I see. So he truly wouldn't be bribable, not because he's so honest, but because he won't remember."

I nodded. I was already looking for a public phone. I went to one, dropped in a few coins, and spoke Bill's commcode into the receiver. It took fifteen rings, but at last Bill answered. He was sitting at his customary place, just beyond the Budayeen's eastern gate, on the Boulevard il-Jameel. It took a couple of minutes for Bill to recall who I was, despite the fact that we'd known each other for years. He said he'd come to the airfield to pick us up.

"Now," said Friedlander Bey, "we must decide carefully on our destination."

I chewed a fingernail while I thought. "No doubt Chiri's is being watched."

Chiri's was a nightclub on the Street. Papa had forced Chiriga to sell it to him, and then he'd presented it to me. Chiri had been one of my best friends, but after the buyout she could barely bring herself to speak to me. I had persuaded her that it had been all Papa's idea, and then I'd sold her a half-interest in the club. We were pals again.

"We dare not contact any of your usual friends," he said. "Perhaps I have the answer." He went to the phone and spoke quietly for a short while. When he hung up, he gave me a brief smile and said, "I think I have the solution. Ferrari has a couple of spare rooms above his nightclub, and I've let him know that I need help tonight. I also reminded him of a few favors I've done for him over the years."

"Ferrari?" I said. "The Blue Parrot? I never go in there. The place is too classy for me." The Blue Parrot was one of those high-toned, formal attire, champagne-serving, little Latin band clubs. Signor Ferrari glided among the tables, murmuring pleasantries while the ceiling fans turned lazily overhead. Not a single undraped bosom to be seen. The place gave me the creeps.

"Just that much better. We'll have your driver friend take us around to the back of Ferrari's place. The door will be unlocked. We're to make ourselves comfortable in the rooms upstairs, and our host will join us when he closes his nightclub at 2 A.M., *inshallah*. As for young bin Turki, I think it would be better and safer if we sent him ahead to our house. Write out a brief note on one of your holocards and sign it without using your name. That will be enough for Youssef and Tariq."

I understood what he wanted. I scribbled a quick message on the back of one of the Damascene holocards—"Youssef and Tariq: This is our friend bin Turki. Treat him well until we return. See you soon. [signed] The Maghrebi." I gave the card to bin Turki.

"Thank you, O Shaykh," he said. He was still quivering with excitement. "You've already done more than I can ever repay."

I shrugged. "Don't worry about repaying anything, my friend," I said. "We'll find a way to put you to work." Then I turned to Friedlander Bey. "I'll trust your judgment concerning Ferrari, O Shaykh, because I personally don't know how honest he is."

That brought another smile to Papa's lips. "Honest? I don't trust honest men. There's always the first time for betrayal, as you have learned. Rather, Signor Ferrari is fearful, and that is something I can depend on. As for his honesty, he's no more honest than anyone else in the Budayeen."

That wasn't very honest. Papa had a point, though. I thought about how I'd pass the time in Ferrari's rooms, and my own agenda began to take shape. Before I could discuss it with Friedlander Bey, however, Bill arrived.

Bill glared out of his cab with insane eyes that almost seemed to sizzle. "Yeah?" he said.

Papa murmured, "In the name of Allah, the Beneficent, the Merciful."

"In the name of Christy Mathewson, the dead, the buried," growled Bill in return.

I looked at Papa. "Who is Christy Mathewson?" I asked.

Friedlander Bey just gave me a slight shrug. I was curious, but I knew it was wrong to start a conversational thread with Bill. He would either blow up in a rage and leave, or he'd start talking unstoppably and we'd never get to the Blue Parrot before dawn.

"Yeah?" said Bill in a threatening voice.

"Let's get in the cab," said Friedlander Bey calmly. We climbed in. "The Blue Parrot in the Budayeen. Go to the rear entrance."

"Yeah?" said Bill. "The Street's not open to vehicular traffic, which is what we are, or soon will be, as soon as I start moving. Actually, we'll all start moving, because we're—"

"Don't worry about the city ordinance," said Papa. "I'm giving you permission."

"Yeah? Even though we're transporting fire demons?"

"Don't worry about that, either," I said. "We have a Special Pass." I just made that part up.

"Yeah?" snarled Bill.

"*Bismillah,*" prayed Papa.

Bill tromped the accelerator and we shot out of the

airport lot, zooming and rocketing and careening around corners. Bill always sped up when he came to a turn, as if he couldn't wait to see what was around the corner. Someday it's going to be a big delivery wagon. Blammo.

"Yaa Allah!" cried bin Turki, terrified. *"Yaa Allah!"* His cries died away to a constant fearful moan through the duration of the journey.

Actually, our ride was fairly uneventful—at least for me. I was used to Bill's driving. Papa pushed himself deep into the seat, closed his eyes, and repeated *"bismallah, bismillah"* the whole time. And Bill kept up a nonsensical monologue about how baseball players complained about scuffed balls, you should have to hit against an *afrit* once, see how hard *that* is, trying to connect with a ball of fire, even if you do, it won't go out of the infield, just break up in a shower of red and yellow sparks, try *that* sometime, maybe people would understand . . . and so forth.

We turned off the beautiful Boulevard il-Jameel and passed through the Budayeen's eastern gate. Even Bill realized that the pedestrian traffic on the Street was too dense for his customary recklessness, and so we made our way slowly to the Blue Parrot, then drove around the block to the rear entrance. When Papa and I got out of the cab, Friedlander Bey paid the fare and gave Bill a moderate tip.

Bill waved one sunburned arm. "It was nice meeting you," he said.

"Right, Bill," I said. "Who is Christy Mathewson?"

"One of the best players in the history of the game. 'The Big Six,' they called him. Maybe two hundred, two hundred fifty years ago."

"Two hundred fifty years!" I said, astonished.

"Yeah?" said Bill angrily. "What's it to ya?"

I shook my head. "You know where Friedlander Bey's house is?"

"Sure," said Bill. "What's the matter? You guys forget where you put it? It just didn't get up and *walk* away."

"Here's an extra ten kiam. Drive my young friend to Friedlander Bey's house, and make sure he gets there safely."

"Sure thing," said the cab driver.

I peered into the back seat, where bin Turki looked horrified that he'd have to ride with Bill, all alone and lost in the big city. "We'll see you in a day or two," I told him. "In the meantime, Youssef and Tariq will take care of you. Have a good time!"

Bin Turki just stared at me with wide eyes, gulping but not actually forming any coherent words. I turned on my heel and followed Papa to the unlocked door at the rear of the Blue Parrot. I was sure that Bill would forget the entire conversation soon after he delivered bin Turki to the mansion.

We went up a stairway made of fine polished hardwood. It twisted around in a complete circle, and we found ourselves on a landing, faced by two doors. The door to the left was locked, probably Ferrari's private apartment. The door to the right opened into a spacious parlor, decorated in a European style with lots of dark wood paneling and potted palms and a piano in one corner. The furniture was very tasteful and modern, however. Leading off from the parlor were a kitchen and two bedrooms, each with its own bathroom.

"I imagine we can be comfortable here," I said.

Papa grunted and headed for a bedroom. He was almost two hundred years old, and it had been a long and tiring day for him. He shut the bedroom door behind him, and I stayed in the parlor, softly knuckling bits of music at the piano.

In about ten or fifteen minutes, Signor Ferrari came upstairs. "I heard movement up here," he explained in an apologetic manner, "and I wanted to be sure it was you. Did Signor Bey find everything to his liking?"

"Yes, indeed, and we both want to thank you for your hospitality."

"It's nothing, nothing at all." Ferrari was a grossly fat man stuffed inside a plain white linen suit. He wore a red felt fez with a tassel on his head, and he rubbed his hands together anxiously, belying the suave, almost oily tone of his voice.

"Still," I said, "I'm sure Friedlander Bey will find some way to reward your kindness."

"If that is his wish," said Ferrari, his little pig eyes squinting at me, "then I would be honored to accept."

"I'm sure."

"Now, I must get back to my patrons. If there's anything you need, just pick up the phone and call 111. My staff has orders to bring you anything you desire."

"Excellent, Signor Ferrari. If you'll wait a moment, I'd like to write a note. Would one of your staff deliver it for me?"

"Well . . ."

"Just to Chiriga's, on the Street."

"Certainly," he said.

I wrote out a quick message to Chiri, telling her that I was, in fact, still alive, but that she had to keep the news secret until we cleared our names. I told her to call Ferrari's number and get extension 777 if she wanted to talk to me about anything, but she shouldn't use the phone in the club because it might be tapped. I folded the note and gave it to Ferrari, who promised that it would be delivered within fifteen minutes.

"Thank you for everything, signor," I said, yawning.

"I will leave you now," said Ferrari. "You no doubt need to rest."

I grunted and shut the door behind him. Then I went to the second guest room and stretched out on the bed. I expected the phone to ring soon.

It didn't take long. I answered the phone with a curt "Where y'at?"

It was Chiri, of course. For a few seconds, all I could hear was gibberish. Then I slowly began to separate words from the hysterical flow. "You're really alive? This isn't some kind of trick?"

I laughed. "Yeah, you right, Chiri, I set this all up before I died. You're talking to a recording. Hey, *of course* I'm alive! Did you really believe—"

"Hajjar brought me the news that you'd been picked up on a murder rap, both you and Papa, and that you'd been flown into exile from which you couldn't possibly return."

"Well, Chiri, here I am."

"Hell, we all went through a terrible time when we thought you were dead. The grieving was all for nothing, is that what you're telling me?"

"People grieved?" I have to admit the notion gave me a perverse sort of pleasure.

"Well, I sure as hell grieved, and a couple of the girls, and . . . and Indihar. She thought she'd been widowed a second time."

I chewed my lip for a few seconds. "Okay, you can tell Indihar, but no one else. Got that? Not Saied the Half-Hajj or any of my other friends. They're all still under suspicion. Where you calling from?"

"The pay phone in the back of Vast Foods." That was a lunch counter kind of place. The food wasn't really vast. That was a sign painter's error that they never bothered to correct.

"Fine, Chiri. Remember what I said."

"How 'bout if I give you a visit tomorrow?"

I thought that over, and finally I decided that there was little risk, and I really wanted to see Chiri's cannibal grin again. "All right. You know where we are?"

"Above the Blue Parrot?"

"Uh huh."

"This black girl happy-happy, see you tomorrow, Bwana."

"Yeah, you right," I said, and I hung up the phone.

My mind was crammed with thoughts and half-formed plans. I tried to go to sleep, but I just lay there for an hour or so. Finally, I heard Friedlander Bey stirring in the kitchen. I got up and joined him.

"Isn't there a teapot around here?" Papa grumbled.

I glanced at my watch. It was a quarter after two in the morning. "Why don't we go downstairs?" I said. "Ferrari will be closing up the place now."

He considered the idea. "I'd like that," he said. "I'd like to sit and relax with a glass or two of tea."

We went downstairs. I carefully checked to make sure all the patrons had left the Blue Parrot, and then Papa took a seat at one of the tables. One of Ferrari's flunkies brought him a pot of tea, and after the first glass, you'd never have known that Papa had just returned from a grim and dangerous exile. He closed his eyes and savored every drop of tea. "Civilized tea," he called it, longing for it every time he'd had to swallow the thin, alkaline tea of the Bani Salim.

I stayed by the door, watching the sidewalk outside. I flinched two or three times as police patrol cars rattled by on the stone-paved street.

Finally, the fatigue caught up with us, and we bid Signor Ferrari good night once more. Then we climbed the stairs to our hiding place. I was asleep within a few minutes of undressing and climbing into Ferrari's comfortable guest bed.

I slept about ten hours. It was the most refreshing, luxurious night's sleep I could remember. It had been a long while since I'd enjoyed clean sheets. Again, I was jolted awake by the phone. I picked up the extension beside my bed. "Yeah?" I said.

"Signor Audran," said Ferrari's voice, "there are two young women to see you. Shall I send them up?"

"Please," I said, running my hand sleepily through my rumpled hair. I hung up the phone and dressed hurriedly.

I could hear Chiri's voice calling from the stairwell, "Marîd? Which door? Where are you, Marîd?"

I hadn't had time to shower or shave, but I didn't care, and I didn't think Chiri would, either. I answered the door and was surprised to see Indihar, too. "Come on in," I said in a low voice. "We'll have to keep it down, because Papa's still asleep."

"All right," murmured Chiri, coming into the parlor. "Nice place Ferrari has up here."

"Oh, these are just his guest rooms. I can only imagine what his own suite is like."

Indihar was wearing widow's black. She came up to me and touched my face. "I am glad to see that you're well, husband," she said, and then she turned away, weeping.

"One thing I gotta know," said Chiri, dropping heavily into an antique wing chair. "Did you or did you not kill that policeman?"

"I did not kill a cop," I said fiercely. "Papa and I were framed for that, and we were tried *in absentia,* and cast out into the Empty Quarter. Now that we're back—and you can be damn sure that somebody never expected us to get back—we have to solve that crime to clear our names. When we do, heads will roll. Quite literally."

"I believe you, husband," said Indihar, who sat beside me on an expensive couch that matched Chiri's wing chair. "My . . . my late husband and I were good friends with the murdered patrolman. His name was Khalid Maxwell, and he was a kind, generous man. I don't want his killer to get away unpunished."

"I promise you, my wife, that won't happen. He'll pay dearly."

There was an awkward silence for a moment. I looked uncomfortably at Indihar and she stared down at her hands, folded in her lap. Chiri came to our rescue. She coughed politely and said, "Brought something for you, Mr. Boss." I looked toward her; she was grinning, her tattooed face wrinkled up in delight. She held out a plastic moddy rack.

"My moddies!" I said happily. "It looks like all of them."

"You've got enough weirdo stuff there to keep you occupied while you're laying low," said Chiri.

"And here is something else, husband." Indihar was offering me a tan plastic item on the palm of her hand.

"My pillcase!" I was more happy to see it than the moddy rack. I took it and opened it, and saw that it was crammed full of beauties, sunnies, Paxium, everything a working fugitive needed to keep sane in a hostile world. "Although," I said, clearing my throat self-consciously, "I am trying to cut down."

"That's good, husband," said Indihar. The unspoken text was that she still blamed me and my substance abuse for the death of her first husband. She was making a large gesture by giving me the pillcase.

"Where did you get these things?" I asked.

"From Kmuzu," said Chiri. "I just sweet-talked that pretty boy until he didn't know which direction was up."

"I'll bet," I said. "So now Kmuzu knows I'm back, too."

"Hey, it's just Kmuzu," said Chiri. "You can trust him."

Yes, I did trust Kmuzu. More than just about anyone else. I changed the subject. "Wife, how are my step-children?"

"They're all fine," she said, smiling for the first time. "They all want to know where you've gone. I think little Zahra has a crush on you."

I laughed, although I was a little uneasy about that bit of news.

"Well," said Chiri, "we should be going. The Maghrebi here has to get to work on his plans of vengeance. Right, Marîd?"

"Well, sort of. Thanks so much for coming by. And thanks for bringing the moddies and the pillcase. That was very thoughtful."

"Not at all, husband," said Indihar. "I will pray to Allah, thanking Him for returning you." She came to me and gave me a chaste kiss on the cheek.

I walked them to the door. "And the club?" I asked.

Chiri shrugged. "Same old story. Business is dead, the girls are still trying to rob us blind, you know the rest."

Indihar laughed. "The rest is that the club's probably making money like crazy, and your share will need a tractor-trailer to haul it to the bank."

In other words, all was right with the world. Except in the area of personal freedom for myself and Friedlander Bey. I had some ideas on how to improve things along those lines, however. I just needed to make a few important phone calls.

"*Salaamtak,*" said Indihar, bowing before me.

"*Allah yisallimak,*" I replied. Then the two women left, and I closed the door.

Almost immediately, I went to the kitchen and swallowed a few sunnies with a glass of water. I promised myself that I wouldn't get back into my old habits, but that I could afford to reward my recent heroic behavior. Then I'd put the pillcase away and save it for emergencies.

Out of curiosity, I browsed through my rack of moddies and daddies, and discovered that Chiriga had left me a little gift—a new sex-moddy. I examined it. The label said it was *Inferno in the Night,* one of Honey Pílar's early moddies, but it was recorded from her partner's point of view.

I went into the bedroom, undressed, and lay down on the bed. Then I reached up, murmured *"Bismillah,"* and chipped the moddy in.

The first thing Audran noticed was that he was much younger, much stronger, and filled with an anticipation that bordered on desperation. He felt wonderful, and he laughed as he took off his clothes.

The woman in the bedroom with him was Honey Pílar. Audran had loved her with a consuming passion ever since he met her, two hours ago. He thought it was a great privilege to be allowed to gaze at her and compose clumsy poems in her honor. That he and she might jam was more than he could've hoped for.

She stripped slowly and enticingly, then joined Audran on the bed. Her hair was pale blond, her eyes a remarkable green like clean, cool waves in the ocean. "Yes?" she said. "You are much hurt?" Her voice was languid and musical.

Inferno in the Night was one of Honey's earliest sex-moddies, and it had a vestigial story line. Audran realized that he was a wounded hero of the Catalonian struggle for

*independence, and Honey was playing the courageous
daughter of the evil Valencian duke.*

"I'm fine," said Audran.

"You need bad massage," she murmured, moving her
fingertips gently across his chest and stopping just at the
top of his pubic hair. She waited, looking at him for permission.

"Oh, please go ahead," Audran said.

"For the revolution," she said.

"Sure."

And then she caressed his prick until he could stand it
no more. He ran his fingers through her fragrant hair,
then grabbed her and turned her on her back.

"Your wounds!" she cried.

"You've miraculously healed me."

"Oh good!" she said, sighing as Audran entered her.
They jammed slowly at first, then faster and faster until
Audran burst with exquisite pleasure.

After a while, Honey Pílar sat up. "I must go," she said
sadly. "There are others wounded."

"I understand," Audran said. He reached up and
popped the moddy out.

"Jeez," I muttered. It had been a long time since I'd
last spent any time with Honey Pílar. I was beginning to
think I was getting too old for this stuff. I mean, I wasn't a
kid anymore. As I lay panting on the bed, I realized I'd
come dangerously close to pulling a hamstring. Maybe
they had sex-moddies recorded by couples who'd been
married twenty years. That was more my speed.

There was a knock on my room's door. "My nephew,"
called Friedlander Bey, "are you all right?"

"Yes, O Shaykh," I answered.

"I ask only because I heard you exclaim."

Yipe. "A nightmare, that's all. Let me take a quick shower, and then I'll join you."

"Very good, O Excellent One."

I got off the bed, ran a quick shower, dressed, and went out into the parlor. "I'd like to get some clean clothes," I said. "I've been wearing this same outfit since we were kidnapped, and I think it's finally dead."

Papa nodded. "I've taken care of that already. I've sent a message to Tariq and Youssef, and they will be here momentarily with fresh clothing and a supply of money."

I sat in the wing chair, and Papa sat on the couch. "I suppose your businesses have been purring along just fine with them at the wheel."

"I trust Tariq and Youssef with my life and more: I trust them with my holdings."

"It will be good to see them again."

"You had visitors earlier. Who were they?"

I gulped. I suddenly realized that he might interpret the visit from Indihar and Chiri as a serious breach in security. Worse that that, he might see it as a punishable stupidity. "My wife and my partner, Chiriga," I said. My mouth went suddenly dry.

But Papa only nodded. "They are both well, I pray?" he said.

"Yes, praise Allah, they are."

"I am glad to hear it. Now—" He was interrupted by a knock on the front door of the apartment. "My nephew," he said quietly, "see who's there. If it's not Tariq and Youssef, do not let them in, even if it's one of your friends."

"I understand, O Shaykh." I went to the door and peered through the small peephole. It was indeed Tariq and Youssef, Papa's valet and butler, and the managers of his estate.

I opened the door and they were enthusiastic in their greetings. "Welcome home!" cried Youssef. "Allah be thanked for your safe return! Not that we believed for an instant that story that you both had died in some distant desert."

Tariq carried a couple of hard-sided suitcases into the parlor and set them down. *"As-salaam alaykum, yaa Shaykh,"* he said to me. He turned to Papa and said the same.

"Alaykum as-salaam," said Friedlander Bey. "Tell me what I must know."

They had indeed been keeping business matters up to date. Most of what they discussed with Papa I knew nothing about, but there were two situations in which I'd become involved. The first was the Cappadocian attempt to win independence from Anatolia. I'd met with the Cappadocian representatives—how long ago? It seemed like many months, but it couldn't have been more than a few weeks.

Youssef spoke up. "We've decided that the Cappadocians have a good chance of overthrowing the Anatolian government in their province. With our aid, it would be a certainty. And it would not cost us very much, relatively speaking, to keep them in power long enough."

Long enough? Long enough for what? I wondered. There was still so much I had to learn.

When all the geopolitical issues had been discussed and commented on, I asked, "What about the datalink project?"

"That seems to be stalled, Shaykh Marîd," said Tariq.

"Unstall it," said Papa.

"We need someone who is not in our household to accept an executive position," said Tariq. "Of course, the executive position will have no real power or influence—

that will remain in the household—but we need a, uh, a—"

"Fall guy," I said.

Tariq just blinked. "Yes," he said, "precisely."

"You're working on that, aren't you, my nephew?" asked Papa.

I nodded. "I'm developing someone for that position, yes."

"Very well," said Friedlander Bey, standing. "Everything seems to be in order. I expected no less. Still, you will be rewarded."

Youssef and Tariq bowed and murmured their thanks. Papa placed his left hand on Tariq's head, and his right on Youssef's. He looked like a saint blessing his followers.

"O Shaykh," I said, "isn't there one more thing?"

"Hmm?" he said, glancing at me.

"Concerning Shaykh Mahali," I said.

"Ah yes, O Excellent One. Thank you for reminding me. Youssef, I want you to make an appointment for my grandson and me to meet with the amir. Tell him that we realize that we're fugitives, but also remind him that we were denied our lawful chance to appeal the verdict of our contrived trials. We think we can persuade him that we're innocent, and beg only for an opportunity to plead our case."

"Yes," said Youssef, "I understand. I will be done as you wish."

"As Allah wishes, rather," said Papa.

"As Allah wishes," Youssef murmured.

"Did the boy arrive safely?" I asked.

"Bin Turki?" said Tariq. "Yes, we've installed him in an empty suite of rooms, and he's rather overawed by everything he's seen. He has struck up a friendship with Umm Jirji, your wife."

My mouth twisted. "Wonderful," I said.

"One more thing," said Friedlander Bey, the ruler of half the city. "I want one round-trip suborbital ticket to the town of Najran, in the kingdom of Asir."

That made my blood run cold, let me tell you.

10

It seemed as if a year had passed since the first time I visited the prince's palace. In fact, it couldn't have been more than a few weeks. I, however, had changed somewhat in that time. I felt that my vision was clearer and that I'd been stripped of my intellectual objections to direct action. Whether that would be a help or a hindrance in my future in the city was yet to be seen.

The amir's estate was even more beautiful in the daylight than it had been on the evening of my wedding reception. The air was clean and the breeze was cool and refreshing. The liquid gurgling of the fountains relaxed me as I walked through Shaykh Mahali's gardens. When we got to the house, a servant opened the door.

"We have an appointment with the amir," said Friedlander Bey.

The servant looked at us carefully, decided we weren't madmen or assassins, and nodded. We followed him down a long gallery that bordered an inner courtyard. He opened the door to a small audience chamber, and we entered and took seats and waited for the shaykh to arrive. I felt very uncomfortable, as if I'd been caught cheating on a test and was now waiting for the principal to come in and punish me. The difference was that I hadn't been caught cheating; the charge was murder of a police officer. And the penalty wouldn't be just ten swats, it would be death.

I decided to let Papa handle the defense. He'd had a century and a half more practice at verbal tap dancing than I had.

We sat there in anxious silence for about a quarter hour. Then, with more bustle than ceremony, Shaykh Mahali and three other men entered. The shaykh was handsome in white *gallebeya* and *keffiya*, and two of his attendants wore European-style dark gray business suits. The third man wore the robes and dark turban of a scholar of the noble Qur'ân; he was evidently Shaykh Mahali's vizier.

The prince took his seat on a handsomely carved chair, and turned toward us. "What is this matter?" he asked quietly.

"O Prince," said Friedlander Bey, stepping forward, "we were wrongfully accused of the death of a police officer, Khalid Maxwell. Then, without benefit of public trial, or even an opportunity to confront our accusers and present a defense, we were kidnapped—right from Your Highness's own grounds, after the wedding reception you gave for my great-grandson. We were forced aboard a suborbital ship, and presented with the news that we'd already been tried. When we landed in Najran, we were taken aboard a helicopter, and then pushed out into the Arabian Desert, in the southern, most dreadful portion known as the Rub al-Khali. We were most fortunate to survive, and it took great courage and sacrifice on the part of my beloved great-grandson to keep us alive until we were rescued by a nomadic tribe of Bedu, may the blessings of Allah be on them. It is only now that we've been able to make our way back to the city. We beg your attention on this matter, because we believe we have the right to ask for an appeal, and a chance to clear our names."

The amir consulted quietly with his adviser. Then he turned back to us. "I knew nothing of this," he said simply.

"Nor I," said the vizier, "and your file should have crossed my desk before your trial. In any case, such a verdict and sentence cannot be legal without the concurrence of Shaykh Mahali."

Friedlander Bey stepped forward and gave the vizier the copy of the charges and verdict that he'd gotten from the qadi. "This was all we were allowed to see. It bears the signatures of the qadi and Dr. Sadiq Abd ar-Razzaq."

The vizier studied the paper for a few moments, then passed it on to the prince. The prince glanced at it and said, "There is neither my signature upon this warrant, nor that of my vizier. It is not a valid order. You will have your appeal, one month from today. At that time, I will assemble Lieutenant Hajjar, Dr. Abd ar-Razzaq, and this qadi, who is unknown to me. In the meantime, I will investigate why this matter was passed along without our knowledge."

"We thank you for your generosity, O Prince," said Friedlander Bey humbly.

The amir waved a hand. "No thanks are necessary, my friend. I am only performing my duty. Now, tell me: did either or both of you have anything to do with the death of this police officer?"

Friedlander Bey took a step nearer and looked the prince in the eye. "I swear upon my head, upon the life of the Prophet—may the blessings of Allah be on him and peace—that we had nothing to do with Officer Maxwell's death. Neither of us even knew the man."

Shaykh Mahali rubbed his carefully trimmed beard thoughtfully. "We shall see. Now return to your home, because your month's grace is already beginning to slip away."

We bowed low and backed out of the audience chamber. Outside, I released the deep breath I'd been holding. "We can go home now!" I said.

Papa looked very happy. "Yes, my nephew," he said. "And against our resources, and a month's time to prepare, Hajjar and the imam cannot hope to prevail."

I didn't know exactly what he had in mind, but I intended to dive back into my normal existence as soon as possible. I was hungry for a quiet life, familiar little problems, and no threats greater than a mouse in the ladies' room of my nightclub. However, as a great Franji poet of the dim, dark past once wrote, "The best-laid plans of mice and men often get jammed all to hell."

It would happen in its own time, I knew it instinctively. It always did. That's why I avoided making plans of any kind now. I could wait for Allah in His infinite benevolence to waft His intentions my way.

Sometimes, though, it takes a few days for the Lord of the Worlds to get around to you. In the meantime I just relaxed in Chiri's, comfortable in my usual seat at the curve of the bar. About four or five nights later, long after midnight, I watched Chiriga, my partner and night barmaid, scoop a meager tip from a customer. She gave him a dismaying look at her filed teeth and drifted down to my end of the bar. "Cheap bastard," she said, stuffing the money into a pocket of her tight jeans.

I didn't say anything for a while. I was in a melancholy mood. Three o'clock in the morning and many drinks always do that to me. "You know," I said at last, staring up at Yasmin on stage, "when I was a kid, and I imagined what it would be like to be grown up, this wasn't it. This wasn't it at all."

Chiri's beautiful black face relaxed in one of her rare smiles. "Me, too. I never thought I'd end up in this city. And when I did, I didn't plan to get stuck in the Budayeen. I was aiming at a higher-class neighborhood."

"Yet here we are."

Chiriga's smile faded. "Here *I* am, Marîd, probably forever. You got great expectations." She took my empty glass, threw a few fresh ice cubes into it, and mixed me another White Death. That's what Chiri had named my favorite drink, gin and bingara with a slug of Rose's lime juice. I didn't need another drink, but I wanted one.

She set it in front of me on an old, ragged cork coaster, then headed back up the bar toward the front of the club. A customer had come in and sat down near the door. Chiri shrugged at him and pointed toward me. The customer got up and moved slowly down the narrow aisle between the bar and the booths. When he got a little closer, I saw it was Jacques.

Jacques is very proud of being a Christian in a Muslim city, and conceited about being three-quarters European where most people are Arab. That makes Jacques dumb, and it also makes him a target. He's one of my three old buddies: Saied the Half-Hajj is my friend; I can't stand Mahmoud; and Jacques is in the middle. I don't give a phony fîq about what he does or says, and neither does anyone else I know.

"Where you at, Marîd?" he said, sitting beside me. "You had us all worried for a few weeks."

"All right, Jacques," I said. "Want something to drink?" Yasmin had danced her third song, and was grabbing up her clothes and hurrying off the stage, to wring tips from the few morose customers we still had.

Jacques frowned. "I don't have much money with me tonight. That's what I want to talk to you about."

"Uh huh," I said. In the months that I'd owned the club, I'd heard it all. I signaled to Chiri to draw a beer for my old pal, Jacques.

We watched her fill a tall glass and bring it down the bar. She put it in front of Jacques but said nothing to him. Chiri can't stand him. Jacques is the kind of guy, if his house was burning in the night, most people in the Budayeen would write him a postcard and drop it in the mail to warn him.

Yasmin came up to us, dressed now in a short leather skirt and a black, lacy brassiere. "Tip me for my dancing, Jacques?" she said with a sweet smile. I think she's the sexiest dancer on the Street, but because Jacques is strictly heterosexual and Yasmin wasn't quite born a girl, I didn't think she'd have any luck with him.

"I don't have much money—" he began.

"Tip her," I said in a cold voice.

Jacques gave me a quick glance, but dug in his pocket and pulled out a one-kiam bill.

"Thanks," said Yasmin. She moved on to the next lonely customer.

"You gonna keep ignoring me, Yasmin?" I said.

"How's your *wife*, Marîd?" she called, without turning around.

"Yeah," said Jacques, smirking, "honeymoon over already? You hanging out here all night?"

"I own this place, you know."

Jacques shrugged. "Yeah, but Chiri could run it just fine without you. She used to, if I remember right."

I squeezed the little wedge of lime into my drink and

gulped it down. "So you just felt like dropping in this late for a free beer, or what?"

Jacques gave me a weak grin. "I do have something I want to ask you," he said.

"I figured." I waved my empty glass back and forth at Chiri. She just raised her eyebrows; she thought I'd been drinking too much lately, and that was her way of letting me know.

I wasn't in the mood for her disapproval. Chiri was usually a noninterventionist, meaning that she believed every person was intitled to his own flaming stupidity. I signaled again, more sharply this time, and she finally nodded and put together another White Death in a fresh glass. She marched down to my end of the bar, dropped it heavily in front of me, and marched away again without saying a word. I couldn't see what she was so upset about.

Jacques sipped slowly at his beer, then put his glass down in the very center of the coaster. "Marîd," he said, his eyes on a pretty sexchange named Lily who was tiredly doing her bit on stage, "would you go out of your way to help Fuad?"

What can I say about Fuad? His nickname on the Street was il-Manhous, which means "The Permanently Fucked," or words to that effect. Fuad was a tall, skinny guy with a big mop of hair that he wore in a greasy pompadour. He'd suffered some kind of degenerative disease as a kid, because his arms were as thin and frail-looking as dry sticks, with huge, swollen joints. He meant well, I suppose, but he had this pitiful puppy-dog quality. He was so desperate to be liked and so anxious to please that he sometimes got obnoxious about it. Some of the dancers in the clubs exploited him, sending him off to fetch food and run other errands, for which they neither paid nor thanked him. If I thought about him at all—which I didn't do very often—I tended to feel a little sorry for the guy.

"Fuad's not very bright," I said. "He still hasn't learned that those hookers he falls in love with always rob him blind at the first opportunity."

Jacques nodded. "I'm not talking about his intelligence, though. I mean, would you help him out if money was involved?"

"Well, I think he's kind of a sad person, but I can't remember him ever doing anything to hurt someone else. I don't think he's smart enough. Yeah, I guess I'd help him. It depends."

Jacques took a deep breath and let it out slowly. "Well, listen," he said, "he wants me to do him a big favor. Tell me what you think."

"It's about that time, Marîd," called Chiri from the other end of the bar.

I glanced at my watch and saw that it was almost half past three. There were only two other customers in the club now, and they'd been sitting there for almost an hour. No one but Jacques had come in during that time. We weren't going to do any more business tonight. "Okay," I announced to the dancers, "you ladies can get dressed now."

"Yay!" shouted Pualani. She and the four others hurried to the dressing room to put on their street clothes. Chiri began counting out the register. The two customers, who had been having deep, meaningful conversations with Kandy and Windy just a moment before, stared at each other in bewilderment.

I got up and tapped on the overhead lights, then sat down again beside Jacques. I've always thought that there is no lonelier place in the city than a bar in the Budayeen at closing time. "What's this that Fuad wants you to do?" I said wearily.

"It's a long story," said Jacques.

"Terrific. Why didn't you come in eight hours ago, when I felt more like hearing long stories?"

"Just listen. Fuad comes up to me this afternoon with this long, mournful look on his face. You know the look I mean. You'd think the world was coming to an end and he'd just found out he hadn't been invited. Anyway, I was having a little lunch at the Solace with Mahmoud and the Half-Hajj. Fuad comes up and drags a chair over and sits down. Starts eating off my plate, too."

"Yeah, sounds like our boy, all right," I said. I prayed to Allah that Jacques would get to the point in less time than it had taken Fuad.

"I slapped his hand and told him to go away, because we were having an important discussion. We weren't, really, but I wasn't in the mood to put up with him. So he says he needed somebody to help him get his money back. Saied says, 'Fuad, you let another one of those working girls steal your money again?' And Fuad says no, it wasn't anything like that.

"Then he takes out this official-looking paper and hands it to Saied, who glanced at it and handed it to me, and I looked at it and passed it on to Mahmoud. 'What's this?' Mahmoud says.

" 'It's a cashier's check for twenty-four hundred kiam,' says Fuad.

" 'How'd you get it?' I ask.

" 'It's a long story,' he says."

I closed my eyes and held the ice-cold glass against my throbbing forehead. I could've chipped in my pain-blocking daddy, but it was sitting in a rack in my briefcase on my desk in my suite in Friedlander Bey's mansion.

"Jacques," I said in a low, dangerous voice, "you said this is a long story, and now *Fuad's* said this is a long story, and I don't want to listen to a long story. Okay? Can you just kind of go over the high points from here on?"

"Sure, Marîd, take it easy. What he said was that he'd been saving up his money for months, that he wanted to buy a used electric van from some guy in Rasmiyya. He said he could live in the van cheaper than renting an apartment, and he also planned to go on a trip to visit his folks in Tripoli."

"That where Faud's from? I didn't know that."

Jacques shrugged. "Anyway, he said the guy in Rasmiyya quoted him a price of twenty-four hundred kiam for this van. Fuad swears it was in great shape and only needed a little work here and there, and he'd gotten all of his money together and had a bank check drawn up in the other guy's name. That afternoon, he walked all the way from the Budayeen to Rasmiyya, and the guy had sold the van to somebody else, after promising he'd hold it for Fuad."

I shook my head. "Fuad, all right. What a hopeless son of a bitch."

"So Fuad trudges all the way back through the eastern gate, and finds us at the Café Solace and tells us his tale of woe. Mahmoud just laughed in his face, and Saied was wearing Rex, his ass-kicker moddy, so Fuad was totally beneath his notice. I kind of felt sorry for him, though."

"Uh huh," I said. I had trouble believing that Jacques felt sorry for Fuad. If that were true, the heavens would have split open or something, and I didn't think they had. "What did Fuad want you to do?"

Jacques squirmed uneasily on his bar stool. "Well, apparently Fuad has never had his own bank account. He keeps his money in cash in an old cigar box or something. That's why he had to have a bank check drawn up. So here he was, stuck with a cashier's check made out to somebody else, and no way to get his twenty-four hundred kiam back."

"Ah," I said. I began to see the predicament.

"He wants me to cash it for him," said Jacques.

"So do it."

"I don't know," said Jacques. "It's a lot of money."

"So *don't* do it."

"Yeah, but—"

I looked at him in exasperation. "Well, Jacques, what the hell do you want *me* to do?"

He stared down into his empty beer glass for a few seconds. He was more uncomfortable than I'd ever seen him. Over the years, he's derived a lot of fierce glee by reminding me that I was half-French and half-Berber, while he was superior to the tune of one whole European grandparent. It must have cost him a lot of self-esteem to come to me for advice.

"Maghrebi," he said, "you're getting quite a reputation lately as someone who can fix things. You know, solve problems and stuff."

Sure, I was. Since I became Friedlander Bey's reluctant avenger, I've had to deal directly and violently with some vicious bad-guy types. Now many of my friends looked at me differently. I imagined they were whispering to each other, "Be careful of Marîd—these days, he can arrange to have your legs broken."

I was becoming a force to be reckoned with in the Budayeen—and beyond it as well, in the rest of the city. Occasionally I had misgivings about that. As interested as I was in the tasks Papa gave me, despite the glamorous power I could now wield, there were still many days when all I really wanted was to run my little club in peace.

"What do you want me to do, Jacques? Strong-arm the guy who screwed Fuad? Grab him by the throat and shake him until he sells the van to him?"

"Well, no, Marîd, that's silly. The guy doesn't even have the van anymore."

I'd come to the end of my patience. "Then *what*, goddamn it?"

Jacques looked at me and then immediately looked away. "I took the cashier's check from Fuad and I don't know what to do with it. Just tell me what you'd do."

"Jeez, Jacques, I'd deposit it. I'd put it in my account and wait for it to clear. When the twenty-four hundred kiam showed up on my balance, I'd withdraw it and give it to Fuad. But not before. Wait for the check to clear first."

Jacques's face widened in a shaky smile. "Thanks, Marîd. You know they call you Al-Amîn on the Street now? 'The Trustworthy.' You're a big man in the Budayeen these days."

Some of my poorer neighbors had begun referring to me as Shaykh Marîd the Trustworthy, just because I'd loaned them a little money and opened a few soup kitchens. No big deal. After all, the holy Qur'ân requires us to look after the welfare of others.

"Yeah," I said sourly, "Shaykh Marîd. That's me, all right."

Jacques chewed his lip and then came to a decision. "Then why don't you do it?" he said. He pulled the pale green check from his shirt pocket and put it down in front of me. "Why don't you go ahead and deposit it for Fuad? I really don't have the time."

I laughed. "You don't have the *time?*"

"I got some other things to worry about. Besides, there are reasons why I don't want the twenty-four hundred kiam showing up on my bank balance."

I stared at him for a moment. This was just so typical. "Your problem, Jacques, is that tonight you came *real close* to doing someone a good deed, but you're catching yourself in the nick of time. No, I don't see any reason why I should."

"I'm asking you as a friend, Marîd."

"I'll do this much," I said. "I'll stand up for Fuad. If you're so afraid of being stiffed, I'll guarantee the check. Got something to write with?" Jacques handed me a pen and I turned the check over and endorsed it, first with the name of the guy who'd broken Fuad's heart, then with my own signature. Then I pushed the check back toward him with my fingertips.

"I appreciate it, Marîd," he said.

"You know, Jacques, you should've paid more attention to fairy stories when you were young. You're acting like one of the bad princes who pass by the old woman in distress on the road. Bad princes always end up getting eaten by a *djinn*, you know. Or are you mostly European types immune to folk wisdom?"

"I don't need the moral lecture," said Jacques with a scowl.

"Listen, I expect something from you in return."

He gave me a weak smile. "Sure, Marîd. Business is business."

"And action is action. That's how things work around here. I want you to take a little job for me, *mon ami*. For the last few months now, Friedlander Bey has been talking about getting involved with the datalink industry. He told me to watch out for a bright-eyed, hard-working person to represent his new enterprise. How would you like to get in on the ground floor?"

Jacques's good humor disappeared. "I don't know if I have the time," he said. His voice was very worried.

"You'll love it. You'll be making so much money, *inshallah*, you'll forget all about your other activities." This was one of those cases when the will of God was synonymous with Friedlander Bey.

His eyes shifted back and forth like a small animal in a trap. "I really don't want—"

"I think you *do* want to, Jacques. But don't worry

about it for now. We'll discuss it over lunch in a day or two. Now I'm glad you came to me with your problem. I think this will work out very nicely for both of us."

"Got to deposit this in the bank machine," he said. He got up from his stool, muttered something under his breath, and went back out into the night. I was willing to bet that he deeply regretted passing by Chiri's tonight. I almost laughed at the look on his face when he left.

Not much later, a tall, strong black man with a shaven head and a grim expression came into the club. It was my slave, Kmuzu. He stood just inside the door, waiting for me to pay Chiri and the dancers and lock up the bar. Kmuzu was there to drive me home. He was also there to spy on me for Friedlander Bey.

Chiri was always glad to see him. "Kmuzu, honey, sit down and have a drink!" she said. It was the first time she'd sounded cheerful in at least six hours. She wouldn't have much luck with him, though. Chiri was seriously hungry for Kmuzu's body, but he didn't seem to return her interest. I think Chiri'd begun to regret the ritual scars and tattoos on her face, because they seemed to disturb him. Still, every night she offered him a drink, and he replied that he was a devout Christian and didn't consume alcohol; he let her pour him a glass of orange juice instead. And he told her that he wouldn't consider a normal relationship with a woman until he'd won his freedom.

He understands that I *intend* to free him, but not just yet. For one thing, Papa—Friedlander Bey—had given Kmuzu to me, and he wouldn't permit me to announce any free-lance emancipations. For another, well, as much as I hate to admit it, I liked having Kmuzu around in that capacity.

"Here you go, Mr. Boss," said Chiri. She'd taken the day's receipts, pocketed half off the top according to our agreement, and now slapped a still-healthy stack of kiam on the bar in front of me. It had taken me quite a while to overcome my guilt at banking so much money every day without actually working, but in the end I'd succeeded. I was no longer bothered by it, because of the good works I sponsored, which cost me about 5 percent of my weekly income.

"Come get your money," I called. I wouldn't have to call twice. The assortment of real girls, sexchanges, and pre-operation debs who worked on Chiri's nightshift lined up to get their wages and the commissions on the drinks they'd hustled. Windy, Kandy, and Pualani took their money and hurried out into the night without a word. Lily, who'd harbored a crush on me for months, kissed me on the cheek and whispered an invitation to go out drinking with her. I just patted her cute little ass and turned to Yasmin.

She flipped her beautiful black hair over her shoulder. "Does Indihar wait up for you?" she said. "Or do you still go to bed alone?" She grabbed the cash from my hand and followed Lily out of the club. She'd never forgiven me for getting married.

"Want me to straighten her out, Marîd?" asked Chiri.

"No, but thanks anyway." I was grateful for her concern. Except for a few brief periods of unfortunate misunderstanding, Chiri had long been my best friend in the city.

"Everything okay with Indihar?" she asked.

"Everything's just fine. I hardly ever see her. She has an apartment for herself and the kids in the other wing of Papa's mansion. Yasmin was right about me going to bed alone."

"Uh huh," said Chiri. "That won't last long. I saw the way you used to stare at Indihar."

"It's just a marriage of convenience."

"Uh huh. Well, I got my money, so I'm going home. Though I don't know why I bother, there's nobody waiting there for me, either. I got every sex-moddy Honey Pílar ever made, but nobody to jam with. Guess I'll just pull my old shawl around my shoulders and sit in my rocking chair with my memories, and rock and rock until I fall asleep. Such a waste of my sexual prime, though." She kept looking at Kmuzu with her eyes all big and round, and trying real hard to stifle her grin but not having much success. Finally, she just scooped up her zipper bag, downed a shot of *tende* from her private stock, and left Kmuzu and me alone in the club.

"You're not really needed here every night, *yaa Sidi*," said Kmuzu. "The woman, Chiriga, is fully able to keep order. It would be better for you to remain at home and tend to your more pressing concerns."

"Which concerns are those, Kmuzu?" I asked, tapping off all the lights and following him out onto the sidewalk. I locked up the club and began walking down the Street toward the great eastern gate, beyond which lay the Boulevard il-Jameel and my car.

"You have important work to do for the master of the house."

He meant Papa. "Papa can get along without me for a little longer," I said. "I'm still recuperating from my ordeal."

I did not in any way want to be a heavy hitter. I did not want to be Shaykh Marîd Audran al-Amîn. I desperately wanted to go back to scrabbling for a living, maybe missing a meal now and then but having the satisfaction of being my own man, and not being marked for doom by all the other heavy hitters in the game.

You just couldn't explain that kind of thing to Friedlander Bey. He had an answer for everything; sometimes the answer was bribes and rewards, and sometimes it was physical torture. It was like complaining to God about sand fleas. He has more important things on His mind.

A warm breeze offered conflicting fragrances: roasting meat from the cookshops, spilled beer, the scent of gardenias, the stink of vomit. Down the block, a starved-looking man in a long white shirt and white cotton trousers was using a green plastic hose to wash the night's trash from the sidewalk into the gutter. He grinned toothlessly at us as we approached, turning the stream of water to the side as we passed. "Shaykh Marîd," he said in a hoarse voice. I nodded to him, sure that I'd never seen him before.

Even with Kmuzu beside me, I felt terribly forlorn. The Budayeen did that to me sometimes, very late at night. Even the Street, which was never completely quiet, was mostly deserted, and our footsteps echoed on the bricks and flat paving stones. Music came from another club a block away, the raucous noise worn to a mournful smoothness by the distance. I carried the dregs of my last White Death in a plastic go-cup, and I swallowed it, tasting only ice water and lime and a hint of gin. I wasn't ready for the night to be ending.

As we walked nearer to the arched gate at the eastern end of the walled quarter, I felt a great, expectant hush settle over me. I shuddered. I wasn't sure if what I felt was some mysterious signal from my unconscious mind, or merely the result of too many drinks and too much tiredness.

I stopped in my tracks on the sidewalk at the corner of Third Street. Kmuzu stopped, too, and gave me a questioning look. Bright blood-red neon zigzags framed a holo display for one of the inexpensive Kafiristani bodmod clinics on the Street. I glanced at the holo for a moment, watching a plump, slack-featured boy metamorphose into a slender, voluptuous girl. Hurray for the miracles of time-lapse holography and elective surgery.

I turned my face up to the sky. I suddenly understood that my few days of respite were coming to an end, that I'd have to move along to the next stage of my development. Of course, I've had this sensation before. Many times, as a matter of fact, but this was different. Tonight I had no illicit drugs in my system at all.

"Jeez," I muttered, feeling a chill in that desert summer night, and leaning against the clinic's plate-glass front.

"What is it, *yaa Sidi?*" asked Kmuzu.

I looked at him for a moment, grateful for his presence. I told him what had just passed through my dazzled mind.

"That was no message from the stars, *yaa Sidi*. That was what the master of the house told you this morning. You'd taken an unfortunate number of Sonneine tablets, so perhaps you don't remember. The master of the house said he had decided what the next step of his vengeance should be."

"That's what I was afraid of, Kmuzu. Any idea what he means?" I liked it better when I thought the crazy notion had come from outer space.

"He does not share all his thoughts with me, *yaa Sidi.*"

I heard a low rustling sound and I turned, suddenly afraid. It was only the wind. As we walked the rest of the way down the Street, the wind grew stronger and louder, until it was whipping scraps of paper and fallen leaves in fierce whirling gusts. The wind began to drag sullen clouds across the night sky, covering the stars, hiding the fat yellow moon.

And then the wind died, just as we emerged from the Budayeen onto the boulevard beyond the wall. Suddenly everything was quiet and calm again. The sky was still overcast, and the moon was a pale glow behind a silver cloud.

I turned to look back at the eastern gate. I don't believe in prescience or premonitions, but I do recall the disquiet I felt as Kmuzu and I headed toward my cream-colored Westphalian sedan parked nearby. Whatever it was, I said nothing of it to Kmuzu. He is in every situation almost repellently rational.

"I want to get home quickly, Kmuzu," I said, waiting for him to unlock the passenger door.

"Yes, *yaa Sidi.*" I got into the car and waited for him to walk around and get behind the wheel. He tapped in the ignition code and steered the electric car north on the broad, divided street.

"I'm feeling pretty strange tonight," I complained, leaning my head back against the seat and closing my eyes.

"You say that almost every night."

"I mean it this time. I'm starting to feel very uncomfortable. Everything seems different to me now. I look at these tenements and I see they're like human ant farms. I hear a scrap of music, and suddenly I'm listening to somebody's cry of anguish lost in the void. I'm not in the mood for mystical revelations, Kmuzu. How do I make them stop?"

He uttered a low-pitched laugh. "You could sober up, *yaa Sidi.*"

"I told you, it's not that. I am sober."

"Yes, of course, *yaa Sidi.*"

I watched the city slide by beyond my window. I wasn't up to arguing with him any further. I did feel sober and wide-awake. I felt filled with energy, which at four o'clock in the morning is something I hate a lot. It's the wrong time of day for enthusiasm. The solution to that was simple, of course: a largish dose of butaqualide HCL when I got home. The beauties would give me a few minutes of delicious confusion, and then I'd fall out for a good night's sleep. In the morning, I wouldn't even remember this unpleasant interlude of clarity.

We rode in silence for a while, and gradually the weird mood left me. Kmuzu wheeled the car toward Friedlander Bey's palace, which lay just beyond the city's Christian quarter. It would be good to get home, stand under a hot shower for a few minutes, and then read a little before going to sleep. One of the reasons I'd been staying in Chiri's until closing time every night was that I wanted to avoid running into anyone at the house. At four o'clock, they'd all be sound asleep. I wouldn't have to face them until morning.

"Yaa Sidi," said Kmuzu, "there was an important call for you this evening."

"I'll listen to my messages before breakfast."

"I think you ought to hear about it now."

I didn't like the sound of that, although I couldn't imagine what the trouble could be. I used to hate answering my phone, because I owed money to so many people. Nowadays, though, other people owed *me* money. "It's not my long-lost brother, is it? He hasn't shown up expecting me to share my good fortune with him, has he?"

"No, it wasn't your brother, *yaa Sidi.* And even if it were, why wouldn't you be glad to—"

"I wasn't serious, Kmuzu." Kmuzu's a very intelligent guy, and I've come to depend on him quite a lot, but he has this huge blind spot where other people have a sense of humor. "What was the message, then?"

He turned from the street into the gate to Papa's mansion. We paused long enough at the guard's post to be identified, then rolled slowly up the curving driveway. "You've been invited to a celebratory dinner," he said. "In honor of your return."

"Uh huh," I said. I'd already endured two or three of those in recent days. Evidently, most of Friedlander Bey's minions in the Budayeen felt obliged to fete us, or risk having their livelihoods stripped away. Well, I'd gotten some free meals and some decent gifts out of it, but I thought all that had come to an end. "Who is it this time? Frenchy?" He owned the club where Yasmin used to work.

"A man of much greater significance. Shaykh Reda Abu Adil."

I just stared in disbelief. "I've been invited to have dinner with our worst enemy?"

"Yes, *yaa Sidi.*"

"When is this dinner, then?" I asked.

"After evening prayers tonight, *yaa Sidi.* Shaykh Reda has a busy schedule, and tonight was the only possible time."

I let out a deep breath. Kmuzu had stopped the car at the foot of the wide marble stairs leading up to the mahogany front door. "I wonder if Papa would mind if I slept late this morning, then," I said.

"The master of the house gave me specific instructions to make certain you attended him at breakfast."

"I'm definitely not looking forward to this, Kmuzu."

"To breakfast? Then eat lightly, if your stomach is still upset."

"No," I said with some exasperation, "to this dinner party with Shaykh Reda. I hate being off-balance. I don't have any idea what the purpose of this meeting is, and it's fifty-fifty that Papa won't see fit to tell me about it."

Kmuzu shrugged. "Your judgment will see you through, *yaa Sidi.* And I will be there with you."

"Thank you, Kmuzu," I said, getting out of the car. Actually, I felt better about having him around than I did about my judgment. But I couldn't very well tell *him* that.

11

I'll always remember it as "The Day of Three Meals."

Actually, the meals themselves were not memorable—in fact, I can't remember much about what I actually ate that day. The significance comes from what happened and what was said across the three tables.

The day began with Kmuzu shaking me awake a full half hour earlier than I'd planned to get up. My alarm-clock daddy was set for half past seven, but Friedlander Bey had moved up the breakfast hour by thirty minutes. I hate getting up, whether it's bright-eyed, high-stepping, and resentful thanks to the chip, or sluggish, yawning, and resentful thanks to Kmuzu. I figured if Allah had wanted us up that early, He wouldn't have invented noon.

I also hate breakfast. Lately, however, I'd been sharing an early morning meal with Friedlander Bey about four times a week. I imagined that things would only get worse, as Papa loaded me with more and more responsibility.

I always wore conservative Arab dress to those meetings. I spent more time in a *gallebeya* than I did in blue jeans, work shirt, and boots. My former standard of dress hung on a hook in the closet, and silently reproached me every time I glanced that way.

The jeans were a constant reminder of what I'd given up since Papa'd tapped me with his magic finger. I'd traded away much of what I formerly called "freedom"; the ironic thing was that every one of my friends would pay that much and more to have the luxuries I now enjoyed. At first, I hated Papa for the loss of my liberty. Now, although I sometimes still had twinges of regret in the dark night, I realized that Friedlander Bey had given me a great opportunity. My horizons had expanded far beyond anything I might have imagined in the old days. Nevertheless, I was acutely aware that I could decline neither the luxuries nor the new responsibilities. In some ways, I was the proverbial bird in the proverbial gilded cage.

The money was nice, though.

So I showered and trimmed my red beard, and dressed in the robe and *keffiya* that Kmuzu had chosen for me. Then we went downstairs to the small dining room.

Friedlander Bey was already there, of course, tended by Tariq, his valet. Kmuzu seated me at my usual place, and then stood behind my chair. "Good morning to you, my nephew," said Papa. "I trust you arose this morning in well-being."

"*Il-hamdu lillah,*" I said. Praise be to God.

For breakfast there was a bowl of steamed wheat cereal with orange peel and nuts; a platter of eggs; a platter of breakfast meats; and, of course, coffee. Papa let Tariq serve him some eggs and roast lamb. "I've given you several days to relax, O Excellent One," he said. "But now the time for rest is over. I wish to know what you've done to advance the datalink project."

"I believe I've got an excellent agent in my friend, Jacques. I did a favor for him, and now I think he's willing to do a small favor for me in return."

Papa beamed at me as if I were a prize pupil. "Very good, my son!" he said. "I'm delighted that you're learning the ways of power so readily. Now let me show you the datalink terminal you'll be using—rather, that your friend will be using." Tariq left the room and returned shortly with what appeared to be a hard-sided briefcase. He placed it on the table, snapped its latches, and raised the lid.

"Wow," I said, impressed by the compact design of the terminal, "that's a little beauty."

"Indeed," said Friedlander Bey. "It has its commlink built-in, as well as the conventional datalink printer. To save on cost, this model doesn't accept voice commands. Everything must be keyed in manually. I expect, however, that the datalink project will earn out its set-up expenses within six months to a year, and then we can begin replacing these terminals with voice-activated models."

I nodded. "And it's up to me to sell the owners of every bar, nightclub, and restaurant in the Budayeen on the idea of renting one of them from me. I don't get it. I don't see why people will pay twenty-five fiqs for an information service that's now provided free by the city."

"We've been contracted by the city," Tariq explained. "The amir's special commission decided that it couldn't afford to run Info any longer. Within weeks, all the free Info terminals will be replaced by our machines, *inshallah.*"

"I know that," I said. "What I meant was what do I do if the bar owners flat-out refuse?"

Friedlander Bey flashed a cold smile. "Don't worry about that," he said. "We have specialized technicians who will persuade those reluctant proprietors."

"Specialized technicians." I loved the euphemism. All of Papa's technicians have names like Guido and Tiny and Igor.

Papa went on. "It would be best if you and your friend worked as a team for a few days, before you send him off on his own. When we have the whole Budayeen covered, we can begin to exercise even closer control. We can tell who is using the service, and what questions they're asking. Because they have to use an official identification card to log on, we can monitor the dispensing of information. We could even prevent certain information from getting to some individuals."

"But surely we won't do that," I said.

Papa was silent for a second or two. "Of course not," he said at last. "That would be contrary to the principles of the holy Prophet."

"May the blessings of Allah be on him and peace," I responded automatically.

Tariq laid a booklet in front of me. "Here is the complete set of commands," he said, "and in the back of the book is a pocket with a special ID card, so that you won't have to pay for calls."

"Thank you," I said. "I'll familiarize myself with these commands today, and tomorrow I'll go with Jacques to talk to the club owners on the Street."

"Excellent, my nephew," said Papa. "Now, as to our vengeance. It would be best if it combined the discovery of the real murderer of Khalid Maxwell, as well as the disposition of those who plotted against us. I will accept only the most elegant solution."

"What if Dr. Sadiq Abd ar-Razzaq wasn't actually involved?" I asked. I was referring to the imam who'd given permission for Hajjar and his goons to kidnap us.

Papa flew into a rage. "Don't talk to me about that son of a diseased camel!" he cried. I'd never seen him show so much emotion. His face turned blood red, and his fists shook as his fury carried him away.

"O Shaykh—"

"The people of the Budayeen are crazy with worry!" he said, pounding the table. "All they can think about is what might happen if we're kidnapped again, and if this time we don't return. There are ugly rumors going around that we've lost control, that our associates no longer enjoy protection. The last few days, all I've done is calm and soothe my troubled friends. Well, I swear on the life of my children that I will not be weakened, nor will I be pushed aside! I have a plan, my nephew. Wait and see if that cursed imam can separate me again from the people who love me. If he is not involved, then *make* him involved."

"Yes, O Shaykh," I said.

Jeez. That's the way things worked around *that* breakfast table. Punishments and rewards were handed out with a blithe disregard for appropriateness. Sometimes Friedlander Bey reminded me of the whimsical Greek gods in the works of Homer—whimsical in that they often disturbed entire human nations because of some imagined slight, or out of boredom, or for no particular reason at all.

Even while Papa spoke about the datalink project, I could see that he was now controlled by hate, and it would continue until he could strike a deadly blow against those who'd conspired against us. Friedlander Bey's motto was "Getting even is the best revenge." Nothing else would do, no forgiveness for the sake of moral superiority, no intensely ironic symbolic acts.

It wasn't only the Bani Salim who demanded proper retaliation. That concept was stated explicitly in the noble Qur'ân, and it was part of the Muslim point of view, something the Western world had learned the hard way on numerous occasions. Someone would die—Hajjar, Shaykh Mahali, Dr. Abd ar-Razzaq, the actual murderer of Khalid Maxwell—and it seemed to be up to me to choose whom.

Friedlander Bey frowned in concentration. "There's another stone in my shoe," he said at last. "I'm speaking of Police Lieutenant Hajjar. Fortunately, it's very simple to rid oneself of such an irritation."

"Didn't he work for you, once upon a time?" I asked.

Papa turned his head and pretended to spit on the floor. "He's a traitor. He goes with whoever offers the most money at the time. He had no honor, no loyalty. I'm glad he works for Shaykh Reda now and not for me. I couldn't trust him when he was my man. Now I know where he is, and I suspect that I could buy him back at any time, if I wished. I may do that; and then when I have him, I can empty my shoe of him at my leisure."

He was talking murder here. Once upon a time I might have been appalled at the casual way Papa discussed terminating someone, but no longer. I looked at the situation as one of the Bedu might, and I knew Papa was entirely correct. It was just a matter of planning. All the details had yet to be worked out, but that was not difficult. I was only concerned that first Papa talked about eliminating the imam, and now Lieutenant Hajjar. I didn't think we ought to get into depopulating the city in our rightful wrath.

A few minutes later I was in my office, tapping trial commands into the data deck. I found that I could learn just about anything about anybody in the city with that little machine. With my special, confidential commands, I had free access to information the average citizen didn't even know had been recorded. I got a dizzying sense of power as I pried into the private lives of both friends and enemies. I felt like a high-tech snoop, and the feeling was delicious.

When I'd gotten proficient with the datalink terminal, I was able to get a list of all of Dr. Abd ar-Razzaq's phone calls for the last two months, incoming and outgoing. The incoming calls were identified by their commcodes only. Then I did the same for Lieutenant Hajjar's commcode at the police station. I found that Hajjar and the imam had spoken together eleven times during those eight weeks. There were probably other calls from other phones, but I didn't need to track them all down. This evidence would never have to be admitted in a court of law.

About half an hour before I planned to have lunch, Kmuzu announced that I had visitors. They were Indihar and bin Turki, the Bani Salim youth.

"Morning of well-being," I said to them.

"Morning of light, husband," said Indihar. "I hope we're not interrupting your work."

I indicated that they could get comfortable on my couch. "No, not at all. It gives me pleasure to see you. And I was going to knock off for lunch in a little while, anyway. Is there something you need?"

"I bring you words of greeting from your mother," said Indihar. "She wonders why you've only visited her once since your return."

Well, the truth was that she still made me uncomfortable. She'd arrived in the city several months ago, looking brassy and blowsy. She'd been a hooker for most of her life, but I'd taken her in and given her a suite of rooms in the eastern wing, and she'd worked hard to tone down her style and be acceptable in Friedlander Bey's house. We'd talked at great length and finally reconciled, but she still embarrassed me. I understood that was my problem, not hers, and I'd tried to overcome my feelings. I wasn't all the way there yet, despite the good works my mother was doing in the city, using my money to establish and run soup kitchens and shelters. Her behavior was certainly laudable, but I couldn't erase the memory of how shocked I was to see her after a long time.

"Tell Umm Marîd that I've been very busy trying to catch up with all that happened while I was gone. Tell her that I'll come to see her very soon. Give her my love and ask her forgiveness for my inattention."

"Yes, husband," said Indihar. I don't think she was satisfied by my response, but she said nothing more.

Bin Turki cleared his throat. "I have much to be thankful for, O Shaykh," he said. "Every day brings wonder upon wonder. I see things that my brothers would not believe, even if I told them myself. Yet I wish to be free to explore your world as I wish. I have no money, and because of that I have no liberty. We Bani Salim are not used to imprisonment, even under such pleasant conditions as these."

I chewed my lip in thought. "You really think you're ready to step outside these walls? You've learned enough already to protect yourself against the well-dressed wolves of the city?"

The young man shrugged. "Perhaps I don't know how to keep out of trouble, but I claim the right to learn for myself."

Then I had a sudden inspiration. "You will need money, as you say. Would you consider doing some work for me, for which I'll see that you're rewarded with a moderate weekly salary?"

Bin Turki's eyes opened wider. "Certainly, O Shaykh,"

he said, his voice trembling. "I thank you for the opportunity."

"You don't know what I want yet," I said grimly. "Do you recall the story of our kidnapping and transporting to the Rub al-Khali?"

"Yes, O Shaykh."

"Do you remember how I spoke of the unnecessarily cruel sergeant in the town of Najran? How he beat the old shaykh for no reason?"

"Yes, O Shaykh."

I opened my desk drawer and took out the suborbital ticket. I pushed it across the desk. "Here, then," I said. "His name was Sergeant al-Bishah. You can leave tomorrow morning." That was all.

Indihar's hand went to her mouth. "Marîd!" she exclaimed. She'd guessed what sort of mission I was sending the young man on, and she was clearly shocked.

Bin Turki hesitated a moment, then accepted the ticket.

"Good," I said. "When you get back, there will be five thousand kiam for you, and a weekly allowance of two hundred kiam. With that you'll be able to rent a house or an apartment and lead your own life as you wish, but you'll always have the gratitude of Friedlander Bey and myself."

"That is worth more to me than any amount of money," murmured bin Turki.

"Indihar," I said, "would you mind taking our young friend under your wing? Help him find a place to live, and give him advice to keep him and his money safe?"

"I'd be happy to, husband," she said. Her expression was troubled. She hadn't seen the new me before.

"I thank both of you," I said. "Now, I have work to do."

"Good day to you, then, husband," said Indihar, rising.

"Yes, thank you, O Shaykh," said bin Turki. I pretended to be engrossed in some papers, and they left quietly. I was shaking like a newborn lamb. I hadn't seen the new me yet, either.

I waited for five minutes, for ten minutes. I was waiting for my sense of moral outrage to make itself heard, but it never happened. One part of my mind sat aloof, judging me, and what it discovered was unsettling. Apparently, I had no moral qualms at all about dispatching people on grim assignments. I tried to work up some sense of sadness, but it was impossible. I felt nothing. It wasn't something to be proud of, and I decided it was not something I could tell anyone about. Like Friedlander Bey, I had learned to live with what I had to do.

I told my data deck to quit, and when the screen of the monitor went dark, I began to make plans for lunch. I'd seen Jacques since I'd been home, but I hadn't run into Mahmoud or Saied. I knew they'd probably be sitting on the patio of the Café Solace, playing cards and gossiping. Suddenly that seemed like just what I needed. I called Kmuzu, and told him that I wanted to be driven to the Budayeen. He nodded wordlessly and went to get the Westphalian sedan.

We parked on the Boulevard il-Jameel, and walked through the eastern gate. The Street was filled with daytime tourists who would soon regret the fact that they'd ignored their hotel manager's advice that they should avoid the walled quarter. If they didn't leave soon, they'd be hustled for every loose kiam in their pockets and purses.

Kmuzu and I walked to the Solace, and just as I suspected, I saw my three friends sitting at a table near the patio's iron railing. I went through the small gate and joined them.

"Hullo, Marîd," said Jacques in a dull voice. "Hullo, Kmuzu."

"Where y'at, Marîd?" said Mahmoud.

"I been wondering what happened to you," said Saied the Half-Hajj. He'd been my best friend at one time, but he'd betrayed me to Shaykh Reda Abu Adil, and since then I'd kept a close eye on him.

"I'm fine," I said. "I suppose you've all heard the story."

"Yeah, we heard it," said Mahmoud, "but we haven't heard it from you. You were snatched, right? Out of the amir's palace? I thought Papa had more on the ball than that."

"Papa's pretty shrewd," said the Half-Hajj. "It's just that Shaykh Reda is shrewder than they gave him credit for."

"I have to admit that's true," I said.

"Kmuzu, sit down," said Jacques. "You don't have to play slave with us. We like you. Have a drink or something."

"Thank you," said Kmuzu in a flat voice. "I prefer to remain standing."

"We insist," grumbled Mahmoud. "You're making us nervous." Kmuzu nodded, then got a chair from another table and sat behind me.

Old Ibrahim came to take my order, and I just had a plate of *hummus* and bread, and a gin and bingara to wash it all down.

"Bleah," said Mahmoud.

I turned to respond, but I was interrupted by a man who came to the iron railing. "Shaykh Marîd," he said in an urgent voice, "do you remember me?"

I looked at him for a moment, but although I knew I'd seen him before, I couldn't place precisely where. "I'm sorry," I said.

"My name is Nikos Kouklis. A few months ago, you lent me the money to open my own gyro-souvlaki shop on Ninth Street. Since then, I've done better than I'd ever dreamed. My shop is successful, my wife is happy, my children are well fed and well dressed. Here. It gives me great pleasure to return to you your investment, and my wife made a pan of baklava for you. Please accept it, with my undying gratitude."

I was taken aback. I'd loaned lots of people a little money here and there, but this was the first time one of them had made a big deal out of paying me back. Indeed, it made me a little uncomfortable. "You keep that money," I said. "Save it for your wife and children."

"I'm sorry, O Shaykh," said Kouklis, "but I insist on repaying you."

I understood the man's pride, and I took the money with a courteous nod. I also accepted the plate of baklava. "May your success continue," I said. "May your fortunes increase."

"I owe everything to you," said the Greek restaurant owner. "I will be in your debt forever."

"Perhaps someday there will come a chance to discharge it," I said.

"Anything," said Kouklis. "Anytime." He bowed to the four of us and backed away.

"Oh, Mr. Bigshot," said Mahmoud mockingly.

"Yeah," I said, "that's right. What have *you* ever done for anybody?"

"Well—" Mahmoud began.

I cut him off. I'd known Mahmoud since he'd been a slim-hipped girl named Misty, working for Jo-Mama. I knew that I couldn't trust him as far as I could throw him. Nowadays, with the weight he'd put on after his sexchange, that was about a foot and a half.

Instead, I turned to Jacques and said, "You still up to helping us out?"

"Of course." Jacques looked a little frightened. As with most of the people of the Budayeen, he preferred to accept the protection of the house of Friedlander Bey, but he was scared out of his mind when it came time to repay that generosity.

"Then call me tomorrow, about noon," I said. "You have my number at Papa's mansion, don't you?"

"Uh huh," said Jacques nervously.

"Oh," said Mahmoud, "have you sold out now, too?"

"Look who's talking," said Jacques. "Mr. Lackey of Shaykh Reda himself finds room to criticize."

"I'm no one's lackey," said Mahmoud, half-rising from his seat.

"Oh no, of course not," said Saied.

I ignored their childish debate. "I've got the hardware, Jacques," I said, "and I've been playing around with it, and it definitely looks like a good deal for us as well as for the club owners who subscribe. You don't have to worry about doing anything illicit—we have a complete set of permits from the city, and everything's legal and above-board."

"Then why is Friedlander Bey interested?" said Mahmoud. "I didn't think he cared about anything that wasn't at least a little bit bent."

The Half-Hajj leaned back in his chair and regarded Mahmoud for a few seconds. "You know, my friend," he said at last, "someday somebody's going to take care of that mouth of yours. You're going to wish you'd never changed sexes and joined the big boys."

Mahmoud only laughed disdainfully. "Any time you think you're man enough, Saied," he said.

The bickering was interrupted by the arrival of Yasmin. "How y'all are?" she asked.

"Fine," said the Half-Hajj. "We're just sitting here in the sun, drinking and eating baklava and listening to ourselves claw at each other's throats. Have some?"

Yasmin was tempted by the honey pastry, but she exercised more restraint than I gave her credit for. "No," she said, smiling, "can't do it. Hips are just right the way they are."

"I'll second that," said Jacques.

"You bad boy," said Yasmin.

"Listen, Yasmin," I said.

"The hell do *you* want, married man?" she said bitterly.

"I was only wondering when you were going to drop this jealousy thing."

"*What* jealousy thing?" she asked haughtily. "You think I even think about such midges and mites as you and Indihar? I have more important things on my mind."

I shook my head. "As I see it," I said, "Islam gives me the option of marrying up to four wives, if I can support them all equally. That means that I can still date, even though I'm married to Indihar. And I'm married to her in name only."

"Ha!" cried Saied. "I knew it! You've never consummated that wedding, have you!"

I glared at him for a few seconds. "Yasmin," I said, "give me a break, all right? Let me buy you dinner sometime. I think we need to talk."

She frowned at me, giving me no encouragement at all. "We'll talk," she said. "We'll talk at the club tonight, if Indihar gives you permission to go out." Then she grabbed a piece of baklava, turned on her heel, and headed off down the Street.

Not long after she left, I got up and bid my friends good day. Then I had Kmuzu drive me back to Papa's estate. I still had paperwork to attend to.

The third meal of the day, of course, was *chez* Shaykh Reda. When I returned home after my lunch break, I tried to get a little work done. It was very difficult. I knew Friedlander Bey was counting on my contribution to both the datalink project and the on-going business of stabilizing or destabilizing the Muslim nations who came to us for help. Still, on this particular day, I couldn't help worrying a little about what was in Abu Adil's mind. Why had he invited us to dinner? To finish what he'd started when he'd had us kidnapped several weeks ago?

That's why I wore a small needle gun on my belt, turned around so that it rested in the small of my back. I chose the needle gun because it was constructed entirely of plastic, and wouldn't show up on an X-ray. It was loaded with razor flechettes, unpoisoned. Half a clip of those suckers would rip away enough flesh to be memorable, if the target survived.

I'd worn my best outfit to the wedding reception Shaykh Mahali had thrown, and so it had been destroyed by the rigors of our desert travels. I'd also given the valuable ceremonial dagger to Shaykh Hassanein. Tonight I wore my best remaining outfit, a long white *gallebeya* decorated with hand-embroidered flowers in a cream-colored silk thread. It was a beautiful *gallebeya,* and I was very proud of it. It had been a gift from a family in the Budayeen I'd given a little help to.

I wore sandals and a black-and-white checked *keffiya.* I also carried a sheathed dagger in the manner of the Bedu, front and center against my belly. When I put it on my belt, I decided to ask Friedlander Bey if we could bring bin Turki with us to the dinner. We'd already planned to bring Tariq and Youssef. We didn't want to offer ourselves up within Shaykh Reda's stronghold without a small army of our own.

Papa agreed that bin Turki might be useful, so he

accompanied the four of us to Shaykh Reda's mansion in the city's western district, Hâmidiyya. Abu Adil squatted like a toad in the center of one of the worst parts of town. His own estate was rivaled in the city only by Papa's and Shaykh Mahali's, but Shaykh Reda was surrounded by the burned-out, abandoned, fallen-in tenements of Hâmidiyya. It always reminded me of Satan sitting at the center of his hellish realm.

We drove through a gate in the high, brown brick wall that enclosed the mansion and stopped to identify ourselves to a guard. Then we parked the car and the five of us went to the front door. This time we wouldn't permit our party to be separated.

We had no trouble with the man who answered the doorbell. He led us to a small dining hall where places for ten had been set. Our group took seats at one end of the table, and we waited for Abu Adil to make his entrance.

And that's just what he did. A hefty bodyguard type entered first, followed by Shaykh Reda in a wheelchair, which was pushed by his little Kenneth. Following them came two more bruisers. I have no doubt that the shaykh watched our arrival from somewhere and made up a guest list of his employees equal to our number. Five against five.

"I'm happy you've chosen to honor my house," said Abu Adil. "We should do this sort of thing more often. Perhaps then there'd be less tension between us."

"We thank you for the invitation, O Shaykh," I said warily.

Kenneth was looking at me appraisingly. Then he gave a quiet laugh and shook his head. He had nothing but contempt for me, and I didn't know why. Maybe if I broke his fingers and toes for him, he'd lose that smirk. It was a harmless fantasy, I thought.

Servants brought in platters of couscous, kefta kabobs,

roast lamb, and vegetables in wonderful, succulent sauces. "In the name of Allah, the Beneficent, the Merciful, may it be pleasant to you!" said Shaykh Reda.

"May your table last forever, O Father of Generosity," said Friedlander Bey.

Papa and I ate sparingly, watching for any sign of treachery from Abu Adil or his musclemen. Bin Turki ate as if he'd never seen food before. I'm sure he'd never seen such a banquet.

I whispered to him, "Shaykh Reda is probably trying to seduce you away from our household." I didn't really mean it. It was a joke.

Bin Turki turned white. "You don't think my loyalty is for sale, do you?" His hands began to tremble with suppressed emotion.

"I was just kidding, my friend," I said.

"Ah," he said, "good. Your city humor is sometimes incomprehensible to me. In fact, I don't even know what's happening here tonight."

"You're not the only one," I told him.

Abu Adil's goons said nothing, as usual. Kenneth said nothing, either, although he rarely turned his gaze away from me. We ate in silence, as if we were waiting for some dreadful trap to spring shut around us. Finally, when the meal was almost at an end, Shaykh Reda stood and began to speak.

"Once again," he said, "it's my great pleasure to present a little gift to Marîd Audran. Let us give thanks to Allah that he and Friedlander Bey have returned safely from their ordeal."

There was a chorus of "Allah be praised!" around the table.

Abu Adil reached down and got a gray cardboard box. "This," he said, opening it, "is the uniform that befits your rank of lieutenant in the *Jaish*. You command three platoons of loyal patriots, and lately they've grown restive, wondering why you do not attend our rallies and exercises. One reason, I thought, was that you didn't have a proper outfit. Well, you no longer have that excuse. Shaykh Marîd, wear this in good health!"

I was struck speechless. This was even more ludicrous than the original commission. I didn't know what to say, so I just stammered a few words of thanks and accepted the boxed uniform. A lieutenant's insignia had already been added to it.

Shortly thereafter, when none of us could eat another thing, Shaykh Reda excused himself and wheeled out of the dining room, followed by Kenneth and his three goons.

Bin Turki bent toward me and whispered, "What was wrong with him? Why is he in a wheelchair? Surely he's wealthy enough to afford any sort of medical aid. Even in the Rub al-Khali, we heard marvelous tales of the miracles that are wrought by civilized physicians."

I spread my hands. "He's not really an invalid," I explained in a low voice. "His 'hobby' is collecting personality modules recorded from actual sufferers from all sorts of fatal illnesses. It's a perversion called Proxy Hell. He can enjoy—if that's the right word—the worst pain and disablement, and pop the moddy out whenever it gets to be too much. I suppose he's got an unusual tolerance for pain, though."

"That's contemptible," whispered bin Turki, frowning.

"That's Shaykh Reda Abu Adil," I said.

In two or three minutes, we were all walking back to our car. "How about that," exclaimed Tariq. "The one time we're ready for him and come into his house armed to the teeth, he just serves us a dandy meal and drops a uniform on Shaykh Marîd."

"What do you think that means?" asked Youssef.

"I trust we'll find out eventually," said Papa. I knew his words were true. There had to be something devious happening at that meal, but I couldn't imagine what.

And did it all mean that we were now obliged to have *them* over sometime? If this kept going, sooner or later the two houses would end up going to movies and watching prizefights on the holoset and drinking beer together. I couldn't face that.

12

I waited for Yasmin so that we could have our talk, but she never came into work that night. I went home about two o'clock in the morning, and let Chiri close up. There was no breakfast meeting with Papa the next day, so I told Kmuzu I wanted to sleep a little later. He gave me permission.

When I awoke, I eased into the morning. I took a long, hot bath and reread one of my favorite Lutfy Gad murder mysteries. Gad was the greatest Palestinian writer of the last century, and I guess now and then I unconsciously imitate his great detective, al-Qaddani. Sometimes I fall into that clipped, ironic way al-Qaddani spoke. None of my friends ever noticed, though, because as a group they're not terribly well read.

When I emerged from the tub, I dressed and skipped the well-balanced breakfast Kmuzu'd prepared for me. He gave me a grim look, but he'd learned over many months that if I didn't feel like eating, I wouldn't eat. Unless Papa demanded it.

Kmuzu silently handed me an envelope. Inside was a letter from Friedlander Bey addressed to Lieutenant Hajjar, requiring that I be reinstated on the city's police force for the duration of my investigation of Khalid Maxwell's death. I read it through and nodded. Papa had an uncanny ability to anticipate that sort of thing. He also knew that he could "require" something of the police and it would be done.

I put the letter in my pocket and relaxed in a comfortable black leather chair. I decided it was time to check in with Wise Counselor. The Counselor was a personality module that gauged my current emotional state, and offered a super-realistic fantasy that expressed my problems and offered a symbolic—sometimes indecipherable—solution. *"Bismillah,"* I murmured, and reached up to chip the moddy in.

Audran was transformed into the great Persian poet, Hafiz. He'd led a life of luxury, and his poems also contained imagery that stricter Muslims objected to. Over the years, Audran had made a large number of enemies, so that when he died, the strict Muslims argued that his body should be denied the blessing of the traditional funeral prayer. Their reasoning condemned Audran with his own words.

"Has the poet not written about unholy practices such as imbibing alcoholic beverages and indulging in promiscuous sex?" they asked. "Listen to his poetry:

> *"Come here, come here, cup-bearer!*
> *Pass around and give the cup,*
> *For love looked free and easy at first,*
> *But too many troubles have come up."*

This fueled a long debate between Audran's enemies and his admirers. Finally, it was decided that the correct course of action should be dictated by a random reference to his own poems. To that end, a large selection of Audran's verses were written out on slips of paper and thrown into an urn. An innocent child was asked to reach into the urn and pick one verse. This is the couplet that the child drew:

> *In the funeral of Audran gladly take part,*
> *For sinful as he was, for Heaven doth he start.*

The verdict was acknowledged by both sides, and so Audran was given a funeral with all proper ceremonies. When the story came to its end, Audran reached up and popped the moddy out.

I shuddered. Those fantasies that showed me dead and hovering over my own funeral always gave me the creeps. Now I had to decide what it meant, how it related to me. I hadn't written a poem in fifteen years. I filed the vision away as something to discuss Real Soon Now with Kmuzu.

It was time to start digging up information about Khalid Maxwell and his violent death. The first step, I decided, was to go to the copshop that oversaw the activities in the Budayeen, where Lieutenant Hajjar was in charge. I didn't hate Hajjar, he just made my skin crawl. He wasn't the sort of person who derived pleasure from pulling the wings from flies—he was the sort of person who'd go into the next room and watch someone else do it, through a secret peephole.

Kmuzu drove me in the cream-colored Westphalian sedan to the precinct house on Walid al-Akbar Street. As usual, there was a crowd of boys on the sidewalk, and I waded through them flinging coins left and right. Still they begged, chanting, "Open to us, O Generous One!" I liked the kids. It wasn't so long ago that I myself haunted the edges of crowds, pleading for money to feed myself. Somewhere along the line the roles were reversed, and now I was the big rich guy. I was rich, all right, but I never forgot my origins. I didn't begrudge the kids their *baksheesh*.

I entered the police station and headed toward the computer room on the second floor. I was braced a couple of times by uniformed men, but I said nothing, just showing them the letter with Friedlander Bey's signature. The cops all melted aside like phantoms.

I remembered very well how to operate the computers. I even recalled the secret backdoor password, *Miramar*. The staff in this station house had rather relaxed standards, and I was confident they hadn't gotten around to changing that password in months. I guess the risk of an outsider getting into the police files was preferable to making the entire force memorize a new word.

I sat down at the beat-up old Annamese data deck and began murmuring commands. The female sergeant who acted as the data librarian saw me and hurried over. "I'm sorry, sir," she said in a voice that wasn't sorry at all, "but these decks are not accessible to the public."

"You don't remember me, do you?" I asked.

She squinted one eye and considered. "No, so you'll have to leave."

I took out Papa's letter and showed it to her. "I've just got a few minutes' work to do here," I said.

"I'll have to check on this," she said, folding the letter again and giving it back to me. "No one's spoken to me about any of this. I'll call the lieutenant. In the meantime, leave that data deck alone."

I nodded, knowing that I'd have to wait for her to work her way up through the chain of command. It didn't take long. In a few minutes, Lieutenant Hajjar himself came huffing into the data library. "What do you think you're doing, Audran?" he shouted. His expression was a black scowl.

I held out Papa's letter. I wasn't about to stand up or try to explain myself. The letter could speak for me, and I felt like exerting a little dominance. Hajjar needed to be put in his place every once in a while.

He snatched the paper from my hand and read through it once and then again. "What's this?" he said harshly.

"It's a letter. From you know who, you've already read it."

He glared at me and crumpled the sheet of paper into a ball. "This letter don't cut it with me, Audran. Not at all. And what are you doing at large? You were formally exiled. I should take you into custody right now."

I shook my finger at him and smiled. "Nuh uh, Hajjar. The amir's granted us an appeal, and you know it."

"Still," he said.

"Still," I said, taking the crumpled paper and holding it against his temple. "You really don't think this letter cuts it, huh?"

"No way." He sounded much less sure this time.

"Well," I said calmly, "Papa has plenty of people who *could* cut you."

Hajjar licked his lips. "Well, what the hell do you want, then?"

I smiled in a completely phony friendly way. "I just want to use this data deck for a minute or two."

"I suppose that could be arranged. What are you trying to dig up?"

I spread my hands. "I want to clear our names, of course. I want to find out what you know about Khalid Maxwell."

A look of fear came and went in his eyes. "I can't allow that," he said. Now his voice shook noticeably. "It's classified police business."

I laughed. "I'm classified police," I said. "At least for the moment."

"No," he said, "I won't allow it. That case is closed."

"I'm reopening it." I shook the crumpled paper at him.

"Right," he said, "go ahead. But there are going to be repercussions from this. I'm warning you."

"I'm *hoping* for repercussions, Hajjar. I advise you to get out of the way of them."

He stared at me for a few seconds. Then he said, "*Yallah,* your mother must've been a syphilitic camel, Audran, and your father was a Christian bastard."

"Close," I said, and I turned my back on him and continued to murmur commands to the data deck. I suppose Hajjar stalked away.

The first thing I did was call up the file on Khalid Maxwell. I didn't learn much. Evidently, the file had been tampered with and edited until there was very little information left. I did find out that Maxwell had been with the police force for four years, that he'd earned a commendation for bravery, and that he'd been killed while off-duty. According to the cop computer, he died while interceding in a violent argument between Friedlander Bey and myself in front of Maxwell's house at 23 Shams Alley.

That was nonsense, of course. I didn't even know where Shams Alley was; I was sure it wasn't in the Budayeen. Maxwell was the second police officer from Hajjar's precinct to be killed during the year. That didn't look good for Hajjar, but of course it looked even worse for poor Maxwell.

I had the data deck print out the file, and then I passed a little time by poking into other files. Lieutenant

Hajjar's dossier gave even less information than it had the last time I looked. All mention of his own difficulties with the force's Internal Affairs Department had been erased. There wasn't much left but his name, age, and address.

My own file listed me as the killer of Khalid Maxwell (released pending appeal). That reminded me that the clock was running, and there were only a few weeks left of my freedom. It would be very hard to prove my innocence —and Papa's—from inside a prison cell or with my head on the chopping block. I decided to stir things up a little and see what happened.

When I left the station house, I found Kmuzu sitting in the car a little farther up Walid al-Akbar Street. I got into the back seat and told him to drive me to the Budayeen's eastern gate. When we got there, I sent him home because I didn't know how long my business would take. When Kmuzu objected, I told him I could get a cab to come home. He frowned and said he'd rather wait for me, but I just told him in a firm voice to do what I said.

I took with me the portable datalink unit Friedlander Bey and I were marketing, and as I walked up the Street toward the Café Solace, my phone rang. I unclipped it from my belt and said, "Hello."

"Audran?" asked a nasal voice that sounded fat with disgust.

"Yeah," I said, "who is this?"

"Kenneth. Calling on behalf of Shaykh Reda Abu Adil."

That explained the disgust; the feeling was definitely mutual. "Yeah, Kenny, what do you want."

There was a brief pause. "My name is Kenneth, not Kenny. I'd appreciate it if you'd keep that in mind."

I grinned. "Sure, pal. Now what's behind this call?"

"Shaykh Reda has just heard that you're digging around in the Khalid Maxwell case. Don't."

The news sure had traveled fast. "Don't?"

"Right," said Kenneth. "Just don't. Shaykh Reda is concerned for your safety, as you are an officer in the *Jaish*, and he fears what might happen to you if you continue this investigation."

I laughed without humor. "I'll tell you what will happen if I *don't* continue the investigation: Papa and I will lose our appeal and we'll be put to death."

"We understand that, Audran. If you want to save your necks, there are two ways to proceed, the right way and the wrong way. The right way is to establish a bulletproof alibi for yourselves the night of the murder. The wrong way is to go on doing what you're doing."

"That's great, Ken, but to tell the truth, I can't even remember what I did on the night in question."

"It's *Kenneth*," he growled, just before he hung up. I grinned again and put my phone back on my belt.

I found Jacques and Mahmoud playing dominoes at the Café Solace. I pulled up a chair to their table and watched for a while. Finally, old Ibrahim came and asked if I wanted anything. I ordered a White Death, and Mahmoud looked at me curiously. "How long you been here, Marîd?" he asked. "We been playing dominoes and I never saw you come up."

"Not long," I told him. I turned to my other friend. "Jacques," I said, "you ready to start pushing data this afternoon?"

He gave me a look which said he regretted ever agreeing to help me out. "Don't you have more important things to do?" he said. "I mean, like clearing your name and reputation."

I nodded. "Don't worry, I've started taking care of that, too."

"We heard," said Mahmoud.

"The rumor on the Street is that you're looking for someone to pin Maxwell's murder on," said Jacques.

"Instead of proving where you were the night of the crime," said Mahmoud. "You're going about it all wrong. You're trying to do it the hard way."

"That's just what Abu Adil's current Bendable Benny told me," I said slowly. "What a coincidence."

"Kenneth told you that?" said Mahmoud. "Well, see, he's probably right."

I didn't have any specific questions to ask them, so I changed the subject. "Ready to go, Jacques?" I said.

"Well, Marîd, to tell the truth, my stomach hurts today. How 'bout tomorrow afternoon?"

"Oh, you'll be on your own tomorrow," I said, smiling, "but you're also going with me today."

I waited patiently until Mahmoud won the domino game, and then as Jacques settled up his wager. "It's not starting out to be a good day for me," said Jacques. He was well dressed, as usual, but he wore that miffy Christian look that all his friends hated so much. He looked as if he wanted to go somewhere and start a new life under another name.

I looked at him from the corner of my eye and stifled a smile. He was so upset. "What's wrong, Jacques?" I asked.

His upper lip pulled back in disdain. "I'll tell you one thing, Marîd," he said. "This job is beneath me. It's not appropriate for me to act like a . . . a common salesman."

I couldn't help laughing. "Don't think of yourself as a salesman, if that's your problem. Truthfully, you're not. You're much more than that. Try to see the whole picture, O Excellent One."

Jacques didn't look convinced. "I *am* looking at the big picture. I see myself going into a bar or a club, taking out my wares, and trying to wangle money out of the proprietor. That's retail sales. It's demeaning to someone of my blood. Have I ever told you that I'm three-quarters European?"

I sighed. He'd told us nearly every day for the last seven years. "Haven't you ever wondered who works retail sales in Europe?"

"Americans," said Jacques, shrugging.

I rubbed my aching forehead. "Forget sales. You won't be a salesman. You'll be a Data Placement Specialist. And when you get rolling, you'll be promoted to Information Retrieval Engineer. With a suitable increase in your commission percentage."

Jacques glared. "You can't trick me, Marîd," he said.

"That's the great part! I don't *have* to trick you. I've got enough power these days to twist your arm and make you delighted to help me."

Jacques gave a short, humorless laugh. "My arm is untwistable, O Shaykh. You're still street scum, just like the rest of us."

I shrugged. "That may well be true, my Christian friend, but I'm street scum with Habib and Labib at my command."

"Who are they?"

"The Stones That Speak," I said calmly. I saw the color go out of Jacques's face. Everyone in the Budayeen knew about Papa's huge bodyguards, but I was one of the few privileged to know their individual names. Of course, I still couldn't tell which one was which, but that was all right because they always traveled together.

Jacques spat on the ground in front of me. "It's true what they say about power corrupting," he said bitterly.

"You're wrong, Jacques," I said in a quiet voice. "I wouldn't threaten one of my friends. I don't need that power. I'm only counting on you to return a favor. Didn't

I cover Fuad's check for you? Didn't you agree to help me?"

He winced. "Yes, well, if it's a matter of honor, well then, of course I'm happy to return the favor."

I clapped him on the back. "I knew I could count on you."

"Anytime, Marîd." But the look on his face told me his stomach still bothered him.

We arrived at Frenchy's club, which was across the Street and up a block from my own. Frenchy was a huge, burly, black-bearded guy who looked like he ought to be rolling barrels into a warehouse in some sunny French seaport. He was as tough a joker as I've ever met. Disturbances didn't last long in Frenchy's place.

"Where y'at, Marîd?" called Dalia, Frenchy's barmaid.

"Just fine, Dalia. Frenchy around?"

"He's in back. I'll go get him." She tossed her bar towel down and disappeared into the back office. There weren't very many customers, but it was still early in the day.

"Can I buy you a drink?" I asked Jacques while we waited.

"The Lord doesn't approve of liquor," he said. "You should know that."

"I do," I said. "I do know that God disapproves. But He's never said anything directly to me about it."

"Oh no? What do you call vomiting all over yourself? What do you call blackouts? What do you call getting your face smashed in because you were so drunk you said the wrong thing to the wrong person? And you shouldn't be blasphemous."

I couldn't take him seriously. "I've seen you drink your share, too."

Jacques nodded vigorously. "Yes, my friend, but then I

go to confession and do my penance and then everything's all right again."

I was saved from further religious exegesis by Frenchy, who showed up in the nick of time. "What's happening?" he said, taking the bar stool to my right.

"Well, Frenchy," I said, "it's nice to see you, and I'm glad I'm still welcome in your club, but we don't really have time to sit here and chat. I want to sell you something."

"You want to sell me something, *noraf*," he said in his gruff voice. "Wait a minute. I'm impossible to scam when I'm sober."

"I thought you stopped drinking," I said. "On account of your stomach."

"Well, I started again," said Frenchy. He signaled to his barmaid, and Dalia brought him an unopened bottle of Johnnie Walker. I don't know what it is, but most of these ex-seamen won't drink anything but Johnnie Walker. I first noticed it over in Jo-Mama's club among the Greek merchant sailors, and the two Filipino bars on Seventh Street. Frenchy twisted open the bottle and filled a tumbler half full. "Gonna give you a fair chance," said Frenchy, gulping down the whiskey and refilling the tumbler.

"Let me have a gin and bingara," I told the barmaid.

"Want some lime juice in that?" Dalia asked.

I smiled at her. "You never forget."

She shuddered in disgust. "How could I?" she muttered. "What about you, Jacques?"

"You've got that Ecuadorian beer on draft? I'll have one." Dalia nodded and drew Jacques his beer.

Frenchy threw down a second glass of whiskey and belched. *"Eh bien,* Marîd," he said, rubbing his thick beard, "what's in the suitcase?"

I put it up on the bar between us and snapped open the latches. "You're going to love this," I said.

"Not yet," said Frenchy, "but maybe in a few minutes." He downed a third tumbler of Johnnie Walker.

"Whatcha got, Marîd?" said Dalia, resting her elbows on the bar.

Frenchy glared at her, and his head wobbled a little. "Go wipe off some tables," he told her. He was beginning to feel the liquor. That was good.

I opened the lid of the suitcase and let Frenchy look at the datalink. It was a state-of-the-art terminal with just enough memory so that it wouldn't forget its own job. It was useless unless it was connected to a mainframe somewhere. Friedlander Bey had contracted with an electronics firm in Bosnia to supply the datalinks at a price well below the fair market standard. That was because the Bosnian corporation was owned by an industrial conglomerate with its headquarters in Bahrain; both the chief executive officer and the vice president for sales owed their current positions of power, wealth, and comfort to Papa's intervention in local political affairs some ten years before.

I reached over and poured Frenchy a fourth drink. *"Merde alors,"* he murmured.

"Friedlander Bey wants you to be the first in the Budayeen," I told him.

The big Frenchman was sipping his whiskey now, not gulping. "First for what, and will I live through it?" he asked.

I smiled. "You're gonna get the chance to be the first on the Street to have one of these datalinks. You can set it up right down there on the end of the bar, right where people can see it when they first come into the club."

"Uh huh," said Frenchy. "The fuck do I want one?"

I glanced at Jacques to see if he was paying attention.

"These units will access more than the city's Info service," I said. "Your customers will be able to tap into a global data network that will provide almost unlimited information."

Frenchy shook his head. "How much is it gonna cost 'em?"

"One kiam. Just one kiam per data request."

"Minute, papillon! The city's Info service is free. All you got to do is pick up a phone."

I smiled again. "Not for long, Frenchy. Nobody knows this yet, so don't go spreading it around. Friedlander Bey's bought the Info service from the city."

Frenchy laughed. "What did he do, bribe the amir?"

I shrugged. "He persuaded the amir. It doesn't make any difference how. The amir has just come to believe that Papa will administer the service better than the previous Public Service Commission. Of course, Papa's also explained that in order to give the people the service they deserve, there will have to be a small fee for each transaction."

Frenchy nodded. "So the free Info service is being phased out. And these datalink units will take its place. And you and Papa are gonna be in charge, doling out bits of information. What happens if someone wants the scoop on Papa's personal life?"

I turned away and casually drank half my White Death. "Oh," I said calmly, "we're unfortunately going to limit the free access of certain people to certain data."

Frenchy slammed his fist down on the bar and laughed. Actually, it was more like a bellow. "He is magnificent!" he cried. "He's throttled the exchange of information, and he'll decide who may or may not benefit! Wait until Abu Adil finds out!"

Jacques leaned closer. "I didn't know about any of

this, Marîd," he said softly. "You didn't mention any of this to me, and I think that dissolves our agreement."

I indicated that he should drink up his beer. "That's why I came along with you today," I said. "I want you to be clear about all the ramifications. It's the dawn of an exciting age."

"But I don't think I like it. What am I getting into?"

I spread my hands. "One of the greatest commercial enterprises in history," I said.

A customer came into the club just then, a tall man dressed in a European-style business suit. He had gray hair that had been expensively cut and styled, and at his neck he wore a silver brooch set with many diamonds and a cluster of large emeralds in the center. He carried a briefcase not much smaller than my own, and he stood in the doorway letting his eyes adjust to the darkness in Frenchy's bar.

One of Frenchy's dancers went to him and invited him in. I didn't know the girl. She may have been new to the Budayeen, but if she stayed around any time at all I'd eventually learn more than I wanted to know about her. She was wearing a long gown of very sheer material, so that her small breasts and her dark pubic triangle were visible, even in that dim light. "Would you like a drink?" she asked.

The elegantly dressed man squinted at her. "Is your name Theoni?" he asked.

The dancer's shoulders slumped. "No," she said, "but she's over there. Theoni, this is one of yours."

Theoni was one of the sweetest girls on the Street, completely out of place in Frenchy's club. She'd never worked for me, but I'd be overjoyed if she ever came into Chiriga's looking for a job. She was small and lithe and graceful, and she'd had only a moderate amount of surgery. Her bodmods accentuated her natural prettiness without making her into the kind of caricature we saw too often around there. Unlike most of the dancers, she'd never had her brain wired at all, and when she wasn't entertaining a customer, she sat by herself near the back of Frenchy's, drinking Sharâb and reading paperback books. I think it was her reading that I found most attractive about her.

She emerged from the dark rear of the bar and greeted the customer, leading him to a table right behind where Frenchy, Jacques, and I were sitting. Dalia came over to take his order, and he got a beer for himself and a champagne cocktail for Theoni.

Frenchy poured himself another healthy round of Johnnie Walker. "Dalia," he said, "gimme a glass of mineral water." He turned to me. "She's the best barmaid on the Street, you know that? You think Chiri's a good barmaid, I wouldn't trade Dalia for Chiri if you threw in Yasmin as well. Jeez, how do you put up with her? Yasmin, I mean. Always late. She's pretty for a boy and she makes money, but she's got a temper—"

"Frenchy," I said, cutting off his drunken monologue, "believe me, I know all about Yasmin's temper."

"I suppose you would. How does she take working for you now that you're married?" He laughed again, a low rumbling sound from deep within his chest.

"Let's talk about the terminal, Frenchy," I said, trying again to steer the conversation back on course. "You're gonna want one, because everyone else on the Street is gonna have one, and without one you'll lose business. Like not having a phone or a bathroom."

"Bathroom only works on Tuesdays and Thursdays anyway," muttered Frenchy. "What's in it for me?"

I took that to mean what was in it for him if he accepted the terminal. "Well, my friend, we're prepared to loan you some money if you'll do us the favor of letting us install our first datalink here in your club. One thousand kiam in cash, right here and now, and you don't have to do a thing for it. Just sign the order form, and tomorrow a wirecutter will come in and set up the unit on the end of your bar. You won't have to lift a finger."

"A thousand kiam?" he said. He leaned close to me and stared into my eyes. He was breathing heavily in my face, and it wasn't a pleasant experience.

"A thousand. Cash. Right now. And the beauty part, Frenchy, is that we won't ask you to repay it. We're gonna split the take from the datalink with you sixty-five to thirty-five. We'll collect the loan payments out of your thirty-five percent. You won't even miss the money. And when it's all paid back, we'll loan you another thousand, in cash, up front, to do with as you will."

He rubbed his beard some more and squinted his eyes, trying to see what the catch was. "You're going to split the take with me every month?" he said.

"Thirty-five percent is yours," I said.

"So these loans are more—"

"They're more like a gift!" said Jacques. I turned to look at him.

There was silence in the club for a few moments. From the corner of my eye, I saw Theoni sitting very close to the customer with the jeweled brooch. She slipped her hand along his thigh, and he looked very uncomfortable. "Where are you from, then, honey?" she said, sipping her cocktail.

"Achaea," he said. He lifted her hand out of his lap.

Frenchy heaved his huge body up and grabbed two glasses from across the bar. He poured them half full of whiskey, and set one in front of Jacques and the other in front of me. Then he took Jacques's bottle of beer and sniffed it. *"Pipi de chat,"* he said scornfully. "Drink with me."

I shrugged and picked up the glass of whiskey. Frenchy and I tinked glasses and I downed it. Jacques was having more trouble with his. He wasn't much of a drinker.

"Maríd," said Frenchy, suddenly serious, "what happens to me and my bar if I decline your generous offer? What if I refuse? This is my club, after all, and I say what goes and what doesn't go in here. I don't want a datalink. What is Papa gonna think about that?"

I frowned and shook my head. "How long we known each other, Frenchy?"

He just stared at me.

"Take the datalink," I said in a calm voice.

He was big enough to break me in half, but he knew this was a critical moment. He knew that throwing me out of his club was not the appropriate response. With a long, sad sigh he stood up. "All right, Maríd," he said at last, "sign me up. But don't think I don't know what this means."

I grinned at him. "It's not so bad, Frenchy. Here. Here's your thousand kiam." I reached into the pocket of my *gallebeya* and took out a sealed envelope.

Frenchy snatched it from me and turned away. He stalked back toward his office without saying another word. "This afternoon," I told Jacques, "you can offer the same thousand kiam to Big Al and the others, but they get theirs when the datalink terminal is actually installed. All right?"

Jacques nodded. He shoved the unfinished glass of whiskey away from him. "And I get a commission on each terminal?"

"One hundred kiam," I said. I was sure that Jacques would do a fine job selling the project to our friends and neighbors, especially with the inducement of a hundred-kiam commission per sale, and with the weighty endorsement of Friedlander Bey. Papa's influence would make Jacques's job that much easier.

"I'll do my best, Marîd," he said. He sounded a little more confident now. He slowly drank the rest of the Ecuadorian beer in his bottle.

A little while later, the customer from Achaea stood up and opened his briefcase. He took out a slender, wrapped package. "This is for you," he told Theoni. "Don't open it until after I'm gone." He bent and kissed her on the cheek, then went back outside into the warm sunshine.

Theoni began to tear the wrapping paper. She opened the package and found a leather-bound book. As she flipped it open, my belt phone rang. I unclipped it and said hello.

"Is this Marîd Audran speaking?" said a hoarse voice.

"It is," I said.

"This is Dr. Sadiq Abd ar-Razzaq." It was the imam who'd signed our death warrants. I was startled.

Theoni jumped to her feet and pointed after the gentleman from Achaea. "Do you know who that *was?*" she cried, tears streaming down her face. "That was my *father!*"

Dalia, Jacques, and I glanced over at Theoni. Things like that happened all the time in the Budayeen. It was nothing to get excited about.

"I would like to discuss how you intend to clear your name," said Abd ar-Razzaq. "I will not stand for the breaking of any Muslim law. I will grant you a hearing tomorrow at two o'clock." He hung up before I could respond.

I slid the sample datalink terminal in the suitcase down to Jacques, and he closed the lid and went on his way. "Well," I told Dalia, "I've talked with everybody I can think of who might be involved in the Khalid Maxwell case. So I've made the first circuit around the village."

She looked at me and cleaned off the counter with a bar rag. She didn't have any idea what I was talking about.

13

I lay in bed reading another Lutfy Gad novel until it was about three o'clock in the morning. My stomach was upset, there was a loud ringing in my ears, and I realized after a while that I was sweating so much that the bedclothes were soaked. I was in the opening round of a full-fledged anxiety attack.

Well, heroes aren't supposed to go to pieces. Look at al-Qaddani, Gad's unstoppable detective. He never worried himself into helplessness. He never stayed up all night wishing he could run away somewhere and start over again. After a couple of hours of nervous trembling, I decided to get my life back in order, and immediately. I slid out of the drenched bed and crossed my bedroom, where I found my tan plastic pillcase.

It was crammed full of helpful medications, and I had to think for a few seconds about my selection. Tranquilizers, I decided at last. I was trying to end my old habits of recreational drug use, but this was a situation where my favorite pills and caps were legitimately indicated. I went with Paxium, taking twelve of the lavender pills and four of the yellow ones. That should take the edge off my anxiety, I told myself.

I went back to bed, flopped the pillows over, and read another couple of chapters. I waited for the Paxium to hit, and I admit that after half an hour or so, I did feel just the tiniest, most insignificant hint of euphoria. It was laid on top of my mental distress like the sugar frosting on a petit four. Underneath it, I was still eating my guts out with apprehension.

I got up again and padded barefoot to the closet. I opened the pillcase and dug out eight tabs of Sonneine, my favorite painkiller. I wasn't actually in severe pain, but I figured the opiate warmth would blot out the remainder of my anxiety. I swallowed the chalky tablets with a gulp of warm mineral water.

By the time al-Qaddani had been captured by the Israeli villain and received his obligatory once-per-novel beating, I was feeling much better. The anxiety was only an abstract memory, and I was filled with a wonderful confidence that later that day I'd be able to overpower Dr. Sadiq Abd ar-Razzaq with the force of my personality.

I felt so good, in fact, that I wanted to share my joy with someone. Not Kmuzu, however, who would certainly report my late night binge to Friedlander Bey. No, instead I dressed myself quickly and slipped out of my apartment. I went quietly through the dark corridors from the west wing of Papa's palace to the east wing. I stood outside Indihar's door and rapped softly a few times. I didn't want to wake the kids.

I waited a minute, then knocked more loudly. Finally I heard movement, and the door was opened by Senalda, the Valencian maid I'd hired to help Indihar. "Señor

Audran," she said sleepily. She rubbed her eyes and glared at me. She wasn't happy about being awakened so early in the morning.

"I'm sorry, Senalda," I said, "but it's urgent that I speak to my wife."

The maid stared at me for a couple of seconds but didn't say anything. She turned and went back into the dark apartment. I waited by the door. In a little while, Indihar came, wrapped in a satin robe. Her expression was grim. "Husband," she said.

I yawned. "I need to talk with you, Indihar. I'm sorry about the hour, but it's very important."

She ran a hand through her hair and nodded. "It better be, Maghrebi. The children will be awake in a couple of hours, and I won't have time to take a nap after that." She stepped aside, allowing me to brush by her, into the parlor.

By now, I felt terrific. I felt invincible. Fifteen minutes before, I decided to go to Indihar and have her say I was brave and true and strong, because I needed to hear that from someone. Now, though, the Sonneine was telling me everything I needed to know, and I only wanted to discuss my misgivings concerning strategy. I knew I could trust Indihar. I wasn't even concerned that she'd be angry with me for getting her out of her nice, warm bed.

I sat down on one of the couches, and waited for her to sit opposite me. She spent a few seconds rubbing her face with her long, delicate fingers. "Indihar," I said, "you're my wife."

She stopped massaging her forehead and glanced up at me. "I told you before," she said through clenched teeth, "I won't jam with you. If you woke me up in the middle of the night in some drunken—"

"No, that's not it at all. I need to get your honest opinion about something."

She stared at me without saying anything. She didn't look mollified.

"You may have noticed," I said, "that lately Papa has been putting more and more responsibility on my shoulders. And that I've had to use some of his methods, even though I personally deplore them."

Indihar shook her head. "I saw the way you sent bin Turki back to Najran on his . . . assignment. It didn't seem to me that you had any problem at all ordering some stranger's death. Not so long ago, you would have been appalled, and you would've left it to Youssef or Tariq to take care of that loose end."

I shrugged. "It was necessary. We have hundreds of friends and associates who depend on us, and we can't let anyone get away with attacking us. If we did, we'd lose our influence and power, and our friends would lose our protection."

"Us. We. You've subconsciously begun to identify with Friedlander Bey. He's won you over completely now, hasn't he? Whatever happened to your outrage?"

I was starting to get depressed, despite the Sonneine. That meant that I needed to take more Sonneine, but I couldn't. Not in front of Indihar. "I'm going to have to find out who actually murdered Khalid Maxwell, and then I'm going to have to see that he's dealt with the same way as that sergeant in Najran."

Indihar smiled without warmth. "You've also adopted a cute way of speaking around the truth. He'll have to be 'dealt with,' instead of 'killed.' It's like you have your conscience on a goddamn daddy, and you just never chip it in."

I stood up and let out a deep breath. "Thanks, Indihar. I'm glad we had this talk. You can go back to sleep now." I turned and left her apartment, closing the door behind me. I felt bad.

I walked silently down the corridor past my mother's apartment. I turned into the gloomy passageway in the main part of the house, and a dark figure slipped from the shadows and came up to me. At first I was frightened—it was always possible that a very clever assassin might defeat the human guards and electronic alarms—but then I saw that it was Youssef, Papa's butler and assistant.

"Good evening, Shaykh Marîd," he said.

"Youssef," I said warily.

"I just happened to be awake, and I heard you moving about. Is there something you need?"

We continued walking toward the west wing. "No, not really, Youssef. Thank you. You just happened to be awake?"

He looked at me solemnly. "I'm a very light sleeper," he said.

"Ah. Well, I just had something I wanted to discuss with my wife."

"And did Umm Jirji satisfy you with her reply?"

I grunted. "Not exactly."

"Well then, maybe I could be of some help."

I started to decline his offer, but then I thought that maybe Youssef was the perfect person to talk to about my feelings. "Indihar mentioned that I've changed quite a bit in the last year or so."

"She is quite correct, Shaykh Marîd."

"She is not altogether happy about what I seem to have become."

Youssef shrugged in the dim light. "I would not expect her to understand," he said. "It is a very complex situation, one that only persons in administrative roles can understand. That is, Friedlander Bey, you, Tariq, and myself. To everyone else, we are monsters."

"I am a monster in my own mind, Youssef," I said sadly. "I want my old liberty back. I don't want to play an administrative role. I want to be young and poor and free and happy."

"That will never happen, my friend, so you must stop teasing your imagination with the possibility. You've been given the honor of caring for many people, and you owe them all your best efforts. That means concentration unbroken by self-doubt."

I shook my head. Youssef wasn't quite grasping my point. "I have a lot of power now," I said slowly. "How can I know if I'm using that power properly? For instance, I dispatched a young man to terminate a ruffian who brutalized Friedlander Bey in Najran. Now, the holy Qur'ân provides for revenge, but only at the same level as the original injury. The sergeant could be severely beaten without feelings of guilt, but to end his life—"

Youssef raised a hand and cut me off. "Ah," he said, smiling, "you misunderstand both The Wise Mention of God and your own position. What you say about revenge is certainly true, for the average man who has only his own life and the lives of his immediate family to worry about. But just as they say that with privilege comes responsibility, the opposite is also true. That is, with increased responsibility comes increased privilege. So we here in this house are above certain plain interpretations of Allah's commands. In order to maintain the peace of the Budayeen and the city, we must often act quickly and surely. If we are brutalized, as you put it, we don't have to wait for a death to occur before we end the threat against us. We maintain the well-being of our friends and associates by prompt action, and we may go on from there secure in the knowledge that we have not transgressed the *intent* of the teachings of the Holy Prophet."

"May the blessings of Allah be on him and peace," I said. I kept my expression studiously blank, but I was howling on the inside. I hadn't heard such a ridiculous piece of sophistry since the days when the old shaykh who lived in a box in our alley in Algiers tried to prove that the entire Earth was flat because the city of Mecca was flat. Which it isn't.

"I'm concerned that you're still showing such reluctance, Shaykh Marîd," said Youssef.

I waved my hand. "It's nothing. I've always dithered a little before doing what had to be done. But you and Friedlander Bey well know that I've always completed my tasks. Is it necessary that I relish them?"

Youssef gave a short laugh. "No, indeed. As a matter of fact, it is good that you don't. If you did, you'd run the risk of ending up like Shaykh Reda."

"Allah forbid," I murmured. We'd come to my door, and I left Youssef to seek out his own bed once again. I went inside, but I didn't feel like going to sleep. My mind was still unsettled. I paused only long enough to take another four Sonneine and a couple of tri-phets for energy. Then I slowly opened my door again, careful not to wake Kmuzu, and peered into the hall. I didn't see Youssef anywhere. I slipped out again, made my way downstairs, and sat behind the wheel of my electric sedan.

I needed a drink with a lot of laughing people around it. I drove myself to the Budayeen, indulging myself in the peculiar and pleasant loneliness you feel so early in the morning, with no one else on the road. Don't talk to me about driving under the influence—I know, it's stupid and I should be caught and made an example of. I just figured that with all the really terrible things hanging over my head, something like a traffic accident wouldn't dare happen to me. That was the artificial confidence of the drugs again.

Anyway, I arrived outside the eastern gate without incident, and parked my car near the cab stand on the Boulevard il-Jameel. My club was closed—had been for an hour or more—and many of the others were likewise dark. But there were plenty of after-hours bars and twenty-four-hour cafés. A lot of the dancers went over to the Brig when they got off work. You'd think that after drinking with customers for eight hours, they'd have had enough, but that wasn't the way it worked. They liked to sit together at the bar, throw back shots of schnapps, and talk about the idiot guys they'd had to talk to all night.

The Brig was a dark, cool bar hard by the southern wall of the Budayeen on Seventh Street. I headed there. In the back of my mind was the faint hope that I'd run into someone. Someone like Yasmin.

It was smoky and loud in the Brig, and they'd covered the lights with blue gels, so everyone looked dead. There wasn't an open stool along the bar, so I sat in a booth against the opposite wall. Kamal ibn ash-Shaalan, the owner, who also worked behind the bar, saw me and came over. He made a couple of feeble swipes at the tabletop with a rag soaked in stale beer. "Where y'at tonight, Marîd?" he said in his hoarse voice.

"Aw right," I said. "Gin and bingara with a little Rose's lime juice in it, okay?"

"You bet. You lookin' for company this evening?"

"I'll find it for myself, Kamal." He shrugged and walked away to make my drink.

Maybe ten seconds later, a drunk pre-op deb sat down across from me. The name she'd chosen for herself was Tansy, but at work everyone was supposed to call her Nafka. Nobody wanted to tell her what "nafka" meant in Yiddish. "Buy me a drink, mister?" she said. "I could come sit beside you and start your day off with a bang."

She didn't remember who I was. She thought I was just any old mark. "Not tonight, honey," I said. "I'm waiting for someone."

She smiled crookedly, her eyelids half-closed. "You'd be surprised what I could accomplish, While-U-Wait."

"No, I don't think I'd be surprised. I'm just not interested. Sorry."

Tansy stood up and wobbled a little. She closed one eye in a slow wink. "I know what *your* problem is, mister." She giggled to herself and headed back to the bar.

Well, no, she didn't know what my problem was. I didn't have much time to think about it, though, because I saw Yasmin stagger out of the ladies' room in the dark recesses of the club. She looked like she'd downed plenty of drinks at work, and then had a few here, too. I stood up and called her name. Her head swung around in slow motion, like an apatosaurus searching for another clump of weeds to munch.

"Whozat?" she said. She lurched toward me.

"It's Marîd."

"Marîd!" She grinned sloppily and dropped into the booth like a sack of onions. She reached under the table and fiddled under my *gallebeya*. "I've missed you, Marîd! You still got that thing under there?"

"Yasmin, listen—"

"I'm real tired tonight, Marîd. Would you take me back to my apartment? I'm kind of drunk."

"I noticed. Look, I really just wanted to talk with you about—"

She got up again and stood beside me, bending down to wrap her arms around my neck. She started tickling my ear with her tongue. "You used to like this, Marîd, remember?"

"I never liked that. You're thinking of someone else."

Yasmin slid her hand down my chest. "C'mon, Marîd, I want to go home. I live back on Fourteenth Street now."

"All right," I said. When Yasmin got drunk and got an idea in her head, there was no way you could talk your way out of doing what she wanted. I got up, put my arm around her shoulders, made sure she had her purse, and half-led, half-dragged her out of the Brig. It took us half an hour to walk the seven blocks back on the Street.

We finally reached her building and I found her keys in her purse. I opened her front door and led her over to her bed. "Thanks, Marîd," she said in a singsong voice. I took her shoes off for her and then turned to go. "Marîd?"

"What is it?" I was getting sleepy again. I wanted to get home and sneak back into my apartment before Youssef or Tariq or Kmuzu found out I was gone, and informed Friedlander Bey.

Yasmin called me again. "Rub my neck a little?"

I sighed. "All right, but just a little." Well, I started rubbing her neck, and while I was doing that she was slipping down her short black skirt. Then she reached up and tried to throw my *gallebeya* over my head. "Yasmin, you're drunk," I said.

"Do it to me, will ya?" she said. "I don't get a hangover that way." It wasn't the most sensual invitation I'd ever had. She kissed me deep and long, and she hadn't lost any speed in that department. And she knew what to do with her hands, too. In a little while, we were jamming hard and hungry. I think she was asleep before I finished. Then I had a weary climax and crashed right beside her.

How do I describe the beginning of the new day? I slept fitfully, half on and half off Yasmin's bare mattress. I dreamed vivid, crazy dreams as the remainders of the opiates and the speed disappeared from my bloodstream. I woke up once about ten o'clock in the morning, a foul taste in my mouth, a dull throbbing behind my forehead. I couldn't remember where I was, and I gazed around Yasmin's apartment, hopeful of finding a clue. Finally, I examined her graceful back, slender waist, and luscious hips. What was I doing in bed with Yasmin? She hated me. Then I recalled the end of the night before. I yawned and turned away from her, and was almost instantly asleep again.

I dreamed that my mother was shouting at me. I dream that a lot. On the surface, my mom and I have patched up all our differences, and the guilts and resentments have been put away forever. The dreams told me that most of that progress had been only cosmetic, and that deep within, I still had awkward, unsettled emotions where my mother was concerned.

My mother's voice rose in both pitch and volume, but I couldn't quite make out what she was mad about this time. I saw her face turn red and ugly, and she shook her fist at me. With her harsh words echoing painfully in my ears, I ducked as she began beating my head and shoulders.

I woke up. It was Yasmin who was screaming, and who was also punching me in my sleep. Yasmin had started out as a rather large and well-built young man, so that even after her sexchange operation, she was still a formidable opponent. In addition, she had the element of surprise on her side.

"Get out of here! Get out of here!" she cried.

I rolled off the mattress onto the cold floor. I glanced at my watch: it was now about noon. I didn't understand what Yasmin's problem was.

"You're slime, Audran!" she shouted. "You're slug vomit, taking advantage of me in the shape I was in!"

Despite all the many times we'd made love in the past, however long we'd actually lived together, I felt embarrassed to be naked in her presence. I dodged out of range of her fists, then stood kind of hunched over, trying to hide my nude vulnerability. "I didn't take advantage of you, Yasmin," I said. The throbbing behind my forehead started up again, but worse this time. "I ran into you a few hours ago at the Brig. You begged me to make sure you got home all right. I was trying to leave when you started begging me to jam you. You climbed all over me. You wouldn't let me leave."

She held her forehead and winced. "I don't remember anything like that at all."

I shrugged, grabbing my underwear and *gallebeya*. "What can I say? I'm not responsible for what you can or can't remember."

"How do I know you didn't bring me home passed out, and then raped me when I was at your mercy?"

I pulled the *gallebeya* over my head. "Yasmin," I said sadly, "don't you know me better than that? Have I ever done anything that would make you think I was capable of rape?"

"You've killed people," she said, but the steam had gone out of her argument.

I balanced on one foot and slipped on a sandal. "I didn't rape you, Yasmin," I said.

She relaxed a little more. "Yeah?" she said. "How was it?"

I tugged on the other sandal. "It was great, Yasmin. We've always been great together. I've missed you."

"Yeah? Really, Marîd?"

I knelt beside the mattress. "Look," I said, staring into her dark eyes, "just because I'm married to Indihar—"

"I won't let you cheat on her with me, Marîd. Indihar and I been friends for a long time."

I closed my eyes and rubbed them. Then I gazed back at Yasmin. "Even Prophet Muhammad—"

"May the blessings of Allah be on him and peace," she murmured.

"Even the Prophet had more than one wife. I'm entitled to four, if I can support them all equally and treat them all with fairness."

Yasmin's eyes grew larger. "What are you telling me, Marîd?"

I shrugged. "I don't know, honey. Indihar and I are married in name only. We're good friends, but I think she resents me a little. And I really meant what I said about missing you."

"Would you really marry me? And what would Indihar say about that? And how—"

I raised a hand. "I've got a lot to work out in my mind," I said. "And we'd all have to get together and talk about this. And Papa might not approve. Anyway, I have an appointment with the imam of the Shimaal Mosque in two hours. I've got to go get cleaned up."

Yasmin nodded, but she stared at me with her head tilted to one side. I made sure I had my keys and everything else I'd come in with—particularly my essential pillcase. I went to her front door.

"Marîd?" she called.

I turned and looked at her.

"I wouldn't be just your Number Two wife. I won't be a servant to Indihar and her kids. I'd expect to be treated equally, just like the noble Qur'ân says."

I nodded. "We've got plenty of time," I said. I crossed the room and knelt to kiss her good-bye. It was a soft, lingering kiss, and I was sorry to end it. Then I stood up, sighed, and closed her door behind me. *Yaa Allah,* what had those drugs gotten me into *this* time?

Outside on the street, it was a gray and drizzly morning. It fit my mood perfectly, but that didn't make it any more enjoyable. I had a long walk along the Street from Fourteenth to the eastern gate. I lowered my head and strode along close to the storefronts, hoping no one would recognize me. I wasn't in the mood for a reunion with Saied the Half-Hajj or Jacques or any of my other old pals. Besides, I barely had time to get home and shower and change clothes for my appointment with Abd ar-Razzaq.

Of course, as usual, what I wanted didn't seem to matter to the cosmos. I'd gone only about a block and a half, when a high-pitched voice called out "Al-Amîn! O Great One!"

I shuddered and looked behind me. There was a scrawny boy about fifteen years old, taller than me, dressed in a torn, dirty white shirt and white trousers. His filthy feet looked as if they'd never seen shoes or sandals. He had a purple and white checked *keffiya* knotted around his grimy neck. "Morning of light, O Shaykh," he said happily.

"Right," I said. "How much do you need?" I reached into my pocket and pulled out a roll of bills.

He looked astonished, then glanced around in all directions. "I didn't mean to ask you for money, Shaykh Marîd," he said. "I wanted to tell you something. You're being followed."

"What?" I was honestly startled by the news, and very unhappy. I wondered who'd set the tail on me, Hajjar or Abd ar-Razzaq or Abu Adil.

"It's true, O Shaykh," said the boy. "Let's walk together. On the other side of the Street, about a block behind us, is a fat *kaffir* in a sky-blue *gallebeya*. Don't look for him."

I nodded. "I wonder if he sat outside Yasmin's apartment all night, waiting for me."

The boy laughed. "My friends told me he did."

I was astonished. "How did you—they—know where I was last night?"

"Buy me something to eat, O Father of Generosity?" he asked. It sounded good to me. We turned around and walked back to Kiyoshi's, a better-than-average Japanese cookshop on South Fourteenth Street. I got a good look at the big man who was trying desperately to be inconspicuous. He didn't appear dangerous, but that didn't mean anything.

We sat in a booth, watching the holographic rock band that appeared between us. The cookshop owner also fancied himself a musician, and his band entertained at every table, whether you wanted it to or not. The boy and I split a double order of hibachi chicken. It seemed safe enough to talk.

"You are our protector, *yaa Amîn*," said the boy between greedy gulps of food. "Whenever you come to the Budayeen, we watch over you from the moment you step through the eastern gate. We have a system of signals, so we always know where you are. If you needed our help, we'd be at your side in a moment."

I laughed. "I knew nothing of this," I said.

"You've been good to us, with your shelters and soup kitchens. So this morning, my friends sat up while you visited that sexchange, Yasmin. They noticed the *kaffir* doing the same. When I awoke this morning, they told me all the news. Listen: whenever you hear this tune"—and he whistled a familiar children's song well known to all the youngsters in the city "—you'll know that we're there, and that we're telling you to be careful. You may be being followed, or possibly the police are looking for you. When you hear that tune, it would be good to become invisible for a while."

I sat back, taking in his words. So I had an army of children guarding my back. It made me feel great. "I am unable to express my thanks," I said.

The boy spread his hands. "There is no need," he said. "We wish we could do more. Now my family, of course, is in greater want than some of the others, and that means that I can't devote as much time to—"

I understood immediately. I took out my roll again

and dealt out a hundred kiam. I shoved the money across the table. "Here," I said. "For the ease of your blessed parents."

The boy picked up the hundred kiam and stared at it in wonder. "You are even nobler than the stories say," he murmured. He quickly tucked the money away out of sight.

Well, I didn't feel noble. I gave the kid a few bucks out of self-interest, and a hundred kiam doesn't hurt my bankroll very much. "Here," I said, standing up, "you finish the food. I've got to get going. I'll keep an eye out. What's your name?"

He looked me directly in the eye. "I am Ghazi, O Shaykh. When you hear two quick low notes followed by a long high note, that means that one boy is passing responsibility for you to the next boy. Be careful, Al-Amîn. We in the Budayeen depend on you."

I put my hand on his long, dirty hair. "Don't worry, Ghazi. I'm too selfish to die. There are too many beautiful things in God's world that I haven't yet experienced. I have a few important things holding me here."

"Like making money, drinking, playing cards, and Yasmin?" he asked, grinning.

"Hey," I said, feigning shock, "you know too much about me!"

"Oh," said the boy airily, "everyone in the Budayeen knows all about that."

"Terrific," I muttered. I walked by the fat black man, who'd been lingering across the way from the Japanese cookshop, and headed east along the Street. Behind me and high overhead I heard someone whistle the children's tune. The whole time I walked with my shoulders slightly hunched, as if at any moment I might be struck from behind by the butt of a pistol. Nevertheless, I made it all the way to the other end of the walled quarter without being jumped. I got into my car, and I saw my tail dive for a taxi. I didn't care if he followed me further; I was just going home.

I didn't want to run into anyone as I slunk upstairs to my apartment, but once again luck was against me. First Youssef and then Tariq crossed my path. Neither of them said anything to me, but their expressions were grave and disapproving. I felt like the useless, drunken sot of a son wasting the resources of a great family. When I got to my rooms, Kmuzu was waiting in the doorway. "The master of the house is very angry, *yaa Sidi*," he said.

I nodded. I expected as much. "What did you tell him?"

"I said that you'd risen early and gone out. I told the master of the house that I didn't know where you'd gone."

I sighed with relief. "Well, if you speak to Papa again, tell him that I went out with Jacques, to see how well he was coming along with the datalink project."

"That would be a lie, *yaa Sidi*. I know where you've been."

I wondered how he knew. Maybe the fat black man who'd followed me wasn't working for the bad guys, after all. "Can't you bring yourself to tell one little falsehood, Kmuzu? For my sake?"

He gave me a stern look. "I am a Christian, *yaa Sidi*," was all he said.

"Thanks anyway," I said, and pushed past him to the bathroom. I took a long, hot shower, letting the hard spray pound my aching back and shoulders. I washed my hair, shaved, and trimmed my beard. I was starting to feel better, even though I'd had only a few hours of sleep. I stared into my closet for a long while, deciding what to wear to my appointment with the imam. Feeling a little perverse, I chose a conservative blue business suit. I almost never wore Western-style clothing anymore, and even when I did, I steered away from business suits. I had to have Kmuzu tie my necktie; not only did I not know how, I obstinately refused to learn.

"Would you care for something to eat, *yaa Sidi?*" he asked.

I glanced at my watch. "Thanks, Kmuzu, but I barely have time to get there. Would you be so kind as to drive me?"

"Of course, *yaa Sidi.*"

For some reason, I felt no anxiety at all about facing Dr. Sadiq Abd ar-Razzaq, the imam of the greatest mosque in the city and one of our leading religious thinkers. That was good, because it meant that I didn't feel the need to pop a few tabs and caps in preparation for the meeting. Sober, and with my wits about me, I might come away from the appointment with my head still attached to my shoulders.

Kmuzu double-parked the car on the street outside the mosque's western wall, and I hurried through the rain and up the well-worn granite steps. I slipped off my shoes and made my way deeper through the shadowy spaces and chambers that formed an asymmetric network beneath high, vaulted ceilings. In some of the columned areas, robed teachers taught religious lessons to groups of serious-faced boys. In others, individuals or small congregations prayed. I followed a long, cool colonnade to the rear of the mosque, where the imam had his offices.

I spoke first to a secretary, who told me that Dr. Abd ar-Razzaq was running a bit late that afternoon. He invited me to sit in a small waiting room to the side. There was one window looking out over the inner courtyard, but the glass was so grimy that I could barely see through it. The waiting room reminded me of the visits I'd made to Friedlander Bey, in the time before I came to live in his mansion. I'd always had to cool my heels in a waiting room very much like this one. I wondered if it was a common psychological ploy of the rich and powerful.

After about half an hour, the secretary opened the door and said the imam would see me now. I stood up, took a deep breath, pressed my suit jacket with my hands, and followed the secretary. He held open a heavy, wonderfully carved wooden door, and I went in.

Dr. Sadiq Abd ar-Razzaq had placed his large desk in the darkest corner of the room, and as he sat in his padded leather chair, I could barely make out his features. He had a green-shaded lamp providing light on the desk, but when I took the seat he indicated, his face sank once again into the indistinguishable shadows.

I waited for him to speak first. I squirmed a little in the armchair, turning my head a little from side to side, seeing only shelves of books reaching up out of sight toward the ceiling. There was a peculiar odor in the room, compounded of old, yellowing paper, cigar smoke, and pine-scented cleaning solutions.

He sat observing me for some time. Then he leaned forward, bringing the lower part of his face into the light from the lamp. "Monsieur Audran," he said in an old, cracked voice.

"Yes, O Wise One."

"You dispute the evidence that has been gathered, evidence that clearly proves you and Friedlander Bey murdered Officer Khalid Maxwell." He tapped a blue cardboard folder.

"Yes, I dispute it, O Wise One. I never even met the murdered patrolman. Neither I nor Friedlander Bey have any connection to this case."

The imam sighed and leaned back out of the light. "There is a strong case against you, you must know that. We have an eyewitness who has come forward."

I hadn't heard that before. "Yes? Who is this eyewitness, and how do you know he's reliable?"

"Because, Monsieur Audran, the witness is a lieutenant of police. Lieutenant Hajjar, as a matter of fact."

"Son of an ass!" I cried. Then I caught myself. "I apologize, O Wise One."

He waved a hand in dismissal. "It comes down to this: your word against that of a high-ranking police official. I must make my judgments according to Islamic law, according to proper civil procedure, and using my somewhat limited faculties to sort truth from lies. I must warn you that unless you can provide conclusive proof of your innocence, the case will no doubt be judged against you."

"So I understand, Imam Abd ar-Razzaq. We have avenues of investigation yet to explore. We're hopeful of presenting sufficient evidence to change your mind."

The old man coughed hoarsely a few times. "For your sakes, I hope you do. But be assured that my primary motive will be to see that justice is done."

"Yes, O Wise One."

"To that end, I wish to know what your immediate plans are, as far as investigating this sad event."

This was it. If the imam was too shocked by my intention, he could very well veto it, and then I'd be up the proverbial dune without a sunshade. "O Wise One," I began slowly, "it has come to our attention that no proper autopsy was performed on the corpse of Khalid Maxwell. I wish your permission to exhume the body, and have a thorough study done by the city's coroner."

I could not see the man's expression, but I could hear his sharp intake of breath. "You know that it is a commandment from Allah that burial follow death immediately."

I nodded.

"And exhumation is permitted only in the most extreme and urgent situations."

I shrugged. "May I remind you, O Wise One, that my life and the life of Friedlander Bey may depend on the results of an autopsy. And I'm sure that Shaykh Mahali would agree, even if you don't."

The imam slammed his wrinkled hand down on the desk. "Watch your words, boy!" he whispered. "You threaten to go over my head on this matter? Well, there is no need. I will grant permission for the exhumation. But in return, I will say that your proof must be gathered in two weeks, not the month you were given previously. The people of the city cannot tolerate a longer delay for justice to be done." He bent over his desk and found a clean sheet of paper. I watched him write out a short paragraph and sign it.

Abd ar-Razzaq was making it almost impossible for us to clear our names. Two weeks! I didn't like that at all. We could have used twelve. I merely stood, bowed my head slightly, and said, "Then if you will excuse me, O Wise One, I will go directly to the coroner's office in the Budayeen. I do not wish to take up any more of your time."

I could not see him, and he said nothing more to me. He just handed me the sheet of paper. I glanced at it; it was an official order for Khalid Maxwell's autopsy, to be performed within the next two weeks.

I stood there in his darkened office for a few seconds, feeling more and more uncomfortable. Finally, I thought to myself, "Fuck him," and turned around. I hurried back through the sprawling mosque, regained my shoes, and got back in the car behind Kmuzu.

"Do you wish to go home now, *yaa Sidi?*" he asked.

"No," I said. "I need to go to the Budayeen."

He nodded and started the car. I sat back in the seat

and thought about what I'd learned. Hajjar was claiming to be an eyewitness, huh? Well, I suspected I could shake his testimony. All in all, I wasn't feeling too bad. I was even congratulating myself for the way I'd handled myself with Abd ar-Razzaq.

Then I got two phone calls that tracked mud across my nice, fresh mood.

The first one was about money. My phone rang and I unclipped it. "Hello," I said.

"Mr. Marîd Audran? This is Kirk Adwan from the Bank of the Dunes."

That's the bank where I kept my own accounts. "Yes?" I said warily.

"We have a check here made out to a Farouk Hussein in the amount of twenty-four hundred kiam. It has your endorsement on the back, as well as Mr. Hussein's in what appears to be your handwriting."

Uh huh. The check that poor Fuad had given to Jacques. Jacques had waited for the check to clear, then he'd withdrawn the twenty-four hundred kiam and given it to Fuad.

"Yes?" I said.

"Mr. Audran, Mr. Hussein has reported that check as stolen. Now, we're not eager to prosecute, but unless you can cover the twenty-four hundred kiam by five o'clock tomorrow, we'll be forced to call the police on this matter. You can visit any of our branches for your convenience."

"Uh, just a minute—" Too late. Adwan had hung up.

I closed my eyes and cursed silently. What was this, some kind of sting? Fuad was too dumb to pull off anything this complicated. Was Jacques in it, too? I didn't care. I was going to get to the bottom of it, and whoever was responsible was going to be sorry. He'd better get used to breathing fine yellow sand.

I was furious. The situation even had me muttering to

myself. Maybe an hour passed. Kmuzu and I were getting something to eat at the Café Solace when the phone rang again. "Yeah?" I said impatiently.

"Yeah, yourself, Audran." It was Lieutenant Hajjar, the expert eyewitness himself.

"I got something I need to go over with you, Hajjar," I said gruffly.

"Take your turn, *noraf*. Tell me, didn't you have an appointment to see Imam Sadiq Abd ar-Razzaq this afternoon?"

My eyes narrowed. "How did you know that?"

Hajjar snorted. "I know lots. Anyway, I was wondering if you could tell me how, less than an hour after your visit, the next time his secretary went in to see him, the holy man ended up dead, sprawled all over his floor with half a dozen poisoned needle-gun flechettes in his chest?"

I just stared at Kmuzu's face.

"Hello?" said Hajjar sweetly. "Mr. Suspect? Would you mind dropping by the office here at your earliest convenience?"

I just clipped the phone back on my belt. Now that I had only two weeks instead of a month to establish our innocence, I had more trouble to take care of than ever. I reached into my suit jacket for my pillcase—after all, this was another one of those moments when illicit drugs were definitely indicated—but I had left it behind in my *gallebeya*.

I asked myself, *What would Shaykh Hassanein do in a situation like this?* Unfortunately, the only answer was *Hightail it back into the untrackable wastes of the Rub al-Khali.*

Say, maybe that wasn't such a bad idea. . . .

14

I took care of both the major problems that very afternoon, which is further proof of how much I've matured. In the olden days, I would've hidden in my bedroom, deep within a fog of Sonneine, and put off thinking about my troubles for a day or two, until the matters became critical. I'd since learned that it was much easier to deal with hassles while they're still in the yellow-alert stage.

I had to decide, first of all, which crisis was the more pressing. Was it more important to save my life, or my credit rating? Well, I've always been on good terms with my banker—especially since I'd become Papa's junior executive, and the beneficiary of frequent fat envelopes stuffed with money. I supposed that the Bank of the Dunes could wait an hour or two, but that Lieutenant Hajjar might not have the same patience.

It was still raining as Kmuzu drove me to the police

station on Walid al-Akbar Street. As usual, I had to pass through a crowd of dirty-faced young boys, all of whom were pressing against me and loudly clamoring for *baksheesh*. I wondered why the kids hung out here at the copshop, instead of, say, the Hotel Palazzo di Marco Aurelio, where the rich tourists were. Maybe they thought people going in and out of the police station had other things on their minds, and might be more generous. I don't know; I just flung a few kiam down the block, and they all chased after the money. As I climbed the stairs, I heard one boy whistle the familiar children's tune.

I found my way upstairs to Lieutenant Hajjar's glassed-in office in the middle of the detective division. He was on the phone, so I just let myself in and sat in an uncomfortable wooden chair beside his desk. I picked up a stack of Hajjar's mail and began sorting through it, until he grabbed it back with an angry scowl. Then he barked a few words into the phone and slammed it down. "Audran," he said in a loud, greedy voice.

"Lieutenant," I said. "What's happening?"

He stood up and paced a little. "I know you're gonna get shortened by one head-length even sooner than you thought."

I shrugged. "You mean because Abd ar-Razzaq cut two weeks off the time we had to clear our names."

Hajjar stopped pacing, turned to face me, and let his face widen slowly in an evil grin. "No, you stupid motherfucker," he said, "the whole city's gonna come after you and hang you by your heels for the murder of the holy man. With blazing torches, they'll drag you out of bed and separate you into little piles of internal organs. You and Friedlander Bey both. And it's about time, too."

I closed my eyes and sighed wearily. "I didn't kill the imam, Hajjar."

He sat down again behind his desk. "Let's look at this

scientifically. You had an appointment with the imam at two o'clock. The secretary said you went in to see him about quarter past the hour. You were in Abd ar-Razzaq's office a little more than fifteen minutes. There were no more appointments until half past three. When the secretary looked in on the imam at three-thirty, Dr. Abd ar-Razzaq was dead."

"There's a solid hour there when someone else could've gotten by the secretary and killed the son of a bitch," I said calmly.

Hajjar shook his head. "It's an open-and-shut case," he said. "You won't live long enough to find out anything about Khalid Maxwell."

I was starting to get annoyed. Not frightened or worried—just annoyed. "Did you ask the secretary if he left his desk anytime during that hour? Did you ask him if he saw anyone else during that time?"

Hajjar shook his head. "No need," he said. "Open-and-shut case."

I stood up. "What you're telling me is that I have to prove myself innocent of *two* murders now."

"In a hell of a hurry, too. We're not going to release the news about the imam until morning, because the amir wants us to get ready for the riots and demonstrations first. There *are* going to be terrible riots and demonstrations, you know. You're going to get to witness them from the very middle, from inside an iron cage, is my prediction. If Friedlander Bey wants to clear his name as far as Maxwell is concerned, he's gonna have to do it without you. You're gonna be a stiff in a few days, unless you skip town. And believe me, you're gonna have a tough time doing that, 'cause we're watching you every minute."

"I know," I said. "The fat black guy."

Hajjar looked embarrassed. "Well," he said, "he's not one of my best."

I headed for the door. These visits with Hajjar were never very rewarding. "See you later," I called over my shoulder.

"I wouldn't be in your shoes for nothin'. Been waiting a long time for this, Audran. Where you going now?"

I turned and faced him. "Oh, I was planning to drop by the medical examiner's office in the Budayeen. I got permission from the imam to have Khalid Maxwell exhumed."

He turned red and blew up like a balloon. "What?" he cried. "No such thing! Not in my jurisdiction! I won't allow it!"

I smiled. "Life is hard, Lieutenant," I said, letting him look at the official okay I'd gotten from Abd ar-Razzaq. I didn't trust Hajjar enough to let him touch it, though. "This is all I need. If worse comes to worst, I can get Shaykh Mahali to hold your leash if I have to."

"Maxwell? Exhumed? What the hell for?" shouted Hajjar.

"They say a murder victim keeps an imprint of his murderer's face on his retinas, even after death. Ever hear that before? Maybe I'll find out who killed the patrolman. *Inshallah.*"

Hajjar slammed his fist on his desk. "That's just superstition!"

I shrugged. "I don't know. I thought it was worth a peek. See ya." I escaped from the lieutenant's office, leaving him fuming and sucking in air and blowing it out.

I climbed into the car, and Kmuzu turned to look at me. "Are you all right, *yaa Sidi?*" he asked.

"More trouble," I grunted. "There's a branch of the Bank of the Dunes around the corner on the boulevard, about ten blocks down. I need to see someone there."

"Yes, *yaa Sidi.*"

As we made our way through the congested traffic, I

wondered if Hajjar really could pin the imam's murder on me. After all, I did have the opportunity, as well as a kind of bent motive. Was that enough to build a legal case? Just the fact that, except for the murderer himself, I was probably the last to see Dr. Sadiq Abd ar-Razzaq alive?

My next thought was sobering. Hajjar didn't *need* to build a tight legal case. Starting tomorrow, there were going to be two hundred thousand anguished Muslims mourning the brutal murder of their religious leader. All somebody had to do was whisper in enough ears that I was responsible, and I'd pay for the crime without ever standing before an Islamic judge. And I wouldn't even be given a chance to speak in my own defense.

I'd stopped caring about the rain. With this latest development of Hajjar's, I'd even stopped caring about the twenty-four hundred kiam. I stepped into the bank and looked around. There was soft music playing, and the faint fragrance of roses on the air. The lobby of the bank was all glass and stainless steel. To the far right was a row of human tellers, and then a row of automatic teller machines. Across from me were the desks of several bank officers. I went to the receptionist and waited for her to acknowledge my presence.

"Can I help you, sir?" she said in a bored tone of voice.

"I got a call earlier today from a Mr. Kirk Adwan—"

"Mr. Adwan's with a customer right now. Take a seat and he'll be right with you."

"Uh huh," I said. I slouched on a sofa and rested my chin on my chest. I wished again that I had my pillcase with me, or my rack of moddies. It would've been good to escape into somebody else's personality for a while.

Finally, the customer with Adwan got up and left, and I stood and crossed the carpet. Adwan was busy signing papers. "I'll be right with you," he said. "Take a seat."

I sat. I just wanted to get this stupid business over with.

Adwan finished his busywork, looked up blankly, let my face register for a split second, then flashed me his official smile. "Now," he said in a charming voice, "how may I help you?"

"You called me earlier today. My name is Marîd Audran. Some confusion over a twenty-four-hundred-kiam check."

Adwan's smile vanished. "Yes, I remember," he said. His voice was very cold. Mr. Adwan didn't like me, I'm afraid. "Mr. Farouk Hussein reported the cashier's check stolen. When it came through the bank, there was only his name on the front, and yours on the back."

"I didn't steal the check, Mr. Adwan. I didn't deposit it."

He nodded. "Certainly, sir. If you say so. Nevertheless, as I mentioned on the phone, if you're unwilling to repay the money, we'll have to turn this matter over for prosecution. I'm afraid that in the city, this sort of grand theft is punished harshly. Very harshly."

"I fully intend to repay the bank," I said. I reached inside my suit coat and took out my wallet. I had about five thousand kiam in cash with me. I sorted out twenty-four hundred and slid the money across the desk.

Adwan scooped it up, counted it, and excused himself. He got up and went through a door marked No Admittance.

I waited. I wondered what was going to happen next. Would Adwan come back with a troop of armed bank guards? Would he strip me of my ATM and credit cards? Would he lead all the other bank employees in a chorus of public denunciation? I didn't fuckin' care.

When Adwan did return to his desk, he sat down and

folded his hands in front of him. "There," he said, "we're glad you chose to take care of this matter promptly."

There was an awkward silence for a moment. "Say," I said, "how do I know that there was ever a stolen check? I mean, you called me up, you told me the check was stolen, I came in here and handed you twenty-four hundred kiam, you got up and disappeared, and when you came back the money was gone. How do I know you just didn't deposit it in your own account?"

He blinked at me for a few seconds. Then he opened a desk drawer, removed a thin file in a cardboard cover, and glanced through it. He looked me straight in the eye and murmured a commcode into his telephone. "Here," he said. "Talk to Hussein yourself."

I waited until the man answered. "Hello?" I said.

"Hello. Who is this?"

"My name is . . . well, never mind. I'm sitting here in a branch of the Bank of the Dunes. Somehow, a check with your name on it ended up in my possession."

"You stole it," said Hussein gruffly.

"I wasn't the one who stole it," I said. "One of my business associates was trying to do a favor for a friend, and asked me to endorse the check and cover it."

"You're not even lying good, mister."

I was getting annoyed again. "Listen, pal," I said in a patient voice, "I've got this friend named Fuad. He said he wanted to buy a van from you, but you sold it to—"

"Fuad?" Hussein said suspiciously. And then he described Fuad il-Manhous from the greasy hair down to the worn-out shoes.

"How do you know him?" I asked, astonished.

"He's my brother-in-law," said Hussein. "Sometimes he stays by me and his sister. I must've left that check laying around, and Fuad thought he could get away with something. I'll break his fuckin' arms, the scrawny bastard."

"Huh," I said, still amazed that Fuad could come up with such a plausible story. It was a better scam than I thought he was capable of. "It looks like he tried to swindle both of us."

"Well, I'm getting my money back from the bank. Did you cover the check?"

I knew what was coming. "Yeah," I said.

Hussein laughed. "Then good luck trying to recover your money from Fuad. He never has two kiam to rub together. If he's blown that twenty-four hundred, you can just sing in the moonlight for it. And he's probably left town already."

"Yeah, you right. I'm glad we got this all sorted out." I hung up the phone. Later, when I'd cleared up all my major troubles, Fuad would have to pay.

Although, in a way, I half-ass admired him for pulling it off. He used my own prejudice against me—me and Jacques both. We trusted him because we thought he was too stupid to pull a fast one. Weeks ago, I'd been taken by Bedu con men, and now by Fuad. I still had plenty to be humble about.

"Sir?" said Adwan.

I gave him back his phone. "All right, I understand it all now," I told him. "Mr. Hussein and I have a mutual friend who tried to play both ends against the middle."

"Yes, sir," said Adwan. "The bank only cared that it was properly repaid."

I stood up. "Fuck the bank," I said. I even toyed with the idea of withdrawing all my money from the Bank of the Dunes. The only thing was, they were just too convenient. I would've liked to have slugged that snotty Kirk Adwan just once, too.

It had been a very long day, and I hadn't gotten much

sleep at Yasmin's apartment. I was beginning to run down. As I got into the car again, I told myself that I was going to make one more little visit, and then I was going to sit on the end of the bar in my club and watch naked female-shaped creatures wiggle to the music.

"Home, *yaa Sidi?*" asked Kmuzu.

"No rest for the wicked, my friend," I said, leaning my head back and massaging my temples. "Take me back to the eastern gate of the Budayeen. I need to talk with the medical examiner there, and after that I'm going to sit in Chiriga's for a few hours. I need to relax a little."

"Yes, *yaa Sidi.*"

"You're welcome to come with me. You know that Chiri will be glad to see you."

I saw Kmuzu's eyes narrow in the rearview mirror. "I will wait for you in the car," he said sternly. He really didn't like the attention he got from Chiri. Or maybe he *did* like it, and that's what was bothering him.

"I'll be a few hours," I said. "In fact, I'll probably stay until closing."

"Then I will go home. You may call me to get you when you wish."

It only took a few minutes to drive back along the boulevard to the Budayeen. I got out of the car, leaned down, and said good-bye to Kmuzu. I stood in the warm drizzle and watched the cream-colored sedan drive away. To be honest, I was in very little hurry to meet the medical examiner. I have a low tolerance for ghastliness.

And ghastliness was just what I saw when I entered the morgue, which was just inside the gate on the corner of First and the Street. The city operated two morgues; there was one somewhere else to handle the city in general, and there was this office to take care of the Budayeen. The walled quarter generated so many dead bodies that it rated its own cadaver franchise. The only thing I never understood was, why was the morgue at the eastern end of the Budayeen, and the cemetery against the western wall? You'd think it would be more convenient if they were closer together.

I'd been in the morgue a few times in the past. My friends and I called it the Chamber of Horrors, because it bore out every horrible expectation one might have. It was dimly lighted, and there was very poor ventilation. The air was hot and dank and reeked of human wastes, dead bodies, and formaldehyde. The medical examiner's office had twelve vaults in which to store the corpses, but natural death, misadventure, and old-fashioned mayhem delivered that many bodies before noon daily. The later ones waited on the floor, stacked in piles on the broken, grimy tiles.

There was the chief medical examiner and two assistants to try to keep up with this constant, grim traffic. Cleanliness was the next greatest problem, but none of the three officials had time to worry about swabbing the floors. Lieutenant Hajjar occasionally sent jailed prisoners over to work in the morgue, but it wasn't a coveted assignment. Because the builders of the body vaults had neglected to include drains, they had to be mopped out by hand every few days. The vaults were wonderful hatcheries for many varieties of germs and bacteria. The unlucky prisoners often returned to jail with anything from tuberculosis to meningitis, diseases which were eminently preventable elsewhere.

One of the assistants came up to me with a harried look on his face. "What can I do for you?" he asked. "Got a body or something?"

Instinctively, I backed away from him. I was afraid he'd touch me. "I have permission from the imam of the Shimaal Mosque to proceed with the exhumation of a body. It was a murder victim who never received an official autopsy."

"Exhumation, uh huh," said the assistant, beckoning me to follow him. I passed through the tiled room. There was a naked corpse stretched stiff on one of the two metal autopsy tables. It was illuminated by a dirty, cracked skylight overhead, and by a row of flickering fluorescent fixtures.

The formaldehyde was making my eyes burn and my nose drip. I was thankful when I saw that the assistant was leading me toward a solid wooden door at the far end of the examination room.

"In here," he said. "The doc will be with you in a few minutes. He's having lunch."

I wedged myself into the tiny office. It was lined with file cabinets. There was a desk piled high with stacks of folders, files, books, computer bubble plates, and who knew what else. There was a chair opposite it, surrounded by more mounds of papers, books, and boxes. I sat in the chair. There was no room to move it. I felt trapped in this dark warren, but at least it was better than the outer room.

After a while, the medical examiner came in. He glanced at me once over the top of his thick-rimmed spectacles. New eyes are so cheap and easy to get—there are a couple of good eyeshops right in the Budayeen—that you don't see many people with glasses anymore. "I'm Dr. Besharati. You're here about an exhumation?"

"Yes, sir," I said.

He sat down. I could barely see him over the litter on his desk. He picked up a trumpet from the floor and leaned back. "I'll have to clear this through Lieutenant Hajjar's office," he said.

"I've already been to see him. I was given permission

by Imam Abd ar-Razzaq to have this posthumous examination performed."

"Then I'll just call the imam," said the medical examiner. He tootled a few notes on his trumpet.

"The imam is dead," I said in a flat voice. "You can call his secretary, though."

"Excuse me?" Dr. Besharati gave me an astonished look.

"He was murdered this afternoon. After I left his office."

"May the blessings of Allah be on him and peace!" he said. Then he murmured for a while. I assumed he was praying. "That's most horrible. It's a terrible thing. Do they have the murderer?"

I shook my head. "No, not yet."

"I hope he's torn to pieces," said Dr. Besharati.

"About Khalid Maxwell's autopsy—" I handed him the written order from the late Dr. Abd ar-Razzaq.

He put his trumpet back on the floor and examined the document. "Yes, of course. What is the reason for your request?"

I filled him in on the entire story. He stared at me with a dazed expression during most of it, but the mention of Friedlander Bey's name snapped him out of it. Papa often has that magical effect on people.

At last, Dr. Besharati stood up and reached across his desk to take my hand. "Please give my regards to Friedlander Bey," he said nervously. "I will see to the exhumation myself. It will be done this very day, *inshallah*. As to the autopsy itself, I will perform it tomorrow morning at seven o'clock. I like to get as much work done before the heat of the afternoon. You understand."

"Yes, of course," I said.

"Do you wish to be present? For the autopsy, I mean?"

I chewed my lip and thought. "How long will it take?"

The medical examiner shrugged. "A couple of hours."

Dr. Besharati's reputation suggested that he was someone Friedlander Bey and I could trust. Still, I intended to let him prove himself. "Then I'll come by about nine o'clock, and you can give me a report. If there's anything you think I ought to see, you can show me then. Otherwise, I don't see the need for me to get in your way."

He came out from around his desk and took my arm, leading me back out into the Chamber of Horrors. "I suppose not," he said.

I hurried ahead of him to the outer waiting room. "I appreciate your taking the time to help me," I said. "Thank you."

He waved a hand. "No, it's nothing. Friedlander Bey has helped me on more than one occasion in the past. Perhaps tomorrow, after we've finished with Officer Maxwell, you'll permit me to give you a tour of my little domain?"

I stared at him. "We'll see," I said at last.

He took out a handkerchief and wiped his nose. "I understand completely. Twenty years I've been here, and I hate it just as much now as when I first saw it." He shook his head.

When I got back outside, I gulped fresh air like a drowning man. I needed a couple of drinks now more than ever.

As I made my way up the Street, I heard shrill whistles around me. I smiled. My guardian angels were on the job. It was early evening, and the clubs and cafés were beginning to fill up. There were quite a few nervous tourists around, all wondering if they'd be taking their lives in their hands if they just sat somewhere and had a beer. They'd probably find out. The hard way.

The night shift had just taken over when I walked into Chiri's. I felt better immediately. Kandy was on stage, dancing energetically to some Sikh propaganda song. That was a trend in music that I wished would hurry up and disappear.

"*Jambo*, Mr. Boss!" called Chiri. She flashed a grin.

"Where you at, sweetheart," I said. I took my seat at the far curve of the bar.

Chiri threw together a White Death and brought it to me. "Ready for another wonderful, exotic, exciting night on the Street?" she said, plopping down a cork coaster and setting my drink on it.

I frowned. "It's never wonderful, it's never exotic," I said. "It's just the same damn boring music and the same faceless customers."

Chiri nodded. "The money always looks the same, too, but that don't make me kick it out of bed."

I looked around the club. My three pals, Jacques, Saied the Half-Hajj, and Mahmoud, were sitting at a table in the front corner, playing cards. This was rare, because the Half-Hajj got no kick from watching the dancers, and Jacques was militantly straight and could barely speak to the debs and sexchanges, and Mahmoud—as far as I knew—had no sexual predilections at all. That's why they spent most of their time at the Café Solace or on the patio at Gargotier's place.

I walked over to welcome them to my humble establishment. "How y'all doin'?" I said, pulling up a chair.

"Just fine," said Mahmoud.

"Say," said Jacques, studying his cards, "what was all that excitement in Frenchy's with that girl Theoni?"

I scratched my head. "You mean when she jumped up and started yelling? Well, the customer she was working on so hard gave her a present, remember? After he left Frenchy's, she opened the package and it turned out to be a baby book. Lots of cute pictures of this adorable baby girl, and a kind of diary of the kid's first few months. Turns out the guy was Theoni's real father. His wife ran off with her when Theoni was only eight months old. Her father's spent a lot of time and money tracking the girl down ever since."

The Half-Hajj shook his head. "Theoni must've been surprised."

"Yeah," I said. "She was embarrassed to have her father see her working in there. He tipped her a hundred kiam and promised to come back soon. Now she knows why he acted so uncomfortable when she was trying to get him excited."

"We're trying to play cards here, Maghrebi," said Mahmoud. He was about as sympathetic as a rusty razor. "Heard you was gonna exhume that dead cop."

I was surprised the news had gotten around already. "How do you feel about it?" I asked.

Mahmoud looked at me steadily for a couple of seconds. "Couldn't care less," he said at last.

"What you guys playing?" I asked.

"Bourré," said Saied. "We're teaching the Christian."

"It's been an expensive lesson so far," said Jacques. Bourré is a quiet, deceptively simple game. I've never played another card game where you could lose so much money so fast. Not even American poker.

I watched for a little while. Evidently, none of the three had any thoughts at all concerning the exhumation. I was glad of that. "Anybody seen Fuad lately?" I asked.

Jacques looked up at me. "Not for a couple days at least. What's the matter?"

"That check was stolen," I said.

"Ha! And you got stuck for it, right? I'm sorry, Marîd. I didn't have any way of knowing."

"Sure, Jacques," I said in a grim voice.

"What you guys talking about?" asked Saied.

Jacques proceeded to tell them the whole story, at great length, with many oratorical devices and changes of voice, exaggerating the truth and making me look like a complete and utter fool. Of course, he minimalized his own participation in the affair.

All three of them broke down in helpless laughter. "You let *Fuad* rip you off?" gasped Mahmoud. *"Fuad?* You're never going to live this down! I gotta tell people about this!"

I didn't say a word. I knew I was going to hear about it for a long time, unless I caught up to Fuad and made him pay for his foolish crime. Now there was nothing to do but get up and go back to my seat at the bar. As I walked away, Jacques said, "You've got a datalink in here now, Marîd. You notice? And you owe me money for all the other ones I've sold so far. A hundred kiam each, you said."

"Come in sometime with the signed delivery orders," I said in a cold voice. I squeezed the slice of lime and drank a little of the White Death.

Chiri leaned toward me across the bar. "You're gonna exhume Khalid Maxwell?" she said.

"Might learn something valuable."

She shook her head. "Sad, though. The family's been through so much already."

"Yeah, right." I swallowed more of the gin and bingara.

"What's this about Fuad?" she asked.

"Never mind. But if you see him, let me know immediately. He just owes me a little money, is all."

Chiri nodded and headed down the bar, where a new customer had sat down. I watched Kandy finish up her last song.

I felt a hand on my shoulder. I turned around and saw

Yasmin and Pualani. "How was your day, lover?" said Yasmin.

"All right." I didn't feel like going through it all.

Pualani smiled. "Yasmin says you two are gonna get married next week. Congratulations!"

"What?" I said, astonished. "What's this next week business? I haven't even formally proposed. I just mentioned the possibility. I've got a lot to think about first. I've got a lot of trouble to take care of. And then I have to talk to Indihar, and to Friedlander Bey—"

"Oops," said Pualani. She hurried away.

"Were you lying to me this morning?" asked Yasmin. "Were you just trying to get out of my house without the beating you deserved?"

"No!" I said angrily. "I was just saying that maybe we wouldn't be so bad together. I wasn't ready to set a date or anything."

Yasmin looked hurt. "Well," she said, "while you're dicking around and making up your mind, I've got places to go and people to meet. You understand me? Call me when you take care of all your so-called problems." She walked away, her back very straight, and sat down beside the new customer. She put her hand in his lap. I took another drink.

I sat there for a long time, drinking and chatting with Chiri and with Lily, the pretty sexchange who was always suggesting that we get together. About eleven o'clock, my phone rang. "Hello?" I said.

"Audran? This is Kenneth. You remember me."

"Ah, yes, the apple of Abu Adil's eye, right? Shaykh Reda's little darling. What's up? You having a bachelor party and want me to send over a few boys?"

"I'm ignoring you, Audran. I'm always ignoring you." I was sure that Kenneth hated me with an irrational ferocity.

"What did you call for?" I asked.

"Friday afternoon, the *Jaish* will parade and demonstrate against the gruesome murder of Imam Dr. Sadiq Abd ar-Razzaq. Shaykh Reda wishes you to appear, in uniform, to address the *Jaish* at this historic moment, and also to meet the unit under your command."

"How did you hear about Abd ar-Razzaq?" I asked. "Hajjar said he wasn't gonna tell anybody until tomorrow."

"Shaykh Reda isn't 'anybody.' You should know that."

"Yeah, you right."

Kenneth paused. "Shaykh Reda also wishes me to tell you he's unalterably opposed to the exhumation of Khalid Maxwell. At the risk of sounding threatening, I have to pass along Shaykh Reda's feelings. He said that if you go ahead with the autopsy, you will earn his undying hatred. That is not something to dismiss lightly."

I laughed. "Kenny, listen, aren't we already fierce rivals? Don't we hate each other's guts enough by now? And aren't Friedlander Bey and Abu Adil already at each other's throats? What's one little autopsy between archenemies?"

"All right, you stupid son of a bitch," said Kenneth shortly. "I did my job, I passed along the messages. Friday, in uniform, in the Boulevard il-Jameel outside the Shimaal Mosque. You better show up." Then he cut the connection. I clipped my phone back on my belt.

That concluded the second trip around the village. I looked at Chiri and held up my glass for a refill. The long night roared on.

15

I got a good four hours' sleep that night. After the short rest I'd got the night before, I felt exhausted and almost completely worn down. When my sleep daddy woke me at seven-thirty, I swung my feet out of bed and put them down on the carpet. I put my face in my hands and took a few deep breaths. I really didn't want to get up, and I didn't feel like jumping into battle with the forces arrayed against me. I looked at my watch; I had an hour before Kmuzu would drive me to the Budayeen for my appointment with the medical examiner. If I showered, dressed, and breakfasted in five minutes, I could go back to sleep until almost eight-thirty.

I grumbled a few curses and stood up. My back creaked. I don't think I'd ever heard my back creak before. Maybe I was getting too old to stay up all night, drinking and breaking up fights. It was a depressing thought.

I stumbled blearily to the bathroom and turned on the shower. Five minutes later, I realized that I was staring straight up into the hot spray with my eyes wide open. I felt asleep on my feet. I grabbed the soap and lathered my body, then turned slowly and let the stinging water rinse me. I dried myself and dressed in a clean white *gallebeya* with a dark red robe over it. As for breakfast, I had a decision to make. After all, I was going back to the Chamber of Horrors. Maybe food could be put off until later.

Kmuzu gave me his blank look, the one that's supposed to pass for emotionless, but was in fact transparently unfavorable. "You were quite drunk again last night, *yaa Sidi*," he said, as he set a plate of eggs and fried lamb patties in front of me.

"You must be thinking of someone else, Kmuzu," I said. I looked at the food and felt a wave of queasiness. Not lamb, not now.

Kmuzu stood beside my chair and folded his well-muscled arms. "Would you be angry if I made an observation?" he asked.

Nothing that I could say would stop him. "No. Please make your observation."

"You've been lax in your religious duties lately, *yaa Sidi*."

I turned and looked into his handsome, black face. "What the hell do you care? We're not even of the same faith, as you keep reminding me."

"Any religion is better than none."

I laughed. "I'm not so sure. I could name a few—"

"You understand what I mean. Has your self-esteem fallen so low again that you don't feel worthy to pray? That is a fallacy, you know, *yaa Sidi*."

I got up and muttered "None of your business." I went back into the bedroom, looking for my rack of moddies and daddies. I hadn't touched a bite of the breakfast.

The neuralware wasn't in the bedroom, so I went into the parlor. It wasn't there, either. I finally discovered it hiding under a towel on the desk in my study. I sorted through the small plastic squares. Somewhere along the line, I'd really put together an enviable collection. The ones I wanted, however, were the special ones, ones that I'd had ever since I'd originally had my skull amped. They were the daddies that fit onto my special second implant, the daddies that suppressed unpleasant bodily signals. It was the software that had saved my life in the Rub al-Khali.

I chipped them in and rejoiced at the difference. I was no longer sleepy, no longer hungry. One daddy took care of my growing anxiety, too. "All right, Kmuzu," I said in a cheerful voice. "Let's get on the road. I've got a lot to do today."

"Fine, *yaa Sidi*, but what about all this food?"

I shrugged. "There are people starving in Eritrea. Send it to them."

Kmuzu customarily failed to appreciate that sort of humor, so I just made sure I had my keys and went out into the corridor. I didn't wait for him to follow; I knew he'd be along immediately. I went downstairs and waited for him to start the car and bring it around to the front door. During the ride to the Budayeen we said nothing more to each other.

He let me out by the eastern gate. Once more I had a lot of plans that didn't involve Kmuzu, so I sent him home. I told him I'd call when I needed a ride. Sometimes it's great to have a slave.

When I got to the morgue, I had an unpleasant surprise. Dr. Besharati hadn't even started on the corpse of Khalid Maxwell. He looked up at me as I entered. "Mr. Audran," he said. "Forgive me, I'm running a little late this morning. We had quite a bit of business last night and early today. Unusual for this time of year. Usually get more murders during the hot months."

"Uh huh," I said. I hadn't been in the place two minutes, and already the formaldehyde was irritating my eyes and nose. The suppressor daddies didn't help me at all with something like that.

I watched as the M.E.'s two assistants went to one of the twelve vaults, opened it, and lifted out Maxwell's body. They wrestled it awkwardly to one of the two work tables. The other one was already occupied by a cadaver in an early stage of disassembly.

Dr. Besharati pulled off one pair of rubber gloves and put on another. "Ever watched an autopsy before?" he asked. He seemed to be in great spirits.

"No, sir," I said. I shuddered.

"You can step outside if you get squeamish." He picked up a long black hose and turned on a tap. "This is going to be a special case," he said, as he began playing the water all over Maxwell. "He's been in the ground for several weeks, so we won't be able to get quite as much information as we would with a fresh body."

The stench from the corpse was tremendous, and the water from the hose wasn't making any headway against it. I gagged. One of the assistants looked at me and laughed. "You think it's bad now," he said. "Wait until we open it up."

Dr. Besharati ignored him. "The official police report said that death came about as the result of being shot at close range by a medium-sized static pistol. If the range had been greater, the proper functioning of his nerves and muscles would've been interrupted for a brief time, and he'd have been rendered helpless. Apparently, though, he was shot close up, in the chest. That almost always leads to immediate cardiac arrest." While he was talking, he selected a large scalpel. *"Bismillah,"* he murmured, and made a Y-shaped incision from the shoulder joints to the sternum, and then down to the top of the groin.

I found myself looking away when the assistants lifted the skin and muscle tissue and sliced it free of the skeleton. Then I heard them snapping the rib cage open with some large implement. After they lifted the rib cage out, though, the chest cavity looked like an illustration in an elementary biology book. It wasn't so bad. They were right, though: the stink increased almost unbearably. And it wasn't going to get better any time soon.

Dr. Besharati used the hose to wash down the corpse some more. He looked across at me. "The police report also said that it was your finger on the trigger of that static pistol."

I shook my head fiercely. "I wasn't even—"

He raised a hand. "I have nothing to do with enforcement or punishment here," he said. "Your guilt or innocence hasn't been proved in a court of law. I have no opinion one way or the other. But it seems to me that if you were guilty, you wouldn't be so anxious about the outcome of this autopsy."

I thought about that for a moment. "Are we likely to get much useful information?" I asked.

"Well, as I said, not as much as if he hadn't spent all that time in a box in the ground. For one thing, his blood has putrefied. It's gummy and black now, and almost useless as far as forensic medicine is concerned. But in a way you're lucky he was a poor man. His family didn't have him embalmed. Maybe we'll be able to tell a thing or two about what happened."

He turned his attention back to the table. One assistant was beginning to lift the internal organs, one by one, out of the body cavity. Khalid Maxwell's shriveled eyes stared at me; his hair was stringy and straw-like, without luster or resiliency. His skin, too, had dried in the coffin. I think he'd been in his early thirties when he'd been murdered; now he wore the face of an eighty-year-old man. I experienced a peculiar floating sensation, as if I were only dreaming this.

The other assistant yawned and glanced at me. "Want to listen to some music?" he said. He reached behind himself and flicked on a cheap holosystem. It began to play the same goddamn Sikh propaganda song that Kandy danced to every time she took her turn on stage.

"No, please, thank you," I said. The assistant shrugged and turned the music off.

The other assistant snipped each internal organ loose, measured it, weighed it, and waited for Dr. Besharati to slice off a small piece, which was put in a vial and sealed. The rest of the viscera was just dumped in a growing pile on the table beside the body.

The medical examiner paid very special attention to the heart, however. "I subscribe to a theory," he said in a conversational tone, "that a charge from a static pistol creates a certain, unique pattern of disruption in the heart. Someday when this theory is generally accepted, we'll be able to identify the perpetrator's static pistol, just as a ballistics lab can identify bullets fired by the same projectile pistol." Now he was cutting the heart into narrow slices, to be examined more thoroughly later.

I raised my eyebrows. "What would you see in this heart tissue?"

Dr. Besharati didn't look up. "A particular pattern of exploded and unexploded cells. I'm sure in my own mind that each static pistol leaves its own, unique signature pattern."

"But this isn't accepted as evidence yet?"

"Not yet, but someday soon, I hope. It will make my

job—and the police's job, and the legal counselors'—a lot easier."

Dr. Besharati straightened up and moved his shoulders. "My back hurts already," he said, frowning. "All right, I'm ready to do the skull."

An assistant made an incision from ear to ear along the back of the neck, just below the hairline. Then the other assistant pulled Maxwell's scalp grotesquely forward, until it fell down over the corpse's face. The medical examiner selected a small electric saw; when he turned it on, it filled the echoing chamber with a loud burring sound that set my teeth on edge. It got even worse when he began cutting in a circle around the top of the skull.

Dr. Besharati switched off the saw and lifted off the cap of bone, which he examined closely for cracks or other signs of foul play. He examined the brain, first in place, then he carefully lifted it out onto the table. He cut the brain in slices, just as he'd done the heart, and put one piece in another vial.

A few moments later, I realized that the autopsy was finished. I glanced at my watch; ninety minutes had sped by while I was wrapped in a kind of gruesome fascination. Dr. Besharati took his samples and left the Chamber of Horrors through an arched doorway.

I watched the assistants clean up. They took a plastic bag and scooped all the dissected organs into it, including the brain. They closed the bag with a twist-tie, pushed the whole thing into Maxwell's chest cavity, replaced the pieces of rib cage, and began sewing him back up with large, untidy stitches. They set the top of the skull in place, pulled Maxwell's scalp back over it, and stitched it back down at the base of the neck.

It seemed like such a mechanical, unfeeling way for a good man to end his existence. Of course it was mechanical and unfeeling; the three employees of the medical examiner's office would have twenty or more autopsies to perform before suppertime.

"You all right?" asked one of the assistants with a sly grin on his face. "Don't want to throw up or nothing?"

"I'm fine. What happens to him?" I pointed to Maxwell's corpse.

"Back in the box, back in the ground before noon prayers. Don't worry about him. He never felt a thing."

"May the blessings of Allah be on him and peace," I said, and shivered again.

"Yeah," said the assistant, "what you say."

"Mr. Audran?" called Dr. Besharati. I turned around and saw him standing in the doorway. "Come back here and I'll show you what I was talking about."

I followed him into a high-ceilinged workroom. The lighting was a little better, but the air was, if anything, even worse. The walls of the room were entirely taken up with shelves, from floor to ceiling. On each twelve-inch shelf were a couple of thousand white plastic tubs, stacked four high and four deep, filling every available inch of volume. Dr. Besharati saw what I was looking at. "I wish we could get rid of them," he said sadly.

"What are they?" I asked.

"Specimens. By law, we're required to keep all the specimens we take for ten years. Like the heart and brain samples I removed from Maxwell. But because the formaldehyde is a danger, the city won't let us burn them when the time is up. And the city won't permit us to bury them or flush them down the drain because of contamination. We're about out of room here."

I looked around at the roomful of shelves. "What are you going to do?"

He shook his head. "I don't know. Maybe we'll have to start renting a refrigerated warehouse. It's up to the city, and the city's always telling me it doesn't have the money to fix up my office. I think they'd just rather forget that we're even down here."

"I'll mention it to the amir the next time I see him."

"Would you?" he said hopefully. "Anyway, take a look through this." He showed me an old microscope that was probably new when Dr. Besharati was first dreaming of going to medical school.

I peered through the binocular eyepieces. I saw some stained cells. That was all I could see. "What am I looking at?" I asked.

"A bit of Khalid Maxwell's muscle tissue. Do you see the pattern of disruption I mentioned?"

Well, I had no idea what the cells were supposed to look like, so I couldn't judge how they'd been changed by the jolt from the static pistol. "I'm afraid not," I said. "I'll have to take your word for it. But *you* see it, right? If you found another sample that had the same pattern, would you be willing to testify that the same gun had been used?"

"I'd be willing to testify," he said slowly, "but, as I said, it would carry no weight in court."

I looked at him again. "We've got something here," I said thoughtfully. "There's got to be a way to use it."

"Well," said Dr. Besharati, ushering me out through the Chamber of Horrors, to the outer waiting room, "I hope you find a way. I hope you clear your name. I'll give this job special attention, and I ought to have results for you later this evening. If there's anything else I can do, don't hesitate to get in touch with me. I'm here twelve to sixteen hours a day, six days a week."

I glanced back over my shoulder. "Seems like an awful lot of time to spend in these surroundings," I said.

He just shrugged. "Right now, I've got seven murder victims waiting to be examined, in addition to Khalid Maxwell. Even after all these years, I can't help wondering who these poor souls were, what kind of lives they had, what kind of terrible stories led to their ending up on my tables. They're all people to me, Mr. Audran. People. Not stiffs. And they deserve the best that I can do for them. For some of them, I'm the only hope that justice will be done. I'm their last chance."

"Maybe," I said, "here at the very end, their lives can acquire some meaning. Maybe if you help identify the killers, the city can protect other people from them."

"Maybe," he said. He shook his head sadly. "Sometimes justice is the most important thing in the world."

I thanked Dr. Besharati for all his help and left the building. I got the impression that he basically loved his work, and at the same time hated the conditions he had to work in. As I headed out of the Budayeen, it occurred to me that I might end up just like Khalid Maxwell someday, with my guts scattered about on a stainless steel table, with my heart and brain sliced up and stored away in some little white plastic tubs. I was glad I was on my way anywhere, even Hajjar's station house.

It wasn't far: through the eastern gate, across the Boulevard il-Jameel, south a few blocks to the corner of Walid al-Akbar Street. I was forced to take an unplanned detour, though. Papa's long black car was parked against the curb. Tariq was standing on the sidewalk, as if at attention, waiting for me. He wasn't wearing a cheerful expression.

"Friedlander Bey would like to speak with you, Shaykh Marîd," he said. He held the rear door open, and I slid in. I expected Papa to be in the car, too, but I was all alone.

"Why didn't he send Kmuzu for me, Tariq?" I asked.

There was no answer as he slammed the door shut and walked around the car. He got behind the wheel, and we started moving through traffic. Instead of driving toward the house, though, Tariq was taking me through the east side of the city, through unfamiliar neighborhoods.

"Where are we going?" I asked.

No answer. Uh oh.

I sat back in the seat, wondering what was going on. Then I had a horrible, icy suspicion. I'd come this way once before, a long time ago. My suspicions mounted as we turned and twisted through the poverty-ridden eastern outskirts. The suppressor daddy was doing its best to damp out my fear, but my hands began to sweat anyway.

At last Tariq pulled into an asphalt driveway behind a pale green cinderblock motel. I recognized it at once. I recognized the small, hand-lettered MOTEL NO VACANCY sign. Tariq parked the car and opened the door for me. "Room 19," he said.

"I know," I said. "I remember the way."

One of the Stones That Speak was standing in the doorway to Room 19. He looked down at me; there was no expression on his face. I couldn't move the giant man, so I just waited until he decided what he was going to do with me. Finally he grunted and stepped aside, just far enough for me to squeeze by him.

Inside, the room looked the same. It hadn't been decorated since my last visit, when I first came to Friedlander Bey's attention, when I was first made a part of the old man's tangled schemes. The furnishings were worn and shabby, a European-style bed and bureau, a couple of chairs with rips in their upholstering. Papa sat at a folding card table set up in the middle of the room. Beside him stood the other Stone.

"My nephew," said Papa. His expression was grim. There was no love in his eyes.

"*Hamdillah as-salaama, yaa Shaykh,*" I said. "Praise God for your safety." I squinted a little, desperately trying to find an escape route from the room. There was none, of course.

"*Allah yisallimak*," he replied bluntly. He wished the blessings of Allah on me in a voice as empty of affection as a spent bullet.

As I knew they would, the Stones That Speak moved slowly, one to each side of me. I glanced at them, and then back at Papa. "What have I done, O Shaykh?" I whispered.

I felt the Stones' hands on my shoulders, squeezing, tightening, crushing. Only the pain-blocking daddy kept me from crying out.

Papa stood up behind the table. "I have prayed to Allah that you would change your ways, my nephew," he said. "You have made me unutterably sad." The light glinted off his eyes, and they were like chips of dirty ice. They didn't look sad at all.

"What do you mean?" I asked. I knew what he meant, all right.

The Stones kneaded my shoulders harder. The one on my left—Habib or Labib, I can never tell which—held my arm out from my side. He put one hand on my shoulder and began to turn the arm in its socket.

"He should be suffering more," said Friedlander Bey thoughtfully. "Remove the chips from his implants." The other Stone did as he was told, and yes, I began suffering more. I thought my arm was going to be wrenched loose. I let out one drawn-out groan.

"Do you know why you're here, my nephew?" said Papa, coming closer and standing over me. He put one hand on my cheek, which was now wet with tears. The Stone continued to twist my arm.

"No, O Shaykh," I said. My voice was hoarse. I could only gasp the word out.

"Drugs," said Papa simply. "You've been seen in public too often under the influence of drugs. You know how I feel about that. You've scorned the holy word of Prophet Muhammad, may the blessings of Allah be on him and peace. He prohibits intoxication. *I* prohibit intoxication."

"Yes," I said. It was clear to me that he was angrier at the affront to him than the affront to our blessed religion.

"You had warnings in the past. This is the last. The last of all time. If you do not mend your behavior, my nephew, you will take another ride with Tariq. He won't bring you here, though. He'll drive away from the city. He'll drive far into the desert wastes. He'll return home alone. And this time there will be no hope of your walking back alive. Tariq won't be as careless as Shaykh Reda. All this despite the fact that you're my great-grandson. I have other great-grandsons."

"Yes, O Shaykh," I said softly. I was in severe pain. "Please."

He flicked his eyes at the Stones. They stepped away from me immediately. The agony continued. It would not go away for a long time. I got out of the chair slowly, grimacing.

"Wait yet a moment, my nephew," said Friedlander Bey. "We're not finished here."

"*Yallah,*" I exclaimed.

"Tariq," called Papa. The driver came into the room. "Tariq, give my nephew the weapon."

Tariq came to me and looked into my eyes. Now I thought I could see a touch of sympathy. There had been none before. He took out a needle gun and laid it in my hand.

"What is this gun, O Shaykh?" I asked.

Papa's brow furrowed. "That, my nephew, is the weapon that killed the imam, Dr. Sadiq Abd ar-Razzaq. With it, you should be able to discover the identity of the murderer."

I stared at the needle gun as if it were some unearthly alien artifact. "How—"

"I have no more answers for you."

I stood up straighter and looked directly at the white-haired old man. "How did you get this gun?"

Papa waved a hand. It evidently wasn't important enough for me to know the answer to that. All I had to do was find out who owned it. I knew then that this interview was over. Friedlander Bey had come to the end of his patience, with me, with the way I was handling the investigation.

I realized suddenly that he could well be lying—the needle gun might not actually have been the murder weapon. Yet in the vast, complicated web of intrigues that surrounded him and me and Shaykh Reda, perhaps that was irrelevant. Perhaps the only important thing was that the gun had been so designated.

Tariq helped me outside to the car. I maneuvered myself slowly into the backseat, holding the needle gun close to my chest. Just before he slammed the door, Tariq reached in and handed me the suppressor daddies. I looked at him, but I couldn't find anything to say. I reached up and chipped them in gratefully.

"Where shall I drive you, Shaykh Marîd?" said Tariq, as he got behind the wheel and started the engine.

I had a short list of three choices. First, I wanted to go home, climb back in bed, and take a few medicinal Sonneine until my tormented arm and shoulders felt better. I knew, however, that Kmuzu would never permit it. Failing that, I preferred to go to Chiri's and knock back a few White Deaths. My watch told me that the day shift hadn't even arrived yet. In third place, but the winner by default, was the police station. I had an important clue to check out.

"Take me to Walid al-Akbar Street, Tariq," I said. He

nodded. It was a long, bumpy ride back to the more familiar districts of the city. I sat with my head tilted back, my eyes closed, listening to the gray noise in my head from the suppressors. I felt nothing. My discomfort and my emotions had been planed off electronically. I could have been in a restless, dreamless sleep; I didn't even think about what I'd do when I got to my destination.

Tariq interrupted my respite. "We're here," he said. He stopped the car, jumped out, and opened my door. I climbed out quickly; the pain suppressor made it easy.

"Shall I wait for you here, Shaykh Marîd?"

"Yes," I said. "I won't be long. Oh, by the way, do you have some paper and something to write with? I don't want to take this needle gun in there. I need to write down the serial number, though."

Tariq searched his pockets and came up with what I needed. I scribbled the number down on the back of some stranger's business card and put it in the pocket of my *gallebeya*. Then I hurried up the stairs.

I didn't want to run into Lieutenant Hajjar. I went straight to the computer room. This time, the female sergeant on duty only nodded to me. I guess I was getting to be a familiar fixture around there. I sat down at one of the streaked and smudged data decks and logged on. When the computer asked me what I wanted, I murmured, "Weapons trace." I passed through several menus of choices, and finally the computer asked me for the serial number of the weapon in question. I took out the business card and read off the combination of letters and digits.

The computer mulled it over for a few seconds, then its screen filled with enlightening information. The needle gun was registered to my pal Lieutenant Hajjar himself. I sat back and stared at the computer. Hajjar? Why would Hajjar murder the imam?

Because Hajjar was Shaykh Reda Abu Adil's tame cop. And Shaykh Reda thought he owned Abd ar-Razzaq, too. But the imam had made a dangerous mistake—he'd permitted me to proceed with the exhumation of Khalid Maxwell, against Abu Adil's strongest wishes. Abd ar-Razzaq had apparently had a few shreds of integrity left, a tarnished loyalty to truth and justice, and Abu Adil had ordered his death because of it. Shaykh Reda was watching helplessly as his plan to get rid of Friedlander Bey and myself slowly unraveled. Now, to save his own ass, he had to make sure that he wasn't connected in any way to the death of Khalid Maxwell.

There was more data on the computer screen. I learned next that the needle gun hadn't been stolen, that it had been properly registered by Hajjar three years ago. The file listed Hajjar's residence, but I knew for a fact that it was long out of date. More interesting, however, was that the file included Hajjar's complete rap sheet, detailing every misstep and misdemeanor he'd committed since coming to the city. There was an extensive recitation of all the charges that had been brought against him, including those for drug dealing, blackmail, and extortion on which he'd never actually been convicted.

I laughed, because Hajjar had worked so carefully to erase all this information from his entry in the personnel files and from the city's criminal information database. He'd forgotten about this entry, and maybe someday it would help to hang the stupid son of a bitch.

I had just cleared the screen when a voice spoke in Hajjar's Jordanian accent. "How much more time you got before the axman takes you, Maghrebi? You keepin' track?"

I swiveled the chair around and smiled at him. "Everything's falling into place. I don't think we've got anything to worry about."

Hajjar bent toward me and sucked his teeth. "No? What did you do, forge a signed confession? Who you pinning the rap on? Your mama?"

"Got everything I need right out of your computer. I want to thank you for letting me use it. You've been a good sport, Hajjar."

"The hell you talkin' about?"

I shrugged. "I learned a lot from Maxwell's autopsy, but it wasn't conclusive."

The lieutenant grunted. "Tried to warn you."

"So I came here and started poking around. I accessed the city's police procedure libraries and found a very interesting article. It seems there's a new technique to identify the killers of victims done by static pistols. You know anything about that?"

"Nah. You can't trace back a static pistol. It don't leave evidence. No bullets or flechettes or nothing."

I figured a couple more lies in a good cause couldn't hurt. "This article said every static pistol leaves its individual trace in the cells of the victim's body. You mean you never read that? You're not keeping up with your homework, Hajjar."

His smile vanished, replaced by a very worried expression. "You making all this up?"

I laughed. "What do I know about this stuff? How could I make it up? I told you, I just read it in your own library. Now I'm gonna have to go to Shaykh Mahali and ask to have Maxwell exhumed again. The M.E. didn't look for those static pistol traces. I don't think he knew about 'em, either."

Hajjar's face turned pale. He reached out and grabbed the material of my *gallebeya* below my throat. "You do that," he growled, "and every good Muslim in the city will tear you to pieces. I'm warning you. Let Maxwell alone. You had your chance. If you don't have the evidence by now, you're just out of luck."

I grabbed his wrist and twisted it, and he let go of me. "Forget it," I said. "You get on the wire and tell Abu Adil what I said. I'm only one step away from clearing my name and putting somebody else's head on the block."

Hajjar reached back and slapped me hard across the face. "You've gone too far now, Audran," he said. He looked terrified. "Get out of here and don't come back. Not until you're ready to confess to both murders."

I stood up and pushed him backward a step. "Yeah, you right, Hajjar," I said. Feeling better than I had in days, I left the computer room and ran down the stairs to where Tariq was waiting for me.

I had him drive me back to the Budayeen. I'd gotten a lot done that morning, but it was lunchtime now and I felt I'd earned myself some food and a little relaxation. Just inside the eastern gate, on First Street across from the morgue, was a restaurant called Meloul's. Meloul was a Maghrebi like me, and he owned another cookshop not far from the police station. It was a favorite of the cops, and he'd done so well that he'd opened a second location in the Budayeen, managed by his brother-in-law.

I took a seat at a small table near the rear of the restaurant, with my back to the kitchen so I could see who came in the door. Meloul's brother-in-law came over, smiling, and handed me a menu. He was a short, heavy-set man with a huge hooked nose, dark Berber skin, and a bald head except for thin fringes of black hair over each ear. "My name is Sliman. How do you do today?" he asked.

"Fine," I said. "I've eaten at Meloul's place. I enjoyed the food very much."

"I'm happy to hear it," said Sliman. "Here I've added

some dishes from all over North Africa and the Middle East. I hope you will be pleased."

I studied the menu for a little while and ordered a bowl of cold yogurt and cucumber soup, followed by broiled skewered chicken. While I waited, Sliman brought me a glass of sweet mint tea.

The food came quickly, and it was plentiful and good. I ate slowly, savoring every mouthful. At the same time, I was waiting for a phone call. I was waiting for Kenneth to tell me that if I went ahead with the phony second exhumation, Shaykh Reda would condemn me to all the agonies of Hell.

I finished my meal, paid my bill, and left Sliman a hefty tip, and went back outside. Immediately, I heard a boy whistling the child's tune. I was being watched. After the meal, and with the suppressor daddies still chipped in, I didn't really care. I could take care of myself. I thought I'd demonstrated that time and time again. I started walking up the Street.

A second boy began whistling along with the first. I thought I heard a hint of urgency in their signal. I stopped, suddenly wary, and looked around. From the corner of my eye I caught a blur of movement, and when I looked, I saw Hajjar running toward me, as fast as his legs could carry him.

He raised his hand. There was a static pistol in it. He fired, but he didn't hit me squarely. Still, there was a horrible moment of disorientation, a flush of heat through my body, and then I collapsed on the sidewalk, twitching and quivering spasmodically. I couldn't get my body to respond to my wishes. I couldn't control my muscles.

Beyond me, one of the boys also fell to the ground. He didn't move at all.

16

They took out the suppressor daddies and put me to bed, and I was unaware of anything else for about twenty-four hours. When I began to gather my scattered wits the next day, I was still trembling and unable even to grasp a glass of water. Kmuzu tended me constantly, sitting in a chair beside my bed and filling me in on what had happened.

"Did you get a good look at whoever shot you, *yaa Sidi?*" he asked.

"Whoever shot me?" I said in astonishment. "It was Hajjar, that's who. I saw him plain as day. Didn't anyone else?"

Kmuzu's brow furrowed. "No one would come forward with an identification. There was apparently only one witness willing to speak, and that was one of the two boys who were trying to warn you. He gave a sketchy description that is completely without value, as far as identifying the killer."

"Killer? Then the other boy—"

"Is dead, *yaa Sidi.*"

I nodded, greatly saddened. I let my head fall back on the pillows, and I closed my eyes. I had a lot to think about. I wondered if the murdered boy had been Ghazi; I hoped not.

A few minutes later, I had another idea. "Have there been any calls for me, Kmuzu?" I asked. "Especially calls from Shaykh Reda or his peg boy, Kenneth."

Kmuzu shook his head. "There've been calls from Chiriga and Yasmin. Your friends Saied and Jacques even came to the house, but you were in no condition to receive them. There were no calls from Shaykh Reda."

That was deeply meaningful. I'd fed Hajjar the lie about a second exhumation, and he'd reacted violently, even running after me to stop my investigation with a pop from a static gun. I suppose he thought he could make it look as if I'd just had a heart attack right there on the sidewalk in the Budayeen. The trouble with Hajjar was, he just wasn't as hot as he though he was. He couldn't bring it off.

I'm sure he passed along my plans to his boss, Shaykh Reda; but this time, there was no warning call from Kenneth. Maybe Abu Adil knew I was only bluffing. Maybe he figured that there couldn't be anymore useful information to be gained by examining Khalid Maxwell's corpse again. Maybe he was just so confident that he didn't care.

This amounted to the third trip around the village, and this time there was only one interested party: Hajjar. I was certain in my heart that he was guilty of both murders. It came as no surprise. He'd killed Khalid Maxwell under orders from Abu Adil, and tried to pin the murder on me; he'd assassinated Dr. Sadiq Abd ar-Razzaq; and he'd wiped out an innocent boy, probably unintentionally. The problem was, as well as I knew the truth, I still didn't have anything I could take into court and wave under his nose.

I couldn't even hold a book, so I watched the holoset all afternoon. There was coverage of the slain imam's funeral, which had been held the day before, after he lay in state for twenty-four hours. Hajjar had been right; there were riots. The streets around the Shimaal Mosque were choked with hundreds of thousands of mourners, day and night. Some of them got a little carried away, and stood outside the mosque, chanting and slashing their own arms and scalps with razors. The crowds surged in one direction and then another, and scores of people were killed, either smothered or trampled.

There were constant, shrill outcries for the murderer to be brought to justice. I waited to see if Hajjar had given my name to the newsmen, but the lieutenant was helpless to fulfill his threat. He didn't even have a murder weapon to connect a suspect to the crime. All he had was some extremely thin circumstantial evidence. I was safe from him, at least for a while.

When I tired of watching the coverage, I turned it off and watched a performance of the mid-sixteenth century A.H. opera, *The Execution of Rushdie*. It did nothing to cheer me up.

My inspiration came just as Kmuzu brought in a tray of chicken and vegetable couscous and prepared to feed me. "I think I've got him now," I said. "Kmuzu, would you please ask Info for the medical examiner's office number, and hold the phone up to my ear for me?"

"Certainly, *yaa Sidi.*" He got the number and murmured it into the receiver. He held the phone so that I could hear and speak into it.

"*Marhaba,*" said a voice on the other end. It was one of the assistants.

"God be with you," I said. "This is Marîd Audran. I was the one who ordered the autopsy on Khalid Maxwell a couple of days ago."

"Yes, Mr. Audran. When you didn't come back, we mailed the results to you. Is there anything else we can do?"

"Yes, there is." My heart started to beat faster. "I was slightly affected by a pulse from a static pistol in the Budayeen—"

"Yes, we heard about that. A young boy was killed in the same attack."

"Exactly. That's what I want to talk to you about. Was an autopsy done on the boy?"

"Yes."

"Now, listen. This is very important. Would you ask Dr. Besharati to compare the cell rupture pattern in the boy's heart with that of Khalid Maxwell? I think there might be a match."

"Hmm. That is interesting. But, you know, even if there is, it won't do you any good. Not in any legal sense. You can't—"

"I know all about that. I just want to find out if my suspicion is correct. Could you ask him to check on that soon? I'm not exaggerating when I say it's a life-and-death matter."

"All right, Mr. Audran. You'll probably be hearing from him later today."

"I am quite unable to express my thanks," I said fervently.

"Yeah," said the assistant. "What you say." He hung up.

Kmuzu put down the telephone. "Excellent reasoning, *yaa Sidi,*" he said. He almost smiled.

"Well, we haven't learned anything yet. We'll have to wait for the doctor's call."

I took a short nap, and was awakened by Kmuzu's hand on my shoulder. "You have a visitor," he told me.

I turned my head, realizing that I was beginning to get some control back over my muscles. There were footsteps in the parlor, and then my young Bedu friend, bin Turki, entered the bedroom. He sat down in the bed beside the chair. "*As-salaam alaykum, yaa Shaykh,*" he said seriously.

I was overjoyed to see him. "*Wa alaykum as-salaam,*" I said, smiling. "When did you get back?"

"Less than an hour ago. I came here directly from the airfield. What has happened to you? Are you going to get better?"

"Someone took a shot at me, but Allah was on my side this time. My attacker will have to do better than that next time."

"Let's pray there is no next time, O Shaykh," said bin Turki.

I just spread my hands. There would be a next time, almost certainly. If not Hajjar, then someone else. "Now, tell me, how was your journey?"

Bin Turki pursed his lips. "Successful." He took something out of his pocket and set it on the blanket by my hand. I cupped it in my curled fingers and brought it closer to get a better look at it. It was a plastic name tag that read *Sgt. al-Bishah.* That was the name of the bastard in Najran who'd beaten both Friedlander Bey and me.

I'd put it out of my mind, but yes, I'd ordered a murder. I'd calmly condemned a man to death, and this name tag was all that remained of him. How did I feel? Well, I waited a few seconds, expecting cold horror to seep into my thoughts. It didn't happen. Sometimes other people's deaths are easy. I felt nothing but indifference and an impatience to get on with business.

"Good, my friend," I said. "You'll be well rewarded."

Bin Turki nodded, taking back the name tag. "We spoke about a position that would provide me with a regular income. I'm coming to appreciate the sophisticated ways of the city. I think I will stay here for a while, before I return to the Bani Salim."

"We will be glad to have you among us," I said. "I wish to reward your clan, too, for their boundless hospitality and kindness, when we were abandoned in the Sands. I was thinking of building a settlement for them, possibly near that oasis—"

"No, O Shaykh," he said. "Shaykh Hassanein would never accept such a gift. A few people did leave the Bani Salim and build houses of concrete blocks, and we see them once or twice a year as we pass through their villages. Most of the tribe, however, clings to the old ways. That is Shaykh Hassanein's decision, too. We know about the luxuries of electricity and gas ovens, but we are Bedu. We would not trade our camels for trucks, and we would not trade our goat-hair tents for a house that bound us to one place."

"I never thought the Bani Salim would live the whole year at the settlement," I said. "But maybe the tribe might like to have comfortable quarters at the end of its yearly migration."

Bin Turki smiled. "Your thoughts are well intentioned, but the gift you imagine would be deadly to the Bani Salim."

"As you say, Bin Turki."

He stood up and grasped my hand. "I will let you rest now, O Shaykh."

"Go with safety, my nephew," I said.

"Allah yisallimak," he said, and left the room.

———— • ————

About seven o'clock that evening, the phone rang. Kmuzu answered it. "It's Dr. Besharati," he said.

"Let me see if I can hold the phone," I said. I took it from him and was clumsily able to put it to my ear. *Marhaba,* I said.

"Mr. Audran? Your suspicions are correct. The cardiac rupture patterns of Khalid Maxwell and the boy are identical. There is no doubt in my mind that they were murdered with the same static pistol."

I stared across the room for a few seconds, lost in thought. "Thank you, Dr. Besharati," I said at last.

"Of course, this doesn't prove that the same individual was using the gun in both cases."

"No, I realize that. But the chances are very good that it was. Now I know exactly what I have to do, and how to do it."

"Well," said the medical examiner, "I don't know what you mean, but again I wish you luck. May peace be with you."

"And upon you be peace," I said, putting down the phone. While I was punishing my enemies and rewarding my friends, I decided to think about something I could do for Dr. Besharati. He'd certainly earned some kind of thanks.

I went to sleep early that night, and the next morning I'd recovered enough to get out of bed and shower. Kmuzu wanted me to avoid any kind of exertion, but that wasn't possible. It was Friday, the Sabbath, and I had a parade of the *Jaish* to go to.

I ate a hearty breakfast and dressed in the dove-gray uniform Shaykh Reda had given me. The trousers were well tailored, with a black stripe down each leg, and cut to fit into high black jackboots. The tunic was high-necked, with lieutenant's insignia already sewn on. There was also a high-peaked cap with a black visor. When I was completely dressed, I looked at myself in a mirror. I guessed that the uniform's resemblance to a Nazi outfit was not coincidental.

"How do I look, Kmuzu?" I asked.

"It's not you, *yaa Sidi*. It's definitely not your style."

I laughed and removed the cap. "Well," I said, "Abu Adil was kind enough to give me this uniform. The least I can do is wear it for him once."

"I don't understand why you're doing this."

I shrugged. "Curiosity, maybe?"

"I hope the master of the house doesn't see you dressed like that, *yaa Sidi*."

"I hope so, too. Now, bring the car around. The parade is being held on the Boulevard il-Jameel, near the Shimaal Mosque. I imagine we'll have to leave the car somewhere and walk a few blocks. The crowds are still huge near the mosque."

Kmuzu nodded. He went downstairs to get the Westphalian sedan started. I followed behind him after deciding not to take either narcotics or moddies with me. I didn't know exactly what I was walking into, and a clear head seemed like a good idea.

When we got to the boulevard, I was startled to see just how great the throng was. Kmuzu began weaving through side streets and alleys, trying to inch his way nearer to the *Jaish*'s gathering place.

After a while, we just had to give up and go the rest of the way on foot. We cut our way through the mass of people; my uniform helped me a little, I think, but progress was still very slow. I could see a raised platform ahead, with a speaker's stand draped in flags decorated with the emblems of the *Jaish*. I thought I could see Abu Adil and Kenneth there, both in uniform. Shaykh Reda was standing and chatting with another officer. He wasn't wearing one of his Proxy Hell moddies. I was glad of that —I didn't want to deal with an Abu Adil suffering the effects of a make-believe terminal illness.

"Kmuzu," I said, "I'm going to see if I can get up on the platform to talk with Shaykh Reda. I want you to work your way around to the back. Try to stay nearby. I may need you all of a sudden."

"I understand, *yaa Sidi,*" he said with a worried look. "Be careful, and take no unnecessary chances."

"I won't." I knifed slowly through the crowd until I reached the rear-most ranks of the *Jaish,* which was arrayed on the neutral ground of the boulevard in orderly companies. From there it was easier to make my way to the front. All along the way, I received nods and salutes from my fellow militiamen.

I walked around to the side of the platform and mounted three steps. Reda Abu Adil still hadn't seen me, and I walked up to him and saluted. His uniform was much more elegant than mine; for one thing, I think his buttons were gold, where everyone else's were brass. On his collar, instead of brass crescents, he wore golden curved swords.

"Well, what is this?" said Abu Adil, returning my salute. He looked surprised. "I really didn't expect you to come."

"I didn't want to disappoint you, sir," I said, smiling. I turned to his assistant. "And how's it going, Kenny?" Kenneth was a colonel, and loving every minute in the jackboots.

"I warned you about calling me that," he snarled.

"Yeah, you did." I turned my back on him. "Shaykh Reda, surely the *Jaish* is a Muslim paramilitary force. I remember when it was a group dedicated to ridding the city of foreigners. Now we proudly wear the symbols of the Faith. I was just thinking: Is your Kenneth one of us? I would have bet that he's a Christian. Or maybe even a Jew."

Kenneth grabbed my shoulder and spun me around. "I testify that there is no god but God," he recited, "and Muhammad is the Prophet of God."

I grinned. "Great! You're coming along real well with that. Keep it up!"

Abu Adil's face clouded. "You two stop your infantile bickering. We have more important things to think about today. This is our first large, public demonstration. If all goes well, we'll get hundreds of new recruits, doubling the size of the *Jaish*. That's what really counts."

"Oh," I said, "I see. What about poor old Abd ar-Razzaq, then? Or is he just a stiff now?"

"Why are you here?" demanded Abu Adil. "If it's to mock us—"

"No, sir, not at all. We have our differences, of course, but I'm all in favor of cleaning up this city. I came to meet the three platoons I'm supposed to be leading."

"Good, good," said Abu Adil slowly. "Splendid."

"I don't trust him," said Kenneth.

Abu Adil turned to him. "I don't either, my friend, but that doesn't mean we can't behave in a civilized manner. We're being watched by a lot of people today."

"Try to hold your animosity in for a little while, Kenneth," I said. "I'm willing to forgive and forget. For now, anyway." He only glared at me and turned away.

Abu Adil put a hand on my shoulder and pointed down to a unit of men assembled at the foot of the platform, on the right side. "Those are your platoons, Lieutenant Audran," he said. "They make up the Al-Hashemi Detachment. They're some of our finest men. Why don't you go down there and meet your noncommissioned officers? We'll be getting ready to start the drills soon."

"All right," I said. I climbed down from the platform and walked up and down before my unit. I stopped and said hello to the three platoon sergeants, then went through the ranks as if I were inspecting them. Most of the men seemed out of shape to me. I didn't think the *Jaish* would make much of a showing against a real military force; but then, the *Jaish* was never intended to go into battle against an army. It was created to bully shopkeepers and infidel intellectuals.

Maybe a quarter of an hour later, Abu Adil spoke into a microphone, commanding the parade to begin. My unit had no part in it, other than to keep the civilians from interfering. Some of the specially trained companies showed off their stuff, marching and turning and juggling rifle-shaped pieces of wood.

This went on for an hour under the hot sun, and I began to think I'd made a serious mistake. I was starting to feel weak and wobbly, and I really just wanted to sit down. Finally, the last showcase company snapped back to attention, and Abu Adil stepped forward to the speaker's podium. He harangued the *Jaish* for another half an hour, going on about the horror of Dr. Abd ar-Razzaq's murder, and how we all had to swear allegiance to Allah and the *Jaish,* and never rest until the brutal assassin had been captured and executed according to the dictates of Islamic law. I could tell that Shaykh Reda had roused every man in uniform to a barely contained frenzy.

Then, surprisingly, he called on me to speak. I stared at him for just a second or two, and then I hurried back up to the platform. I stood at the microphone, and Abu Adil backed away. An anxious hush fell over the uniformed men assembled before me, but beyond them I could see the hordes of tens of thousands of men and women whose pent-up fury was still seeking an outlet. I wondered what I was going to say.

"My fellow Soldiers of Allah," I began, raising my arms to include not only the *Jaish*, but also the mob beyond. "It is too late for anything but vengeance." A loud cry went up from the onlookers. "As Shaykh Reda said, we have a sacred duty, authorized in many places in the noble Qur'ân. We must find the person who struck down our holy imam, and then we must make him taste our keen-edged justice." Another cry, this one a strange, hungry, ululating sound that made me shiver.

I went on. "That is our task. But honor and faith and respect for the law demand that we control our anger, for fear that we revenge ourselves upon the wrong man. How, then, shall we know the truth? My friends, my brothers and sisters in Islam, I *have* the truth!"

This drew a loud shout from the mob, and a surprised sound from behind me, where Abu Adil and Kenneth were standing. I opened a few buttons of my tunic and brought out the needle gun, holding it high for everyone to see. "*This* is the murder weapon! *This* is the horrible instrument of our imam's death!" Now the reaction was long and frightening. The hysterical crowds surged forward, and the foot soldiers of the *Jaish* struggled to keep the people from rushing the platform.

"I know whose needle gun this is!" I shouted. "Do *you* want to know? Do *you* want to know who murdered Dr. Sadiq Abd ar-Razzaq, shamefully in cold blood?" I waited a few seconds, knowing the uproar would not subside, but pausing only for effect. I saw Kenneth start toward me, but Abu Adil grabbed his arm and stopped him. That surprised me.

"It belongs to Police Lieutenant Hajjar, a Jordanian immigrant to our city, a man with many past crimes that have long gone unpunished. I do not know his motives. I do not know why he stole our imam from us. I only know that he did that evil deed, and he sits this very moment, not far from here, in the police precinct on Walid al-Akbar Street, content in his sinful pride, certain that he is safe from the just retribution of the people."

I'd thought of a few more things to say, but it was impossible. From that point on, the mob became a terrifying thing. It seemed to shift and sway and shake itself, and voices were raised in cries that no one could understand, and chants and curses went up all around us. Then, in only a few minutes, I could see that a bewildering organization had taken place, as if leaders had been chosen and decisions made. Slowly, the mob animal turned away from the platform and the *Jaish*. It began to move southward along the lovely Boulevard il-Jameel. Toward the police station. It was going to claim Lieutenant Hajjar.

Hajjar had foreseen the behavior of the outraged mob. He had foreseen the terror of its mindless rage. He had only failed to foresee the true identity of its victim.

I watched, fascinated. After a while, I stepped back, away from the microphone. The afternoon parade of the *Jaish* was over. Many of the uniformed men had broken ranks and joined the wrathful rabble.

"Very well done, Audran," said Abu Adil. "Excellently played."

I looked at him. It seemed to me that he was entirely sincere. "It's going to cost you one of your most useful hirelings," I said. "Paybacks are a bitch, aren't they?"

Abu Adil only shrugged. "I'd written Hajjar off already. I can appreciate good work, Audran, even when it's done by my enemy. But be warned. Just because I'm congratulating you, don't think I'm not already planning a way to make you pay. This whole matter has been a disaster for me."

I smiled. "You brought it on yourself."

"Remember what I said: I'll make you pay."

"I suppose you'll try," I said. I climbed down the steps

at the back of the platform. Kmuzu was there. He led me away from the boulevard, away from the surging mob, toward our car.

"Please take off that uniform, *yaa Sidi*," he said.

"What? Ride home in my underwear?" I laughed.

"At least the tunic. I'm sickened by everything it stands for."

I complied, and tossed the tunic into a corner of the backseat. "Well," I said, stretching out, "how did I do?"

Kmuzu turned around briefly, and he gave me one of his rare smiles. "Very fine, *yaa Sidi*," he said. Then he turned his attention back to driving.

I relaxed and leaned back against the seat. I told myself that the slight interruption in my life caused by Abu Adil and Lieutenant Hajjar and Imam Abd ar-Razzaq was over, and now life could get back to normal. The matter was closed. As for Shaykh Reda himself, any plans of paying that son of a bitch back the way he deserved had to be tabled until sometime in the hazy future, after Friedlander Bey was gathered by Allah into His holy Paradise.

In the meantime, Papa and I restored our good names. We met the next day with the amir and presented him with information and evidence concerning the deaths of Khalid Maxwell, Abd ar-Razzaq, and Lieutenant Hajjar. I didn't feel it necessary to go into detail about the sudden demise of Sergeant al-Bishah in Najran, or certain other pertinent points. Shaykh Mahali then ordered one of his administrative deputies to clear us of the false charges, and expunge any mention of Khalid Maxwell's murder from our records.

I was rather gratified by how easily I slipped back into my old routines. I was soon back at my desk, reviewing information concerning a revolutionary party that was gaining strength in my homeland of Mauretania. Kmuzu stood beside my desk and waited for me to notice him. I looked up. "What is it?" I asked.

"The master of the house wishes to speak with you, *yaa Sidi*," said Kmuzu.

I nodded, not knowing what to expect. With Papa, it was sometimes impossible to predict whether you were being summoned to receive reward or punishment. My stomach began to churn; had I earned his disfavor again? Were the Stones That Speak waiting with him to break my bones?

Fortunately, that proved not to be the case. Friedlander Bey smiled at me as I entered his office, and indicated that I should sit near him. "I commanded you to find an elegant solution to our difficulties, my nephew, and I am well pleased with what you accomplished."

"It makes me glad to hear it, O Shaykh," I said, relieved.

"I have what I believe is adequate recompense for all you have suffered, and for all the labor you performed on my behalf."

"I ask no reward, O Shaykh," I said. Well, I like rewards as much as the next guy, but it was good form to offer a token refusal.

Papa ignored me. He pushed a thin envelope and a small cardboard box toward me. I looked up at him questioningly. "Take them, my nephew. It pleases me greatly to give them to you."

The envelope contained money, of course. Not cash, because the sum was too large. It was a bank draft for a quarter-million kiam. I just stared at it for a few seconds, swallowed, and set it down again on the desk. Then I picked up the box and opened it. There was a moddy inside. Friedlander Bey was strongly opposed to personality modules on religious grounds. It was highly unusual for him to give me one.

I looked at the label. The moddy was a re-creation of my favorite fictional character, Lutfy Gad's detective, al-Qaddani. I smiled. "Thank you, my uncle," I said softly. The moddy meant more to me than the huge amount of money. There was a kind of warm significance to it that I couldn't put into words.

"I had the module created specially for you," said Papa. "I hope you enjoy it." He looked at me for a few seconds more. Then his expression grew serious. "Now tell me about how the datalink project is going. And I need a report on the final disposition of the Cappadocian situation. And further, now that Lieutenant Hajjar is dead, we must decide on a reliable replacement."

Months of torment, relieved at the end by a single minute of good cheer. What more could anyone want?

"Captain Jack Zodiac suggests what might have happened if Voltaire's Candide had gotten shipwrecked inside a Tex Avery cartoon."—James Morrow, author of *Only Begotten Daughter*

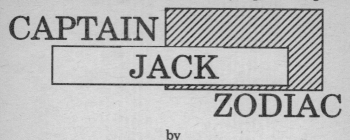

CAPTAIN JACK ZODIAC

by
Michael Kandel

Cliff Koussevitsky has some terrible problems: his son's a drug-taking space cadet, his daughter's a mall zombie, and his fiance's dead mother won't let the love-birds get married. Furthermore, his world is in terrible trouble: the greenhouse effect is running rampant, America's in the midst of a nuclear war, and radiation is causing mutations galore—superheroes from suburbia, and a man-eating lawn. From trippy pills pushed by a drug-dealer named Captain Jack Zodiac to magic subway tokens that open the doorway to hell, Cliff Koussevitsky is in for the ride of his life...and Michael Kandel is ready to take you along for the ride.